DEAD
RINGER

Also by Lisa Scottoline

DEAD RINGER

LISA SCOTTOLINE

DOUBLEDAY LARGE PRINT HOME LIBRARY EDITION

HarperCollins*Publishers*

DEAD RINGER. Copyright © 2003 by Lisa Scottoline. All rights reserved. Printed in the United States of America. No part of this book may be used or reproduced in any manner whatsoever without written permission except in the case of brief quotations embodied in critical articles and reviews. For information, address HarperCollins Publishers Inc., 10 East 53rd Street, New York, NY 10022.

ISBN 0-7394-3518-3

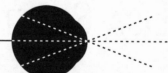

This Large Print Book carries the
Seal of Approval of N.A.V.H.

For my father

There are some things you learn best in calm, and some in storm.

—WILLA CATHER

DEAD
RINGER

1

Bennie Rosato had waited for more than a hundred jury verdicts in her career, but the waiting never got easier. The courtroom was empty, the air still. Bennie could hear the clock ticking on the paneled wall, but it could have been her sense of drama. She was sitting next to her client, Ray Finalil, who was gnawing his cuticles. If they lost this trial, Ray's company would have to pay three million dollars in damages. Three million bucks buys a lot of cuticles.

Bennie set aside her own case of nerves to cheer him up. "Yo, Ray. How do you stop a lawyer from drowning?"

"How?"

"Take your foot off his head."

Ray didn't smile. His gaze remained fixed

on the vacant jury box, with its black leather chairs swiveled in different directions. The jury had been charged on the law this morning and they'd been out deliberating all day. That meant Ray and Bennie were entering their sixth hour of small talk. To Bennie, that was as good as married.

"Okay, no more jokes," she said. "Tell me about your son's baseball game. I'll pretend I don't know about the home run or the catch at third base."

"*Second* base."

"See?"

Ray's chin dropped to his hand. His brown eyes were bloodshot from three weeks of sleepless nights and his cheeks hollow from the ten pounds he'd shed during the trial, even though he was completely innocent. Being a defendant was no-win; if you lost, you paid the plaintiff, and if you won, you paid your lawyer. This was known as the American Rule. Only Americans tolerate law without justice.

"Look, Ray, we don't have to stay here. I have my cell phone, and the deputy clerk has my number. How about we take a field trip? We can go see the Liberty Bell. It's only a block away."

"No."

"This land is your land, Ray. This land is my land."

"No."

"Come on, it'll do you good to go out and walk around." Bennie rose, stretched, and took a personal inventory. She thought she was good-looking for a lawyer, even though she stood six feet tall and her proportions were positively Amazonian. Her khaki suit was still pressed and her white Gap shirt fairly clean. Her long, disobedient blond hair had been piled into a twist with a tortoise-shell barrette, but no makeup maximized the blue of her eyes or minimized the crow's-feet at their corners. An old boy-friend had told her that her mouth was gen-erous, but she suspected it was a sneaky way of saying she had a big mouth. At the moment, it was shaped into a sympathetic frown. "You don't wanna take a walk?"

"When do you think they'll come back?" Ray didn't have to explain who "they" were. The jury.

"End of today." Bennie sat back down. At least the stretch had shaken off some of her stress. She couldn't remember the last time she'd exercised. This trial had consumed every available minute for the past two months, but her law firm needed the dough. The slump in the economy had hit lawyers, too, and people had stopped suing each other. Could world peace be far behind?

"I can't take another day of this. You sure they'll come back today?"

"Positive. This is a simple fraud case, in federal court only through the miracle of diversity jurisdiction. And Thursday is a good day for juries to go out. They get it over with if they come back today, then they go home and make it a three-day weekend. They won't go to work on a Friday after jury duty."

"How do you know?"

"Trial wisdom. The elders pass it down in a secret ceremony. We call it the bar exam to fool gringos like you."

"But what are they *doing* in there for so long?" Ray rubbed his forehead with left-over fingernails. He looked older than his fifty-one years, and oddly, he'd become more nervous as the trial wore on, not less. Ray wasn't a lover *or* a fighter. He was an accountant.

"A day is nothing. We just had a fifteen-day trial with one hundred twenty-six exhibits and twenty-eight witnesses. You want them back sooner?" Bennie pointed to the empty jury box. "Keep watching those chairs. It works every time."

Suddenly, the paneled door next to the dais opened and the deputy clerk entered. He was tall and fit, and his polyester blazer made an officially swishy sound when he walked. When Bennie realized he was heading for her, she rose. "They back?" she asked, her heart beginning to thump, but the deputy clerk shook his head.

"They got a question. They sent a note. Court's in session in five minutes. Plaintiff still in the attorney's conference room?"

"Yes," Bennie answered, and as soon as the deputy clerk took off down the aisle, Ray jumped up and clutched her sleeve.

"What does he mean, a question? The jury has a question? What question?"

"Relax. Sit down." Bennie unpeeled Ray's fingers and eased him down into his chair. "The judge is coming out to read us the question. Then we—"

"A question? How typical is that? I don't understand. What does he mean, a question?"

"It happens from time to time. The jury

sends the judge a question about the evidence or the law. It's nothing to be—"

"I mean, what do they have to know?" Ray raked his free hand through his thinning hair. At the beginning of this trial he had looked like a Chia Pet. Okay, maybe that was an exaggeration. "Who said they could ask questions? Why do they get to ask questions?"

"Because this is America. Now stay cool. Curtain's up." Bennie gestured behind him, where the courtroom had come abruptly to life. The court reporter returned, cracking his knuckles before he took his seat straddling the stenography machine. The deputy clerk and a young female law clerk entered through the paneled door and bustled to their posts at the side and the front of the courtroom. The plaintiff and his lawyer hustled up the aisle and sat down at their counsel table, and the lawyer nodded, acknowledging Bennie.

Bennie nodded back, but that was as friendly as she ever got with opposing counsel, if you didn't count giving them the finger behind her legal pad. She wasn't trying to win friends; she was trying to win cases. Her loyalty remained with her client, even one as panicky as Ray. Especially one as panicky as Ray, who leaned over and started whispering so close she could smell lunch on his breath. Ray Finalil was the only person in the world still eating liverwurst and onions.

"What do you think they'll ask? What could they not understand?"

"Quiet. Stand up." Bennie rose as Judge William Delburton, a gray-haired Carter appointee who'd been tough if evenhanded during the trial, swept into the courtroom. He sat in his high-backed leather chair on the paneled dais, underneath the thick golden seal of the United States Courts. In his hands rested a single piece of folded paper, which he studied as the deputy clerk said his lines.

"All rise!" cried the deputy clerk, needlessly. The parties were already on their feet and the gallery was empty. "Court is now in session, the Honorable Judge William Delburton presiding."

"You may be seated," the judge said. "Good afternoon, everyone." He glanced at Bennie as she sat down, then at plaintiff's counsel table. "Counsel, as you may have heard, our jury has a question. I'll read it to you."

Ray grabbed Bennie's hand. She pretended not to notice. Litigation reduced men to little boys, and women to Gloria Allred.

Judge Delburton slipped on black reading glasses that matched his robe. "The question reads, 'Judge Delburton, are we allowed to give the plaintiff more than the three million dollars he is asking for?'"

Oh my God. Bennie's mouth went dry. This couldn't be happening. It was a runaway jury. Ray slumped in his seat like a crash-test dummy.

Judge Delburton gestured to plaintiff's table. "Counsel, what is plaintiff's position on the answer to this question?"

"Thank you, Your Honor." Plaintiff's counsel rose and couldn't hide a giddy chuckle. "The answer to the question is yes. In addition to the three million dollars in compensatory damages, plaintiff is entitled to punitive damages. We put on substantial evidence of the invidious nature of the misconduct and fraud perpetrated by the defendant company and its owner, Mr. Finalil.

An award in excess of the three million in damages is more than justified."

"Thank you." Judge Delburton slipped off his glasses and turned to Bennie. "Ms. Rosato, for the defense, your thoughts on this matter."

"Thank you, Your Honor." Bennie swallowed with difficulty and rose on weak knees. "The answer to the jury's question should be no. The jury may not extend damages to a figure that plaintiff's evidence doesn't factually support. The jury should be charged again and told that they are required to base their verdict on the evidence, not on anything else."

"Thank you, Counsel." Judge Delburton slipped his glasses back on and placed the jurors' note neatly on his desk. The document would be nice and flat for the appeal that would surely follow, either way. "I have your arguments, and I hold that we will answer the question in the affirmative. The plaintiff did request punitive damages, so the jury may award damages in excess of the compensatory amount of three million. I will so instruct them."

"Objection for the record," Bennie said reflexively. She glanced over at Ray, who looked as if he were ready to hurl. The deputy clerk brought the jury back into the courtroom, and the judge answered their question and sent them out to deliberate again. Then the judge and his staff left the courtroom, the plaintiff and his lawyer gloated down the aisle, and Bennie turned to Ray. But by now she had her bearings.

"Ray, don't freak," she said, but it was too late.

"How can I not? Didn't you hear what they said?" Ray tore off his glasses and slapped a hand to his face, rubbing reddish streaks into his cheek. "They're gonna give him *more* than three million dollars!"

"No, that's not necessarily so. I admit this looks bad, but you never know with a jury question. They—"

"This is a disaster! A *disaster!* How can they do this to me?"

"Ray, wait, calm down." Bennie reached across counsel table for a gray plastic pitcher, shook a Styrofoam cup from the up-side-down stack, and poured him some water. "Please listen to me. We don't know where that question came from and we don't know what it means. It's not necessarily a question the whole jury has, and it most likely isn't. Somebody could have a stray hair. It happens—"

"But the *question!*" Ray gulped water and some splashed over the rim. "Didn't you hear that question? What am I gonna do? This is unreal! This is a catastrophe!"

"I don't think the plaintiff proved his case. You didn't think so either, remember? We thought that they lost, and nothing has changed except for the jury question. So my opinion remains the same." Bennie looked directly into his stricken eyes, which were peering over the Styrofoam like Kilroy. "Scharf was a lousy witness, remember? He was angry on the stand, not sympathetic, and angry plaintiffs never win. Remember my Angry Plaintiff Theory?"

"No!"

"Yes you do." Bennie leaned over. "Ray, look. I've seen this before. Everybody goes crazy when the jury asks a question. Everybody tries to read the tea leaves. People run and scatter. Don't lose your head."

"But they asked the question!"

"Forget the question. We don't know what it means and we can't do anything about it. Our defense went in very nicely. You were a great witness, and so were Jake and Marty. We're in the right. We told the truth. So stay the course."

"The *course* is what got me here! The *course* is gonna kill me!" Ray set down the cup, spilling water on the table. "Shouldn't I settle? Maybe I can still settle!"

"They wanted five hundred grand last time we asked, and you didn't have it. You knock over a gas station since then?" Bennie didn't wait for an answer. "And I'm sure their demand just went up. So we have no choice but to wait."

"But it's like waiting to get hit by a train! I'm tied to the tracks here!"

"Wait, and stay calm."

"Easy for *you* to say!" Ray exploded, his voice echoing in the empty courtroom. His eyes flashed with sudden anger. "If I lose, you won't have to pay a dime! You just go on to the next case! You're a typical fucking lawyer!"

Bennie felt stung. Silence fell between them. The clock on the wall ticked away. This time, she was sure of it. "We're in this together, Ray," she said, after a minute.

She didn't expect him to believe it.

But it was true.

Only half an hour later, court was back in

session, and the jury was entering the jury box. The jury foreman held a piece of white typing paper in his hand. It was the verdict sheet, which contained a single question and answer. The courtroom went completely quiet as everyone scrutinized the jurors, including Bennie. She noticed that they avoided eye contact with her, and she tried not to take it as a bad sign. She could hear Ray sucking wind. At least he wasn't green anymore.

Judge Delburton was sitting in his black leather chair atop the dais, eyeing the jurors over his reading glasses. When they were resettled and looking at him, he addressed them. "Has the jury reached a verdict?"

"We have, Your Honor," answered the foreman. He rose and handed the verdict sheet to the deputy clerk.

Bennie held her breath. Ray clenched his fists. The deputy clerk handed the verdict sheet to Judge Delburton, who opened and read it to himself, his expression impassive. Then he handed it back to the deputy clerk, who puffed out his chest, held the paper high, and read it aloud:

"Question: Do you find the defendant is liable to the plaintiff, and if so what are his damages? Answer: We find the defendant not liable."

Yes! Yes! Yes! Bennie felt like shouting for joy. They had *won!* She nodded toward the jury in gratitude as Ray grabbed her hand and squeezed it hard. She looked over, and he'd burst into a broad grin, which didn't let up even as the jurors were polled by a shocked plaintiff's lawyer, answered "not liable" one by one, then were dismissed by the judge, who left the room with his staff, closing the door behind them.

"Congratulations!" Bennie shouted when they were alone again, and Ray leapt into her arms. She gave him a heartfelt hug. She couldn't remember the last time she'd felt so happy. Or so relieved. "We won, Ray! Thank God!"

"I won! I won!" Ray yelled, and when she broke their embrace, his eyes were welling up behind his glasses.

"Aw, it's all over, Ray!" Bennie gave him another hug. She'd never seen a grown accountant cry. So what if he'd gotten a little jerky in the clutch? Served her right for telling lawyer jokes. "Enjoy it! We won!"

"I know, I can't believe it." Ray took off has glasses and squeezed his eyes with his thumb and index finger, trying to regain his composure. "You said I would, and I did."

"I won't even say I told you so." Bennie clapped him on the back and picked up her briefcase and bag. "Come on, let's go cele-brate! Drinks on you!"

But when Ray removed his hands from his eyes and replaced his glasses, he still looked miserable. His forehead creased with anxiety, his eyes brimmed with tears, and his lower lip trembled.

"Ray, cheer up! We won! It's all over!"

"It's not that." Ray cleared his throat and met her gaze with wet eyes. "I have some-thing to tell you."

"What?"

"I can't pay."

Bennie smiled. "I was only kidding, Ray. Drinks on me."

"No, I mean, I can't pay you." Ray squared his narrow shoulders. "What I owe you. Your fee."

Bennie blinked. "Sure you can."

"No, I can't. I feel terrible about this, but I can't pay you. I don't have the money."

"Of course you do." Bennie set down her briefcase and purse in bewilderment. "You're a good client. You paid me last quarter and the ones before that. Your business is healthy."

"Not really. I borrowed the money to pay you last quarter, and I thought I could pay you this quarter because my two biggest clients were going to pay me. But last month they told me they can't, since their customers didn't pay them." Ray ran a tongue tip over dry lips. "They're both filing for Chapter Eleven. In fact, I'm about to file myself."

"You're filing for *bankruptcy*?"

"Yes."

Bennie's mouth dropped open. "This can't be!"

"It is."

"But you're an accountant, for God's sake! I mean, how could this happen?"

"I'm a good accountant, a good businessman. But with this recession, it's like a domino effect."

"Ray, I'm counting on this fee!" Bennie had put in almost 250 hours on this case this quarter, with trial preparation and trial. Even if she billed him fifty bucks an hour for her time, she was still cheaper than a plumber. "You owe me almost fifteen thousand dollars. I can't absorb that kind of loss. I have a payroll to meet."

"I can't pay you, Bennie."

"You can pay *some,* can't you?"

"Not a penny. I'm sorry."

"How about you pay in installments?" Bennie felt desperate. No wonder he'd been getting more nervous as the trial went on; he was facing bankruptcy. And now, so was she. "Listen, Ray, I can work with you. I'll work with you. You're my client."

"No. My company is your client, not me. This is a corporate debt, and I can't make side deals." Ray shook his head. "When I put it into bankruptcy, you'll have to get in line."

"Am I first, at least?"

"Frankly, you're not even the first lawyer. My business lawyers take before you, and my tax guys."

"But what about the experts we hired, for the trial? You have to pay them. I promised you'd pay them. I'm not allowed to, even if I had the money."

"Sorry."

Bennie reeled. She couldn't process it fast enough. She was still feeling residually happy about the victory. She had won and lost in the same moment. She didn't know what to say or do. There was no trial wisdom about this. Nobody wise ever let this happen. And Ray looked so stricken, she didn't have the heart to kill him.

On autopilot, Bennie picked up her briefcase and bag. "I gotta get back to work," she said.

But she was talking more to herself than to him.

2

Friday morning, Bennie squirmed in her desk chair and crossed one strong leg over the other. No matter what she did, she couldn't get comfortable. Her calves itched, her thighs hurt, and her underwear felt vacuum-sealed. She *hated* pantyhose, and she had more important things than lingerie to think about, like the new client coming in. She needed a new case desperately after yesterday's debacle with Ray Finalil. But at the moment, the fashion police were at the door. And they had a warrant.

"Open up!" Anne Murphy called through the door, and in the next second burst into the office. Anne had long red hair, the gorgeous features of a runway model, and a law degree from Stanford. Naturally everybody had hated her instantly when she joined Rosato & Associates, and they were only now starting to forgive her her DNA. Anne clapped her hands together like a drill sergeant with a French manicure. "Stand up! Let's see 'em!"

"No, I have to get ready for the meeting," Bennie said, but she wasn't sure she could stand anyway. The control-top waistband bisected her ovaries like a do-it-yourself hysterectomy.

"Lemme see." Anne strode around the side of Bennie's desk in heels high enough to cause nosebleeds and a black knit dress that outlined her curves. At twenty-something, she had yet to learn that knit dresses were the enemy. She appraised Bennie's legs with a delighted eye. "Awesome! They totally finish your look."

"What, the sausage-in-natural-casing look?" Bennie struggled to her feet to discourage the formation of blood clots and caught sight of her pained expression in her office window. Otherwise, she had on the same khaki suit as yesterday, with her hair a little neater. "These stockings are too tight, Murphy."

"Thank God I had them. The ones you

had were way thick." Anne waved at the wastebasket beside Bennie's desk, which contained pantyhose molted like snakeskin. "I can't believe you put that crap on your body. Note to Bennie: Don't wear anything they sell in the grocery store."

"But the tube socks are a deal."

"I hope you're kidding. Those pantyhose you have on, they're from Nordstrom's." Anne handed Bennie a shiny package. "If you insist on wearing pantyhose, which I told you are so over, these are the only ones that don't suck."

"Don't say 'suck' in the office," Bennie corrected.

"You say 'suck.'"

"Not anymore. I'm on a curse diet."

" 'Suck' is not a curse."

"Shh." Bennie was scanning the empty package, which pictured a completely naked woman lounging beneath the price tag. She didn't know which surprised her more, the full frontal or the price. "Murphy, you buy pantyhose that cost seventeen dollars?"

"Of course. Wear them. You want the new client to think you're a loser?"

"I'm not a loser," Bennie shot back, unaccountably defensive. She was one of the best trial lawyers in Philadelphia, practically undefeated in both civil and criminal cases. It was beside the point that she was almost broke, had failed at two serious relationships, and bought her pantyhose at Acme. "Damn it, it's okay to buy pantyhose at Acme."

"But look at the ones I gave you. The color is perfect."

Bennie looked down and double-checked. Her legs were strong and muscular from years of rowing, and a thick vein snaked down the side of one calf, with a valve like a tiny knot. But she couldn't see any color in her legs, undoubtedly owing to the lack of circulation to her extremities. "These stockings don't have a color."

"Of course they do. They're 'nude.'"

"Nude isn't a color, it's a misdemeanor."

"Nude is the new nude."

"Oh, please." Sometimes Bennie doubted whether Anne Murphy had ever *seen* Stanford Law. "Who buys pantyhose to look like they're not wearing pantyhose?"

"Everybody but you." Anne folded arms skinny as licorice sticks, but Bennie couldn't stop thinking about the seventeen dollars. She hadn't paid herself a salary in two months and was rapidly losing her sense of humor. And Ray Finalil wasn't the only one of her clients in deep financial trouble; the recession had already bankrupted two of her bread-and-butter corporate clients, Caveson, Inc., and Maytel. As a result, Bennie had been up most of last night, going over the books. Her firm couldn't survive on her personal savings for more than two months. She'd already cut their expenses to the bone, and at the moment she was looking into the guileless green eyes of her newest associate, who would be the first lawyer to be laid off.

Just then laughter came from the open door, where the other young associates, Mary DiNunzio and Judy Carrier, had materialized. At least Bennie thought it was Judy Carrier, but she had to do a double take. The associate was wearing Judy's artsy corduroy smock and white T-shirt, and a familiar grin warmed her round, pretty face. But her formerly lemony hair had been hacked off around her ears and the entire moplet had been colored a hot pink. Bennie was horrified.

"Carrier, you dyed your hair!" she said,

instead of the profane alternative she favored. It was hard not to curse at work. Maybe she could just cut down. Did they have a patch or something? "What possessed you? You're a lawyer!"

"I'm an artist, too. I'm my own work in progress!" Judy wiggled her hips and bopped her Bubblicious head. "Besides, lawyers can have fun."

"No they can't. It carries federal penalties."

Murphy was bounding over to Carrier in delight. "Jude, it's so cute! Lipstick pink! I love it!"

Even DiNunzio was squealing. "I love it too, it's so cool! I wish I had the guts to do it!" She ruffled Carrier's shorn locks wistfully, though her own dark blond hair was pulled back into a sleek French twist. Mary DiNunzio looked compact and conventional in a navy blue suit, since she thought the term "business casual" was an oxymoron. But in no time, Mary and the other two associates were clucking and cooing in girl overdrive. The only problem with an all-woman firm was the estrogen.

"Yo! Ladies!" Bennie called out, and the girls turned in a startled little row. She put her hands on her hips. "Carrier, have you lost your mind? Pink hair doesn't belong in a law office. How are you going to meet the new client?"

"Like I would with my old hair." Judy's blue eyes flashed defiantly, but under her pink bangs she looked like a psycho baby shower. "My friend Ellen had green hair the last time I saw her in court. The jury went her way, and afterward they all asked her about it." Suddenly the telephone intercom beeped; Marshall, the secretary, signaling that the new client had arrived. Everybody straightened up, Bennie most of all.

"That's him!" she said, and hurried for the office door, frowning at Judy on the way. "Carrier, can you put a hat on that? Or a briefcase?"

"Aw, come on, boss." Judy sounded hurt, so Bennie let it go.

"Okay, we'll live with it. You and Murphy sit in on this meeting. If we get this case, I'll need you both. Carrier, tell Murphy the drill."

Judy turned to Anne. "Take lots of notes, say nothing at all, and don't go changin' to try and please me."

"Funny," Bennie said, giving her a playful hip check.

Judy laughed. "What kind of matter did you say it was? Corporate?"

"Yes."

"No murder or mayhem?"

"Corporate mayhem. We're taking a break from crime scenes and blood spatter. And no whining, van Gogh." Bennie left the associates and charged down the hall toward the reception area. She forgot about the costly pantyhose and the artistic hair. Her chest swelled with a hope familiar to chronic gamblers and the self-employed.

Ten minutes later, they were all settled at the round conference table in Bennie's office. The morning sun shone brightly through the large windows on the north side, illuminating white walls dotted with the rowing series by Thomas Eakins. Diplomas from the University of Pennsylvania, awards for trial advocacy, and plaques for civil rights work blanketed another wall. Casebooks, law reviews, and ABA magazines crammed the bookshelves, and fresh coffee brewed on a small Braun machine atop an oak credenza, filling the office with its aroma. Bennie had wanted them to meet here instead of the conference room because it was chummier and she wanted to build owner loyalty.

"Mr. St. Amien, would you like a cup of coffee?" she offered, going to the credenza. She had no qualms about getting coffee for a client, even as a woman professional. Especially as a woman professional. A professional served her client. Period.

"Black would be fine, thank you," he answered with a polite smile. Robert St. Amien was an elegant fifty-five years old, tall and lean, with dark silver hair and blue eyes sharp behind tortoiseshell glasses. He spoke with an accent from the best arrondissement in Paris, and his manner was almost courtly. A charcoal suit draped expensively on his shoulders, and his print tie reflected the dull shine of silk threads.

"Coffee coming right up."

"And please, as I said, call me Robert. All of you." St. Amien glanced around the table at a seated Judy, then Anne next to her. Bennie noted it as a polite thing to do, even though his gaze lingered a little too lovingly on gorgeous Anne. St. Amien was French; maybe he was a French manicure fan.

"Robert it is, then," Bennie said. She grabbed the only plain coffee mug, bypassing ones that read FEMINAZI, HEAD BITCH, and HELP, I'M TURNING INTO MY MOTHER, filled the cup with hot brew, and handed it to him. She went with Styrofoam for herself, pouring as she spoke. "Now, Robert, tell me what brings you here, and how I can help you."

"*Eh bien,* to begin." St. Amien took a neat sip of coffee, then set it down. "As I believe I mentioned on the telephone, I own a medical-lens manufacturing company, which just built and opened a U.S. facility in Philadelphia last year. We have one hundred fifty employees in King of Prussia, and we make specialized lenses for medical equipment and instrumentation, such as fiber-optic microscopes, among other things."

Bennie took a seat at the table. St. Amien had told her much of this on the telephone. Clients loved to talk about their businesses, and they hired lawyers who shared their enthusiasm. Bennie could be very enthusiastic to get a new client. By the end of this meeting, fiber optics would bring her to orgasm.

"The medical equipment and instrumentation business is undergoing a boom in the Philadelphia area, thanks to the concentration of hospital and research facilities here, and the current changes in health insurance, which increase demand for diagnostic tools."

"I see," Bennie said. Sometimes it was good to say stuff, even dumb stuff.

"In connection with my new facility, last month I happened to attend a convention of the national trade association of lens manufacturers, though I hadn't yet joined the association. I stopped by the meeting to learn, to hear. They were holding various seminars and such. I believe they are called 'breakout sessions.'"

Bennie sipped her coffee. "I hate breakout sessions. I always want to break out of breakout sessions."

St. Amien laughed. "Me, too. *Par hasard,* I wandered into the wrong session, there were so many in the various ballrooms, and I took a seat at the back of the room, just at the moment when the young man at the lectern said something about competition from foreign lens manufacturers. In fact, he said, quite openly, 'Americans should not buy foreign lenses this summer, no matter how low they go on price. No foreign lenses! We have to stick together as Americans, now more than ever!'"

"That's terrible!" Bennie said. She felt embarrassment at the behavior of her fellow citizens and anger at the injustice to St. Amien. But she couldn't deny this was good news for Rosato & Associates. The statement was direct evidence of wrongdoing, the proverbial "smoking gun" testimony, and St. Amien's case was a sure winner. Blood rushed to Bennie's head, but it could have been the pantyhose, squeezing it upward like a thermometer.

"The one who was speaking was the vice president of the association. I have his name, it was in the program. I could not believe he would be so bold!"

"It happens. Trade associations get sloppy because their members don't always know the antitrust laws, and criminals are arrogant, whether their collars are blue or white." Bennie leaned forward. "What happened next?"

"The room applauded, three hundred persons, perhaps, and the week thereafter, I lost a multimillion-dollar contract, my biggest, with Hospcare." St. Amien frowned, two deep furrows appearing on his high forehead. "The Hospcare contract was the very reason I decided to build a facility here. Two other contracts canceled in the three days after Hospcare, and my last remaining bidder is now showing signs of unease." He spread his hands palms up. "Well, suddenly I find myself in the position of having no income and no new contracts coming in, in my U.S. operation. As if the rug had been . . ." He faltered.

"Pulled out from under you?" Bennie supplied.

"Précisément."

She knew the feeling, if not the French. "I see. Your losses must be significant. Can you put a number on the damages? Lost revenue from the contracts?"

"The Hospcare contract was worth almost three million dollars. The other two contracts total slightly over five million. My entire investment in the U.S. facility is now in grave jeopardy, and the costs for the new facility are well in excess of fifty million." St. Amien rattled it off as if money were his first language. "My losses are approximately sixty million dollars."

The numbers stunned Bennie. She couldn't add with all that blood rushing to her brain. She couldn't add even when blood wasn't rushing to her brain. She used to think she was just bad at math until she convinced herself she had math anxiety, which upgraded basic stupidity to disability level and made her feel better about herself.

"I am gathering a legal wrong has been perpetrated," St. Amien said, watching her with an obviously amused smile.

"Well, yeah. Sure. Absolutely. Right you are." *Focus, girlfriend.* "In addition to breach-of-contract claims against the trade association, there is a significant antitrust claim, which would be far easier to prove, given the statement at the conference. I have to get all the facts and investigate, but basically we're talking dead to rights, Robert."

" 'Dead to' . . ." St. Amien's voice trailed off. He was obviously unfamiliar with the idiom, so Bennie decided against "cold-cocked."

"Let me explain, briefly." The law centered her when caffeine failed. "Under our antitrust laws, anyone may refuse to do business with anyone else, but what they cannot do is agree as a group not to do business with someone. That's a group boycott and it violates federal law. Damages are tripled under the antitrust law, and your recovery would more than make you whole."

"That's excellent news." St. Amien permitted himself another smile.

"Frankly, you have a case that even my dog could win, but I doubt it will ever get to trial. The evidence is so clear and the damages so lethal that the trade association will surely settle, maybe even in six months."

"Even better."

"I'll say," Bennie blurted out, then caught herself. She realized something she had overlooked in her greed attack. "Wait a minute. Robert, the speaker mentioned all foreign lenses, not just yours. Are there other foreign manufacturers he was referring to, do you know?"

"Ah, *oui*. There are many others like me, though my losses are the greatest. I have many colleagues who have been harmed, three from Germany, several from the Netherlands. Also from the Far East, the Japanese in particular, and I know they plan to seek an attorney."

"How many other lens manufacturers do business here?"

"Perhaps thirty or more across the country, who would all be affected. It is a national trade association, not just local."

Uh-oh. Bennie took the bad news like a man. In nylons. "That changes things, Robert. I'm not sure I should represent you."

"What?" St. Amien's finely etched lips fell apart slightly. Next to him, Judy and Anne exchanged confused glances.

"You don't have an individual claim, you have a class action." Bennie took a sip of coffee so she didn't burst into hysterical tears. That would definitely *not* be professional. "I'm not a class-action lawyer, and your needs would be best served by one of them. They could represent you and the others against the trade association."

"A class action?" St. Amien inclined his silvery head.

"A class action is a lawsuit designed for people in your situation, when there are lots of people who have the same case against the same entity, and there is basically the same fact pattern. Technicalities aside, that is," Bennie added, but she didn't know them herself. She had just told the man all she knew about class-action law, which was the problem. "I'm not a class-action expert, but I can help you find one."

Across the table, Murphy was shaking her head in disagreement. Her shiny auburn mane swung back and forth as if in a Pantene commercial. "I'm sure we can handle a class action, Bennie. I did class-action work before I came here."

Next to her, Judy looked equally unhappy. "Boss, we can maintain a class action. We've done tons of antitrust work, and we can read the class-action rules as well as anybody. It's only a procedural difference."

Bennie was about to throttle them both when St. Amien joined in. "I truly wish that you represent me, Benedetta. I have heard of your reputation as a trial lawyer, of your abilities and your experience. My son is being educated in this country and he told me that you even judged his moot-court competition, at Harvard Law School. He told me about you, and he says you are something of an outsider. A maverick, no?"

Mavericks don't wear seventeen-dollar pantyhose. "I don't know . . ."

"You *are* a maverick. Your office is not pretentious. Your manner is honest." St. Amien gestured at the associates. "Consider Mademoiselle Carrier. She is permitted to express herself freely, in her ideas, and even in her appearance. This speaks volumes about you."

Bennie fell speechless. She couldn't even think of anything dumb to say, which was a first.

Judy grinned. "It's true, she's always been that way. And she *loves* my hair."

St. Amien continued, "I am an outsider also. A French national, making my new home in Philadelphia. Making my way here, until this association blocked me. Ruined my business, merely because I am not one of them. For many reasons, I want you to represent me."

"Robert, wait a minute," Bennie said. "To represent you, I'd have to represent the entire class, and your damages are so great, you'd probably be the lead plaintiff, the most important member of the class." *Lead counsel!* It would not only be interesting, but if she was lead counsel, she'd represent all the members of the class who didn't opt out, and most didn't. And the legal fees in class actions ranged from Mars to Pluto. "I've never been lead counsel to a class.

I've never even represented a class member."

St. Amien shrugged. "So, represent the class then. I'm sure you will do an excellent job."

"Boss, are you really having a crisis in confidence?" Judy asked in disbelief.

"Dude!" Anne's mascaraed eyes widened. "You're *the* Bennie Rosato!"

"It's not that easy, girls," Bennie said evenly. She gritted her teeth and tried to glare them into silence. She should have had DiNunzio here instead of these two crazies. DiNunzio understood that family conversations never left the dinner table. Bennie turned to St. Amien. "Under the federal rules, I can't just anoint myself class counsel. I have to apply for court approval. Lawyers who want to represent a class have to *prove* their adequacy and their experience."

"I could write that brief, easy," Judy said. "Let's take the case!"

Bennie gritted her teeth. "Carrier, we're not qualified."

"We always take cases we're not qualified for!"

Oh, great.

"We weren't murder experts when we started taking murder cases, and now we do them all the time. We learned." Carrier was on a tear. "Bennie, you're superqualified as a trial lawyer, and I can't imagine a judge in the Eastern District who would go against you. They love you on that bench. They've appointed you to two separate committees."

St. Amien nodded. "Excellent, then, my decision is made. I agree with your young ladies. So." He slipped a hand inside his jacket and extracted a checkbook bound in burgundy leather and a merlot Montblanc. He flipped open his checkbook and began to write a check, which was when Bennie's pantyhose exploded.

"Robert, please, don't do that." *Don't. Stop. Don't stop.* "Don't."

"I trust you'll forgive me," St. Amien said, with a sly smile. He finished writing and tore the check from the checkbook, then replaced his checkbook and pen. "I leave the money, in hoping you will accept my representation. Consider it 'earnest money,' as you say."

"Robert, even if I took the case, which I'm

not, it would be on a contingency basis. Please keep your check."

"Consider it for expenses and costs, *alors*."

"Class-action lawyers front those expenses. They're an exception to the professional rules. But please, don't do this." *Please. Don't. Stop.*

"Represent my interests. Will you do it, please?" St. Amien placed the check on the table in front of him like a trump card.

No. Yes. No. Yes. Then Bennie heard a sound. The siren song of solvency. Her heart leapt up. Maybe her firm wasn't doomed! Maybe the class action would settle fast! If she didn't get appointed as class counsel, it wouldn't be for lack of trying! Why should she defeat herself, when there were so many qualified people ready to do it for her? "Okay, you convinced me!" she said, and St. Amien laughed.

"*Merci beaucoup*. I couldn't be happier. I will take my leave." He rose, bowing at Judy and Anne. "Thank you, ladies, for your assistance."

"Thank you," Judy said, and Anne nodded.

"Yes, it was our pleasure."

Bennie got up. "Let me walk you out," she offered, taking St. Amien outside her office and into the empty hallway, where he turned.

"You needn't escort me all the way. Thank you again, for everything. *À bientôt.*" Suddenly St. Amien leaned over and gave her a deft kiss on the cheek, then turned and left.

"See ya." Bennie blinked, caught off balance. She'd never had a client kiss her, but she couldn't say she disliked it. She watched him catch the elevator, feeling vaguely as if they'd begun dating. Then she went back to her office to go holler at the associates. "Girls! The next time you disagree with me in front of—"

"This check is for ten thousand dollars!" Anne squealed, and Judy couldn't stifle a giggle. They had been joined by Mary Di-Nunzio, and their young faces were alive with excitement. In their hot little hands was St. Amien's check.

"*Ten grand?* Gimme that," Bennie said, taking the check. The watery ink had barely dried and the lettering was European, but it was made payable to Benedetta Rosato. She tried to remember the last time she'd seen her name on a payee line, and couldn't. And ten grand was double her usual retainer. It would employ two associates through the next month, and she could keep Murphy with her savings. *"Sacré bleu!"*

"It sounds like a really interesting case," Mary said, and Anne nodded.

"St. Amien is hot, for an old dude."

"And we could really use the work," Judy blurted out. "Since Caveson and Maytel went belly-up, I don't have anything to do. I mean, I have no work at all."

Bennie froze looking at the check, her face flushed. That no new business was coming in was evidently an open secret, but she felt too embarrassed to talk about it with the associates. How could she have let herself get into this position? Had she mismanaged the firm? Why hadn't she killed Ray Finalil? She let the moment pass, then walked stiffly around her desk for her purse. "Let me get you your seventeen bucks, Murphy. I can't get these stockings off without a sandblaster."

Anne waved her off. "Don't worry about the money, I charged them."

Mary looked at her with disapproval. "That doesn't mean they're free, Murph."

"For a month it does."

Judy was shaking her flame-retardant head. "The federal-government school of asset management."

Gulp. Bennie kept her thoughts to herself. She was in no position to lecture anybody. St. Amien's check would make a dent, but it wouldn't solve the problem. She had to keep the firm alive long enough to get to that class-action settlement. She opened her purse, a well-worn Coach barrel bag, and rummaged inside for her wallet. House keys, old Kleenexes, and a silver Motorola tumbled by, but her wallet wasn't there. She used a black pocket Filofax as a wallet: a chubby little organizer that held her credit cards, cash, and change.

"Bennie, you don't have to reimburse me," Anne said. "Buy me a T-shirt next time you go food shopping."

But Bennie wasn't listening. She'd reached the bottom of the bag, and her wallet wasn't in it. She dropped the bag heavily on her desk chair, eyeballing her desk. Marked-up briefs, stacks of correspondence, Xeroxed cases, and a rubber-band gun covered its surface, snowing in a laptop and an empty coffee mug. She moved the stuff aside, searching. "Please tell me I didn't lose my wallet. I can't function without that thing."

"When did you have it last?" Mary asked, but Bennie was already mentally retracing her steps.

"It's Friday. I walked the dog, then I got dressed and left for work. I stopped off at Dunkin' Donuts for a coffee. Extra cream, extra sugar."

"Maybe you left it at the Dunkin'?"

"No." Bennie shook her head. Usually, she didn't take her wallet out of her purse at a Dunkin' run. She would just slide out two bills, so she didn't have to juggle wallet, purse, and briefcase. Then she'd pay and leave the change in the tip cup. "This is odd. I know it was in my purse. I remember seeing it."

Mary folded her arms. "Maybe you're remembering wrong. You were probably thinking about your meeting this morning."

"Maybe." Bennie flashed on the scene in the Dunkin' Donuts. It had been crowded. She'd been preoccupied with thoughts of Ray and money. She'd skimmed the headlines of the newspapers on the metal rack near the counter. MORE BUSINESS DOWNTURNS

EXPECTED. LAYOFFS CONTINUE. The news had depressed her. "I must have left it there."

"I'll call the store for you," Murphy offered. "Is it the one near the office?"

"I'd cancel your credit cards too, Bennie," Mary said.

Judy was studying her boss's face with care. "You have been kind of forgetful lately, Coach. Is something the matter?"

"Not at all," Bennie answered. She faked a smile and slipped St. Amien's check into the side pocket of her purse. "What could be the matter? We just scored a huge class action!"

"Go, us!" Carrier cheered, and the associates all clapped. "Musta been the pink hair, huh, boss?"

"Musta been," Bennie agreed, and this time her smile was genuine.

3

Bennie had taken her lunchtime run to Dunkin' Donuts, looking for her wallet. It hadn't been there, and she'd run back to the office, cooling down along the route she took into work, jogging in the prematurely warm weather past happy crowds, budding trees, and air that was clean, for Philadelphia. She kept scanning the curb in case she'd dropped the wallet, but no dice. She'd have to cancel the credit cards when she got back to her desk.

She ended up at her office building, extracted a promise from the front security guard to keep an eye out for the missing wallet, and scooted inside the elevator. She scanned the empty cab for her wallet, then leaned against the wall as the steel doors slid closed. She bent down to catch her breath, leaning over her ratty tank top, loose Champion gym shorts, and old Sauconys with the curled-up toes. The only sound was her panting until the elevator reached her floor, where there was quite a ruckus. The elevator doors slid open, and fifty people were mobbing the reception area. She prayed they weren't her creditors.

Bennie stepped off the elevator into the crowd, but it was so thick nobody noticed her. They occupied all of the waiting-room chairs and stood talking and laughing among themselves. They were of all shapes and sizes—young, very old, men and women—and many of them carried tiny synthetic flags of a merry red, white, and green. They sipped coffee from Styrofoam cups and her JAVA DIVA mug while they ate biscotti and pignoli cookies from a huge bakery-style tray on her coffee table. Apparently, Rosato & Associates had been transformed into an Italian wedding. The only thing missing was the accordion.

"Uh, hello," she said as excited faces began to turn toward her. The receptionist wasn't around, but one muscular young man, wearing a T-shirt that read SOUTH PHILLY

ROCKS, broke into a grin when he spotted Bennie.

"You gotta be Bennie Rosato!" he exclaimed. He extended a hand and pumped hers so hard she was glad she was wearing a sports bra. "I'm Art DiNobile. It's so great to meet ya, and I can't thank ya enough for helping us out."

"You can't?" Bennie asked. She had no idea what he was talking about, she was half naked, and strangers were using her coffee mugs. Other than that, she was completely in control.

"Yo, everybody, this is Bennie! Bennie Rosato's here!" the young man shouted, turning to the crowd, which reacted instantly. The decibel level skyrocketed and the throng surged forward, pressing Bennie back against the elevator. Women tried to hug her, men offered their handshake, and someone passed her a cup of coffee and a plate of pignoli cookies. South Philly Rocks released her hand long enough to catch the cookies before they slid off the flimsy paper plate. "Have some, Bennie! They're from my father's bakery. Also I brought a nice rum cake and some *sfogliatelle*. It's the least we can do."

"It is?" Bennie asked, completely bewildered until Mary DiNunzio made her way though the crowd. Her hair was straying from its neat twist and her brown eyes were dancing the tarantella.

"Bennie!" DiNunzio was so excited she was almost short of breath. "Wait'll you see. I got us a case, a wonderful case!"

"A wonderful case?" Bennie repeated, fully aware that three thousand pairs of tarantella eyes were focused on her. She couldn't help feeling that her back was against the wall, or at least the elevator. "What kind of case?"

"The kind of a case you love! A once-in-a-lifetime case!" Mary shouted, and everybody behind her took up the cry like a Greek, er, Roman, chorus.

"Thank you!" they said, and "We appreciate your help" and "Ya gotta know the facts" and "We must bring it to light"—all manner of justice-sounding noises that made Bennie suspect she wasn't going to earn a dime in fees.

"DiNunzio, maybe we should talk about this in the conference room?"

"Great! Great idea! The client's in there."

"These people aren't the client?"

"No, this is the Circolo, from the neighborhood."

"The Circolo." *Of course. Whatever-o.* "DiNunzio, who's the client?"

"Mr. Brandolini, but he's dead. The client is really a lawyer, and he's dying to meet you."

"Huh?" Bennie was confused about who was dead and who was dying, but let it go. "Where's Murphy and Carrier?"

"In the conference room, with everybody else. The Circolo called while you were out, and I told them all to come right over. Marshall's still out at her gyno for a checkup."

"I'll see you inside in two minutes. I have to change out of my running clothes."

Bennie hustled to her office, skipped her usual shower, and put clean clothes on her sweaty body and slid reddish toes into her pumps. She'd wanted to call and cancel her credit cards, but Sicily awaited her in the conference room. She sent their secretary an E-mail listing her credit cards and asking her to cancel them when she got back from the doctor. Then she hurried out of her office and down the hall, into the crowd that spilled into the reception area. She shook their hands and greeted them as she passed, and they parted for her with a reverence usually reserved for Frank Sinatra.

"Brava, Bennie Rosato! Bravissima!" someone shouted, startling Bennie as she crossed the threshold into the conference room, when the entire room burst into resounding applause. The place was packed wall to wall, crammed with cheering, hollering, applauding people, and Bennie laughed and took a spontaneous bow.

"Thank you, thank you," she said, and pulled out the seat at the head of the long walnut table. Murphy and Carrier stood against a wall lined with happy Italians, which Bennie was beginning to understand was redundant. Mary sat beaming, catty-corner to her, next to a middle-aged man in a three-piece suit. He had thick dark hair and a brushy mustache, sharp brown eyes, and a pleasant smile. Bennie extended a hand. "I'm Bennie Rosato. Pleased to meet you, Mr. . . ."

"Cavuto, Frank Cavuto," he supplied, rising. "I'm a lawyer, representing the estate of Tony Brandolini."

"Welcome." Bennie nodded him into his seat, and the boisterous crowd deigned to settle down to business, with residual smiles—except for a tiny older woman who scowled inexplicably from the far end of the table. She looked immersed in a brown wool coat, despite the balmy day, and her salon pink-gray hair had been teased into a very feminine wren's nest. Thick glasses magnified her round dark eyes, fixed so hard on Bennie that she had to look away. "Now, Mr. Cavuto, what brings you here?"

"I'm Frank, please, and I've known the Di-Nunzio family since the day Mary was baptized. In fact, I'm her godfather's son."

Bennie didn't know that Italians really did have godfathers, and in truth didn't know much about Italians at all, despite her surname. "So you came to us through Mary."

Mary took over. "Frank came to see me when he probated the will of Tony Brandolini, who died last month, of cancer. Tony was a contractor, and his father, Amadeo Brandolini, was interned in 1942, as part of the internment during World War II. Mr. Brandolini was a fisherman, from the days when you could fish right off the port of Philadelphia."

Bennie raised a palm. "Slow down, wait a minute. What do you mean by 'interned'?

Interned means confined during war. Imprisoned."

"Yes, exactly. Well, you know that Japanese people living in this country were interned during World War II, even if they were citizens. Their property was taken, and their homes."

"Yes." Bennie remembered the historic *Korematsu* case, which held that it was constitutional to seize the property of American citizens who had the misfortune of being Japanese during wartime. The stirring dissent by Justice Brennan was renowned by fans of civil liberties. By the way, having pink hair wasn't a civil liberty. "I remember the time. Not a nice chapter in our history."

"Ours, either," Frank added, and heads nodded around the table, except for that of the old lady with the magnified glare. She fingered a gold necklace with a tiny horn charm as she looked daggers at Bennie, like a Neapolitan Madame Defarge. She sat next to a heavyset, balding man who appeared to be her husband but, unlike her, was dressed normally and was kind-eyed behind bifocals.

Mary cleared her throat. "Well, more than ten thousand Italians, citizens and legal immigrants, were interned in this country. They were covered by the same act and declared enemy aliens, even if they'd lived here for twenty years or more. They were ordered to register and sent away to internment camps in Missouri, Texas, and other states."

It was news to Bennie, even with her background in civil rights work, but it didn't surprise her. The government assumed all sorts of powers in wartime and used them to their fullest extent, for good and sometimes not-so-good reasons.

"The impact on Italians was biggest on the West Coast, and on fishermen on both coasts. The FBI considered fishermen especially dangerous because they had access to the sea, submarines, and enemy vessels." Mary glanced at her notes. "The government confiscated flashlights and shortwave radios so nobody could signal the enemy."

"It's all true," interrupted an elderly man near the door to the conference room. "My father and mother were both taken to the camp, even though they were living thirty-two years in this country. Even though I was enlisted and served. They weren't enemy aliens or what they called them, *traitors*. They were patriots! They never got their papers because they couldn't read and write in English."

"How's that for irony?" called out a woman near him. She had an academic air, with reading glasses dangling on a chain. "The son was fighting for this country while the parents were considered enemies by the same government. Did you know that Joe DiMaggio's father wasn't even allowed to go to his own son's restaurant in San Francisco? He was confined to a special zone."

Mary set her stack of papers on the table. "People lost businesses and homes. Families were split up and left without anyone to support them. And some, like Amadeo Brandolini, killed themselves in the camp. Amadeo couldn't live with the shame he felt he had brought upon his family."

"What shame? He didn't do anything wrong. He was a victim."

Cavuto raised a finger. "You look at it from a modern perspective, Bennie. Maybe even a woman's. But that wasn't the way Amadeo saw it, according to his son. His business was taken from him. His fishing boats. His livelihood. He had failed to support his family or to protect them. It made him feel ashamed, as a man." Cavuto cocked his head. "What kind of Italian are you, you don't know that? You just married one?"

"I'm single," Bennie answered, fighting the need to apologize for her condition. Being single after age thirty defined defensive. "I understand what took place. What I don't get is what you want us to do."

"Tony Brandolini wasn't a wealthy man, but he had some means and he never forgot his father or forgave his government." Cavuto bent over, reached into his thick briefcase, and retrieved a manila file folder. "Tony started to research what happened to his father's business, but then he got cancer and was too sick to finish the job. He provided in his will that when he died, his estate should hire a lawyer to recover the damages incurred by his father. We came to hire Mary and your firm to do this."

"You mean sue the government? Recover damages? Reparations?"

"That's what my client wanted. He was divorced, he had no children, and he left his entire estate to this cause." Cavuto gestured around the table. "It's a very important issue to all of us, and that's why we're all here. We'll help you any way we can."

"I second that emotion!" yelled South Philly Rocks, with a wink at Bennie. "Anything you need, you got it! And Mary, too. Alla youse!" Heads around him nodded in instant agreement.

"Thank you," Bennie said, pulling the case file over while the Circolo resettled, hopefully permanently. She opened the file, skimmed Brandolini's will, and read the bequest with a sinking heart. The will earmarked nine thousand dollars to fund the litigation. It was a lot of money, but it wasn't enough to take on the United States.

Mary read her mind. "Bennie, I told Frank how expensive it is to sue the government, and the Circolo has taken up a collection to raise money for the lawsuit. They've already pledged to match the funds in the will. That's almost twenty thousand dollars."

From across the table, South Philly Rocks was nodding again. "We got three Easter raffles going at church. And Goretti and St. Monica's are gonna do a real big basket of cheer. We got three different parishes working on it!"

Bennie sighed inwardly. *You can't stage a lawsuit with a bake sale.* "Frank, this is a very complex question. I'm not even sure the Brandolini estate has standing to bring suit, and there are issues of sovereign immunity and constitutional law. This is an expensive—"

"Bennie," Mary interjected, "I would donate all my time and do it pro bono. I would even work on my own time, outside of regular business hours."

Bennie didn't have the lira to let an associate work for free. "Mary, I'm sorry but—" she began to say, when there was a loud shout from the back of the room.

"Vide! Vide!" a woman shrieked, and Bennie jumped. The hard-eyed old woman at the end of the table was on her feet, yelling in Italian and pointing at Bennie with an arthritic finger. Bennie didn't understand anything until the end, when the woman lapsed into broken English. "You! You, Benedetta Rosato! You are evil! *Evil!*"

Bennie's eyes widened. She had no idea what she'd done. She'd never even met the woman. Who was she?

"Mom!" Mary shouted, leaping to her feet. "No, please! Mom!"

Mom? Bennie looked dumbfounded from her associate to the shouting woman and back again. *Madame Defarge is DiNunzio's mother?*

"Mom, no! Dad, please! She promised!" Mary was rushing over to the woman, whose thin skin had turned red as marinara. "Ma, no! You promised! Dad, she promised!"

Mom? Dad? Bennie watched as the older man got to his feet and tried to hug his wife into a state less hysterical. She kept waving her finger at Bennie, even as the rest of the Circolo tried to calm her down with help from Mary.

"Mom, please, be quiet!" she kept saying, joined by Carrier, who sprang from the side wall and hurried over to Mrs. DiNunzio. Fuchsia hair blossomed like a petunia among the brunettes. Murphy was right behind her.

Bennie rose to her feet, amazed. The conference room had gone nuts. Everybody left their chairs. People shouted at one another, and Mrs. DiNunzio was on a Neapolitan tear. Bennie turned to Cavuto. "Frank, do you speak Italian? What is she saying?"

Cavuto grabbed Bennie's elbow and took

her aside. "Well, she says that you're evil and she hates you."

"How can she hate me when she doesn't even know me?" Bennie was confounded. "You have to know me to hate me."

"She says that you don't care about nobody but yourself. Sorry, but Italian uses the double negative." Cavuto translated as the raving intensified. "You don't appreciate Mary. You don't care about nothing but yourself. Again the double negative."

"*Me?* I don't care about Mary?"

"You aren't good enough to her daughter. Or to her daughter's friends."

"Carrier and Murphy?"

"Yes. You almost got them all killed on some murder case." Cavuto's dark eyes narrowed in accusation. "Is this true?"

Ouch. "Well, yes. But it was on three different murder cases."

Cavuto turned away. "She says you don't pay them enough."

Bennie had no immediate reply. Mrs. DiNunzio was in the zone.

"She says your hair is always a mess."

"Does this matter?"

"And you walk like a man."

"I'm trying to get somewhere!"

"You're all alone. No man will ever marry you."

Whoa. Bennie bristled. "Now she's getting personal."

"You should leave immediately."

"She has nerve, throwing me out of my own conference room."

Cavuto met Bennie's eye. "She didn't say you should leave, I did."

"Why? It's *my* conference room. *She* should leave, not me." Bennie folded her arms. "I'm as capable as anyone of being childish. I have a First Amendment right to be childish."

Cavuto shook his head. "Rethink your position. I know Vita DiNunzio. She can go on like this for an hour or more. She only gets stronger as she goes, like a house on fire."

Bennie eyed the scene. The group was practically wrestling Mrs. DiNunzio to the ground, and she was still yelling. Her finger stuck up from the throng, like the Statue of Liberty in a hurricane.

Cavuto *tsk-tsk*ed. "At some point, she gets completely out of control. A whole city block can be consumed. She's a natural force."

Bennie snorted. "Okay, tell Mary I'll meet

her in my office. I'll get back to you about the Brandolini representation. You put me on the spot here, you know."

"Forgive me, but it's for a good cause. *Buona fortuna.*"

"For that I don't need a translation." Bennie gave him a pat on the back, then went back to her office to find her goddamn wallet.

4

Bennie combed the dhurrie rug and crawled under her desk and chairs. She wasn't giving up on that Filofax. She didn't have time to replace her driver's license, and she needed an organizer to feel organized. She went over every cluttered surface, then peeked under stacks of correspondence, old court decisions, and law books. She rummaged through every drawer in her desk and didn't find the wallet, but did find an old picture of her ex-boyfriend, Grady Wells, from a weekend trip to Cape May. She stopped at the sight of the photo. Maybe if they'd spent more weekends together. That was what he'd said anyway, but she'd had a business to run.

Just then came a timid knock on the door,

and Bennie didn't have to guess who it was. The secretary was out, Carrier knocked like a freight train, and Murphy never knocked at all. Bennie shoved the photo in the drawer and closed it quickly, so as not to reveal that she had Normal Human Emotions and/or Chinks in the Armor. She called out, "You're fired, DiNunzio!"

No laughter came from outside the door.

"I'm only kidding! Come in, silly!"

The door opened slowly, and a stricken Mary DiNunzio peeked inside. "I'm not coming in if you're going to fire me."

"I'm not going to fire you." Bennie waved her inside. "Come in and sit down."

"Thank you, thank you so much, Bennie, I can explain everything. First off, I'm really sorry and my mother is not crazy." DiNunzio hurried to the club chair across from the desk, perching on the edge of the seat cushion. Her words tumbled over each other and she gestured as rapidly as sign language. "She's really great, and I love her a lot, but I never would have let her come to the meeting if I had known she was going to act that way. She said she'd behave, but I guess she couldn't control herself, because she's very old school, you heard her accent, she wasn't even born here, and she gets a little upset and emotional because she loves me and she worries about me, and I'm really sorry. I can't believe she did that and I'm so embarrassed and so sorry. Really sorry. Did I say that already?"

"Yes. You—"

"I feel just awful. I'm so embarrassed, I know you must be so embarrassed. It was just so *embarrassing*."

"No, I'm an adult, and a lawyer. I can deal—"

"I mean, to have someone yelling at you, right in front of everybody, right in the office, and the whole thing was like a nightmare, I couldn't believe it was happening. It was awful! My mother says she's sorry and my father says *he's* sorry and we're all so upset that it happened." Mary teared up, but all Bennie had was a cup of cold coffee, so she handed it across her desk. The associate drank some and made a face. "Ugh! This tastes terrible."

"I know. I'm trying to shut you up."

"It worked." She set down the mug. "I'm sorry."

"Me, too. Now can we get over it? You

know I'm not good at the comforting thing. I—"

"But *I* should be comforting *you*." Mary's eyes welled up again. "You didn't do anything wrong. You were just trying to help me and—"

"Please *shut up!*" Bennie shouted, startling the associate into a tearstained silence. "Thank you. Now, settle down and listen. Your mother has good cause to be angry at me. I gather it's because of the trouble I've gotten you into on some of our cases."

"But that's not your fault, and I tried to explain it to her. Working on those cases was my decision, and things happened. She just worries because I work here. She wants me to quit."

"You can do whatever you like." Bennie couldn't imagine the place without DiNunzio, but she wasn't about to guilt-trip the kid. "Do you want to work somewhere where your mom wouldn't worry?"

"That's impossible. She'd worry no matter what I did. She worried about my sister Angie, and she was a nun in a cloistered convent."

Bennie said nothing. She was thinking

about her mother, who had been so ill and had passed two years ago. Bennie still missed her every day.

"Besides, I like the work we do, even if sometimes I get into trouble. I mean, we're doing justice. We actually do justice." The associate's mouth set with determination. "I think I'm getting better at being a lawyer, over time. I know I'm trying, and I don't want to stop. And today I brought in a new client, all by myself."

Bennie smiled. She'd never heard DiNunzio speak with such pride. It seemed like a cue for Bennie to say something she'd never said, even at the associate's performance reviews, when maybe she'd been too bogged down in the details of brief writing. "DiNunzio, I think you're a far better lawyer than you know. You have the mind, and the heart, to be one of the best of your generation."

Mary almost started crying again.

"Also your hair doesn't glow in the dark."

Mary smiled, but tears threatened still.

"Don't give a second thought to what just happened with your mom. I'm sure we can work it out. I'll take her to lunch and have a little chat."

"No!" Mary's eyes flared with new alarm. "I mean, thanks, but I don't think so. My mother doesn't go out to lunch."

"Why not?"

"It's outside."

"Outside what?"

"Her kitchen."

"Of course it is." Bennie thought again of her own mother. Depression had kept her confined to bed, often for months, in the era before Prozac and Paxil, when nothing seemed to work. "Why doesn't she go out? Is she ill?"

"No way. You saw her."

"Is she agoraphobic?"

"No, she's Italian."

Bennie let it go. "Okay. Then I'll take her to an Italian restaurant. Get her a nice plate of pasta."

"No, she would never eat someone else's gravy. Unless it was a blood relative."

"Okay, we won't go out. I'll go over to see her. That's in."

"No." Mary shuddered. "No talking, no seeing."

"Why not?" To Bennie, the whole thing seemed unusually complicated. "I want to make peace. We can reason together. I have great faith in the power of words."

"Take it from me, you two don't speak the same language. Bennie, you may not realize this, but my mother has lots of superstitions. Beliefs she brought over from the old country."

"Like that I'm the devil incarnate? Because of our cases?"

Mary swallowed hard. "It's not what you do, it's more who you are. It's what you stand for, the way you wear your hair, that you're tall, that you're so unlike her, what she thinks a woman should be, that you're not married, that you're not really lady-like—"

Don't hold back now.

"—and also it's not completely rational. Like, she's mad at you because I grew up, because I work, because I don't live at home, because my sister is a nun and I'm a lawyer and all and—"

Bennie stopped the word flow like a traffic cop. Funny thing was, she sort of understood. "Okay, so what do I do about it?"

"Letting it go will be the best course."

"That's not like me."

"Sometimes it's good to step back."

From the mouths of babes. Bennie straightened up. "Okay, fine. Now then, about the Brandolini case—"

"Can we keep it? If I promise to walk it and feed it and work it on my own time?" Mary jumped off the chair, fell to her knees on the dhurrie rug, and clasped her hands together in prayer. "Please, please, please?"

"You nut! Get up!" Bennie burst into laughter.

"I'm not a nut, I'm a Catholic, and we do this all the time. Please, please, *please* can we take the case? It's so important. It would be righting a terrible wrong. I'll work it on my own, I swear, and the Circolo will help with the bill. They can sell a lot of cannoli. The ricotta with the chocolate chip is beyond belief."

The associate's dark eyes pleaded with such deep and undisguised emotion that Bennie realized there was more than just a case at stake. Mary had brought in her first real client and was growing up before her eyes, as a lawyer and as an adult. Bennie felt herself respond, caught by surprise as something wrenched within her chest. Between Murphy's pantyhose and Carrier's hair and Mary's new case, she had lost any and all authority with these girls. The inmates were taking over the asylum, and for some reason, Bennie found herself smiling.

"So this is what it's like to have kids," she muttered.

And Mary exploded with joy.

Bennie had given up on the Filofax and was just about to call about her driver's license when the phone rang and she picked up reflexively. "Bennie Rosato," she answered, and the voice on the other end of the line laughed.

"Gotcha!" It was Dale Gondek, the rental agent for her office building. "Bennie, you been ducking my calls for two weeks!"

Busted. Bennie flushed. It was true. Caller ID wasn't made to evade landlords, it was more a by-product. "You're not going to believe this, but I have great news. I just got a big case, and I should have some dough for you this week."

"Who fell, Bill Gates?"

"Very funny. I can send you three grand as soon as the check clears." She had already earmarked the St. Amien and Brandolini money for payroll, utilities, and Iams MiniChunks.

"Three grand? That's one month rent. You owe us for three months, Bennie. You said you would get current when your jury trial ended. Did it end yet?"

Bennie winced. *Ray Finalil.* "It did, but my client went bankrupt and couldn't pay me. Can you take the three grand, and I'll get you the rest later?"

"When's later?"

"Soon later."

"Huh?"

Bennie rubbed her forehead. She was confusing herself. And she couldn't lie. She was the worst liar in the bar association. "Realistically? In six months, when the big case settles. Then I'll never fall behind again, I swear."

"*Six* months?" Dale sighed. "Not good enough. You know I like you, Bennie, but I'm gettin' all kinda heat from upstairs."

"I know that, and I appreciate it." Bennie had thought of moving her offices east of Broad Street, where the rents were lower, but at this point she couldn't make the security deposit. "Can you remind them I've been a tenant for five years, and I've never missed a month until recently? It's just a cash-flow problem."

"I know, and that's why you're still there. I got you the three months' leeway because of that trial you were on."

Ouch. "Maybe if I could talk to them myself and explain."

"No way, that's what they hire me for. Just between us, they ain't doin' so hot either. They need the money. Can't you borrow the dough somewhere?"

"No, I'm already leveraged out the wazoo." Bennie had already maxed out a commercial loan and a personal line of credit. She had a last resort, but broke a sweat at the prospect. "I'll get it to you, I swear."

"Ben, I'm up against it here. Don't make me send you an eviction notice."

"You did that already. It's pink." Bennie's gaze traveled to the notice, which was sticking out from underneath a stack of papers on her desk and was the same shade as Carrier's hair. Eviction Notice Pink. "Just let me slide a little longer, please?"

"No can do."

"I get thirty days on the eviction anyway. I'll have plenty of money as soon as this case settles. Send me the final eviction notice. The orange one." *Oops.*

"I'll see what I can do, but I'm not promisin' anything."

"Dale, thanks so much! You're the best!" Bennie said.

She hung up before he could change his mind.

5

It took only a weekend to transform the firm's large conference room into a war room. Documents from St. Amien & Fils, Xeroxed cases, and scribbled notes cluttered its long walnut table, law books sat stacked on its matching chairs, and a modern oak credenza overflowed with empty lo mein containers and a coffeemaker brewing on an endless loop. Windows lined the north wall, dark squares of shiny onyx, now that it was well past eight o'clock at night, and four weary lawyers ringed the table.

"Well, I understand class-action law better and I almost have a complaint drafted." Bennie leaned back in her chair, in a blue work shirt and khaki shorts, with her long curly hair twisted into a topknot by a dull pencil. Things were bad when your sole fashion accessory was a Dixon Ticonderoga. "And this fee business is amazing."

"How so?" Judy looked up from behind a mountain of open casebooks. Her orange T-shirt was wrinkled, and the stubby strands of her candy-coated hair were pinned away from her face by about two hundred clips. Her eyes had dark circles around them but came to life when she spoke. "You mean the amounts?"

"Yes. Under the lodestar approach, lead counsel can charge five to six times more than the hourly rate for representing the class, because of the benefit bestowed on the class as a whole." Bennie tried not to drool. "That's why there is such a battle over who gets to be lead counsel. It should be called the mother lode approach."

Anne looked up, next to Bennie. She managed to look fresh and crisp in a white cotton dress, with a coppery French braid running down her back. "What would the fees be in this case, for example?"

"If there's sixty million in damages in this case, then we can make twenty percent in fees. That's more than ten million dollars!" The number took Bennie's breath away.

She'd never thought she could be so mercenary, but being broke can turn a girl. "Thirty percent, which would still be kosher, would yield even more. If we represent the class, we get a ton of new clients, almost automatically, and my head explodes."

"Yowza!" Judy said, and Bennie agreed.

"The hard part is getting to be lead counsel. Lawyers usually decide among themselves who will be lead counsel. It's called 'private ordering.' The lawyer representing the biggest fish generally becomes lead counsel, which I have to believe is us, in St. Amien. And you know another way lead counsel is picked?"

"I do," Anne answered, raising her hand like the law student she'd been not long ago. "It's auction bidding. The qualified law firms submit secret bids on their fees, under seal, and the judge chooses the lowest bidder."

Judy looked over. "Are you serious? Lawyers submitting bids, like contractors? That's absurd! How can a judge choose who should be someone's lawyer? Whose lawsuit is it anyway?"

Bennie sipped ice-cold coffee. "It works well for cases like St. Amien's. It leaves more money for the class and gives lawyers like us, who don't usually represent class actions, a fighting chance. That's the rationale, but the Third Circuit found that auction bidding should be used only in special circumstances."

"Bidding is commerce, not law." Judy curled her nose. "The law should be pure, like art. It evolves like a painting, created step by step, until the whole can be seen."

Bennie smiled. The associates could be so surprising. They had worked their butts off this weekend, especially Mary, who had screened out the world as she researched her Brandolini case. Yellow, orange, and blue Hi-Liters lay on the table at her side, and she had filled three legal pads with tricolor notes. She was dressed to work in an oxford shirt and jeans, her hair pulled back into a tight ponytail, and wore her tortoiseshell glasses instead of contacts. Bennie found herself touched by the young associate's effort.

"DiNunzio?" she said. "It's late. Maybe you should stop now. We all should."

"Huh?" The associate looked up after a minute, her gaze preoccupied behind her glasses. "Gimme another ten minutes."

"No, I think we're all finished. We have to go to work tomorrow. You've all busted your butts this weekend, and I appreciate it. Time to go get some dinner."

Mary set down her pen only reluctantly, avoiding eye contact. Silence fell for a minute, and everybody noticed it.

Carrier looked over at her friend. "Hey, Mare. Something the matter?"

"Not at all. It's nothing. Not really." She turned to Bennie. "By the way, did you find your wallet?"

"No, but Marshall canceled the cards. Is that what's bothering you, my wallet?" Even Bennie could see that Mary needed to be drawn out, but she was almost as bad at drawing out as she was at comforting. "You've been quiet all weekend. Not that I'm not grateful, given the disorderly conduct of your fellow associates. But is something the matter? You want to talk about it?"

Mary looked away. "I don't know."

Bennie wondered if it was the thing with her mother. "Listen, we're a firm of four women. A hardy few, a happy few, I'm too tired to remember the quote. We should be able to talk about anything."

Mary wet her lips. "Well, it's just that

there's something I wish we could talk about." Her soft brown eyes found Bennie's. "With you, Bennie. It's about the firm, and money." She cleared her throat. "I mean, I know that Caveson and Maytel went out of business. How exactly does that affect us financially, and will St. Amien and Brandolini make it better? For example, I tried to call long distance on Friday and couldn't. I called AT&T to check the line but they said they'd talk only to the person whose name is on the account. Is something wrong with the bill?"

Anne nodded gravely. Her artful makeup had worn off by now, leaving her even lovelier. "And laying off Marie last month. You loved her, and she was our only other secretary. You wouldn't have done that unless you had to. And there's other cutbacks. No magazine and reporter subscriptions. Only double-sided copying. We're not supposed to take clients to dinner anymore, only lunch. And we share everything but toilet paper."

Judy chimed in, "You just won a jury verdict for Ray Finalil, and we should be flush. Celebrating. But you don't even seem that happy about it. What's going on? We have a right to know."

"Wait just one minute." Bennie felt herself stiffen. She didn't want to discuss this with them. She had let herself get too close, somewhere between the pantyhose and the lo mein. They weren't her colleagues; they were her employees. "I don't agree that you have a right to know. As a matter of fact, you most certainly do *not* have a right to know. It's my business. Literally."

Judy's cheeks turned as pink as her bangs, and Mary bit her lip. "Bennie, I'm not sure we have a right to know, but we want to know. It's our burden to share."

"Right," Murphy agreed.

Bennie considered it, only reluctantly. "Okay, I do have a cash-flow problem. Ray Finalil is going bankrupt, and he didn't pay us or his experts. St. Amien's case is great, but frankly, he may come too late. I don't know if I can keep the wheels on this thing until it settles, and there's always a chance that it won't settle at all." Bennie gathered her papers and rose stiffly, stowing them quickly in her briefcase. "You don't have to worry about your jobs for the next two months, but that's all I can guarantee. At this point, that's all I can promise you. Two months."

The three associates looked thunderstruck, and Bennie was fairly sure none of them had considered her job in jeopardy until this very moment. She looked down, fumbling with the latch of her briefcase, willing the lump from her throat. Then she forced herself to meet their eyes dead-on and steeled herself to say what was best for them, and not what she wanted to say at all:

"So now you know. I think things will change when we settle this class action, but I've learned enough law this weekend to know that that may take a long time. I will understand if any one of you wants to leave. Feel free to put out your résumé. I wish you all the best and will give you nothing but the highest recommendations. And I will manage without you. So if you need to leave the firm, please go."

"We don't want to leave!" Judy blurted out, and Anne was shaking her head.

"No way. I just got here."

Mary looked stricken; her lips parted. "I didn't mean it that way, Bennie. Let's just go to dinner. Forget about the whole thing. We have two great cases, in the class action and Brandolini, too. We can make it work. Bridge the gap somehow—"

"No, you guys go to dinner without me." Bennie shook her head quickly. "I'm beat. I'll see you tomorrow morning. Thanks again, for everything." She managed a fraudulent smile and headed for the exit. Her face felt hot, her mouth dry. Words she'd heard earlier that day flashed into her mind, about Amadeo Brandolini: *He had failed to support his family, or to protect them. It made him feel ashamed, as a man.* She understood now exactly how Brandolini had felt. The feeling wasn't confined to men. She left the associates quickly, and without another word.

Outside the office, the night air was dark, humid, and cool. The streets were deserted even though it wasn't that late. An empty SEPTA bus traveled down Chestnut Street, rocking from side to side with a hydraulic hissing. The bus didn't bother to stop at the kiosk at the corner, since nobody was waiting there, but accelerated, belching gray exhaust into the street. Bennie took a right turn onto a side street to lose herself in the narrow colonial streets of the city. She usually took them for her walk home because she liked the different sights they afforded, an insider's view. But tonight her route wasn't a matter of preference. She simply felt like hiding. From her associates, from herself.

She headed down a backstreet too narrow for a streetlight. An almost complete darkness lay ahead of her, interrupted only by the pool of a mercury-vapor streetlight at the far end of the block. It must have rained hard while they were working, and the asphalt of the street glimmered slick and black. Her Sauconys squished on the wet sidewalk. Then she heard a funny sound right behind her.

She turned, but there was no one there. Maybe she was just tired. Stressed. Still, she picked up the pace, hoisting her heavy briefcase a little higher. Something made her glance again over her shoulder. But there was nothing there. Bennie, usually so fearless, felt suddenly uncomfortable.

Enough already. Loser.

She held her head up and inhaled deeply. The wet air had a heavy odor that was hard to explain. Maybe it was her imagination, or maybe it was something else, which she identified next. Cooking oil? She had walked northeast, far enough to find herself

approaching Chinatown. The scent of saturated fats wafted down the block, spewed
into the air by whirling fans atop a score of
restaurants.

She walked on, and brightly lit signs with
red lettering—PEKING DUCK, DIM SUM, SHANG-
HAI GARDEN—surrounded her, and she remembered she had only cereal to eat for
dinner at home. Her dog could wait a little
for his walk; she felt oddly that she needed
to be around people. She ducked into one
of the bigger restaurants, hoping to get a
table quickly.

The restaurant bustled with suburban
families and couples, raising the noise level
and steaming up the front window. It
wouldn't be the peaceful meal Bennie had
pictured. She was turning to leave when a
waiter in a black jacket grabbed her elbow.
"One seat at bar," he said, urging her with a
pushy little yank.

"Is it ready now?"

"Right now," the waiter replied, and Bennie followed him through the packed restaurant to a seat at the bar, which was busy
since this was one of the few Chinese
restaurants with a liquor license. The waiter
read her mind. "You want drink?"

"Please, yes. A glass of zinfandel." The waiter nodded and took off, and Bennie set her briefcase at her feet and glanced around. The lights were low, but she could make out some familiar faces at a long table in the back of the restaurant. There was Judge William Tepper, of the federal district court, his glasses reflecting the tiny white lights at the center of the table, near a huge pu-pu platter. Next to him sat Judge Lynne Maxwell, also of the district court, then Judge Lucien Favata and Judge Ernest Calhoun Eadeh. It was a huge party, full of judges from the Eastern District bench. Judges often lunched in Chinatown because it was so close to the courthouse, but Bennie wouldn't have expected to see them here on a Sunday night.

Damn. She looked away, but thought better of it. The St. Amien complaint would be randomly assigned to one of these judges. She should start politicking if she wanted to be approved as class counsel. And her seat was close enough to the table that she couldn't avoid being seen. In fact, Chief Judge Kathryn Kolbert was already motioning to her to come over.

"Bennie, Bennie, over here!" the chief

judge was calling. She was in her late six-
ties, with frosted hair cropped in a chic lay-
ered cut, and she wore her laugh lines with
pride. Bennie had always admired Judge
Kolbert, who came from an era when
women burned bras and promoted other
women, which made her almost extinct.

Bennie got up, put on a smile, and
wedged her way to the table of judges.
"Well, here's quite a brain trust! What brings
you all together? Splitting the atom?"

Chief Judge Kolbert laughed, waving a
manicured hand at the head of the table. "It's
Ken's birthday. He's the big six-oh today."

"Sixty, can it be?" Bennie asked, smiling
at Judge Kenneth Sherman. She genuinely
liked Judge Sherman, though she could
never bring herself to call him Ken. Judges
for her held a certain mystique and they always would, even without their robes. They
were true public servants, making far less
than they could have in private practice, for
the good of everyone. She bowed slightly
from the waist, trying to summon some dignity in her khaki shorts. "Congratulations,
Judge Sherman!"

"Ms. Rosato, one of my favorite Democrats!" Judge Sherman exclaimed, and Bennie laughed.

"That's right. Now don't die on me, Judge. It's only you, me, and the chief on the home team."

"You got that right!" Judge Sherman laughed, and so did the others, good-naturedly. Everybody knew that the string of Republican presidents, starting with Bush senior, had changed the face of the federal judiciary, making it older, whiter, and more conservative. But the appointments were generally smart and fair, and evidently had a decent sense of humor. Even if they didn't realize that sisterhood is powerful.

"Well, I don't want to disturb you," Bennie said. "I'll leave you to your revelry. Enjoy!" She left with a short wave and a round of good-byes and went back to her seat at the counter, where the waiter greeted her with her glass of wine. She sat down, nursed her wine, and tanked up on the fried things they brought free while she memorized her draft complaint. Her only other choice was looking at all the happy people around her, who undoubtedly paid their long-distance bills. When her meal came, she finished it quickly and left the restaurant.

Bennie emerged into the night, and the air had thickened, heavier with an expectant humidity. She pulled her sweatshirt closer around her and glanced up at the sky, opaque with storm clouds, and moonless. It was going to rain again, from the look of it, any minute. She looked around for a cab but there was none in sight. The sidewalks were empty. Philadelphians stayed home on Sunday nights, and every other night. It was only one of the things she loved about her hometown.

She turned west toward her neighborhood and picked up the pace. If she had to walk home, she would. It would take only a half an hour. But her stomach felt uncomfortably full, and she couldn't shake the spooky feeling she'd had before. She didn't hear a noise, but she glanced back anyway. A drizzle came on, spitting at first and then harder, with cold raindrops pelting the parked cars and city streets.

Bennie tilted her head down and hurried down the street.

Trying not to look behind her.

6

Monday morning, Bennie stepped off the elevator into the reception area of her firm and stood confounded by the sight. Cardboard boxes filled the room, stacked like toy building blocks. There had to be thirty of them, heaped on the carpet and piled atop the coffee table and chairs. What was all this? She tucked her newspapers, bag, and briefcase under her arm, went over to the nearest box, and read the shipping label. NORTH CAROLINA HAMMOCKS (2). She lifted up the second page of the bill for the order line, and it read BENEDETTA ROSATO. *What*?

Bennie went puzzled to the next box, from Neiman Marcus, and skimmed the white shipping bill. CASHMERE SWEATERS, TWO. BENEDETTA ROSATO. She hadn't ordered any cashmere sweaters. She turned to a long, skinny box from Smith & Hawken. GARDEN SHOVELS (2), from France. *Imported shovels?*

Bennie realized what had happened, just as the secretary appeared. Marshall Trow was a bright-eyed woman in a blue cotton maternity dress. Bennie turned to her. "Can you believe this shit?"

"You off the curse diet?"

"Fuck yes! It's my credit cards, right? Whoever has my wallet must have used them before we canceled the cards."

"Right, but don't sweat it. You're not liable for the charges. I called some of the vendors and they verified that your Visa and AmEx cards were used for the purchases. Remember, the credit card companies let me cancel your cards, but only the cardholder can find out about the recent purchases. I told you to call them, in my E-mail. Did you?"

"Didn't get a chance. Sorry." Bennie had been too busy working. She hadn't even replaced the Filofax. All her money, about fifty bucks from her underwear drawer, was stuffed in a Ziploc bag. "I have no time to deal with this, Marsh."

"I'll file a report with the police and call

FedEx to come get these boxes. I'll call about your driver's license."

"Thanks." But Bennie didn't get one thing. "Why would somebody buy all this stuff on my cards and *send* it to me? Why not just keep it? What's the point?"

"It must be a prank." Marshall fingered the paintbrush end of her light brown braid. "Somebody thinks this is funny, like sending twenty pizzas to your house. They want to jerk your chain."

"Well, let 'em laugh." Bennie hoisted up her briefcase, bag, and newspapers. "Onward and upward. How was your weekend?"

"Fine, thanks. Jim and I took it easy, but the baby didn't. He's movin' and groovin.' Only two weeks to go." Marshall rubbed her very pregnant tummy. "It's great news about the new class action. We're playin' in the bigs now, huh?"

"Trying to." Bennie had finished St. Amien's complaint last night and she'd have to file it this morning. They'd meet at eleven o'clock to review it, but she couldn't wait to file. She wanted to get ahead of the curve on the lead counsel thing. "Marshall, can you fill out a civil cover sheet for me to file with the St. Amien complaint?"

"It's already on your desk, for your signature."

"What a woman," Bennie said, meaning it. She didn't know if Marshall would decide to come back to work after the baby was born. It would be a terrible loss for the firm, if there still was a firm. "Now all I have to do is find the hundred and fifty bucks for the filing fee."

"I got it out of petty cash. There's three dollars and two cents left."

"You anticipate my every need. Will you marry me?"

"No."

"Is it because I walk like a man?"

"What?" Marshall's pretty forehead wrinkled.

"Forget it. Any messages?"

"Not yet," she said. It was Marshall's considerate way of saying *Nobody calls here anymore.* "Who's going to file the complaint?"

"I am. I want Carrier and Murphy to keep working on the class-action research, and DiNunzio's on *Brandolini,* so I'll file it. You know my mantra."

"Eat two, they're small?" Marshall smiled crookedly. She had the intelligence, loyalty, and sense of humor God reserved for legal secretaries, because they needed it more than anybody else.

"No. 'If you have more time than money, do it yourself.' Let me check my E-mail, then I'll go." Bennie headed for her office, then stopped. Marshall must have talked to the associates about the conversation last night. She told them everything. She was the one in the office with Warmth and Personality. Bennie turned back. "Marshall, you know the story about the firm's finances, but the associates don't. Or didn't, until last night. I think I surprised the shit out of them. I mean, the crap."

"I would say so." She snorted. "They were in a tizzy this morning, but they'll be okay."

"How bad were they? Did you distribute Prozac?"

"No, they're fine. It's good to share information like that with them. They're old enough, they should know the kind of pressures that the firm is under." Marshall's eyes narrowed. "You're the one I'm worried about. They said you didn't eat dinner with them, that you were really upset when you left. Are you okay? You look tired this morning."

"I worked late, and I wasn't upset. I wanted to draft that complaint. I'm fine."

"You can't do everything alone, Bennie." Marshall clucked. "What'll you do when I have a real baby to take care of?"

"God knows," Bennie answered, then went off to be her own messenger.

A half an hour later, she had arrived at the United States Courthouse, which rose like a red-brick monolith among the historic halls and the new Constitution Center. Lawyers, court employees, jurors, and judges flooded into the courthouse this morning, typically busy for a Monday, when new juries were impaneled. Inside, new security measures had forced the slicing up of the courthouse's formerly generous marble lobby into glass chutes that funneled people to the metal detectors. Bennie joined the back of the line, ending up not far from the courthouse entrance, and was just about to jockey for a faster lane when she felt a hand on her arm. It was Chief Judge Kolbert, but today she appeared stiff in a trim tweed suit, carrying an accordion briefcase.

"Long time no see, Chief," Bennie greeted her. The lawyers in front of her glanced back, jealous. Knowing Chief Judge Kolbert was the legal equivalent of knowing Madonna.

"Good morning, Bennie," the judge replied, but her freshly made-up face wrinkled so deeply her foundation cracked. "I gather you have a rather large headache this morning."

"No, not really. Why do you say that?"

"Your conduct last night." The chief judge leaned over, scented with Shalimar and annoyance. "You had had quite a lot to drink at the restaurant. You certainly tied one on."

"What?" Bennie asked, surprised. "I had only the one glass of wine."

"Please. You disappoint me. Judge Eadeh told me he saw you, in the crowd at the bar. You made quite a scene. He told me they asked you to leave."

"That's not true!" Bennie felt slapped in the face. The lawyer in front of her glanced back to see who was making a fool of herself in front of Madonna. "Nobody threw me out, Judge! What are you talking about?"

"I'm not going to argue with you about it." The chief waved hello at a passing group of lawyers, then returned her attention to Bennie, her whisper thinned to a hissing. "I'd advise more prudence in public. I know you were on your own time, as were we, but really, everybody noticed. You are well known and you represent all of us."

"But, Judge, I didn't get thrown—"

"Judge Eadeh saw you, and so did Judge Sherman. Are you saying they were lying?"

Judge Sherman, too? "No, of course not, but they must have made a mistake. The bar was crowded. Maybe it was someone who looked like me, but it wasn't me, I swear it!"

"Bennie, I tell you as a friend. If you have a drinking problem, attend to it. Now, I must go." The chief judge pivoted on her patent pumps and left bearing her briefcase.

Bennie stood stunned, her face aflame. What was the judge talking about? She hadn't had more than one glass. She hadn't made any scene. She hadn't been thrown out. The line shifted forward, and she shifted with it, on autopilot. She couldn't understand it. There had been a crowd at the restaurant's bar. Maybe someone in the bar area had made a fuss, and the judges had mistakenly thought it was her. Maybe it was someone who looked like her. That had to be it. But what could she do about it? Go to each judge and explain? *Excuse me, Judge, I'm not an alcoholic?*

Bennie passed through the security checkpoints, shoving her briefcase and bag onto the conveyor belts and flashing her laminated court ID, completely preoccupied. There must have been some sort of misunderstanding, simple as that. Best to let it go. Say nothing, and pray that St. Amien's complaint wasn't assigned to a judge who thought she needed Alcoholics Anonymous. It gave a whole new meaning to the term "judicial intervention."

Bennie grabbed the escalator to the second floor, and by the time she reached the blue rug of the landing, she had another theory. She'd said it herself earlier, the thought coming out of its own volition: *Maybe it was someone who looked like me.* Because there was someone who looked like her. It was possible that Alice, her twin, had come back to Philly. They looked identical, but Bennie hadn't seen Alice since the day she'd left town two years ago, and given Alice's lifestyle, Bennie had even wondered if she were still alive. Alice hadn't

wanted a twin, and Bennie hadn't either—
after she'd met hers. The two women hadn't
grown up together, and one had become a
lawyer, while the other had become a criminal. It had all come out in court, when Bennie defended Alice on a murder charge. Was
Alice back in town? And why would she be
in the same Chinese restaurant last night?

Bennie walked distracted down the corridors of the building, through a warren of
bright white halls and past the door to the
United States marshal's office, flanked by
framed movie posters of Kevin Costner as
Wyatt Earp and Tommy Lee Jones in *U.S.
Marshals*. Evidently everybody was having
trouble separating fiction from reality this
morning. Bennie walked on, considering her
situation. It couldn't have been Alice in the
restaurant, could it? She hadn't seen her
there, and she would have noticed her dop-
pelgänger eating dim sum. It seemed impossible, or at least unlikely. No reason to
jump to conclusions. Alice had no business
in town, and she'd said she'd never come
back. The judges had simply made a mistake. They did that all the time, whenever
they ruled against Bennie. She tried to laugh
it off, but she wasn't laughing.

She reached the office of the district court clerk and opened the double doors into the large office, buzzing with characteristic activity. Facing the entrance was a long Formica counter of fake wood, and behind it fifty-odd court employees hustled back and forth with court documents or keyboarded at their desks in maroon cubicles covered with American flags and Eagles calendars. Bennie never lost sight of the fact that even the biggest lawsuit started with a single complaint, which would be accepted by someone, time- and date-stamped, then assigned to somebody in a black robe. The employees in the clerk's office, dressed in rugby shirts and Cherokee jeans, were as integral to the justice business as the guys in the black robes, and Bennie had come to know many of the clerks personally over time. She took a place in line at the counter, suppressing nagging thoughts about Alice.

"Yo, Joe," she said, settling when she reached the front of the line. Joe Grimassi, the clerk at the counter, greeted her with a smile. He was a twenty-five-year-old in a blue oxford shirt and khakis, and he attended Temple Law at night.

"Hey, Bennie. How you been?"

"Good." She reached into her briefcase, slid out a manila folder containing the complaint, the civil cover sheet and the other papers, and her check for the filing fee. "How was your Civ Pro exam?"

"Last semester? I got an A! Thanks for your help. I really appreciate it."

"No problem. Res judicata's a bitch."

"Tell me about it. If it weren't for you, I'd be screwed. So, what do you have for me today?" Joe held out his hand, and Bennie passed him the papers and check.

"A class-action complaint. I'm an old dog, learning new lawsuits."

"I recognize this defendant." Joe nodded, skimming the caption. "I heard this case is gonna be a monster. We already had four other complaints filed in it last week."

Huh? "Already? You're kidding. From who? Whom?"

"The usual suspects. Kerpov, Brenstein, Quinones, and Linette's firm. Linette filed first, of course."

"I shoulda known." Bennie was kicking herself. So much for getting ahead of the curve.

"These class-action jocks, they don't sit

on their thumbs. Not on a case this big, with lead counsel in play. It's a gold rush." Joe leaned over the counter like a co-conspirator. "And you didn't hear it from me, but the word is Bill Linette signed the lead plaintiff."

"The lead plaintiff?" Bennie couldn't believe it. Bill Linette was the heaviest hitter in the class-action bar. He'd supposedly been given the nickname "Bull" because he was so tough, but Bennie knew a better reason. "How can he? I have the lead plaintiff. Robert St. Amien."

"Not according to Linette. His messenger spilled the beans. I forget the plaintiff's name." Joe set aside her papers, filled out a receipt for her check, and assigned her a case number. "Looks like you and Big Bull will have to duke it out. Celebrity Lawyer Deathmatch. Kick his ass for me, would you?"

"Bet on it, Joe." Bennie felt her juices flowing. "Lemme see a copy of Linette's complaint."

"Believe me, it ain't Oliver Wendell Holmes. It took him about ten minutes to write, if that." The clerk went to a desk nearby, looked through a file, extracted a manila folder, and returned to Bennie. "Here we go. You know the rules, give it to the guys in the copy department over there."

"It hasn't been assigned to a judge yet, has it? Say no." Bennie wanted time between her alleged public drunkenness and the case assignment, but one look at the file told her that it wasn't to be. The judge's name had been stamped in large red letters at the top. HONORABLE KENNETH B. SHERMAN. It was Judge Sherman, the birthday judge, who had liked her until he found out she was in rehab. "Thanks a lot, Joe," she said as he motioned for the next lawyer in line.

Bennie moved out of the way with the file folder and joined the long line at the copy department, where she opened the folder. *"Mayer v. Lens Manufacturers Association of Pennsylvania et al.,"* read the caption, and she winced. One Herman Mayer had already been given the lead plaintiff position, at least in the caption. She flipped through the complaint while she waited in line, with increasing anger. It was only three pages long, with just the barest bones of pleading, stating the reasons the case should be a class action and the cause of action. There were no details, no specifics, no dates, no wrongful statements alleged. It wasn't a complaint, it was a bookmark.

Bennie turned the page to the claim for damages, at the end of complaints in capital letters. She had to read the capitals three times before she could convince herself what was really printed there, in black and white: SEVENTY MILLION DOLLARS. Her eyes popped. *Seventy million dollars!* No way was Mayer's case worth that much! He hadn't built a plant, as St. Amien had. It went way beyond the norm, even for kamikaze plaintiff pleading. No wonder Linette had beaten her to the courthouse. If the fee was a standard percentage, he could make as much as 30 percent of seventy million bucks. She'd need a twelve-step program to figure the final total.

"Hey, lady," said a gruff voice from behind her in line, a messenger from one of the big law firms. "You gonna copy that or not?"

"Yes, sorry." *Seventy million!* Shaken, Bennie moved forward and began fishing at the bottom of her purse to find money for the copies, fifty cents a page. She needed to buy a new wallet. But she couldn't get past the request for damages. *Seventy mil-*

lion dollars! "That's a lot of money!" she heard herself say.

"Fifty cents a page, I'll say," the messenger agreed.

Bennie had the complaint photocopied, returned the file, left the courthouse, and stormed rather than walked all the way back to the office. She couldn't shake her terrible mood. It was another unseasonably warm day but she didn't notice. She hadn't eaten but she wasn't hungry. She reached her office building full of steam, worry, and purpose, but all of it vanished when she stepped off the elevator.

And realized what was happening.

7

Near the wall in the reception area, two workmen in the navy blue jumpsuits of the building-management company were posting an eviction notice of a color Bennie hadn't yet seen. White. Laser-printed. No-nonsense. *Eek.* Bennie hurried to the workmen as the associates rushed her like abandoned baby birds.

"Boss!" Carrier said, almost tripping over a new delivery from J. Crew. "They say they're evicting us! We have to get out in thirty days."

DiNunzio had paled as white as her oxford shirt. "They can't do this, can they?"

"Of course not." Murphy folded her arms, seething in a manner perfected by redheads. "I told them they'd be in deep shit when you got back."

"Step aside, girls," Bennie said, coming through. Marshall was already on the phone at the reception desk; she probably already had Dale on the line. This was definitely a mistake. Maybe he hadn't gotten her check, or maybe these guys didn't know he'd gotten it.

"Yo, guys," Bennie said to the workmen. One name patch read GUS and the other, VINCENT, but she didn't need the prompting. She had known them since she'd moved her office here. "Gus, what the hell's going on?"

"Sorry, Bennie," he answered, keeping his head turned away. He was heavyset and looked like a chubby baby in his jumpsuit. His thick hand grasped a ring of gray duct tape. "Believe it or not, this is harder for us than for you."

"We're just doin' our jobs, Ben." Vincent was duct-taping the bottom edge of the eviction notice to the wall. "We got no choice in this matter, you know that."

"Listen, guys, I swear, I sent Dale a check by FedEx. I even paid extra for Saturday delivery. Maybe he didn't get it, maybe something went wrong, I don't know. I'll call him and he'll tell you, so you can save your duct tape."

"I don't think so," Gus said, his tone flat. "They took this outta Dale's hands. This comes from the cheese. He tole us this morning, go out and get it done."

"And don't let you talk us out of it." Vincent was twisting off the end of the duct tape with difficulty. He turned to Gus. "Gimme the X-Acto knife."

"I don't got it. I thought you brought it."

"I thought *you* brought it. Just rip it, stupid."

"Okay," Vincent said, and did. "Sorry, Bennie. You're a great lady, you know that. We all wish you lotsa luck, and the girls, too." He nodded at the associates, looking away from a wet-eyed Mary DiNunzio. The workmen left quickly for the elevator and caught the next cab.

Bennie confronted the eviction notice taped to the wall of the reception area. *Her* reception area. She had painted it with her own hands. Picked the pictures. Bought the furniture. She had even sanded the goddamn floor. This office was her second home, and getting thrown out was unthinkable. Bennie grabbed the eviction notice at the top and ripped it down with a satisfying *shzipp*. "I may not know art, ladies. But I know what I like!"

"Yeah!" Murphy cheered, and Carrier clapped and hooted beside her. Only Mary looked worried still, her young forehead prematurely creased. For her benefit, Bennie plastered a grin on her face and wadded the notice and duct tape into a ball.

"Don't worry, DiNunzio," Bennie said. "We'll have this fixed up in no time."

Marshall had hung up the phone and was waddling hurriedly toward them through the box maze, biting her lip. She held a notepad in her hand. "Dale said he's really sorry but the management wouldn't go for the partial payment."

"No problem," Bennie said, gritting her teeth. Just then an inconvenient *ping* emanated from the elevator bank, and she straightened up instantly. It wasn't eleven o'clock yet. It couldn't be St. Amien. The lawyers snapped to jittery attention, and Marshall looked toward the elevators. It was their good-looking UPS man in his jaunty brown shorts, carrying a large box that read FRAGILE—WATERFORD CRYSTAL.

"Another delivery, Bennie!" he called out, then set down the box on the other boxes and left with a quick wave. It would have been funny, but Bennie couldn't find her smile. Another package, another fake charge. Her credit, a mess. Her wallet, stolen. And her reputation with the judges, ruined. She suddenly knew in her heart what she had been denying all morning. She announced:

"Alice Connelly is back in town, ladies."

DiNunzio groaned, and Carrier's Delft blue eyes flared in alarm. Only Murphy cocked her head, puzzled. "Alice who?"

"Alice Connelly, my twin sister." Bennie paused to collect her thoughts. Her heart hammered against her chest wall. Now that she'd said it, it had become real. "Everybody here except you, Murphy, will remember Alice from that case that we had. She found me—aided and abetted by my wayward father—and asked me to defend her on a murder charge. After it, she did a disappearing act, which apparently runs in my family."

Murphy's green eyes narrowed. Carrier was nodding, and DiNunzio bit her lower lip. Marshall eased onto the L.L. Bean box, her hand protectively on her tummy, and Bennie continued.

"Alice was given up for adoption when we were born, and I didn't know about her until we met as adults. We're identical—at least we look that way. I haven't heard a word from her in two years, since I dropped her off at the train station." Bennie flinched at the memory. She had thought about Alice in the intervening years, with more frequency than she could explain. She'd even tried to find her once, to no avail.

"I thought she'd left Philly for good, but I think she's come back. I think she stole my wallet and ordered all this stuff to jerk my chain, like Marshall said." Bennie's thoughts raced ahead. Suddenly the crazy events of the past few days were making a twisted sort of sense. "There's two of everything, get it? Twins. And I bet she made me look bad to the judges, too. She must have followed me from the office, maybe even pretended to be me in the Chinese restaurant."

"Your twin sister would do that to you?" Murphy asked, astonished.

"This is no ordinary sister," Mary told her. "And no ordinary twin." She sank to the box beside a silent Marshall as Murphy shook her glossy head.

"Whoa. This is so *Port Charles*."

Carrier frowned. "What do you mean, made you look bad to the judges?"

Bennie hadn't told them yet. "Half the Eastern District bench, including Judge Sherman, who picked up St. Amien's case, thinks I was drunk in the restaurant last night."

"Well, were you?" Carrier asked, and Di-Nunzio nodded with sympathy.

"It's no crime if you had a drink or two, Bennie. You've been under a lot of strain lately. You keep it all inside—"

"What?" Bennie looked at them, incredulous. "It wasn't me. I was barely drinking. It had to have been Alice." But if they were doubting her, everybody would. Bennie put it together, and the gravity of her predicament dawned fully. Anger bubbled like lifeblood to her cheeks. She snatched up the phone and punched in the number for information. "In the Philadelphia area, the listing for Alice Connelly, please."

Carrier watched. "She won't be listed."

"I know," Bennie said, and when she got the answer they both expected, she thanked the operator and hung up. "We have to find her. Carrier, I have to get ready for St. Amien, so can you run a computer check on Alice? I want to see if she's back in town, and where she is. Call Lou, too." Lou Jacobs was their veteran investigator, home recuperating from prostate surgery, and Bennie missed him. "He might have some ideas how to find her."

Carrier nodded. "Done."

"Good, thanks." Bennie was fuming. It had to be okay to curse in present circumstances. She slammed a fist down on the desk, and the pencil cup jumped. "*Goddamn it!* She's back!"

"Bennie, relax, want some water?" Marshall offered, rising, but Bennie waved her back onto the box.

"To make matters worse, we're already being outgunned on St. Amien. Bill Linette beat us to the courthouse, and he claims he has the lead plaintiff." The telephone rang on the reception desk just as Bennie was about to get seriously profane. She hit the button for the speakerphone and answered.

"Robert St. Amien here," came the response, a musical accent over the loud speakerphone. "Answering your own tele-phones now, Benedetta?"

"Sure, I'm a maverick, remember?" Ben-nie checked her emotions. "How are you, Robert? I have you on speaker, if that's okay."

"It's fine. Even better. Are your young ladies there?"

"They are." Bennie turned to the associ-ates. "Angels, say hi to Charlie."

"Hi," they all chorused.

"Good morning, ladies," St. Amien called back. "Bennie, I'm on the mobile phone. I am calling because I have been receiving this morning several telephone calls from Mr. William Linette."

Bull! "I know Bill. He's another lawyer in town, who represents one of the other class members in your case. He filed a complaint against the trade association last week." Bennie hoped it would sound like she was up to speed, even though she was strug-gling to play catch-up. "He called you?"

"Several times, as I say, when I didn't re-turn his. He caught me on the last try. He tells me that he is one of the most experi-enced class-action attorneys in the country and that he wishes to represent me and my company."

The associates stood mute, and Bennie swallowed hard. She prayed to God that St. Amien didn't leave her now. "I didn't file our complaint until this morning, so maybe Linette didn't know I was representing you. If he had, I'm sure he wouldn't have called me directly."

"No, he mentioned that he had heard I engaged you."

Bennie laughed, and Carrier held up a silent, yet eloquent, middle finger. So Linette was trying to snake her, trying to steal a represented client. It was a move even lawyers considered low. "I'm not completely surprised. Are you?"

"Of course not." St. Amien chuckled over the speakerphone. "Nevertheless, I told him I am already represented, by you."

"Thank you." Bennie would have kissed the man, but insolvency had killed her libido. "Robert, you're about to become the most popular Frenchman in town. Lawyers will be buying you all the escargot you can eat."

"I'm sure of it." St. Amien chuckled again. "By the way, Mr. Linette said that there would be several other counsel and their clients—men I know—meeting in his office today, at noon. He invited you and me to this meeting. Shall we meet alone as we had planned, or shall we go to Mr. Linette's meeting?"

"We should go to Linette's, absolutely. We have to coordinate with the rest of the class, and I want to establish your position as lead plaintiff." *Jesus.* Bennie had never seen a case move this fast. Linette was wasting no time grabbing power and running with it. She had to deal with Alice, but she couldn't jeopardize St. Amien's interests. "But I'm warning you, I expect there to be a tussle over the lead plaintiff. Linette filed on behalf of someone named Mayer, whom he's touting as lead plaintiff."

"Mayer, Herman Mayer?" St. Amien paused. "Linette did not mention this. Herman Mayer is quite vocal, a troublemaker of sorts. But he is—how do you Americans say—a piker, in comparison with me."

"I suspected as much. And you should also know that Linette's complaint, which I will show you, seeks damages of seventy million dollars."

"Oh." St. Amien paused, and the associates started whispering among themselves until Bennie hushed them. St. Amien was saying, "Mr. Linette is an optimist."

"I think he's nuts, but so be it. It doesn't help the case to ask that much in damages, especially if you can't prove it. But it gets clients. And headlines."

"If I meet you there, I expect I'll be pounced upon the moment I set foot."

"Exactly." Bennie managed a smile. "You'll need a bodyguard, and I recommend an Amazon with messy hair. I'll meet you downstairs in the lobby, and we'll walk over together."

"Perfect, see you there. *À bientôt,* ladies."

"Bye," the associates chorused, and he hung up.

Bennie hit the off button on the phone and her ersatz good mood evaporated. She heard herself sigh and leaned against the desk. She'd have to fight to keep St. Amien, but Alice was back, the landlord was evicting her, and she was out of dog food. She hadn't felt so totally at a loss since the day her mother had passed. And her employees were staring at her, momentarily speechless. They looked like waifs, bewildered and scared—as if *their* mother had passed. It telegraphed to her suddenly what to say, and do. *Be a mother.* Be strong, nurturing, certain, sure. Take control. Run the family. Be all the things her own mother had been, until illness overcame her. That strength had been her only legacy, and in truth, it was the only legacy of value.

"Listen, folks," Bennie began, "there is no reason to panic. It's not a disaster, not yet. As calamitous as this seems, I will deal with it. Fix it. Set it right."

"Sure," Murphy said.

"Absolutely," Carrier said.

"We have faith," DiNunzio said, but none of them sounded completely convinced, and Bennie straightened up.

"First things first. Right now I have a client to meet, and I'm never late." She was beginning to feel better, more in control. She took a deep breath, picked up her bag and briefcase, and went to the elevator bank. "Carrier, if you find Alice, call me right away on the cell."

"Got it," Carrier called back, brightening.

"I'll help her," Murphy added, and even DiNunzio managed a thumbs-up.

Only Marshall couldn't find a smile, but

she knew how serious it was. She was about to be a mother, too.

Bennie grabbed the elevator and was gone.

8

Bennie had visited Lawyer Kingdoms in her day: oases of thick rugs, original oil paintings, and Chippendale chairs like thrones. She had seen plenty of corner offices, some as big as football fields, with patterned runners the length of airport runways, and rare law books that nobody read housed behind glass in mahogany bookshelves. She knew the costly *whoosh* of perfectly calibrated air-conditioning and could identify the dull patina of real brass doorknobs. But Bennie had never seen a law firm as opulent as Bull Linette's.

The floor of the reception area was tiled in black-and-white marble, like the Grand Hall at Versailles, and an overstuffed golden brocade couch was adorned with spun-gold piping, as were matching club chairs. Four-teen-carat swags draped over tall mullioned windows, and the centerpiece of the room was a library table with ornate gold-covered feet, its mahogany surface inlaid with exotic ivory, teak, and yew. Golden damask walls were covered with gilt-framed scenes of French châteaus. Oddly enough, there wasn't an eviction notice in sight.

Bennie was jealous as hell, especially considering the present circumstances. *Somebody has a small penis,* she wanted to say. But she was trying to act classy, so she settled for: "Not too shabby, huh?"

St. Amien chuckled. *"Après moi, le déluge."*

"And that, too."

St. Amien smiled. His silvery hair had been slicked back and he wore an elegant light wool suit of charcoal gray with another silk print tie, and even so looked under-dressed in the fabulous waiting room. He sniffed as he surveyed the surroundings. "This decor, it's costly, certainly. Yet it lacks something."

"Duct tape?"

St. Amien cocked his head. "What is 'duct tape'?"

"Tape for ducks."

St. Amien let it go with a smile. They were getting used to each other. *"Non.* This decor, it lacks taste."

"True. Also fun." *But so much friggin' money.* "Is friggin' a curse, Robert?"

But St. Amien wasn't listening. "I see no women lawyers."

"Some of the lawyers in Philadelphia are men."

"C'est dommage."

"Huh?"

"It means 'Too bad.' "

"I knew that." Bennie stole a sideways glance at her new client. Maybe Robert was a dirty old man. Admiration was one thing, and lechery another.

Just then the receptionist returned. She was a knockout, with Miss Texas hair and a teal sheath Bennie would have saved for the evening-gown competition. She didn't act like a real secretary; she was more like a firm hostess, and she smelled of Beautiful and swished her hand at the hallway like Vanna White. "Ms. Rosato and Mr. St. Amien, please come this way."

"Thank you," St. Amien replied for the both of them, and Bennie kept her thoughts to herself. At this point, the only thing worse than losing her client to Bull Linette would be losing him to Miss Texas.

They walked down a long corridor, also damask-covered, with exquisite offices for associates on both sides of the hall. Bennie tried not to count the number of associate offices—ten in all, five to a side—or to hear the sounds of a hugely successful law firm—phones ringing, fax machines zz-zzt-ing away, Xerox copies ca-thunking, and lawyers on the phone calling each other assholes. Bennie's firm used to sound like that, and she missed it. She sneaked a look at her cell phone clipped to her purse, but the green light wasn't flashing. No message from the kids about Alice.

"Here we are," breathed the hostess, opening a heavy mahogany door. It swung into a huge conference room populated by men in Brioni suits and spread collars. The air was filled with multilingual chatter, and the people milled, talking, eating, and drinking around a glistening conference table covered with platters of cheese Danish, bagels of every type, and thin, oily slices of Nova Scotia salmon. Mounds of cream cheese and fancy jellies filled out the spread on the left-hand side, and flanking it on the right sat a plate of knotted rolls, shiny with egg whites.

"What a spread!" Bennie heard herself say, then winced. Though she was broke, she had to stop acting it. And she could feel St. Amien stiffen beside her.

"Mr. Linette did mention something about food," he said under his breath. "I've already eaten, however."

"Me too." *Yesterday.* Bennie entered the room, noticing that bald spots were turning in their direction. There wasn't a lawyer in the room who wouldn't have cut off his left briefcase to represent St. Amien, and Bennie felt suddenly what it must have felt like to be a man dating Marilyn Monroe. Bull Linette himself was already charging through his guests to meet them.

"Bennie!" Bill boomed, extending a huge hand. He stood a brawny six foot three in his custom dark suit, with the heavy shoulders of a Villanova quarterback. His physical presence impressed friends, enemies, and juries, and he knew as much. His features were proportional, with round blue eyes, a fresh sunburn over a largish nose, and a toothy smile that was broad and overbleached. "Lady, it's so damn good to see you again!"

"You too, Bill." Bennie extended her hand and acted as if it didn't hurt when Linette tried to break it. "Looks like we'll be working together."

"So I hear, and I'm thrilled!" Linette's strawberry blond hair had thinned, but his eyes were bright as he looked down. "I need someone with your street savvy on my team."

My team? Bennie let it go. She had brought the homecoming king to the prom, and that said it all. "Bill, let me introduce you to my client, Robert St. Amien. I believe you've already spoken." *Heh.*

"Bob!" Linette fairly shouted at St. Amien, grinning and pumping his fine hand with vigor. "Great to meet you, just great! Welcome aboard! From what I hear about you, Bob, you could try this case yourself!"

"Nice to meet you, also," St. Amien said, smiling in a well-mannered way. "Please, call me Robert."

"Robert! Great! Have a bagel and a schmear! Meet the gang!" Linette looped his hand around St. Amien's back, scooped him up, and steered him into the room. "You know Herm Mayer, right?"

Bennie tagged along like a fifth wheel, telling herself not to worry. St. Amien was coming home with her because she was a maverick and didn't call him Bob. Also he loved French manicures and didn't know she was flat broke. She checked her cell phone. No green flashing. The kids still hadn't found Alice. *Damn! Shit! Fuck!* She got it out of her system and concentrated on introducing herself to Herman Mayer.

"Pleased to meet you," Mayer said, shaking Bennie's hand. He was tall, about St. Amien's age and of average build in a brownish Brooks Brothers suit. His light brown eyes matched almost exactly the tortoiseshell of his horn-rimmed glasses, and his smile seemed a little stiff. He struck Bennie as being as plain and no-nonsense as St. Amien was classy and full of nonsense. "I understand that you are representing Robert St. Amien," Mayer said.

"I am."

"Then we shall be seeing quite a lot of each other. Robert and I are for many years in this business. We were both greatly wronged by these actions of the trade association."

"Trade associations sometimes get out of line, and they need a reminder now and then," Bennie said, guarded. She had to assume that anything she said would go straight back to Linette.

"Bill feels very optimistic about our chances of an early settlement, perhaps this month, in the neighborhood of fifty million. My wife, who is my adviser in all things, disagrees with him. But she is unfortunately in Germany. We make our home in Osnabrück."

"I see."

"She prefers it, and I can commute easily, twice a month." Mayer's eyes narrowed and his tone lowered. He inclined his head toward Bennie. "I was wondering what you thought about that. If you agreed with this assessment."

"If I agree? With Bill or your wife?" Bennie asked, stalling. Clearly, Mayer wasn't one of Linette's apostles. It would be another lovely aspect of this case; while the lawyers tried to steal each other's clients, the clients went lawyer shopping. This lawsuit was a singles bar where everybody had their eyes on the door. A class action, but nobody was showing any class.

"You aren't sure you agree," Mayer said matter-of-factly.

"I didn't say that." Bennie hated people putting words in her mouth. "I'd love to talk to Bill more about that, and I will. That's the purpose of this meeting, I believe." She didn't contradict Linette, because she was trying to be a good team player. Not that it came naturally to her. There was a reason she rowed a single scull.

"I quite understand," Mayer said, an edge to his tone. If he wanted dirt, he wasn't getting it. He straightened up, and Bennie shifted her attention to Bill. He had finished introducing St. Amien to everyone as his new girlfriend and was cuddling him into a chair to his right, at the head of the conference table. If Bennie didn't watch out, he'd go for second base.

"It was great meeting you, Herman," she said, excusing herself, and made her way to the head of the table. Lawyers jumped for the seats as if they were playing musical chairs, and St. Amien was signaling her to the empty seat next to him. She wedged her way over, checking her cell phone on the fly. No message.

"Thanks, *Bob,*" she whispered, leaning over, and he smiled in response as Linette stood up, towering over the head of the table.

"Friends, Romans, Irishmen," he began, and everybody around the table laughed heartily as they settled down and pulled shiny pens and fresh legal pads from their briefcases.

Bennie did the same, as did the men sitting opposite her, big guns in the class-action bar. Mick Brenstein, in his neat little glasses and precisely knotted rep tie. Zander Kerpov, pale and gaunt, whose sunken eyes expressed all the warmth of Ivan Lendl or Dostoyevsky at his most playful. Next to him was José Quinones, a short man with dark skin, an easy smile, and a thick pinky ring in the shape of a horseshoe. Math anxiety prevented Bennie from totaling their yearly incomes and assets. Hers, she knew with ease. And still no messages.

"This is the first day of the rest of your litigation," Linette continued, pausing for laughter, "and I hope we will finish it by the end of this month!" He beamed with pride and burst into sudden applause. Everybody around the table clapped, too, and Bennie joined in. Why, she didn't know. Because they were gonna get rich quick? Because the home team was gonna beat State? Those who didn't matter enough to get seats at the table were relegated to clapping from their seats along the wall, and Linette was careful to make eye contact with them as he spoke.

"Last week we filed a complaint in federal district court, and you are being provided with a copy right now." He gestured to a male associate who had materialized from behind the lox and was distributing copies around the table. "It states, in relevant part, that as a class we are a hundred strong—and growing!"

More applause.

"That we are all brothers—and sisters—here, and we all share common questions of law and fact."

Applause again.

"And that this action can and should be maintained as a class, and that my client is fully ready, willing, and able to represent the class as a whole."

Applause, except for St. Amien and Bennie. She didn't want to stop Linette now, in front of everyone, and nothing he had said fixed the determination of who would be lead plaintiff, or lead lawyer. The choice would be something she, Bill, and the big guns would hammer out in private, and the court would have to approve. The three guns would vote with their pal, and the contest would be between Linette and Bennie. For now, she held her applause, and her fire.

"Friends, I know we haven't officially determined the class representative so soon," Linette said, pointedly looking at Bennie, "and that is something ultimately for the court to decide. Today, I wanted to bring all of us here, so we can meet each other as friends and break bread together. On another day, we can move on to a discussion of the facts of the case, and the statements the defendant made at the trade association meeting, which gave rise to the wrong committed against all of you. And finally, we will need to determine and quantify the damages you all suffered as a result of the trade association's grossly illegal and unfair acts."

Heads nodded around the table, since

everybody's hands were tired from applauding.

"And we will establish a timetable for this litigation, which, as you know, will be managed more efficiently than most small countries." Linette paused for laughter. "We need a government, and, as usual, at the head will be lead counsel and an executive committee. Reporting to them, as always, will be the briefing committee, the motions committee, the discovery committee, the experts committee . . ."

Bennie stifled a laugh when she realized he wasn't kidding. Was this how class actions ran? She usually tried cases herself or with an associate, sitting second chair. She would have to play well with others. The kids still hadn't called.

". . . the exhibits committee, the damages committee, the fees committee, and although we won't need it, the appellate committee. We will work together to divide and conquer. That's the best way I know to assure a swift, certain, and very healthy settlement."

More heads nodding. From across the table, Quinones interjected, "It worked like a charm in *Bronson Mechanics*."

Next to him, Brenstein added, "Also *Anderson-Wells*. The proverbial well-oiled machine."

Bennie had no idea what they were talking about and assumed the references were the names of cases they'd worked together. She had expected the class-action bar would be clubby, but this was the Mob. She wondered why she didn't recognize any of the case names, at least from her legal research, and realized that none of the cases had made it to the federal reporters. They'd all settled before they got to court. Bennie looked around the table with new eyes. These were trial lawyers who never tried cases. They might have all the money, but they missed all the fun.

At the head of the table, Linette was saying, "So far there are fifteen law firms already signed on to represent various members of the class. As usual, everybody will have to pony up for the war chest. My thought is the usual ante will do, thirty grand in cold cash. I need to collect that from each of you by the end of this week."

More nodding, except for Bennie, who couldn't have nodded if she'd tried. Her neck had locked in place. *Thirty thousand dollars?* How the hell would she get that? What would she do? By the end of the week? She was so stunned she could barely focus. *Thirty grand!*

"At this juncture, we don't know who the bad guys will hire as their mouthpiece, but my best guess is that it'll be Yates & Gumm, in that big black building right across the street." Bill winked as he gestured out the window. "I try to run 'em over when I can, but they're too damn fast."

Louder laughter from around the table.

"But make no mistake, my friends, Yates & Gumm is good. Very good. We may call 'em Stupid & Dumb, but they're not. They're three hundred strong and they got lawyers from Harvard, Penn, and Yale. I hear there's one from my alma mater, Villanova, but nobody likes him much. He does all the real work."

Laughter again.

"Whoever is on the other side of this case makes no difference, because if it ain't Yates & Gumm, it'll be somebody just as smart and experienced. And whoever it is, we'll let 'em know that we mean business from the beginning, and that we will not relent until we have achieved justice for all of you." Linette modulated his tone, bringing his message home. "If we all work together, we can make a just and fair settlement for everyone, no matter how large or small your damages. And that is my—and all of our—one and only goal. Justice, for all!"

Clapping surged in earnest, and Brenstein and Quinones stood up. Dostoyevsky followed, and then Bennie, and soon they all were on their wing tips, flushed and happy that victory was within their grasp, giving themselves and justice a standing ovation.

Inside, Bennie felt like crying. *Thirty grand.* And still no word from the kids.

Ten minutes later, she was walking back to her office, with St. Amien beside her. The sidewalks were crowded with people heading out for lunch, and Bennie eyed them as they walked by, suddenly hyperaware of her surroundings. Was Alice following her now? Could she have followed her to the restaurant? And why would she do any of it?

A gaggle of secretaries passed, laughing and talking, and then a group of first-year associates from one of the big firms hurried along. The ties of the bright young men flew over their shoulders, and the young girls carried tiny little purses. Bennie remembered when she had been one of them, working so hard at Grun & Chase, caring so much about her cases and the hours she billed. She had dreamed of the day when she'd be her own boss, and her life would be completely in her own control. Like now. *Eek.* She double-checked her cell phone, but no dice.

"Bennie, you seem quiet today." St. Amien looked over as they walked. Whatever pomade he put on his gray hair made it glint like stainless steel in the sun. The sky above them was clear and cloudless, and he chose to pollute it by lighting up a cigarette from a superwide red-and-white pack. "Thoughts of the meeting?"

Not exactly. "You go first. What did you think of it?"

"I think Mr. Linette is quite the showman, but I also think we will achieve victory, in the end." The smoke from his French cigarette smelled like burning ozone.

"Right on both counts. Let's go back to my office to talk, and we can look over your complaint." They reached the corner, then turned onto Locust Street, passing a brick rowhouse that had been converted to doctors' offices, then another with green shutters, lawyers' offices. The sidewalks thronged with people enjoying the ridiculously pleasant weather; none of the passersby was Alice. Bennie and St. Amien were closing in on her building when she noticed a crowd collecting. Two white police cruisers idled at the curb in front of her office.

"What's that?" Bennie wondered aloud, and St. Amien looked down the street, squinting slightly through his acrid smoke.

"The police?"

Something's the matter. "Oh, no." Bennie picked up the pace to a light jog, and St. Amien stepped lively on his long legs, loose change jingling unhappily in his pockets. Two cops with light blue shirts stood around the cruiser. Their navy blue hats sat low on their foreheads, but under them Bennie could see the grave set of their mouths.

"Officer!" Bennie yelled when she was only a few feet away, hailing them. Her cell phone started ringing in her purse, but this was no time to answer. She reached the cops, her heart in her throat. "I'm Bennie Rosato. My office is upstairs. What's the matter? Did something happen to one of my—"

"You're Ms. Rosato?" one of the cops asked, rapid-fire. He stepped quickly to her, followed by his partner, a black woman.

"She fits the flash," the female cop said, and Bennie didn't understand. She had always thought that "flash" meant a description of a fleeing offender, broadcast over police radio. Two more cops emerged suddenly from the second squad car.

"Yes, I'm Bennie Rosato, what's the matter? What happened?" she asked as St. Amien caught up with her, his chest heaving, his cigarette gone. The crowd stopped to stare. Her cell phone kept ringing. "Are my people all right?"

"Bennie Rosato, you're under arrest," said the cop in front, and before she could protest, he'd grabbed her arm and spun her around.

"What are you *talking about?*" Bennie asked, stricken. St. Amien looked stunned, his blue eyes wide behind his glasses. The crowd gathered and gaped.

"We know you're an attorney, so we don't expect any trouble." The female cop came up and joined the first cop, blocking Bennie in against the other two. "Take it nice and easy. Just relax for us now." The female cop grabbed Bennie's other arm and together the cops forced her against the car.

"You can't arrest me! I didn't do anything!"

"Take it easy, Ms. Rosato. Gotta pat you down," she said, and Bennie braced her hands against the sun-warmed metal of the cruiser, dropping her briefcase and bag. The female cop recited the Miranda warning as she ran a pair of knowing hands over Bennie's thighs, and hips, and along her legs. Then around her ears and the back of her neck.

"What am I being arrested for?" Bennie demanded. Her face burned with shame, then resentment. "What do you think you're doing? I'm entitled to know why I'm being arrested!"

"Don't make a scene, Ms. Rosato," one of the cops said from behind her. Suddenly powerful hands yanked her arms from the cruiser, jerked them behind her back, and cinched her wrists together, clamping a pair of tight handcuffs over them.

St. Amien stepped forward, shaken. "Officers, you are making a terrible mistake. This is my attorney."

"You're interfering with an arrest, sir." The cop opened the backdoor of the cruiser and placed Bennie neatly inside by pressing down on her forehead. He slammed the door shut, locking Bennie inside the cage car.

"I want to know why you're arresting me!" she was yelling, even as she saw Carrier running from the office building toward her, cell phone in hand. Instantly Bennie's cell began ringing in her purse. Carrier had been calling, not to tell her about Alice, but to warn her about the cops.

But it was too late. The cruiser lurched off bearing her away, and the last face Bennie saw was that of her completely appalled client.

9

Only a telltale latex smell signified that the interrogation room at the Ninth Police District had been freshly repainted; otherwise it was a pre-scuffed blue. The room was small, the gray door closed, and fluorescent lighting glared from a ceiling of white tile. A black TV cart with an old Sony portable and VCR occupied one corner, and the only other furniture, three mismatched chairs and a gray Formica desk, had a scavenged look Bennie had seen only in police stations and freshman dorms. She fidgeted in a stainless-steel chair reserved for suspects, unique in that it was bolted to the floor and had a pair of handcuffs hanging from one arm. Judy sat in a swivel chair beside her, acting as defense counsel. As if Bennie

Rosato would shut up long enough to let anyone else represent her.

"Theft? Assault?" she shouted in disbelief, her voice ricocheting around the tiny closed room. *"Reckless endangerment? Receiving stolen goods?"* Bennie almost jumped out of her chair, but Detective Maloney had told her if she did that again he'd cuff her to it. Since he was one of the so-called Hollywood Detectives from SIU, or the Special Investigations Unit, she believed it. These guys came to play. "What are you talking about? I didn't do—"

"Bennie, please, be quiet," Carrier said, burying her fingernails in her client's padded shoulder. "Let the detective ask his questions, and you can answer only if I say." A sheaf of white papers sat ignored in front of her, the form questionnaire issued by the police, certifying that Bennie had been advised of her right to remain silent. Unfortunately, she was exercising her right to freak out.

"But this is ridiculous! I didn't steal anything! I would *never* steal anything!" Bennie told Maloney and the other SIU detective, a bald, heavyset man whose name she was too upset to remember. He stood against the wall, taking notes; he was the one who had directed that she and her belongings be searched when they'd first brought her in, but they hadn't found whatever they'd been looking for. "I would never break the law, I'm a lawyer!"

Carrier squeezed her shoulder again. "Not your best argument, Bennie. Now please, can you be quiet?"

"Settle down, Ms. Rosato. No reason to get worked up." Detective Maloney remained calm, even relaxed, which was easy because he wasn't in custody. He was trim and tall, about her age, with longish sandy hair and hazel eyes Bennie would have found attractive if he hadn't arrested her. He reached into an accordion file folder on the counter and pulled out a typed form she recognized as an incident report, which was the officer's account of the facts of the crime. He said, "All right, I'll read this aloud, then I'll take your client's statement. If she didn't do it, we can work it out, okay?"

"Fine," Carrier answered. Bennie quieted momentarily, and Detective Maloney bent over the report, his neatly scissored bangs falling forward.

"The crime occurred in the Tiffany store,

in the Park Hyatt on Broad Street. The store manager gave a statement, and so did his assistant, the saleswoman, and three eye-witnesses. According to the store manager, the perpetrator stole a pair of diamond ear-rings—diamond studs, they're called—worth eleven thousand five hundred forty-three dollars from—"

"Earrings?" Bennie asked, dumbfounded. "This is crazy! I didn't steal any earrings! There has to be some—"

"Bennie, quiet!" Carrier snapped, and Bennie bit her tongue.

What the hell is going on?

The detective continued reading. "The perpetrator browsed in the store for approx-imately fifteen minutes, then went to a counter which contained diamond earrings on the first shelf. She asked the sales-woman to show her the earrings, which were more than a carat in weight. The store was very crowded, and customers were waiting to be helped. The perpetrator tried on the earrings. When one of the two secu-rity guards stationed at the door went to as-sist an older lady who had dropped her shopping bag, the perpetrator ran for the exit with the earrings on."

Oh my God. Bennie's mouth went dry. It was *Alice*. Alice had stolen the earrings. Alice posing as Bennie. First the Chinese restaurant, and now this. Bennie knew it in her very marrow, the bones and blood she shared with her twin. The realization shocked her into silence.

"The perpetrator shoved the security guard out of her way, and he fell into a glass display case of Elsa Peretti jewelry, whatever that is. The other security guard gave pursuit down Broad Street, but he lost the perpetrator, who ran down into the Broad Street subway and disappeared."

Bennie's thoughts tumbled over one another in confusion. How had Alice done it? *Why* had she done it? What the *fuck*? This wasn't mischief with credit cards or even tainting her reputation with the judges. These were felony charges. They could ruin her. Alice was upping the ante.

"What evidence do you have that my client committed this robbery?" Carrier was asking, and the detective scoffed.

"Other than the whole shebang on surveillance tape? Tiffany had three cameras on that counter, and your client is on each one."

"I wanna see that tape!" Bennie blurted out. She had to see it for herself. With her own eyes.

Carrier cleared her throat. "Detective, may we see the videotape?"

"Fine." Detective Maloney opened the accordion file and extracted a black Fuji videotape. He got up holding the tape, brushed down his dark slacks with a practiced hand, and walked over to the TV cart with the ancient VHS machine. He slid the tape inside, turned on the TV, and pressed Play.

Everybody turned toward the screen, which showed a busy main room in Tiffany: a grainy view of lush carpeting, attractive shoppers, and display cases full of diamond bracelets and earrings. Suddenly a woman entered from the left side of the picture and threaded her way through the customers. Her face wasn't visible, because her back was turned from the surveillance camera, but the woman was fully as tall as Bennie, her shoulders equally square, and she was wearing the same suit Bennie had on today, her trademark khaki. The woman's hair was Bennie's shade of honey blond, and it had been pinned up in a carbon copy of Bennie's messy twist. She stopped in front of a display case, her back still to the camera.

"The beauty shot is in one, two, three," Detective Maloney counted down, and the woman turned on cue and faced the security camera dead-on for several seconds, as if she were posing for a photograph. The detective snorted. "There you are, Ms. Rosato."

"That's her," Bennie said, voicing her thoughts aloud. It was Alice. She *had* come back. Here was proof positive. Bennie felt stunned. "That's my—"

"Please be quiet and watch the tape, Bennie," Carrier warned, and Bennie looked over. On-screen, Alice was putting on the diamond earrings and examining her face—Bennie's face—in a square mirror sitting on the glass counter, tilted up. An older woman with a cane dropped a shopping bag, spilling its contents of wrapped boxes, and a security guard went to help her. The saleswoman turned away for a moment, and all of a sudden Alice bolted from the counter, knocking over a customer in the process. She punched the guard by the door before he could move to stop her, sending him sprawling backward against a display case, and flew out the door.

Bennie shifted her gaze to the top of the screen, where a black band ran with a date and time. It was today's date, and the time ticked off: 10:30:10, 10:30:11, 10:30:12. Her heart sank. She had no alibi. At that time, she had been walking back from the federal courthouse, alone. Tiffany lay between the courthouse and her office, on the way. It was more than possible for Bennie to have been there at ten-thirty, stealing diamonds. Alice couldn't have planned it that way, could she? Did she have people helping her? And who was that older woman who dropped her shopping bag at the exact right moment? Was she in on it, too?

Detective Maloney reached over and turned off the TV. "Let's get real, Ms. Rosato. It's you on the tape, I can see that with my own eyes. The manager IDed you positively and two of the eyewitnesses recognized you from TV. You're wearing the clothes you have on in the video. Your hair is the same too." He put his hands on his hips. "So cut the shit. Give the earrings back, you'll get a couple years' probation—"

"Detective," Bennie interrupted, "the woman on the tape isn't me, it's my twin. I didn't take the earrings, she did."

Carrier clamped a hand over her client's. "Bennie, please don't make any more statements. You know better than to—"

"But that's not me on that tape!" Bennie knew Carrier was right, but she couldn't help herself. Alice had turned her life upside down. She appealed to Maloney as the bald detective took rapid notes. "Detective, I have a twin, an *identical* twin, named Alice Connelly. This is criminal impersonation, clear and simple. Alice Connelly is pretending to be me. I want these charges dropped!"

Carrier squeezed her hand. "Bennie, please let me handle this. You're not going to convince him. We should just end this interrogation."

But Detective Maloney was looking directly at Bennie, amused, if not intrigued. "Ms. Rosato, are you telling me it's not you on the tape, it's your *twin?*"

"It's a matter of record, Maloney. Her name is Alice Connelly."

Carrier leaned forward. "Detective, this interview is over. My client isn't answering any more questions. Let's get her arraigned so I can post bail and get her out of here."

Detective Maloney snorted. "You really have a twin, Rosato?"

"I do, I defended her on a murder charge, two years ago. It was in all the papers. Her prints are on file, too. If you had just investigated for two minutes before you—"

"Where is she?"

"I don't know, exactly. In town." Bennie turned to her pissed-off associate. "Carrier, did you have any luck in finding her?"

"I'm not discussing this here. You want me to waive attorney-client privilege?" Carrier's eyes flared. "I said, the interview is over!"

"Where does she live?" Detective Maloney was asking Bennie.

"I don't know."

Carrier cleared her throat, interrupting. "Bennie, please, that's enough. Detective Maloney, as I said, it's time to end this interrogation."

Maloney addressed Bennie again. "But she lives in Philly, your sister?"

"I don't think so."

Maloney frowned. "You don't know where your own twin sister lives?"

"We weren't raised together. But she's in town. She's running around town, posing as me."

Carrier jumped to her feet and made a show of gathering her papers. "Bennie, Detective Maloney! Really! This interrogation is over. It's time to—"

"Where does she work?" the detective asked Bennie.

"I don't know."

"What kind of car does she drive? We can run a DMV check."

"I don't know."

"Voter's registration? You don't know." Maloney's eyes narrowed. If he'd believed Bennie at first, he was beginning to doubt it now. "Let me get this straight. Your *twin* did the crime, but you can't tell us anything about her. And we have a positive ID on you, a coupla eyewitnesses, and you got no alibi." Maloney shook his head. "If I were you, I'd give us a complete statement right now, because after we see what the search of your house and office turns up—"

"Search of my *house and office?*" Bennie felt stricken. "You have to be kidding! I just told you, I had nothing to do with it! My twin did it! You're not searching anything!"

"We're already conducting the search, Ms. Rosato."

"You're fucking searching my *house?*" Bennie exploded, even as she knew she shouldn't. Curse or explode, that is. But the cops were at her house! Turning over her mattress. Digging through her underwear drawer. She should have realized. They preferred to search when the owner wasn't there, so they wouldn't be interrupted, and they had more than enough for probable cause to get a warrant. Still. "How dare you search my—"

"Bennie, that's it!" Carrier shouted. "Let the detective produce his warrant! Detective, I'm sure you wouldn't search without a warrant."

"Of course not, I was just about to give it to you." Detective Maloney extracted a warrant from a manila folder under his pad and handed it to Carrier, who grabbed it before her client could. Bennie's one glance at it made her ballistic. Her home address, on the PREMISES line!

"Detective, why didn't you do your fucking homework? I have a twin! The case made major news! You know the press will pick this up from the scanners? You trying to *ruin* me?"

"Rosato, you gotta settle down." Detective Maloney gritted his teeth, and Bennie got hotter.

"Don't tell me to settle down! You're invading my home, my office! You arrested me in front of my most important client! You're pickin' on the wrong lawyer on the *wrong frigging day*."

"That's enough outta you!" Detective Maloney shouted back, pointing a stiff finger in Bennie's face. "I know you're a certified big deal, that's why SIU got stuck with you. But you got no privileges here, no matter who you are!"

"I didn't ask for anything special, I just asked you to do your job like a professional!" Bennie leapt to her feet, and suddenly Carrier stepped in front of her and turned around. The two women stood nose to nose. Bennie wasn't sure if Carrier was protecting the detective or her.

"Sit down, Bennie!" Carrier shouted in Bennie's face. "Sit down, shut up, and let me do *my* job like a professional!"

"But these charges are bullshit!"

"I said, *sit down and shut up!*" Carrier

glowered at Bennie from under a fuchsia fringe that made it impossible to take her seriously, even though Bennie knew she was right.

"I will not!"

"You will, too!" Carrier yelled back, and before Bennie knew what was happening, the associate shoved her down into the seat, grabbed the handcuffs from the chair arm, and slapped the open one onto Bennie's wrist, where it clicked shut. "Ha! *Now* you'll stay put!"

"Ouch!" Bennie's mouth dropped open. She looked at the cuff pinched tight around her wrists, then up at her associate. "You *handcuffed* me?"

"You're hanging yourself! You're giving them free discovery!" Carrier straightened up with satisfaction and turned from an incredulous Bennie toward an equally incredulous detective. "Now, Detective Maloney, this interrogation is *over!*"

"I, for one, am loving this," the detective said, shaking his head with a smile. He leaned back in the chair and gestured to the other detective. "You get a load a this, Shep? The *lawyer* cuffing the client?"

"You go, girl," the bald detective said with a sly grin. "We gonna do anything about it?"

"Better not!" Carrier told them. "If I have no objection, why should you?"

"*I* have an objection!" Bennie felt confounded. *My lawyer is depriving me of my civil rights.* She was pretty sure it was unconstitutional, if not basically the same thing. "Remember me? The one chained to the chair? Woo-hoo, Carrier!"

But everybody, including her own associate, ignored her. "Detective Maloney," Carrier said, "my client is telling the truth, but you wouldn't drop the charges now anyway, would you?"

"Not on your life. You know that's not how it works at this stage. Or maybe you don't." Maloney shrugged. "We got more than enough to charge, so we gotta charge. What do I say to the jewelry store? 'Sorry, but it coulda been her twin'? If you got proof of this twin, you can present it at the preliminary hearing in ten days. Then they'll dismiss the charges, but not now."

"We will." Carrier shot Bennie a look that said, *See?* "And she's not signing anything or making any further statements. So unlock her and let me bail her out."

Bennie looked up. "Bail me out? With what?"

"I'll treat you," Carrier answered. "The bail commissioner will probably set it at ten grand, since you don't have a prior record. I'll get a bond for ten percent."

Bennie flushed, embarrassed. It was a new low to borrow money from the kids. She felt as if she should go to jail and stay there.

But Detective Maloney was smiling. "Unlock her?" he repeated.

"The handcuffs." Carrier gestured at Bennie's chair. "Unlock her. Get her out of the handcuffs."

"I never used those cuffs before." Detective Maloney looked over at the bald detective. "Shep, you ever use those suckers?"

"I thought they were for show," he answered, and the detectives burst into new laughter.

And Bennie started hollering.

Way too many hours later, after Bennie had been fingerprinted, arraigned, and completely humiliated, the lawyers emerged from the Ninth Precinct into a group of reporters lying in wait.

"We have no comment! No comment!"

the associate shouted, and the women broke into a light run ahead of the pack to the curb, where they hailed a Yellow cab, jumped inside, and took off.

When the cab approached their office building, the lawyers weren't surprised to see a new crowd of reporters and photographers thronged on the sidewalk in front. Bennie knew that they'd be following her everywhere until this died down, and she didn't want to think about what this was doing to her reputation. It would kill her business, if she still had a business to kill. She flashed on St. Amien's shocked expression. She was pretty sure Bill Linette had never boosted diamond studs.

Reporters stuck their camera lenses at the cab window, and Carrier finished paying the driver. "We get out of the cab and run for it. That's all. Got it?"

"Not the plan, kid." Bennie's brain was starting to function. "You get out here, go upstairs, and call St. Amien. Tell him it was a mix-up and I'll explain the details to him later. And try to get the office in order if the cops left it a mess."

"But what are you going to do?" Carrier had already cracked the backdoor, and the press surged toward the opening, shouting questions:

"Bennie, you gonna plead guilty?" "Bennie, you receiving treatment for this?" "Bennie, Bennie, over here!" "Bennie, just one picture!" "Confirm or deny! Can you confirm or deny?" "Come on, Ben, give us a statement!"

Bennie ignored them. "Go. Call St. Amien first thing."

Carrier frowned. "Where are you going?"

"I'm going to get my life back."

10

Grun & Chase was one of the largest law firms in the city, with almost four hundred lawyers in its Philly headquarters alone, and its thirty-fourth-floor waiting room was another Lawyer Kingdom. If Linette's offices were France under Louis Quatorze, Grun's were England under King Henry. The carpet at Grun was a rich, woolly maroon, and the overstuffed couches were covered with shiny striped fabric of emerald green and royal blue. The artwork chronicled a series of British tall ships sailing along the Isle of Whatever, with ink-etched rigging and round cannons poking through the gunwales. Bennie had started her legal career at Grun & Chase but hadn't remembered it being so House of Windsor. She was glad she'd escaped before being thrown into debtors prison.

"Mr. Freminet will see you," the receptionist said. She turned from her desk with a jowly frown, like a body double for Queen Victoria. Either she was your basic sourpuss, or she'd heard that Bennie was a diamond thief. "His office is down the hall and on the right, in the corner."

"Thanks," Bennie said, and hurried down the hall. She passed row after row of secretaries typing away on computer keyboards, plugged into Dictaphone earphones, and she wanted to rescue them all. Except that she couldn't pay them. She went to the end of the hall and opened the door of the corner office.

"Bennie!" Sam Freminet was a compact, freckled lawyer with a supershort red haircut, in a neat navy blazer and a Looney Tunes tie, and he leapt delightedly from behind his polished glass desk. He met her at the door with a warm, if slightly bony, hug that smelled too strongly of Calvin Klein. "What's up, doc?"

"Everything, Sam." Bennie broke the clinch after a moment and flopped into one of the leather Eames chairs in front of Sam's desk. The chairs coordinated perfectly with the modern glass desk, the sleek Danish bookshelves and credenza, and a brown leather couch containing a plush Pepé Le Pew, Daffy Duck, Bugs Bunny with a stuffed carrot, and Elmer Fudd in wabbit season. Sam was a Looney Tunes freak, and Bennie's oldest friend in the world. But she still didn't know how to tell him her news. "You'd better close the door."

"Ooh, good dish, huh? I love it!" Sam closed the door and rubbed slim hands together. "As Bugs would say, 'Better start scheming.' That was in 'Now Hare This,' by the way."

Bennie was trying to think of a way to explain. She and Sam had both started at Grun together after graduating from law school, but Sam had survived and become a partner in the bankruptcy department. Now she needed him, personally and professionally. "Well, this isn't dish, it's bad news, and I don't know where to start."

"Aw, *mon petit* corned beef," Sam purred in his best Pepé Le Pew, sliding into the sling chair next to her. He took her hand, and his forget-me-not blue eyes melted with genuine warmth behind hip rimless glasses. "Don't worry, whatever it is, we'll fix it."

"We can't."

"Yes we can. We girls can do anything!"

"Wait, that's not Bugs Bunny, that's Barbie."

"I know. I'm mixing icons, but I do love that girl!" Sam waved a small hand. "I had the pink car, the dream house, the whole complex. How do you think I turned out the way I did?"

"Gay?"

"No, a lawyer."

Bennie laughed, feeling a rush of affection. She stalled in telling him the bad news, not wanting to leave the comfort of the moment. "Sammy, do you look especially good today, or am I just happy to see you?"

"Well, I am positively *caliente* today. Check me out." Sam swiveled his skinny shoulders. "Hugo jacket, Versace shirt, Ralph pants. Now that I'm out of the closet, I'm fierce. I'm flaming. I'm Bankruptcy Queen."

Bennie smiled. "I remember when you had to hide your love away."

"The dark ages. I couldn't believe they fell

for my straight act. I thought only the army had that kind of denial. Or Liza Minnelli."

They both laughed, and Bennie felt her tension ebb away. The only good thing about getting older was that you got to have old friends.

"Now, what's going on, honey?" Sam inched forward on his chair. "What's the matter?"

"Alice is in town."

"The bitch is back?" Sam's tiny eyes blinked behind his tiny glasses, and Bennie began the story, telling about the missing wallet, the double packages, and the diamond earrings, while Sam grew more and more upset, reddening under his freckles. He barely waited for her to finish before he exploded. "Why the *fuck* is she doing this to you? You didn't do anything to deserve this! All you ever did was help her! Why, for fuck's sake?" Sam was never on a curse diet. "She came out of *nowhere,* charged with murder, and you proved she was innocent!"

"I agree, but God knows how she sees it, or me. She's a mess. She's a damaged person."

"Damaged, what does she have to be damaged about?"

"Maybe being put up for adoption instead of me?" Bennie had wondered about it. Their mother, alone with limited emotional and financial resources, couldn't handle raising both of the children she had borne, and had kept Bennie. It had to hurt. "Maybe she felt abandoned. After all, my mother chose me over her."

"Don't even tell me you feel guilty about that."

"I do, a little. Sure."

"*What?* Why? Let's review. You got the family with the sick mom—God rest her soul, but she was very sick—and the father who splits at birth. You raised yourself, put yourself through college and law school, and managed to take care of your mother, too. On the other hand, Alice got the nuclear family in north Jersey, with the Eldorado."

"I don't know about the Eldorado." Bennie couldn't laugh, but it was partly true. Alice had told Bennie that her adoptive parents had been wonderful to her, but she just never felt that she belonged with them.

"Okay, I'll betcha. Now, who got the *good* childhood?"

"I did. I knew my mother, and Alice didn't," Bennie answered, and Sam fell uncharacteristically silent. "She was a loving, wonderful mother before she became completely depressed. It was like watching the sun set on someone, and part of her depression had to be the pain of giving up Alice, and the guilt. Nobody gives up a child without losing something." Bennie wished away the weight on her chest, even as she knew it wouldn't leave. "Anyway, enough. I'll deal with Alice. You tell me what to do about my business. Frankly, I'm going broke."

"It's about time you told me."

"How did you know?"

"Please, I'm a bankruptcy lawyer, you think I don't know?" Sam's phone started ringing but he let his secretary pick up. "Small business is in big trouble in this economy. I read that Caveson and Maytel filed, and I knew they were your house clients. Also, you haven't called for two months, so I know you're in trouble. You're the only friend who calls when she doesn't need anything, and avoids me when she needs help."

Bennie found a smile. "Well, here I am. I have to stay open for business, plus I have to ante up thirty grand to buy into a class action."

"You doing class-action work?"

"I am now. Or I was. This representation will save my ass, if I can keep it. So I guess I need bankruptcy advice."

"No, you need cash, and lots of it. Fast. That's easy." Sam reached inside his Hugo/Versace/ Ralph jacket and extracted his checkbook. "I'll give it to you."

"No, put your money away." Bennie had known he'd offer, but she wouldn't mooch from her best friend. "I won't take it."

"Don't be silly!" Sam leaned forward on his glass desk and started to scribble out a check. "How much do you need? Fifty grand will do it, to start. That will cover the thirty grand you need for the class action, plus your office rent and overhead for the next few months."

"Try years, but it's out of the question."

"Tarnation, Bennie! I won't miss it. The economy goes in the tank, and bankruptcy lawyers get flush." Sam threw his hands up in the air. "I just bought the new 500S, the one with the all-wood package, and the second condo is paid off. I'm having one of the best years I've ever had, and I *owe* you. You stuck by me when I wasn't sticking by myself. You got me back on the straight and narrow, remember? Well, the narrow anyway."

Bennie remembered. "I didn't do it for payback, and I won't take your money. I won't cash the check."

"I'm not listening." Sam was about to tear the completed check out when Bennie snatched the checkbook and chucked it across the room. It bounced off of Daffy Duck, knocked him into the furry lap of Foghorn Leghorn, and landed on the hand-made Heriz rug.

"Oops! 'Ah say, Ah say, Widow Brown,'" Bennie said, doing a lousy Foghorn Leghorn, and Sam shushed her.

"I don't see why you don't just take my money." He was hurrying across the rug to the windowsill, where he righted Daffy and retrieved his checkbook from the rug. "You can pay it back if it makes you feel better."

"No thanks. Now, are you gonna give me

some free legal advice or do I have to find myself another bankruptcy duck?"

"You mean, treat you like a client?" Sam went to his desk, tossed his checkbook on the desk, and flopped into his black leather chair. "That's why you came to me?"

"Yes. I have to stay in business until this class action settles. I have a house, an old Saab, and a golden retriever. I need only the golden."

"God knows why." Sam shuddered. "Dog sheds like a mother."

"It's part of his charm."

"Before we begin, what did your accountant say about all this?" Sam slid out of his jacket, hung it around the back of his chair, and rolled up his shirtsleeves. A fashionably oversized watch looked like a weight on his wrist. "You hired an accountant, didn't you?"

"I couldn't afford one. It's a catch-22."

"You need an accountant. You can hardly add."

"It's all subtracting anyway." Bennie edged forward on the chair. "So, be my lawyer. I'm going to my last resort. What do you think?"

Sam's eyes flared in alarm. "Don't be insane. There has to be money in the business."

"There isn't. And no bank will give me another business loan, with my payment record. I've gone from slow pay to crack addict."

Sam frowned. "You know, you're a great lawyer, but you don't have a head for this. How much money do you need to get through the next month? How much do you pay in salary, legal and support staff? Are you current on your taxes? On withholding payments? Status on credit cards, business and personal? What are your accounts receivable?"

Bennie's mind reeled.

"Have you gotten all the bills out you should have? Can you offer a discount for payment in seven days? Can you make commitments to work on fee arrangements which may not be attractive for the long term? Do you have a lender? Can we offer the lender a security interest in the fixtures of the office? The receivables? Well?" Sam took a breath. "Gimme, gimme, gimme."

"I don't know the answers off the top of my head."

"You should. Grow up. Find out. Call your

office." Sam grabbed his desk phone by the receiver and pushed it at Bennie. "I need the paper. Tax returns, account statements, check registers. You should have that together already, it's tax time. Get everything else sent over. Messenger it all here. We'll work all night if we have to, but we won't have to."

"Do you have time, now?"

"If I didn't, what kind of girlfriend would I be?" Sam asked, and Bennie gathered the question was rhetorical.

An hour later, the glass surface of Sam's desk was cluttered with all of Bennie's financial records. Slippery stacks of smooth canceled checks, piles of trifold bank statements, thin rent bills, and time records on Rosato & Associates stationery. Sam sat behind the debris, ignoring the near-constant ringing of his telephones and expertly hitting keys on his adding machine. He frowned at the numbers on the white tape, which curled onto the rug. Styrofoam cups of coffee dotted the mess, and Bennie drained the cold brew from the closest cup just as Sam looked up from the tape, his eyes reddish from strain.

Bennie knew it was bad news. "How bad is it?"

"It could be worse."

"How?"

Sam thought a minute.

"Told you."

"You were right. You can't get another cent out of this business. You have old receivables that total at most two hundred eighty-three dollars and thirty-four cents. You missed three quarterly tax payments, which you have to get current immediately, the interest and penalties will kill you. Your firm is overextended, heavily leveraged." Sam was shaking his head, looking as forlorn as if it had been his own business. "Frankly, if you file, you can reorganize. Start over. Get back in business. Viable business."

"You want me to file for bankruptcy?" Bennie felt a pang. "Absolutely not."

"Why?"

"It's failing."

"It is not!"

"Then it's cheating."

"It's not that either." Sam's eyes softened, their corners tilting down. "Honey, your business was in trouble before Finalil stiffed

you, and now you have nothing. The bankruptcy laws were enacted for people like
you."

"I never understood the bankruptcy laws.
What about my creditors? I leave everybody
in the lurch? We wave a financial magic
wand and presto? I don't pay what I owe?"

"No, especially not with these new
changes in the law. In simplest terms, your
creditors get parked, in a way. You give
them payout schedules. They settle or they
wait for the full amount is all. Life goes on.
It's not personal, it's just business."

"Business *is* personal."

"No it isn't. You always confuse the two."

"It's easy to do when your name is on the
front door."

"You have no other choice!" Sam flushed
with frustration. "Your office fixtures won't
secure another line of commercial credit.
Nobody will lend you another nickel with the
business as collateral."

"What about my house? I can put it up,
can't I?"

"For a business debt? Why would you?
You don't want to do that."

"Looks like I have to." Bennie shuffled
through the papers on Sam's desk and

found her mortgage note. "This is my mortgage, what does it tell you?"

Sam looked it over. "You should have refinanced when the rates went down."

"Can I borrow against it?"

"Okay, there is equity in the house."

"Equity is good, equitable and all. I bought the house as a shell, what, seven years ago?"

Sam glanced at the paper. "Six, it says here."

"Okay, and I renovated it completely, increased its value. And the neighborhood, which wasn't that hot when I bought in, is trendy now. A house down the street went for sixty grand more than I paid."

"I don't think you should even consider doing this, Bennie. It's deadly to commingle your assets, to use personal funds to pay business debts." Sam set the mortgage aside. "You've been doing it for months now, buying office supplies on personal credit cards. Paying your associates out of personal savings. You're eating your seed corn. Robbing Peter to pay Ramon."

Bennie smiled. "You're seeing him again?"

"No, usually it's dark. Can't see a damn thing."

Bennie laughed, which felt momentarily good. "Now. How much can I get if I hock the house?"

"Ballpark?" Sam punched some numbers into the adding machine, then checked the tape. "I bet you can raise forty-five grand in a hurry, maybe fifty."

"Fifty grand!" Bennie felt happy and sad, at once. She was pretty sure the word for this was "ambivalent," but that didn't begin to convey her internal conflict. "That would be enough to solve my cash-flow problems and keep me in business until the class action settles."

"Don't do it. It's too risky." Sam was shaking his neat little head. Behind him, outside his large office window, the sun was dropping in the sky, singeing the top of the skyscrapers and making fuzzy silhouettes of the Looney Tunes on the windowsill. Sam leaned forward. "This is a business debt, Bennie. Fold the business and start a new one. Keep your house. You love your house, and for Christ's sake, you have to live somewhere. Are you even making the payments now?"

Barely. "Yes. And if I have the equity, why not use it?"

"Because if you don't make the payments on the new loan, which will be higher, your business folds *and* you're out on the street. There will always be another business, another job. They come and go." Sam paused, searching for the words to persuade her. "But your house is your *home*. You *never* put that up. You practically built the damn thing yourself."

"I know that, but—"

"The bank will take it as soon as you go into default. They'll demand full payment and foreclose. Don't think they won't. You'll lose everything."

"Don't worry, it'll be okay. I won't lose everything. I won't lose you," Bennie said, and Sam managed a smile.

"True. You can't lose me. Not ever."

Bennie thanked him, but couldn't feel the sentiment now. She couldn't feel anything. She could only act, and suddenly the last resort had become the only course.

"Make it happen, Sam," she said.

11

Bennie walked home from Grun & Chase, moving faster than the businesspeople who hadn't been charged with felonies. She couldn't wait to get home and see what her house looked like after the cops had tossed the place. She felt anxious. Disoriented. She kept looking behind her for Alice. The twin had to have been following her at least some of the time. She knew what Bennie wore. Alice could be somewhere in the crowd right now, or someone working with her. And it was almost dark.

Bennie checked behind her again. The same young man with spiky black hair, plugged into an MP3 player, with a Jan-Sport backpack slung on one shoulder. Next to him a middle-aged man strode along, carrying his suit jacket over the handle of his briefcase, and a young woman walked behind him in spongy Nikes. Alice was nowhere in sight.

Bennie turned onto the Ben Franklin Parkway into a cool wind whipping down the boulevard from the Schuylkill River, which flowed behind the art museum. The giant multicolored flags of all nations flapped from stainless-steel poles lining the parkway, billowing in the gusts. She put down her head and braced herself against the wind. She'd get back on her feet when she mortgaged the house, and even have some room to breathe. Before she'd left Sam's office, he'd called a gay banker he knew to get her house appraised and draw up the loan papers. With his connection and a little luck, she'd have the money in three weeks, and she could stall Linette that long. She was back in business, at least temporarily.

Crak! The flag flapped in a sudden gust, and Bennie started, glancing around. She didn't see Alice, but there were fewer people around her now, since only those heading toward her Fairmount neighborhood would be going this way. She felt exposed.

Vulnerable. She picked up the pace and found herself on her street in no time, jogging to get to her house. As she got closer, she could see that her front door had been broken. She hustled to her stoop, and the sight hurt her heart.

Wood splintered from two long cracks in the varnished oak of her front door, running almost its length. The cops had sledgehammered the lock to get in, then had nailed the door shut to secure it. Bennie gritted her teeth. She climbed up the stairs, stuffed her briefcase and bag under her arm, and ran a finger over the splintered oak of the door, which she had hung and varnished herself. It had taken almost all day, with Grady's help. Goddamn it! Doggy scratching broke her spate of self-pity, and Bennie felt her smile return. The cops didn't have to break the door; Bennie had a golden retriever who would have unlocked it for them and fixed meat loaf.

"Hang on, Bear!" she said, then stopped. She couldn't get in the front; she'd have to go around the back. So she climbed down the steps, went around to the alley, and hurried back to her house, slipping a key into the back French door. Bear jumped on her instantly with his rag-mop front paws, wondering if this was some new game.

"Bear! No! Bad dog!" she said, but they both knew her heart wasn't in it. She dropped her stuff, closed the door, and scanned her dining room with dismay. Her stereo system in the corner had been torn apart, the cardboard backs taken off the speakers, and the CDs spilled from their teak racks and left all over the floor. The kitchen cabinets hung open, every one, and all of her groceries—cereal boxes, flour and sugar bags, cans of peas, and even a box of baking soda—had been dumped on the counters. All the kitchen drawers had been pulled out, the silverware reshuffled and knives slid from the knife rack. Even the dishwasher was open and the blue plastic racks rolled out. The search warrant had authorized the cops to look in everything, since an item like earrings was so small. She didn't want to think about what they'd done to her mustard.

She walked into the living room, where the scene was the same. The cushion on the sofa had been upended, novels had been torn from the bookshelves, and magazines and newspapers lay scattered on the coffee table. It would take hours to put the place back together, and she hadn't been upstairs yet. Her bedroom. Her bathroom. She even had a tube of Clearasil in her medicine chest. At her age, it was humiliating. Bear bounded obliviously over the debris, a hundred pounds of fur carrying a denuded tennis ball. His wetly pink tongue lolled out behind the ball, challenging both the laws of physics and the rules of etiquette.

"Good boy, good dog," she said, scratching the dog's soft cinnamon head. He responded by scampering on the books, wagging his heavy butt in the air, and setting the tennis ball squarely between her pumps. He wanted to play, and he needed to go out anyway. He didn't care what the house looked like, or that Alice was screwing up her life. Who could say he was wrong?

"You got it, handsome." Bennie bent down and picked up the ball, which set the golden dancing and sliding on the books. She grabbed his red leash and the pooper scooper and hooked him up, and they left the house together through the completely inconvenient backdoor, with Bear holding his ball delicately in his mouth, his lips draped over it on either side like velvet curtains.

Once she got outside onto the street, Bennie glanced around. The street was deserted because most of her neighbors had returned home in this residential section of the city; she hoped they'd been at work when the police went on their treasure hunt. The rowhouses were low here, none taller than three stories, leaving lots of sky. The sun had dropped behind the houses, leaving behind a lovely royal blue wash with undertones of deep rose. It was still light, and would be for about an hour, with spring coming on full bore. Just enough time for a quick game of fetch. Bear trotted alongside her as they walked, stopping only to relieve himself with a tennis ball between his teeth. It was his best trick.

She gave him a pat, feeling herself almost relax in the process. Lights were already glowing through the windows of the rowhouses, and the cooking aromas wafted down the block. "Chicken," she decided, and Bear looked back in agreement as he tugged her along.

The Lame Dog Park was just a few blocks away, so named not because it was for lame dogs, but it was such a lame park. It contained not a single blade of grass, but was simply an abandoned square of rubble and trash leftover where a few houses had been torn down and reconstruction had yet to begin. The dog owners in the neighborhood had picked out all of the glass and dangerous trash, and had taken to using the open lot to run the dogs because it was so convenient and secluded. Bennie wished she could take Bear someplace nicer—Rittenhouse Square, Taney Park, or the Schuylkill River—but they didn't have time before dark. Bear set the ball at her feet, and she picked it up and gave it a good toss. She glanced around but no one appeared to be watching.

Bear came cantering back with the ball, his gait rocking back and forth, his tail wagging. His round eyes were like brown marbles, bright and alert, and he smiled broadly, panting up at her. Bennie felt a rush of warmth for the animal, marveling at how happy he could be with so little. He didn't need anything but an old tennis ball and a trash-strewn vacant lot. There was a lesson in it, even for a woman with two Ivy League degrees: Best not to become too attached to things, even to houses. But then again, the dog didn't employ three young lawyers, in one of the toughest job markets ever.

She threw the ball, preoccupied. She couldn't live her life looking over her shoulder. She wanted to know where Alice was. She knew that Alice wouldn't be found if she didn't want to be, not by conventional methods. There was one way she could track her down, but she hadn't wanted to find her enough before to resort to it. But as distasteful as it was, the time was now. It was the night of last resorts, after all.

Half an hour later, Bennie had consumed a sandwich and was driving out of the city, steering her old white Saab into the dark night, heading southwest onto I-95. She would be there in under an hour, sans driver's license, but she doubted that was a felony. Traffic was light because the rush hour had passed, and the road opened up ahead, its asphalt smooth and dry.

The Saab whizzed past exits for the Philly airport, then the Red Roof Inn, oil refineries, and lighted billboards that had sprung up around the Tinicum Nature Preserve, engulfing it with catalytic converters. Bennie hadn't come this way for about two years, since the last time she saw her father. Which was also the first time she saw her father. Bennie hadn't known any of her own history until Alice surfaced two years ago, and her mother had been too ill by then to speak, much less explain their past, or her secrets. But what Bennie learned when she uncovered the truth made her understand why her mother had kept it a secret. In particular, the truth about her father, William Winslow.

Bennie gritted her teeth at the memory. Two years ago, Bennie had traced Winslow to the Wilmington area, where he worked as a gardener for a wealthy family on a country estate. His blond hair had thinned and turned gray, and his eyes were a light blue color that matched hers exactly, but for the odd chill behind them. He'd kept track of her and Alice in his own crazy fashion, and he was Alice's only tie to Philadelphia. If anyone would know where Alice was, he would, but first Bennie had to find him. She had tried the last phone number she had for him before she'd left, but there had been no answer. She didn't know if he still lived in Delaware, but maybe the family would, and stopping there had helped her last time.

"Ready or not, here I come," she said aloud, not terribly surprised at the anger underlining her tone. She probably should have gone to therapy about her feelings, but she'd been too busy, then too broke. She'd read self-help books about dysfunctional families, but she wasn't self-helped.

Her fingers tensed around the hard steering wheel, and she noticed her speedometer jitterbugging at eighty miles an hour. She passed a red Miata, then a long McDonald's truck with a mile-high hamburger on the side. She was feeling more nervous the closer she got to her father. She accelerated, ignoring the speedometer and the other cars. She felt as if she were a bullet streaking toward a target, the trajectory flat, straight, and true. She would see her father and go right through to Alice.

She checked the Saab's clock: 8:22. She'd be at his house in half an hour. She whipped past strip mall after strip mall, their neon signs glowing in the dark, the way she had remembered it. Soon the landscape would change to the lovely countryside right outside Wilmington. The estate her father lived on was in the middle of gorgeous horse country, with acres of rolling hills and rustic split-rail fences. Bennie remembered the last time she visited; it had been almost twilight then, and scattered bay horses had been grazing the pastures, the feathery edges of their black tails flicking at invisible flies. She had resented the fact that her father had lived amid such beauty while she and her mother had gone from block to block in the city, chasing lower rents. Her poor mother.

God rest her soul. Bennie ached inside, missing her, and knew that if she permitted that pain to stay, she would be lost. She'd have to pull over and cry, and she wasn't sure if or when she would stop. There were many nights she didn't, at home in her bed, and the notion seemed fitting. Her mother had sacrificed so much for her, Bennie owed her a few sleepless nights. It was all she could give her now.

Go, a voice said, and Bennie wasn't sure if it was hers or her mother's. She didn't know if her mother would approve of this mission. But she knew she would understand. And Bennie obeyed.

Over a half hour later, she'd arrived at a large white sign that stood where her father's mailbox used to be. HUNT COUNTRY

ESTATES, it read in Olde English letters, and a curved brass horn flanked the words. Bennie got out of the Saab, dismayed. She looked behind her, then ahead. Fake Victorian gaslights illuminated the place. She had the right street. This was the place. She'd circled and circled and ended up here. But where was her father's house?

She blinked, trying to remember the place two years ago. There had been a gravel road right on this spot, with a fork on the left that led to her father's cottage and garden, and an almost paved road on the right, tree-lined, that had led to the main house. The main house of the estate had stood on the hill—a huge white mansion with colonial shutters and separate wings, like an embrace. A maid who had answered the door had helped Bennie, the last time.

But Bennie stood now on a smooth single road with too high curbs and iron grates for public water. The new road was lined with bright streetlights and curled to a guardhouse and a grand entrance with its tall iron gates fixed open. Through the gates lay about two billion brick, stone, and stucco-fronted houses, with sculpted terraces and lighted water fountains. The houses looked brand-new, and the slim trees planted on the perimeter were hardly leafy, with lights illuminating the slimmest of trunks, still paper-wrapped for protection. The land had to have been developed right after she'd seen her father. How could so much have changed so fast? They had taken away the hunt country and built the Hunt Country Estates.

Bennie strode to the guardhouse, of white clapboard with a cedar shake roof. On its front a small sign read Master of the Hunt in the same Olde English letters, and inside the guardhouse sat a young man watching baseball on a portable TV. He was dressed in a fake riding helmet and red hunt jacket. Even foxhunters loved the Phillies.

"Tallyho!" the young man called out when he spotted Bennie at the window, and gave a white-gloved wave.

"Tallyho?"

"They make me say that. Doesn't it blow?" He twisted a toothpick in his teeth, and an eyebrow pierce peeked subversively from under his velveteen brim. "This is the dumbest job I ever had."

"I used to waitress in a green dirndl. I had to say 'Welcome to Little Tyrol.'" Bennie shuddered at the memory. Even being a bankrupt lawyer was better.

The young man smiled. "You lost or something? I-95 is up there three blocks, then take a right."

"I'm not lost, but didn't there used to be a big estate here? A huge white main house, a white cottage, and at least fifty acres of land. In fact, this whole area used to be horse farms."

"I dunno. I just work here."

"Damn! When did you start?"

"Six months ago. It's still not sold, all the way. They're asking a million bucks for these cribs." The young guard's attention was diverted by an onyx Porsche Carrera rumbling through the gates, and he gave his little wave and called out, "Tallyho!" Then he turned back to Bennie.

"So you don't know the name of the people who owned the farm, do you? Or where they moved to?"

"A farm that used to be here? No way, sorry. I didn't even know a farm used to be here."

Bennie thought a minute. A neighbor might know where the family had moved, but there were no neighbors in sight. And the post office might have a forwarding address, but they'd be closed now. She got another idea. "Who's the developer of these homes?"

"Simmons Brothers." The toothpick twisted. "They're outta Jersey."

"Where in Jersey, do you know?"

"Someplace fancy."

Bennie avoided the Jersey joke. Bruce Springsteen was from Jersey, so she loved the entire state. "Princeton?"

"Princeton! That's it."

"Thanks, I appreciate it." Just then a yellow Hummer squeezed through into the gate. "Tallyho!" Bennie and the guard called out in unison, and they both waved.

She scooted back to the Saab, grabbed her cell phone, and called Princeton information. They found the number and connected her to Simmons Brothers Developers. The developer would know from whom they'd bought the tract of land, and if they wouldn't tell her, she'd have to go to the office of the recorder of deeds. The owner would be public record. She waited nervously for the call to connect, then got a recording: "You have reached the headquarters of Simmons Brothers Developers. Our office hours are eight to five. . . ."

Bennie pressed End and tossed the phone aside. She'd have to wait until tomorrow.

She threw the Saab into gear and took off, cruising to make sure there were no neighbors left. Night had fallen, but Bennie could see how much the terrain had changed. Streetlights lined the newly paved roads, and large homes rose from formerly verdant horse pastures. Chandeliers shone through curved Palladian windows in the darkness, and the air didn't smell of manure anymore, which wasn't necessarily an improvement. The shiny brown horses had been replaced by shiny brown Jaguars. She took a left and right, then stopped at a light. She signaled for a right turn and was about to head toward the highway when she saw a handmade sign stuck into the new curb by the side of the road.

MACK'S TACK SHOP CLOSEOUT—EVERYTHING MUST GO, it read, with a hand-drawn picture of a horse. Bennie considered it as the Saab's breathy engine idled. A tack shop was where they sold stuff for horses, wasn't it? The family that had owned the farm where her father had lived had owned horses. Maybe someone at the tack shop would know the family, and maybe even where they'd moved. Also Bennie's father had been their caretaker. Maybe he'd gone in there for hay or whatever food horses eat. It was possible. Bennie switched her blinkers to signal left, and when the traffic light turned green, followed the hand-drawn arrow on the sign.

Giddyap!

12

Bennie got to the tack shop fifteen minutes before nine o'clock, the closing time on the door. It was a small and chummy store; three small rooms joined together, with a plain green rug, and no-frills fluorescent lights on the ceiling illuminating a dwindling supply of horse supplies. At least, Bennie assumed it was horse supplies, since she was from Philly. A golden retriever was the closest she'd come to wildlife.

"Be with you in a minute!" called out a young girl in a green polo shirt that read MACK'S TACK. Her dark ponytail swinging, she hit the keys on the cash register with a rhythmic beat, *hunka-hunka-hunka,* and was concentrating too hard to look up. "I'm just cashing out. Can you hang in there for two minutes?"

"Sure," Bennie said, and looked around to kill time. To her left, on a wall of Peg-Board hooks hung a few ropes of leather straps looped around horse bridles, and to her right, the Peg-Board held a group of silvery metal things she guessed must be the bits, some qualifying as cruel and unusual punishment. Orange crates of shiny stirrups lined the floor, and a funny odor emanated from an open basket of weird brown cookies.

The cashier behind the counter glanced up. She had intelligent blue eyes behind her glasses and her nametag read Michelle. "Thanks for being so patient."

"No problem. You're the first person perceptive enough to call me patient." Bennie crossed to the counter, a rectangular wooden affair beside a magazine rack filled with titles like *Dressage, Practical Horseman,* and *Equus.* Next to the cash register sat a bin of clear soaps labeled Soapy Ponies, apparently because little toy ponies were cryogenically frozen inside. Bennie picked the last one up with a pang. This could be her business in a few weeks. "So you're going out of business, huh? All the horse farms gone?"

"Yeah," the girl said with a sigh. "The county got a new board of supervisors and everybody sold. The land goes for two hundred thousand dollars an acre now. No horses, no tack."

"I'm sorry."

"It's sad, but people gotta live somewhere." Michelle shrugged.

"Actually, I'm looking for someone who used to live around here, a family who used to own one of the horse farms nearby. It stood where the development is now, Hunt Country Estates. This would be about two years ago."

"I don't know." The cashier shook her head, setting her ponytail swinging. "I've only worked here a few months."

"Damn." Bennie was tired of saying damn all the time. It just didn't go far enough. "They had horses, and a caretaker, and I was guessing they came in here for their horse stuff, or for horse food, like hay. Don't horses eat hay?" She was pretty sure horses didn't eat Iams.

"They do, and grain, but we're not feed or hay dealers. We sell tack, bridles and saddles, and gift items like books, mugs, and computer games." The young woman gestured helpfully at a shelf behind Bennie.

"Well, do you have records of customers, or mailing lists I can look at? I know the family's address, but not their name."

"No, I think any mailing lists are all packed up, if the owner even kept them. He's retiring, and our lease is up in two weeks, then we're outta here. The mailing lists wouldn't have helped anyway, they were only in order of names. If you didn't know their name, you'd have to look through every entry."

"I've done dumber things," Bennie said. "You think the mailing lists have been sold to anyone? It would seem like too valuable a thing to throw away."

"Maybe Janet would know. She's worked here forever." Michelle gestured behind Bennie, to a petite older woman walking toward them with a thick key ring that jingled *closing time*. Her gray hair was cut in a neat feathery bob, and with her green Mack's Tack polo shirt she wore loose jeans and tan Birkenstocks. The cashier waved her over. "Janet, you know what happened to our mailing lists?"

Bennie turned around. *The older woman has worked here forever.* "Or did you know the family who owned the horse farm that became Hunt Country Estates?"

"Hi, I'm Janet, and sure, I knew the Rices," the woman answered, and Bennie's heart leapt up.

"The Rices? They lived on Owen Road? They had a horse farm?"

"Of course, Peg Rice came in here all the time. A very active horsewoman, even at her—our—age. She hunted regularly with her son. They even hunted in Ireland, with the Galway Blazers." Janet thought a minute. "Yes, they had a thoroughbred and an old paint pony, Buddy. Cute, and a good little mover. The pony was her daughter's. She was a pony clubber."

She clubbed ponies? Bennie knew that wasn't right. Horse people had a language of their own. She was feeling more left out than St. Amien.

"And Peg's husband had the Apps. Four Apps."

Forget the Apps, Bennie could barely believe her luck. "Janet, do you know where they moved? Maybe they mentioned it?"

"Ocala, Florida."

"Great! Then it would be no trouble to find them."

"Not at all, I have their address. We just sent Peg a new bridle she'd ordered for Sewanee. He's in between a horse and a cob and it makes her crazy."

Bennie was too happy to ask what a cob was. She always thought it came with corn. "The Rices had a caretaker, right? For the estate?"

"Bill?"

"Yes, Bill Winslow!" Bennie was astounded. It was the break she'd been waiting for! "You know him?"

"Sure, he used to come in here all the time, to pick up orders for Peg. A quiet man. I don't think he ever said two words to anyone."

"That's him, all right," Bennie said, with a tight smile of recognition. Practically the only words he'd said to Bennie were "hello" and "good-bye." And she remembered how he'd recoiled from her touch when they'd met. "Very quiet."

"A bookish man, too." Janet was gesturing at the wall of books behind her. "In fact, most of the books behind you belonged to

Bill, the used ones. We're trying to sell them."

"They're his?" Bennie turned to the wall she hadn't looked at before. It was full of horse books, obviously used, and worn in a friendly way. *Centered Riding, A Horse of Your Own,* and *A Horse Around the House.* She flashed on her father's small white cottage, filled with every sort of book imaginable, many bought at library sales. She doubted that he'd been a rider, and she remembered him collecting the classics and lots of other books, almost randomly. She ran an index finger along the spines of the books, as she had the time she'd seen him at the cottage.

"They're yours for a song," Janet said. "Most of them are his, I believe. *Were* his. Peg donated them to us after Bill died."

Bennie's finger froze on the spine of one of the books. She wasn't sure she'd heard correctly. She turned from the bookshelf and found that she couldn't speak.

"I'm sorry," Janet said quickly. Her hooded eyes searched Bennie's from behind her bifocals, and her expression softened, her wrinkled mouth turning down at the corners. "You didn't know that Bill had passed. It happened last year, of a heart attack."

Bennie was trying to find her voice, to get over the awkwardness of learning from a complete stranger that her father had died. When her father was no more than a complete stranger, in fact. She experienced the moment outside her own body, where she saw herself standing, hollow, in a tack store in the middle of Delaware, holding a Soapy Pony and hearing this news. Feeling it rock her to her foundations, even as she knew that it could not. She struggled to absorb the information, only vaguely aware that the women were staring at her.

"Did you know Bill well?" Janet asked.

Not really. He was only my father. Bennie had momentarily misplaced her voice. Her heart hammered away. The little store seemed suddenly so quiet, the fluorescent lights white-hot. She shook her head.

"Well, Bill did keep very much to himself. He was taciturn." Janet and the young cashier exchanged tense looks. "Would you like a glass of water?"

Bennie finally swallowed. "No, thanks. I'm okay. It's just . . . I didn't know." *Know what? Him? That he had died? Anything?* She couldn't specify.

"Bill worked for the Rices for decades, tending the grounds."

Maybe they have the wrong man. Bennie had to make sure it was him they were talking about. Maybe it wasn't him. Maybe he was still alive. "He was tall, right? Real tall, maybe six three. With blond hair, used to be before it went gray."

"Yes, that's him. We saw quite a bit of him. He worked for them for a long, long time."

"But he took some time off, not too long ago, right?" When Alice had been arrested for murder, their father had come to Philly to tell Alice about Bennie, so Alice could get the best defense on the charge. He saw it as taking care of his daughters, but given what had happened next, Bennie saw it as something else.

"Yes, he did disappear for a while. Said he was taking some time off. Peg was quite concerned. When he returned to work, he wasn't the same."

"How so?" Bennie asked, though she wasn't sure enough what "the same" was to know what qualified as different.

"He seemed tired the times he came in here. Thinner. He had aged quickly. I guess it was his heart. You understand." Janet gave a final sigh and walked to the counter, picked up a sales slip, and slid a pencil from a pencil cup. "Now, if you tell me your name and address, I can contact the Rices and perhaps they'll give you a call."

Bennie noted she had just been demoted from getting the Rices' address to giving her own. The saleswoman must have thought she was some kind of nut. She doubted the Rices would call her, but she told Janet her name and address anyway. It was something to say. An answer she knew.

"Good, I'll let them know." Janet folded the slip and slid it into her back pocket, then checked her watch. The movement set the keys jingling on her ring. "Now, if you don't mind, we really should be closing. Will you be okay?"

Bennie nodded. The Soapy Pony clenched in her hand made a hard fist. "How much do I owe you for the soap?"

"You needn't. It's only a dollar."

"No, I insist. And . . . I want the books, too."

"Which ones?" Janet asked.

Bennie turned and scanned the titles. *Beginning Horsemanship, A Complete Medical Guide to Horse Care, Grooming from A to Z.* "All of them," she answered impulsively.

"You're a horse lover."

"No," Bennie answered, and turned away.

It wasn't until Bennie reached the Tinicum exit ten minutes from the Center City that she became aware of a thought. She had driven for an hour to get back to Philly, yet she couldn't remember a thing. Had her head gone blank for sixty miles? It didn't seem possible. She had steered the Saab onto I-95, shifted gears and accelerated properly, and had seen cars, trucks, hotels, strip malls. Roadside lights had blurred as she'd whizzed past them; neon signs, lighted billboards, lights illuminating exit signs, red taillights flashing on and off, all of them bright holes puncturing the blackest of nights, like stars punched into the sky. She had seen these things and somehow she had made it home, but she couldn't remember how this had happened exactly.

The Saab sped forward as if it were driving itself, turned on its blinkers and switched into the correct lane for the exit off of I-95, and headed into the oldest part of town, then turned north, straight toward the Fairmount section. The tight turn shifted the books in their box on the backseat, but Bennie didn't notice the sound. She didn't think about the fact that her father was dead. That she wouldn't be able to mourn him. That she had missed his funeral and didn't even know where he was buried.

She wiped unexpected wetness from her eyes and swung the Saab onto the parkway, between the line of the amber lights limning the broad Ben Franklin Parkway, its asphalt slick with a rain past. A bright red traffic light burned into the night, but Bennie saw its blazing only blurrily, even though she wasn't whizzing past anything, but was stopped there, rolled to a halt at a light and shifted out of gear. It was then that she realized that her mother and her father had died of the same thing. Their hearts had failed; hers from being used too much. And his, too little.

Bennie hit her house lonely, quiet, and depressed, an array of human emotions evidently lost on golden retrievers. Or at least, Bear. He threw himself on her chest the moment she came in the backdoor, licking her face the way he did every day and almost stripping her of the box of books. She told Bear the usual forty-four times to *get down* and *no jumping* and *stop that,* all of which he ignored seriatim, dancing delightedly at her feet, his toenails clicking on the hardwood floor as he tried futilely for traction among the clutter of CDs the cops had left on the dining-room floor. Bennie set the box on the rug amid the mess and, even so, couldn't help but smile.

"Yo, what happened to that legendary intuition of the canine? You're supposed to gauge my mood, then try to comfort me. Don't you watch Animal Planet?"

Bear plopped his furry butt on the floor and pawed at the air until Bennie settled him by scratching the bozo hair behind his ear. The dog pressed his head against her palm in a way that told her the yeast infection had returned to his *ears,* which had to be some cruel gynecological joke. She stepped over the dumped CDs and went to the kitchen for his goopy ointment as he trotted behind her, scooping up his scummy tennis ball on the way and dropping it at her feet when she stopped before the cabinet.

She had to grab his collar before she found the medicine among the cereal and sugar on the counters, or he'd escape.

"Aha, tricked you yet again!" she said with complete satisfaction, plucking aside a rattling bottle of Excedrin and a thin box of heartworm medicine until she located the crimped tube of Panalog. She twisted off the red cap one-handed and squirted a wiggly line of goop into the dog's raggedy ears, then closed and massaged each in turn, holding on to his collar while he wriggled to save face.

"Poor baby, hang in there." She put the crumpled tube back on the counter, and he picked up his ball again and let it drop at her feet, where it bounced and rolled to a stop, as if on cue.

"Nice move," she said with a smile, and when she bent down to retrieve the ball for her thrilled retriever, realized his secret plan. Bear wasn't the kind of dog who sniffed out your lousy mood and shared it; he was the kind of dog who ignored your lousy mood until you surrendered to join his, which was uniformly and consistently terrific. Bennie stroked his soft nose, just beginning to gray, shot through now with tiny spears of dull silver, and she bent down and kissed him on the muzzle more times than she would have in public. Then she whispered to him that she loved him, and when she straightened back up again, she didn't feel like crying anymore. Nor did she feel like cleaning up.

She felt like figuring things out.

Ten minutes later, she was hoisting the box of books onto the tiny kitchen table, covered with paper napkins taken from their ceramic holder and a grainy pile of sugar dumped from a matching bowl. She tore into the books, taking the top one. *Horsemanship* was the first title, a thin green volume, and she opened it to the flyleaf. *Ashleigh Rice,* read a name in a child's hand, and underneath: *Wilmington Pony Club, D-2. Age 6.*

Bennie flipped through the book. Glossy pictures of people jumping things on even glossier horses. Nothing to tell her anything about her father. No secret notes stuck inside, no receipts from stores, no photos or papers of any kind. She went to the next book, *Lessons on the Lunge,* which bore no name in the flyleaf, merely a faintly penciled-in price, $14.95. She flipped through the pages again, not knowing why or even what she was looking for. Just that she was looking.

After the whole box had been emptied and all the books gone through, she still hadn't found anything. She considered that then, with the books lying open on the table. In the back of her mind, she'd always understood that her father was terribly unfinished business in her life, and she'd always thought she'd get back to Delaware when she was ready to deal with him. There was so much she'd wanted to know, about his life, about his decisions, and his acts. And now about Alice.

But as it happened, he couldn't wait for Bennie. Death had intervened, not impatient, merely inevitable. It hadn't known of her intentions and plans, inchoate and well-meaning. It had taken her father on a schedule all its own, denying her her answers, conclusions, and explanations. Some families died with their mysteries still, and Bennie's would be one of those. And though she had lost the chance to know her father, she still felt grief at his passing. Which was the biggest mystery of all.

She considered that, too, letting it lie in

her heart for a minute longer, giving him that much due and no more. Then she closed the book.

And went to clean up her house.

13

The next morning found Bennie in her office at seven o'clock. It had taken her until late to get the house back in order and she hadn't slept much, but with adrenaline and caffeine she was coming around. Marshall and the associates had put the offices back together after the police search, hard work which wasn't in anybody's job description. And for that Bennie felt responsible.

A pale ray of sunlight shone translucent through her window, too weak to warm her, glaring off the hard finish of the papers cluttering her desk. She normally loved to work early in the morning, but she was feeling wretched this morning. She had lost a father she'd never known. It left her feeling oddly restless, and had implications for the present. If the Rices didn't call her, she'd have to find another way to get to Alice. But for the time being she had to concentrate.

Today was the day of fighting back, on all fronts. First, fighting Alice. No way could Alice dress like her today. Bennie had retired the khaki uniform that was too easy to copy, and this morning she was wearing a bright red suit she'd bought on sale at Ann Taylor but had never worn because the color was too Nancy Reagan. Its short jacket cinched in at the waist, and its skirt was high enough to have locked Bennie into shaving above her knees. *Eek*. And she'd brushed her hair and moussed it back into a sleek, if wavy, ponytail, which was disguise enough for the present.

She'd channeled the remainder of last night's angst into work, drafting a discovery, interrogatories, and document requests in support of St. Amien. She had to get this case—and this client—back on track. She'd called St. Amien's office last night, hoping to explain that pesky felony arrest on the street, but he hadn't returned her calls. Concerned, she'd E-mailed him and asked him to meet her today, but he hadn't responded. He wasn't the E-mail type, so she'd assume she wasn't fired and go forward. Asserting his legal interests was the best way to keep him happy, and Bennie was coming out slugging. She swiveled her desk chair to her computer keyboard and opened the file for the draft discovery on the screen, then reviewed it carefully, putting on the finishing touches.

Bennie read the interrogatories, which were one of the better sets she'd written, and hit the Print icon with satisfaction. Usually when she drafted discovery she'd anticipate striking fear into the heart of the opposition, but this time she was thinking about giving a cardiac to her co-counsel. She refused to let Linette and his posse run all over her. She had to get the upper hand on becoming lead counsel, and she knew just how to do it. She imagined Linette's ruddy face when he got her papers—and the other trick she had up her very stylish sleeve—which she would set in motion right now.

She hit a button on her computer and summoned onto the screen a fresh white sheet of computer paper. She was supposed to be a maverick; she'd start acting like one. She tapped away on the keyboard.

She couldn't keep playing nice with Linette, attending meetings that he ran, at his office, on his agenda. His was a closed club and they'd never let her in. Good girls didn't get to be lead counsel. She'd take this battle straight to the top. There was only one place to get justice, and it wasn't from a lawyer.

She had almost finished when Mary Di-Nunzio stuck a head inside her door, reminding Bennie of a turtle peeking out of its shell. "Bennie, can I ask you a dumb question?"

Bennie looked up from her computer with a reflexive frown. "DiNunzio, could you sell yourself any shorter? Don't *ever* begin a conversation that way." Her tone was unnecessarily harsh, but she was in high maverick mode. Unfortunately, it had the effect of driving the associate deeper into her shell.

"Okay. Sorry. Forget it." DiNunzio's head retracted. "I'll come back when you're not busy."

"No!" Bennie shouted, then got up and went to the door in time to catch her. "DiNunzio, come back here." She tried to change her tone from ballbuster to kindergarten teacher, but it had been a long night. "Please, come back here."

"Okay." DiNunzio turned and came back slowly in her conservative print dress, with its high neck and thin leather belt. Either the associate dressed kind of retro or everything old was new again, but Bennie didn't care. "I didn't mean to snap at you. I just don't want you to be so wimpy."

"Sorry."

Bennie smiled. "Stop apologizing for yourself. Don't be such a good girl. You want to be lead counsel someday, don't you? You're tougher than this, aren't you?"

"In my head, I am. But then it disappears when it goes outside."

"Let's give you a lesson. You go over there and sit in my seat, at my desk." Bennie gave the associate a starter shove that propelled her into the office, where she walked around the desk and sat miserably down. "Watch me, DiNunzio. This is how you approach me in my office from now on." Bennie cleared her throat, strode to her own office door, and gave it a stiff rap. "Bennie, you gotta minute?" she asked in a rapid-fire cadence that took the answer for granted.

"Uh, yes. I mean, bring it!"

"Say no, and say it exactly how I would."

"No!" DiNunzio shouted, which Bennie overlooked.

"This is an important question. I have to speak with you, right now." Bennie barged into her own office and took the seat opposite the associate, whose freshly made-up eyes flared with mild alarm. "Get it? See what I'm doing? How I'm acting?"

"Rude?"

"No, in control. Fueled by testosterone."

DiNunzio snorted. "I forgot my injection."

"Pretend. Imagine."

"I can't. I went to Catholic school."

Bennie thought a minute. "Then act caffeinated. It's basically the same thing."

DiNunzio looked dubious.

"Channel Starbucks, and ask me what you came in to ask me."

DiNunzio cleared her throat. In a strong voice she asked, "Can I go to Washington for Brandolini?"

"No."

DiNunzio blinked. "Oh."

"You just going to take no for an answer?"

"Well, yes. You're the boss, and I don't have a choice."

"Bullshit! You have a good reason to go to D.C., don't you?"

"Yes."

"You've never asked to go on a business trip before, have you?"

"No."

"In fact, this would be your very first one, right?"

"Yes."

"Well then, fight for it. Gimme your best argument. Keep it short. People like short."

DiNunzio squared her shoulders behind the desk. "I have to go to Washington. It's my job."

"Not that short."

DiNunzio inhaled deeply. "It's the only way I can find out what happened to Amadeo Brandolini. The records of his internment are there, in the War Department files in College Park, Maryland. I requested them under the Freedom of Information Act, but I have to wait four months unless I want to go there and see them for myself. I know it's a bad time to be leaving the office, but I can't wait that long, so I have to go."

"Well done." Bennie felt a guilty twinge. "But I don't have the money to send you right now."

"I'll pay myself."

Ouch. "You shouldn't have to do that."

"Why not? It's my client and I can invest in it, same as you."

Yowza. "I'll reimburse you. How long will you be gone?"

"Two days."

"Fine. You have my permission."

"Who asked you?" DiNunzio shot back, and Bennie hid her smile, just as the telephone started ringing.

It was St. Amien. "Benedetta. I'm sorry to be returning your call so late. I had a minor emergency to deal with. My son."

"Nothing serious I hope."

"He needs money, *naturellement.* For clothes, food, CDs, books. This week here, that week there. You have no children, am I correct?"

"None without fur."

"Excellent. Keep it that way. Since my wife passed away, Julien has been nothing but trouble. She had a special way with him, which I seem to lack." St. Amien paused, and Bennie could hear the softest *whoosh.* He must be smoking his stinky cigarettes.

"But enough of that. How are you, and what happened with the police yesterday? Judy called to let me know you were all right and that it was a case of mistaken identity. But what a scene that was! And they have you on TV, all over the news I see!"

"You don't know the half of it," Bennie said, but she had already decided to level with him. "My twin sister is back in town, making trouble. But don't worry about it. I can deal with her."

"A twin! How wonderful. You are identical?"

"Yes."

"And she is the black sheep?"

Bennie smiled. A quaint notion. "This flock ain't that uniform, Robert."

"I see. In any event, so you're not going to prison."

"Not at all. They'll be some fussing later, but I can clear that up, too," Bennie answered with a light laugh. Then it occurred to her. Alice could make trouble for St. Amien, as well. "Though, just to be on the safe side, you should know that this twin looks exactly like me and has been running around posing as me. There's even an outside chance she may approach you—as me—at some point. She's taken to dressing like me too. We're completely identical."

"Ah, so she is lovely too."

"Picture me with a criminal record," she said, deflecting the compliment. She flashed on that kiss of the other day. St. Amien was the Pepé Le Pew of clients. "Her name is Alice Connelly and she's a bold sort, Robert. So if I drop by your office unexpectedly, call here to double-check if it's really me. I know this sounds awkward, but it needs saying."

"You're joking."

"Wish I were."

St. Amien blew out some smoke. "Benedetta, if you are in trouble, perhaps I can help you."

Bennie felt touched, but worried. No client would keep that attitude for long. In three days St. Amien would be looking for a lawyer he didn't have to help. She channeled reassurance and caffeine. "Robert, I think you have that backward. Thank you for your very kind offer, but I am here to help *you*. You stay the client and I'll stay the lawyer, okay?"

"*Ça va.*"

"And that, too."

"Also, I did have a surprise visitor this morning, though it wasn't your twin. Herman Mayer came to see me, without an appointment. It was Mayer who told me about you, on the TV. I was dealing with my son and hadn't turned it on."

Bennie felt mortified. "Mayer? What did he want?" she asked, but she was already guessing.

"To speak with me about switching lawyers, from you to Mr. Linette."

Whoa. "Full-court press."

"What means this?"

"It means they're really pressuring you."

"Herman Mayer cannot pressure me to do anything," St. Amien said, his tone changing on a franc. "His opinions are of no moment to me. He and I have history, as you say."

"How so?"

"We have been competitors for some time, he and I. I was going to tell you this when we went back to your office, but the police intervened, unfortunately. Mayer and I were both bidding on the Hospcare contract, the one which eventually fell through, as you know. He wanted it very badly, but they awarded it to us."

Bennie raised an eyebrow, even over the phone. "I didn't know that."

"There you have it. I suspect that Herman is increasing his damages estimate in some artificial way, inflating the revenue from the contract I got. There can be no way his damages are greater than mine. None. He has seventy-five employees only and not even ten million in sales, and he didn't build an entire plant on the strength of certain contracts. Perhaps he is smarter than I." St. Amien laughed.

"Or maybe he just has less faith."

"Perhaps. My company is much older than his, founded by my grandfather. Herman and I expanded our European facilities at the same time. He came to the States first, however. Moved here and gained a small foothold on the market two years before I saw the opportunity. As such he feels as if he were my superior, which is not the case, needless to say."

But it's cute that you said it anyway. Bennie liked this client. He seemed more human to her than when they had first met. Though the kiss by the elevator bank may have had something to do with it. Everybody needs positive reinforcement.

"So Herman and I had a brief, unpleasant meeting. I told him I was quite pleased with my counsel and wouldn't switch."

"Even with me getting arrested? And my wacky sister?"

"Ha! Wait until you meet my wacky brother, then we shall talk again. Ah, he does not work ten hours a week, but for play, his horses, he has much energy. Riding around and around a ring of twenty meters." St Amien chuckled. "Don't worry, Bennie. I stay with you, wacky family and all."

This guy is loyal. Bennie flushed with gratitude. Maybe she could learn to smoke. She knew how to eat, and it was basically the same thing. But back to business. "You think that Linette put Mayer up to seeing you? Linette can't contact you directly at this point, but parties to a lawsuit can always talk to one another."

"I doubt it came from Linette. Mayer is too stubborn to listen to anyone, least of all a blowhard."

Bennie smiled. "Blowhard! Who taught you that word? It sounds like a bad translation of asshole."

"Benedetta, don't be an asshole," St.

Amien said with a soft chuckle, and Bennie laughed.

"Okay, wise guy. You got my letter, you know what's going on this afternoon. Meet me there at one. I'm doing it to shore up your position as lead plaintiff."

"I understand, and I'll see you at one o'clock. But tell me, how will I know you're you and not your twin?"

"I'll be the one you kissed," Bennie said, and hung up with a smile. *Touché*. Then she caught herself. What the hell was she thinking? St. Amien was way too old for her, and he was a client. Was she that desperate? Of course not, right? Bennie rested a hand on the phone and couldn't help but wonder: *Can I get him to stop smoking?*

Then she came to her senses. She had a master plan to set in motion, and kisses didn't figure into it.

14

Bennie felt the familiar whoosh of chilly air rush at her as soon as she opened the door to the courtroom and ushered St. Amien inside. In the federal courthouse in Philadelphia, the government conserves money by air-conditioning only the courtrooms, clerks' offices, and judges' chambers, and saving it in the many hallways of the twenty-odd-floor building, so the refrigerated blast of the courtroom welcomed Bennie as surely as coffee smells did at the office and a golden retriever did at her house. It signaled to her that she was on her turf, even that she was home.

St. Amien was looking around. "No one's here yet, we're so early," he said, his tone hushed by the spaciousness and grandeur of the courtroom. Bennie had noted that the room usually had that effect on clients and witnesses; it was why she always brought witnesses in for a look-see. St. Amien wouldn't have to testify today, but he stopped at the door, uncertain. "Benedetta, may we enter?"

"Of course. It's a courtroom. It's public. It belongs to us."

"It is so different from Paris," St. Amien whispered, eyeing the place, his mouth taut. "Our courtrooms are much smaller. Darker, and much older."

Sounds great. She led him up the carpeted center aisle, and his silvery head swiveled left and right, taking in the huge wood-paneled courtroom, which empty seemed even bigger. An immense modern dais dominated the room, flanked by paneled boxes for the witnesses and jury, and it bore the flag of the United States before a rich maroon backdrop meant to absorb sound. Above the dais, a heavy golden medal of the United States Courts hung like a gilded sun in the sky. Okay, maybe Bennie was idealizing the place, but if a lawyer didn't get a charge in a courtroom, she should get out of the business.

The flag, the dais, the seal, and the jury box—all of these fixtures reassured and thrilled Bennie. They were the stuff of the law, the emblems, accoutrements, and tools used every day to hammer out justice, case by case, verdict after verdict. Bennie wasn't so naive that she thought justice was always perfect, blind, or evenly administered; she knew from bitter experience that judges and juries made mistakes, were bamboozled, or simply went the wrong way, every day. But she also believed that in the main, judges, juries, and lawyers strove together for justice, and that the courthouse remained a citizen's best hope for a truly level playing field. Which was why she had come here today.

"Please sit down, Robert," Bennie said, and gestured him into a seat in the front row of smooth polished wood. He sat down dutifully and placed his cushy leather envelope on his expensive pants. She could have been imagining it, but she sensed a subtle shift in the balance of power between them, as if he were silently ceding her the upper hand. She had become the expert, his Sherpa in the big American courtroom. Now if she could only get him to kick the habit.

"Robert, I have to ask you, have you ever tried to quit smoking?"

St. Amien looked up, puzzled behind his spotless glasses. "I won't smoke here. I know not to smoke in the courtroom. I would never do that."

"It's not about that. Why don't you quit?"

"Quit smoking? Why would I?" He sounded so nonplussed, Bennie almost laughed.

"Because it's bad for you. Haven't you heard that in Paris, where the courtrooms are older and smaller?"

"Yes, of course, they say this, but I enjoy smoking."

Bennie let it go. She had her answer, and it was off the point anyway. "Okay, fine. You stay here and watch. And don't give this seat up for anything. This is the best seat in the house, and you are about to become the lead plaintiff in this lawsuit. I want the judge to see you, and you first. When Mayer and everybody else arrive, let them step over you."

St. Amien smiled. "It seems ill-mannered."

"It is. We call it litigation. Welcome to America. It's time to bang some heads."

Bennie knew that St. Amien would need an explanation for the idiom, but she didn't offer one. She turned to plaintiff's counsel table to take first chair. By the end of the afternoon, St. Amien would understand the term perfectly.

The Honorable Kenneth B. Sherman glared down from the dais, his gray hair slightly frizzy and his dark eyes cranky behind gold-rimmed aviator glasses. He hunched over in his black robe with tiny gathers at the yoke top, and his striped tie was knotted too tight for most liberal Democrats. If he was angry at Bennie because she had requested this conference or because she'd been thrown drunkenly out of a Chinese restaurant *or* because she had been widely reported as guilty of diamond theft, she didn't know. It might have been moot.

"Well, good afternoon, everyone," Judge Sherman said as the courtroom settled down. He nodded briefly around the room, now full to capacity and almost warm with body heat.

"Good afternoon, Your Honor," Bennie responded, in unfortunate unison with Bull

Linette, who shifted unhappily next to her at counsel table. He'd be unaccustomed to second chair at counsel table, which was usually occupied by the second-in-command on a lawsuit. He had barely said a word to her when he stormed in with an equally stony Herman Mayer, and he kept his gaze riveted to the front of the courtroom. She knew she'd pissed him off royally with this move, but she was trying to represent her client, not make friends and influence people.

"Does everyone have a seat on the plaintiff's side?" Judge Sherman asked, eyeing Quinones and Kerpov, who nodded back as they pulled up chairs next to Linette, then the other minor lawyers who formed part of their cabal. More lawyers filled the left side of the courtroom, spilling onto the pews behind counsel table, sitting with their clients, brought for show.

In contrast, the right side of the courtroom, reserved for the defense, was markedly empty, the pews completely vacant. There was no client presence at all, and only a single defense lawyer, an older man, sat at counsel defense table. Bennie knew that the trade association would have retained fleets of lawyers from one of the big, prestigious law firms in the city, but had intentionally sent only a single lawyer, to preempt the underdog position. He wasn't fooling anybody, least of all Bennie, who felt like telling him to save it for the jury. But she'd fight that enemy later. Right now she had to fight her alleged friends.

Judge Sherman shifted his oversized glasses higher onto his nose, and his mouth became a hyphen as he returned his glare to the lawyer directly in his field of vision, Bennie Rosato. "Now, Ms. Rosato, since we are all here on your motion, do tell us, what is an emergency hearing in a class action? Class actions usually move along as quickly as evolution itself. I don't think I've ever heard of such a thing in this context."

It's okay, Judge, neither have I. Bennie didn't require prompting to stand up and take the lectern. This whole proceeding was *about* her taking the lectern. She grasped both sides with sure hands. "May it please the court, my name is—"

"Bennie, for God's sake, I know who you are. What I don't know is why you're here."

Okay, maybe that wasn't a good start.

Bennie's hands shook a little, so she gripped the lectern harder.

"And do tell me, while you're at it, what these papers are. Is this an exercise in creative writing?" Judge Sherman held up a sheaf of white papers at a delicate distance from his nose, as if they smelled really bad. Unfortunately Bennie recognized the motion she'd filed today with the court and had sent to chambers with her letter. Judge Sherman's knitted brow told her he thought she was ready for rehab. "What on earth is an 'Emergency Motion to Determine the Method for Appointment of Class Counsel'? I never heard of such a thing. You on an emergency binge or what?"

"Your Honor, I know this is unorthodox—"

"*Unorthodox!* Unorthodox is Chianti with Dover sole. I *know* unorthodox, Bennie. I *am* unorthodox! This isn't unorthodox, it's nuts!"

"Your Honor, please—"

"Wait, I haven't finished! I know it sounded like I was finished, but that's just the type of zany, unorthodox judge that I am!"

Bennie stood tall. If his wasn't the most judicial tone or demeanor, it was the plain talk for which Judge Sherman was famous. And behind it was concern for her mental state and addictive personality; she could hear the softness in his tone. Bennie flushed with embarrassment, cursing Alice inwardly. Her scam had tainted the judge's view of the motion, and her scheming had infected St. Amien's interests. Bennie gritted her teeth and bore down.

"It's not only nuts, it's premature," Judge Sherman continued. He let her motion papers drop to the dais like trash. "The complaint in this class action landed on my desk last week, and I got your client's complaint just yesterday. Now we all have to meet? Today?"

Bennie was about to respond when Linette leapt suddenly to his feet and muscled the two steps to the lectern. "Your Honor," he said loudly, "if I may say so, I quite agree, and it is vital for the court—"

"Mr. Linette, sit down!" Judge Sherman thundered, and Bennie bit her cheek. Linette eased into his seat. "This is Ms. Rosato's motion, and right now I'm engaged in a colloquy with her. This case has major circus potential, and I will *not* let that happen in my courtroom, so I'm nipping it in the bud. From here on out, when I need your two cents, I'll ask for it, Mr. Linette. Now please remain in your seat."

"Yes, Your Honor," Linette answered. His ruddy face went ruddier, and Bennie felt a rush of satisfaction. She was willing to take the beating she was about to get, but she would keep the floor. If she had to act out to get attention, so be it. It was a lesson every Bad Girl had learned. Mavericks 'R' Us.

"Now, Ms. Rosato, please continue," Judge Sherman said, squaring his puffy black shoulders. "I'd really like to hear you defend this motion. I could have simply denied your request, but I admit, you intrigued me." His gaze softened for a minute, and Bennie realized he *had* been worrying about her. He couldn't contact her ex parte, that would have been unethical, but maybe he'd granted her request for a motion simply to see her in person. He could have denied it without a hearing. As if to confirm her thoughts, the judge flashed a smile that was almost encouraging. "Make it worth the price of admission, Counsel."

"Okay, Your Honor," Bennie began, steeling herself. "As you can see, the lawyers representing the various class members in this lawsuit are all prominent members of the Philadelphia class-action bar, including Mr. Linette. As you are aware, I do not normally do class-action work, but in this suit I represent Mr. Robert St. Amien, the president and CEO of St. Amien & Fils."

Bennie gestured briefly behind her to St. Amien, who was sitting according to her seating chart. "St. Amien & Fils is a French company that manufactures lenses for medical equipment, and it recently expanded to the U.S., opening a subsidiary in the King of Prussia area. Mr. St. Amien should be the lead plaintiff in this lawsuit because his is the biggest company in the plaintiff class, at one hundred and fifty employees, and his damages, at sixty million dollars, far exceed any of the other plaintiffs', including Mr. Linette's client, Herman Mayer. But my client's position as lead plaintiff is currently being jeopardized by the process of private ordering among class counsel."

Bennie ignored the low growling emitted by Linette and the ripple of hostility that reverberated around the plaintiff's side of the courtroom. Defense counsel kept taking notes, and the stenographer tapped silently away on her mysterious black keys. Bennie doubted that she was recording any of these atmospheric changes. That was the problem with a trial transcript; it recorded only the words, not the tone. Like Cliff's Notes to *Portnoy's Complaint*.

"I am therefore moving the court, at this admittedly early juncture, to appoint class counsel by using the auction-bidding method, as opposed to private ordering. This method is particularly appropriate to the case at bar, in which a newcomer to the class-action practice represents the plaintiff with the greatest damages. In addition, because my law firm is so small, I can provide the least expensive legal services to the class as a whole."

Judge Sherman frowned. "Let's be clear. You're not asking me to appoint you class counsel today, or even ultimately. That would not only be unorthodox, it would be insane. Rather, you're asking that I determine that auction bidding be the method whereby I appoint class counsel. Your motion goes to the procedure, not the substance."

"Yes, Your Honor."

"Your co-counsel have not had an opportunity to brief this matter, Ms. Rosato."

"I welcome their briefs, Your Honor. My only intent was to get things rolling." Bennie didn't add that what she had wanted was momentum, the initiative.

But by now Judge Sherman's frown had taken up residence on his forehead. "Normally, a matter like this wouldn't be brought up on motion, Counsel."

"You mean, that's not how it's done, Your Honor."

"Precisely."

"I understand that, but there is no reason why it couldn't be, or shouldn't be, is there?"

"Perhaps not."

"It's in my client's interests to be open and aboveboard about this process, Your Honor. My predicament as his counsel is that I know precisely how it *is* done. Secrecy and closed proceedings do not serve my client, nor does delay. I recognize that this motion and hearing are somewhat unconventional, but my only other choice is to risk my client's rightful position as lead plaintiff to the vagaries of backroom bargaining by powerful members of a very exclusive club—to which I do not belong."

Bennie stopped, almost involuntarily, right there. Her words rang out in the silent courtroom and had a hang time all their own. She had said the unsayable—in open court—and she swallowed hard. She was going public with their behind-the-scenes fistfight, and she knew the implications: Bennie had just declared war on Bull Linette.

Back at second chair, Linette held his breath, red-faced, seething. His bleached teeth were set in a grimace. Quinones and Kerpov looked frozen and pale, as if they'd been cast in plaster death masks. The court stenographer paused in her typing, her fingers poised in midair. The silence deafened until the judge broke it:

"My, my, my. This *is* unusual." Judge Sherman shifted in his seat and replaced his glasses, then took a minute to let his gaze shift down the line to Linette and the other class-action lawyers. It returned to Bennie, and it didn't look as if he thought she was drunk anymore. In truth, he didn't even look angry. But his tongue clucked with concern, and after a minute, he spoke. "Ms. Rosato,

I cannot begin to consider the merits of your motion from the bench, but I am cognizant—"

"What! This is an outrage!" boomed a sudden voice from the back, with a thick accent, and Bennie turned around in surprise. Herman Mayer had jumped to his wing tips in the front row. Next to him, St. Amien looked surprised and drew backward. Mayer's gaunt cheeks were mottled with anger. "Your Honor, my losses are greater than St. Amien's, and I came sooner to the U.S., to Fort Washington! He only followed me here, and through illegal competition and interference, he *stole* my contract with Hospcare—"

Linette was standing up, waving Mayer into his seat. "Herman, sit down. Be quiet. Let me handle this."

"This is *my* business, Lawyer!" Mayer shouted back. His dark eyes flared with indignation. The veins in his stringy neck bulged like an angry rooster's. He waved a hand with a heavy gold wedding ring. "I know my business! I will not sit here silent while that woman lies about my business! My *business!*"

St. Amien had risen to his feet, too, his

lips parted in affront. "How dare you accuse me, Herman!" he said, his voice only slightly raised. "I did *not* steal your contract with Hospcare, you fool! You *had* no contract with Hospcare! They came to me—"

Holy shit. World War II is breaking out. "Robert!" Bennie said firmly. "Please, you don't have to answer him, I will—"

"Fool! Liar!" Suddenly Mayer turned and, red-faced, gave St. Amien a strong shove that almost toppled him.

"Argh!" St. Amien said, struggling to stay on his feet, righting his glasses with dignity.

"Robert!" Bennie shouted in alarm, moving to help him.

Crak! Crak! Crak! "Order! Order!" Judge Sherman shouted, banging his gavel on the dais, as Bennie eased St. Amien into his seat and waited for the judge to restore order. "Mr. Linette, get your client in control! Order! Or I'll throw him out!"

"Herman!" Linette said, pivoting on his slippery Italian loafer. Next to him, Quinones's eyes widened and Kerpov looked embarrassed. Brenstein turned away, and Linette tried to contain his client. "Sit down! Right now!"

"Don't you tell *me* to sit down!" Mayer

shouted back, pointing at Linette with a long index finger. Bennie stayed with St. Amien, who had composed himself, and watched amazed as Mayer turned his anger on his lawyer. "*You* sit down, Linette! You aren't doing anything to help me! How dare you let her malign me and *my business!*"

"Herman, *sit down!*" Linette thundered, instantly red-faced. He took a threatening step forward, which surprised even Bennie. Scenes like this didn't happen in civil lawsuits. That's why they called them civil.

Crak! The judge howled, "Mr. Mayer, you will sit down this minute or I'll have you hauled off!" Mayer obeyed reluctantly then, sinking into the seat beside a grim-faced St. Amien and still shaking visibly from his outburst. But he seemed cowed enough for Bennie to leave St. Amien safely and return to counsel table. Judge Sherman set down the gavel after one final bang, and his glare this time focused on Linette, his eyes searing into him like twin lasers. "Mr. Linette, I hold you responsible for this! This is *exactly* what I meant by circus potential. I won't have it!"

"Understood, Your Honor," Linette said, his expression stoic and his stance stiff as a toy soldier's. "Your Honor, I apologize for my client, but Mr. Mayer is simply reacting to Ms. Rosato's misstatements of fact regarding her client's damages. Mr. Mayer knows his were far greater." He spat out the words, each one precise as a stiletto. If he couldn't take the lectern, he'd turn counsel table into one. "And I strongly object to Ms. Rosato's having filed this motion without consultation with me, running off to tell the teacher—"

"Objection, Your Honor!" Bennie said, because she couldn't resist. She didn't know if you could object to a statement by co-counsel, but she was loving being unorthodox. And unorthodox was a better adjective than mavericky. "And I resent my motion being trivialized as running to the teacher. Every plaintiff is a tattletale. Justice is obtained only by running to the teacher. That's why they call it court."

Linette ignored her. "Your Honor, I would seek the opportunity to brief the method by which the court appoints class counsel. The process of auction bidding has been disapproved by this circuit in the *Cedent* case, and Your Honor is well aware of the task force—"

"Enough, Mr. Linette," Judge Sherman said, waving dismissively. "You needn't argue the point now, and I know all about the task force. You and all parties of record will have the opportunity to respond to Ms. Rosato's brief, with all briefs to be filed within twenty days." Judge Sherman glanced over at defense table to the lawyer sitting alone, like a blind date stood up. "And you, too, Counsel. We haven't forgotten about the defendant trade association, and I couldn't deny defendant the opportunity to be heard, even though it is not necessarily a matter of your direct concern."

The defense lawyer nodded his balding head. "Thank you, Your Honor. We will brief the issue. If the issue concerns this lawsuit, it concerns my client," he said with dignity, and Bennie knew that he was milking the melee in the plaintiff's ranks for all it was worth.

Judge Sherman looked sternly at Bennie and Linette. "Now, obviously there has been infighting—even fisticuffs—between you lawyers, and you clients, and you clients and lawyers. And even you clients and clients." He rolled his eyes. "This is absurd, unprofessional, and not in anyone's interests. So I have some free legal advice for all of you, and it didn't originate with me. A lawyer who was smarter than all of us once said, 'A house divided against itself cannot stand.' Mr. Linette, Ms. Rosato— *and* Mr. Mayer and Mr. St. Amien—you all would do well to heed those words."

"Yes, Your Honor," Bennie answered, again at the same time that Linette did, only he said it louder. *Anything you can do I can do better.* She was hardly optimistic that Linette would be taking any advice from Judge Sherman, much less Abraham Lincoln.

"Good." Judge Sherman banged the gavel, then set it down and rose, arranging his robes around his tall frame. "I'll take the motion under advisement and await briefing by all the parties, to be filed within twenty days. Adjourned, people. Go home and play nice," he ordered, with a grim set to his mouth; then he left the dais.

Bennie couldn't help but smile, and when she turned back to St. Amien, he was grinning from ear to Gallic ear. But next to him, Mayer didn't look so happy. And neither did Linette, who swooped to the front row of the gallery, grabbed his client by the arm, and stalked off without another word. Quinones, Kerpov, and Brenstein departed in a small horde of lawyers, collectively shunning Bennie, but she had expected as much. In fact, she didn't even blame them. She took her time packing her briefcase to let them all go ahead, to avoid them avoiding her in the elevators. Today she'd made herself a player, leveled the playing field, and gotten the ball.

St. Amien caught up with her at counsel table and slipped a congratulatory arm around her shoulder and gave it a squeeze. "*Fantastique,* Bennie! We won, did we not?"

Bennie clicked her briefcase shut with a grin. "They want to kill us, don't they?"

"Yes."

"Then we won," Bennie said, and hardly minded at all when she was rewarded with another peck on the cheek.

15

Bennie left her very satisfied client at the courthouse, grabbed a cab back to the office, and came off the elevator feeling good for the first time in days. She realized when she saw a leftover L.L. Bean box that she hadn't thought about Alice the whole time she was in court, and she resolved not to let that unresolved situation get her down. She had won, or at least she had struck a blow, and she had to celebrate. She threaded her way through the boxes and found Marshall at the reception desk, hanging up the phone.

"Hey, lady!" Bennie called out. She dropped her briefcase at her feet. "The good guys are making a comeback!"

"I'll say!" Marshall looked up from the reception desk with an expectant smile. Though on Marshall, every smile was expectant. "I have good news too."

"What? Tell me."

"You go first," she said, so Bennie told her what had happened in court. Marshall responded with a whoop that sent the associates hurrying from their offices to the reception desk. Mary DiNunzio came running with a legal pad, Judy Carrier bore her afternoon Frappuccino in a transparent plastic cup, and Anne Murphy had wrapped her long red hair into a topknot with a pencil. They asked in happy unison what was going on and made girl noises while Bennie told the whole story for a second time. Not that she minded.

"Unreal, huh?" Bennie said, finishing. "I thought Mayer was going to fire Linette right there! He still may."

"Fire *Bull Linette?*" DiNunzio's rich brown eyes went wide. "That's like firing God!"

Carrier looked over. "God doesn't work for thirty percent."

"Neither does Linette," Murphy cracked, and they all laughed. "And Bennie, did you hear? We're rich!"

"What?" Bennie looked puzzledly at Marshall. "What happened? Is that your news?"

"We got a check!" The receptionist bent her sleek head over her neat desk, set some correspondence aside, and found an envelope, which she handed to Bennie with a huge grin. "This just came in from Pennsy-Bank. We're in the money!"

"Really? So soon?" Bennie opened the envelope and pulled out a check payable to her for fifty thousand dollars. But the check wasn't from her mortgage bank; it was from Sam, with a Post-it attached. She unstuck it and read the note: *Bennie, it turns out there is no gay Mafia. Take my check and reimburse me when yours comes in next month. Love, Wascally Wabbit.* Bennie felt a rush of gratitude.

"Who sent the money?" Carrier asked as the associates grouped around. "Fifty grand! Where'd that come from?"

"I borrowed it," Bennie answered, avoiding anyone's eye. She wasn't about to tell them she was hocking her house and borrowing from her friend in the meantime. Marshall had probably figured it out, but the associates would have a lifetime to learn reality. And Bennie felt too good to focus on the negative. "It'll keep us afloat until St. Amien settles. We can pay the rent and the long-distance bill, and buy a Frappuccino or two!" She looked around at their faces, alive with hope. "Ladies, we're back in business! Carrier, I owe you for my get-out-of-jail card. DiNunzio, I'm paying for your field trip, not you. And Murphy, about your seventeen dollars—"

"Woohoo!" DiNunzio said, clapping, and Murphy brightened.

"We're okay, and I have more good news, Bennie. You know how you asked me to see about your license, with the felony charges against you? I called the disciplinary board, and if you get the charges dropped, there are no repercussions at all. Your license is fine."

"Yeah!" Carrier yelped, and the associates began shaking their butts and doing the butter-churn dance, their generation's reflexive response to any bit of good news, such as Justin Timberlake was single again.

But this time, Bennie joined in.

An hour later Bennie was celebrating Rosato-style, rowing along in a single shell, letting the sights and sounds of the Schuylkill River seep into her bones and soul. She was back to her usual routine of rowing after work every Tuesday and Thursday, and on Sunday morning, and it always felt so good being back in the groove, getting away from courtrooms, clients, and twins. She breathed in the earthy smells of the water, an organic cocktail of muck, minnows, and goose poop, and took another languid stroke, leaning back after dropping her blade into the green-gray water. The late-afternoon sun warmed her sweaty face and shoulders, bare in her white tank.

Sunlight glimmered gold on the tiny ripples of the river, making a gilt edge to the scalloped chop of the waves, as if they were the baroque frame to its glorious natural landscape. On both banks of the river, towering oaks, maples, and cherry trees showed off their new green leaves, reaching into a cobalt blue sky filled with transparent wisps of white clouds, like cotton candy pulled apart by the too-eager hands of children. The grass covering the riverbanks had sprouted a kelly hue, its slender blades weak with youth. Canada geese called in the sky, their honking echoing even in the middle of the river, conducted along the water's smooth surface as surely as an electrical current, if not quite as scientifically.

Psshlp, splashed Bennie's oars, cutting the water and spraying cold water onto the bow deck of her boat, a yellow Empacher. Her boat was twenty-seven feet of beautiful, weighing only thirty pounds; the German-made shell was the favorite of elite rowers, and Bennie had scored hers used. She was too skilled a rower to make such a messy splash, but she wasn't worrying much about her technique today. She was trying to unwind. Get a good mood flowing and forget Linette and Alice. Maybe even her father. And rowing was working its magic, at least by the time she was stroking her way back to the boathouse. She had rowed the seven-mile circuit to the verdigris-colored Falls Bridge and back, but it had taken only two miles for Bennie to feel like herself again.

Psshlp. She leaned back in the hard wooden seat of the scull, pulled the oars into her lower ribs with all her might, and feathered their black rubber handles and pushed them out quickly. A breeze wafted across the water, carrying a chilly undercurrent of winter past and the fresh green gust of spring establishing itself. Bennie breathed it in, let it fill her lungs, and took another powerful stroke. Her thighs ached from the effort, and blood hardened her quads. A rush of good feeling suffused her, flowing like oxygen-rich blood, and she felt almost euphoric. Rowing wasn't a sport, it was a religion.

Psshlp. She looked downriver, where the trees on the banks were giving way to the first edifice of the ten Victorian boathouses that lined Boathouse Row, and to the brick lighthouse known as Sedgeley. The lighthouse marked the place where Turtle Rock lurked just under the Schuylkill's surface, a hazard in a time past, when steamboats cruised down the river. To Bennie, Sedgeley meant that it was time to leave her fugue state and pay attention. The rowing traffic could be dicey going into the boathouses. At any given time, there could be as many as fifty boats on the river, and today, singles, fours, and plenty of school eights were jockeying to get in and get the boats put away by dark. The expressway could be safer; at least if you got out of your lane there, you didn't go over a waterfall.

Bennie stopped rowing, letting her scull coast toward Sedgeley on its own momentum, trailing the tips of her oars in the water to slow her down. There were four other boats on the water, three college eights and a crew from Father Judge High School, heading back toward the boathouses. She decided to let the eights row past her—Penn with its familiar red-and-blue oars, then Drexel and St. Joe, all with coaches shouting from skiffs alongside. She relaxed over her oar handles, dangling her callused hands and listening to her breathing return to normal.

She wiped sweat from her forehead while she waited, and looked around. The dappled grass on the riverbank was dotted now with people who'd ditched work early to take advantage of the unseasonably warm stretch of weather. Cyclists in baby hats with turned-up brims biked on the asphalt paths, their skintight jerseys vivid splotches of color, and runners trotted on the dirt jogging paths, test-driving new running shoes, in telltale white. Lovers smooched on bedspreads, and students tossed cloth Frisbees to mutts in bandannas.

Bennie liked that people liked the river,

and watched the dogs as they fetched their well-loved balls and toys. One black-and-white mutt was an aerial genius, leaping to snag his Frisbee in midarc. A tiny Jack Russell shot after a Nerf football twice his size and as soon as he had captured his prey, plopped down to gnaw it to pieces. A big golden retriever chased a formerly lime green tennis ball, thrown by a man in a red Phillies cap. The dog reminded Bennie of Bear, who was a sucker for a tennis ball, especially a muddy tennis ball. The man was throwing the ball in a bad direction, though. Beyond the bike and jogging paths lay Kelly Drive, on the east side of the river, filled with rush-hour traffic. Instead of tossing the ball away from traffic like everybody else, the man in the cap was tossing it toward traffic.

Bennie frowned like a worried mother. The ball bounced short of traffic, but she would never take a chance like that, not with Kelly Drive so close. The River Drives were the fastest way out of town, and at the end of the day, as now, they were crazy. People drove way too fast, hell-bent on getting home. Still the man tossed the ball toward the street, and the dog went gamely after it, his tongue flying. Bennie shook her head. Golden retrievers were the dumb blonds of the dog world.

"Five, four, three, two, one!" a coxswain shouted through her megaphone, and the high school crew rowed past, their young heads shaved for macho effect. Bennie took up her oars to steady her scull, but she couldn't stop watching the man in the baseball cap on the grass. She loved goldens, and the dog reminded her so much of Bear. His pink tongue lolled out of the side of his mouth in single-minded pursuit of the ball, and he wouldn't drop the ball once he'd retrieved it. Like Bear, the dog danced away once he brought it back, prolonging the tease.

Psshlp. Bennie took a stroke, rowing a little closer to the bank. The man pulled the ball from the dog's mouth and threw it toward traffic again. She rowed past on her way to the boathouse, annoyed. Why would anybody do that? Was the man an idiot? She watched the dog streak toward traffic after the ball, almost upending a jogger on the dirt path. She half considered yelling at the guy from her boat, but it wasn't her business, and she had to get rowing. Other boats were waiting to come in. Still.

Her boat drifted closer to the bank, bobbing on the residual wake, and she rowed a steady course. Closer to the bank she could see the dog's coat, also glossy like Bear's. It was a cinnamon shade considered unfashionable by most golden fans, who preferred the lighter shades, but Bennie loved Bear's coat. It caught the light like this one's, glowing red as an Irish setter's in the sun. The man in the cap threw the ball and the dog dashed after it, but a runner caught the tennis ball before it reached the drive. The runner tossed it back and yelled something Bennie couldn't hear. Probably telling the idiot not to throw it that way. Good.

Psshlp. Bennie had to get going. Three more college eights were rowing toward her, heavyweight crews power-stroking in an impromptu regatta before they reached Sedgeley, their coaches urging them. She took another stroke, but she kept an eye on the jerk in the cap. No sooner had the jogger turned his back than the man threw the ball toward traffic again. But this time the force of the throw caused his baseball cap to fall off. A pile of curly blond hair tumbled to his shoulders.

Bennie did a double take. The hair was

way too long for a man's. It was a woman's, and in the next instant, the woman turned toward the river, looked at Bennie, and waved right at her. Bennie, stricken, recognized the woman instantly.

It was Alice.

Bennie froze over her oars, then grabbed the handles before the water's force drove them into her waist. This couldn't be happening. She couldn't process it. It was Alice, taunting her. And it *was* Bear. It was Bennie's *own dog* racing into traffic after the ball, his pink tongue flying!

"No! Bear! No!" Bennie screamed at the top of her lungs. She dropped her oars, and stood up in the boat, pitching it violently to the right. How had Alice gotten Bear? She was going to kill him! It was impossible to stand in a single, and the boat wobbled dangerously.

"Bear! No! Come!" she yelled, making a megaphone of her hands. Alice was running away, toward the parking lot. She had thrown the tennis ball one last time and it was bouncing on the asphalt of the jogging path, then into the fast lane. Bear bolted after the ball, straight toward traffic.

Suddenly everything was happening at

once. The college eights were racing toward Bennie, unable to stop. They hadn't calculated on her stopping dead in the water. Bennie's boat was rolling like a log. She was going to capsize. She gripped the quick release on her sneakers and plunged into the cold water just as the boat went over.

She began swimming frantically toward shore, a straight-ahead breaststroke. The water was freezing and filled with debris. It tasted like filth but she spit it out. She would never make it in time to save him. Bear would run right in front of the cars. *No, please. No!* She hiccuped with fright and swam as hard as she could, stroke after stroke, barely taking a breath. Her eyes stung. A stick scratched her cheek. She kicked something slimy from her ankle. She came up for air and heard people shouting. Screaming.

Bennie blinked sludge from her eyes and realized why.

She was swimming directly in the path of the college eights. And they were heading straight for her.

Oh my God.

16

"Look ahead, eight! Look ahead!" rowers screamed from the other boats, but the eights rushed toward Bennie, unstoppable. A heavy eight weighed a ton and gathered the momentum of an express train. She swam for her life.

The rowers tried frantically to brake, jamming their oars in the water, spraying water like fountains from both sides. "Hold water! Hold water!" their coxswains screamed and steered but it was no use. One boat's rudder flapped uselessly back and forth. Its lead wire must have been broken by the sudden strain. Bennie could see the point of the boat. Racing at her like a spear.

No! She swam harder. Her lungs felt as if they'd burst. The lead eight was coming right at her, the boyish bowman twisting his trunk around to see her in their path. Bennie saw the terror in his young eyes. She couldn't get out of the way in time. She was going to get run over.

She gulped a final breath of air and dove down deep into the mud and shit, heading for the river bottom. Her chest felt as if it would explode. In the next second, she could feel the powerful current of the eight moving like a whale over her head.

Please, no. Bennie had to stay down long enough for the eight to pass. She couldn't get hit by the boat, the oars, or the riggers. She'd be killed. She leaked precious air from her mouth so she'd stay down. She flailed her arms to get lower, but it was too dark to see anything. Suddenly a wave of water hit her, sending her tumbling end over end in the cold and blackness, like a crumpled paper in a hurricane. Her mouth opened and she took in gulp after gulp of river water. She couldn't breathe. Her nostrils bubbled with water. She felt a bolt of mortal fear. She was going to drown.

But then she saw sunlight, up and to her right. She was sideways. The boat had passed. Out of air, Bennie kicked futilely for the surface. She couldn't make it. She'd never make it. She had nothing left. Her arms ached; her legs gave up. She hiccuped water, gagging. She felt herself lose consciousness.

I don't want to die. Not like this. Not with Alice still alive. And Bear.

Bennie's hands reached for the surface. Her legs kicked with their last effort. She went blindly toward the light, and in the next second broke the water's surface and bobbed into the sunlight, gagging and coughing.

"Wait, wait, there!" she heard a coach yelling, but she was coughing too hard to hear more. She vomited gritty river water and tried to stay afloat.

Bear. She wiped her eyes with cold and trembling hands. She torqued in the water toward the riverbank and saw it through bleary eyes. *Please, God. Let him be alive.*

A crowd formed suddenly on the bank where Bear had been chasing the tennis ball. Traffic stood at a standstill. People jumped out of their cars. The joggers stopped running. The cyclists leapt from their bikes.

The skiff motored closer, and Bennie felt her tears flowing with the river.

She ran soaking and out of breath toward the fringe of the crowd, ignoring the stares and shock of the onlookers. She couldn't see through the crowd to Bear. Dirty spittle covered her chin, and her hair dripped with filthy water. Mud caked her shins, and her socks were soaked. Maybe Bear could still be saved. Maybe if she got him to a vet in time. The vet school at Penn wasn't far way.

"Bear!" she yelled, staggering her way to the front of the crowd, which was breaking suddenly into wild applause. The cyclists in their tiny hats, the runners with the white sneaks, and the lovers and the students were clapping. Bennie felt new tears come to her eyes.

"Bear?" she asked with hope, and as the crowd parted she saw that one of the runners, a huge, well-built man, was carrying her unhappy golden from the path of certain death. It was Bear! Alive! Well! And with a tennis ball in his mouth! The hunky runner set the squirming golden down on the grass.

"Bear!" Bennie shouted with joy, and the startled dog turned, spotted her, and rushed toward her, jumping up on her with soft, gritty paws. Not that she minded. "Bear!" she cried again, smooshing her wet face into his furry one and coming away with hairy cheeks.

"Yeah!" "Way to go, buddy!" "Great job!" shouted the crowd, and the runner waved them off modestly. Bennie reached him just as people began climbing back in their cars, breaking up the gaper block that had stopped traffic on the drive. The cyclists returned to their bikes, the runners to their jogging, and the lovers to their necking.

"Yes, thank you so much for saving my dog," Bennie said to the runner with a rush of gratitude, but oddly, he wasn't smiling.

"No problem," he said tersely. His largish mouth made a businesslike line, and his eyes, large, round, and brown, had gone flinty in the sunlight. He looked to be about Bennie's age, in dark blue gym shorts that read NAVY in yellow letters. A thick white T-shirt hung loose on his broad, muscled chest, and his well-defined biceps were slick with sweat.

An older woman in a blue sweatsuit and

Reeboks was wagging a red-polished finger at Bennie. "Honey, if that's your dog, you owe this man a reward! He just risked his life for that animal! He ran right into the street, stopped traffic with his hands, and scooped up that dog like he was a newborn baby!"

"No, please," the jogger said modestly, but the older woman cut him off.

"Honestly, I've never seen anything like it! He *risked* his life!" She turned to the man. "You should get a medal!" She reached for the man's hand and shook it firmly, then turned again to Bennie. "He deserves a reward for what he did, you hear me? He could have been killed! He carried your dog out of the street and ran with him!"

"You *ran with* my dog?" Bennie looked up at the man, incredulous. Bear weighed over a hundred pounds, all of it peanut butter. It took a crane to lift him onto her bed. "You picked him up and *ran* with him?"

"Yes, it was amazing!" the older woman repeated. "He's a real hero!"

"Please, no!" The jogger dismissed it with a modest wave. "It wasn't anything."

"You're a real hero! A real hero!" the woman said again as she power-walked off, and Bennie felt overwhelmed.

"Thank you again, so much," she said. Bear pawed her soggy socks to get her to throw the ball into traffic again, and she scratched his head with happiness. "Did you really run into traffic to save him?"

"Nah, I was going after the ball."

Bennie laughed. "No, how did you do it? You stopped the traffic and grabbed him? And how did you pick him up?"

"It wasn't hard," he answered offhandedly. He was huge, at least six three, and his physique explained how he had benchpressed a golden retriever.

"I do owe you, that lady was right." Bennie was about to offer the man a reward, but she didn't think he took Visa. "I'm a little strapped right now, but there must be something I can do for you in return. You need some free legal advice? Somebody you want to sue? I can make life hell for your enemies."

"There is something." The jogger's eyes narrowed, and Bennie realized he was angry with her. "Learn a lesson. Take better care of your dog. Don't play fetch near the street."

Oh, no. "No, that wasn't me throwing the ball," Bennie said. She shook her head and grimy droplets flew off, but the man's lips were glued skeptically together.

"Sure it was, I saw you. I told you to stop throwing the ball, and you told me to go fuck myself."

Eek. "No, it wasn't me. I didn't say that. I used to say stuff like that, but I'm on a curse diet." *Sort of.* "You saw my twin sister. My crazy twin sister, who was trying to kill my dog."

"What?" The runner leaned over, frowning in disbelief. His hair was dark and thick, and he pushed lanky bangs from his eyes.

"My twin was the one throwing the ball. She cursed you out. I was out rowing, in that boat." Bennie gestured at the river behind her, and the runner peered past her shoulder.

"What boat?"

"My boat." Bennie turned, but there was no boat floating on the water where she had abandoned hers. She glanced downriver, but her boat wasn't there, either. *Oops.* She turned back to the man and tried to explain. "Well, I had a boat, but it sank. I know I sound like I'm lying, but I'm not. People can always tell when I'm lying."

"I have to go." The runner leaned down

and gave Bear a final pat. "You've got a great dog here. You should take better care of him."

"No, wait, it wasn't me, I swear." Bennie would go crazy if this mistaken-identity thing kept up. At least this time she could prove it. "Think about it. You know it wasn't me throwing the ball because I wasn't wet before. How did I get so wet? And I wasn't wearing these clothes before, was I, when you think you saw me? How did I change my clothes?"

The runner looked Bennie up and down. Listening, not leching.

"I'm not the person you saw with the ball. It really was my twin in the baseball cap. We look exactly alike. She ran away, toward the parking lot." Bennie eyed the lot, but it was too far away. Her eyes welled up with stress and fatigue. "I have to get to a phone and call the police. Do you have a cell?"

"Not on me."

"Shit! She'll get away again!" Bennie glanced around, but the runners were sprinting and the cyclists were cycling. No necking students who might have cell phones were in the vicinity. "I have to get back to the boathouse. I want to call the police, at least to report her."

"You're telling the truth? Your own sister would kill your dog, on purpose?"

"Evidently." Bennie ran a hand through her hair, wet and tangled with leaves and crap from the river. She doubted that it was a good look for anyone but Swamp Thing. But she had to get going. She had to call the cops. "It's only one of the very nice things she's done lately, but it's not your problem. I owe you a reward for saving my dog. He's the sanest member of my family."

The runner smiled, showing teeth that were white and even, and he put his hands on slim hips. He looked like Superman in that pose, but it could have been the fact that he'd saved Bear's life. "I'm David Holland," he said, extending a large hand, and Bennie introduced herself and shook it. His handshake felt strong, sure, and slightly rough. "So where *is* your boat, Bennie?"

"Capsized, I guess." Bennie turned back to the river. She spotted one of her oars rowing merrily down the stream. The old skiff from her boathouse was speeding upriver, toward the spot where her scull had been. "This is probably the recovery operation now. I should go over and see if I can help. Maybe they have a cell phone too."

"I'll join you," David said matter-of-factly, and strode toward the riverbank. Bear trotted after him in adoration. Bennie's socks squished with each step. Her black shorts stuck to her butt. Swamp Thing with back.

"I wonder how you pick up a boat. They probably have to dredge it up, like the *Titanic*," she said to him. On the river, the skiff was nearing the spot where the scull had sunk, and the skiff's Evinrude throttled down to a throaty rumble. Three men from the rowing club rode in the skiff, and they shot Bennie a collective *women drivers* look. David picked up his pace. Bennie straggled after him. "I mean, how do you get a boat off the bottom of a river?"

"Tell you in a sec," he called back, and when he reached the edge of the water, he swung his muscular arms together, bent quickly at the knees, and dived in. Bear barked at the ripples he left behind, then came scampering back to Bennie, wagging his butt and feathery tail and looking up at her with plaintive brown eyes.

"Not unless you walk him," she told the dog.

It was past eight-thirty and already dark by the time Bennie and Bear arrived home, given a ride by David in his khaki brown Jeep, which was neater than any man's should be. Other than that, Bennie couldn't see that he had any faults. He had saved Bear's life. He was hunky, gorgeous, and polite. He'd helped tow her scull to the boathouse, bailed it out, and set it upside down on its rack, almost good as new. Bennie was willing to believe he could have built her a new one with Popsicle sticks. And he liked Steely Dan, which she liked almost as much as Bruce Springsteen, and "Night by Night" was playing softly on the Jeep's CD system. She was trying not to idealize the man, but it was difficult. After all, he was her hero. Or at least Bear's, which was basically the same thing.

David steered the Jeep into a parking space on the block just as a white police cruiser pulled up, double-parking a little ahead of them. It had to be Detective Maloney, whom Bennie had called about what had happened. Meantime, Bennie worried about her house. What had Alice taken? Or had she simply destroyed the place? Trashed it? Bennie boosted herself up in the passenger seat to see her house, but in the half moonlight all she could make out was its flat roofline. At least the place was still standing.

"Well, the cavalry's here," she said, turning to David. It felt strange being in such close quarters with him, and even though their clothes were almost dry, the Jeep's interior smelled of brine and industrial pollution. "Thanks for everything, and most of all, thanks for saving Bear."

"I thought I'd stay until the cops left, to make sure you were safe." David cut the ignition, leaving them in awkward silence, now that "Night by Night" had gone.

"You don't have to do that," Bennie said, and Bear thrust his slobbery muzzle between them from the backseat.

"Bear wants me to. He feels safer with me here." David got out of the Jeep, and Bennie didn't have time to fight about it. She wanted to get into the house. She climbed out, holding on to Bear's collar, and two uniformed officers were emerging from the cruiser.

"Over here, Officers!" she called out, struggling to hold on to the dog as he jumped excitedly at the police, wagging his tail. Nobody else had gotten out of the squad car. "Isn't Detective Maloney with you?"

"The detective sent us out, Ms. Rosato," the first cop said. His voice sounded middle-aged and slightly weary, and he looked heavyset in the dark, the light blue of his shirt puffy at the girth. "I'm Officer Leighton, and this is my partner, Officer Banneman."

"Well, thanks for coming, gentlemen." Bennie introduced herself and tried to prevent Bear from jumping up on his new friends. The dog tugged her this way and that. "But isn't the detective coming? He said he'd be here. He knows about this case, with my sister."

"The detective got held up. He filled us in. It's a B & E, right, and you suspect it was your twin?"

"I know it was my twin. I saw her at the river with my dog. She set me up on theft charges yesterday." Bennie felt David shift beside her and realized this would be news to him. She half expected him to run screaming, but instead she felt him taking the rambunctious dog from her hands. "My door is broken because the cops just searched my house. It's still nailed shut, so you have to go around the back. She must have broken in through the backdoor, taken my dog, and tried to kill him. God knows what else she's done, inside."

"We'll check it out, Ms. Rosato," Officer Leighton said brusquely. "Please, step aside and let us do our job." The cops switched on long-handled black Maglites, making instant pools of jittery light on the gritty city sidewalk, and aimed them at the house. The light circles chased each other up and down, but the splintered wood of the front door looked untouched, just as broken as before. Bennie found it hard to think of it as progress. Officer Leighton *tsk-tsk*ed. "It is nailed shut. How do we get around the back?"

"This way," Bennie said, and led the cops, the flashlights, David, and the dog down the street to the alley, and to the wooden gate in the back of her tiny cement patio, not ten feet by ten. She opened the latch of the gate, wishing now she'd made the time to put a lock on it. They went through the patio to the French doors in the back of the house, when the cops stepped in front of Bennie and shone their Maglites at the French door.

"I don't see any signs of a forced entry," Officer Leighton said. "It's locked."

"It is? How could it be locked?" Bennie asked, surprised.

"Did you leave it that way?"

"Yes, but since then it was broken into, okay?" Bennie couldn't keep the irritation from her tone. "We know this because my dog was taken, and he didn't lock it after himself."

David said, "Do you leave a key with a neighbor?"

"No, the only spare is in the office."

"You have your key on you, Ms. Rosato?" Officer Leighton asked.

"Yes, hold on." Bennie shoved her hand into her purse, fumbled for her keys, and handed them up with the house key drawn. "Maybe she picked the lock."

"Ms. Rosato, please wait here until we secure the premises." Officer Leighton took the key and said to the other cop, in low tones, "I'm primary." He unlocked the door, and it swung open wide in the jittery cone of light. Then he reached inside the door, and the anteroom light went on inside the house, illuminating Leighton's profile. The middle-aged cop had a brushy mustache and a worried expression. "Let's go, Mike."

"Right behind you," the other cop said, and they hurried into the house.

Bennie held her breath. She almost expected gunfire, but all she got was silence. Then talking, then low laughter. Next to her, David was listening intently, even as Bear sat panting, his tail happily brushing the cement. Goldens love new games, even when tennis balls aren't involved. The three of them waited outside while light after light went on in Bennie's house; first the ground floor, then the second floor, and then she heard their heavy shoes pounding down her stairs and back again into the dining room.

"Come on in, Ms. Rosato!" called out one of the cops, and Bennie grabbed Bear's collar and hurried inside, followed by David.

Bennie crossed the threshold, anxious and uncertain, and held her breath, preparing herself mentally for what she might see. She didn't exhale until she'd entered her house and looked around. Her dining and living room were just the way she'd left them that morning, after she'd cleaned up the cops' mess: couch against the wall, bookcases against the other wall, CD and DVD players all in place. Nothing smashed or upended, nothing destroyed or vandalized, not even any scary scrawled writing in red lipstick. But Alice had been here. She had to have been, to steal the dog, and part of Bennie could just *feel* it. That dark vibration.

Officer Leighton switched off his Maglite, and Banneman's hand hung loosely at his side, no longer cocked at his holster. "The premises are secured, and we didn't find any evidence of a B & E, even at the backdoor, Ms. Rosato. Everything looks in order upstairs, too. You'll walk through with me, but everything looks fine."

"That's not possible," Bennie said, confused. Frustrated and angry. Alice was smart. She was fooling them. It was a game for her, a prank with a deadly edge. Bennie had to figure it out, figure *her* out. "The dog didn't let himself out and drive himself to the river."

"Are you sure *you* didn't?"

"Of course not!" Bennie exploded. A long

day of drama and wet underwear was coming to a head. "What do you think, I'm making this up? I have a twin, it's a matter of record!"

"You don't understand what I'm telling you, Ms. Rosato. There's no evidence that any crime has been committed here. You claim that somebody took your dog out of the house, but the backdoor wasn't even unlocked. And the front was nailed shut."

"She exists! Ask *him!*" Bennie gestured at David, who was already stepping forward.

"Everyone settle down," David said, spreading his large hands palms down. He addressed the cops, but Bennie knew he was talking to her, since she was the only one throwing a hissy fit. "Officers, my name is David Holland and I was running along the river when I saw her twin intentionally endangering the dog."

"Tell you what," Officer Leighton said with a slow sigh, like a tire deflating. He reached into his back pocket and withdrew a skinny notepad. "Mr. Holland, you give me the statement for my report while my partner takes Ms. Rosato on a walk-through. This way we get this over with, we file a complete report, and Ms. Rosato makes sure that nothing of value was taken from the premises."

"Fine with me," David answered. "Bennie? Okay with you?"

"Yes, thanks." Bennie stalked to the staircase and went upstairs, going straight to her bedroom. If Alice was going to steal something, it would be here. She entered the bedroom, which looked inviolate, and experienced the same eerie tingle she had downstairs. Alice had been here, too, she just knew it. But not by looking. Everything was in absolute order, or at least a completely familiar disorder, only partly due to the local constabulary.

She hurried to her dresser, a three-drawer chest made of pine, and checked her jewelry box on top. She didn't have much—a tangle of gold chains from when they were the new thing, a few pairs of gold hoops, and three bangles—but all of it was there. She rifled quickly through her drawers—undies, unmatched socks, tattered jeans, and faded T-shirts—but they were in the same mess she'd left behind. She went to the closet, but it was fine. Then she remembered. Her gun.

She hurried to the closet and shoved

aside old running shoes to get to the or-ange-and-brown Nike box, tearing off the lid. There it was. The brown case, a canvas triangle. Bennie unzipped it with shaking hands but was reassured by the weight alone. Her Smith & Wesson revolver lay un-touched. She zipped it closed and tucked it safely away.

She closed the closet door with relief and hurried past the cop to her office, a second, smaller bedroom just off the hall. An old Bianchi bike leaned against the wall in the corner, and clutter covered her daybed and her IKEA workstation. Her computer was still there, and a Bose radio/CD player. She'd left the only things of value. Bennie didn't get it.

"It all here?" Officer Banneman asked, and Bennie nodded slowly, wondering.

How the hell did Alice get in? And get out with Bear?

She couldn't think of an immediate an-swer and returned downstairs with the cop.

17

Bennie did a double take when David came into the kitchen wearing her ex-boyfriend's clothes. It wasn't only the confluence of past and present men; it was the way the clothes fit, or more accurately, didn't fit. Grady's old Duke sweatpants were puffy Capris on David, and the leftover T-shirt stretched tight across his chest and biceps, making him look like an oddly butch ballet dancer.

"These were the clothes you left outside the bathroom door," David said, holding out his arms with a faint smile. The armholes rolled up along each mound of shoulder cap. "You were joking, right?"

"Sorry, I thought they'd fit." Bennie had always thought that her ex was big, but

David was bigger. She could tell because she had to look up to see his eyes, qualifying him as one of the two men on earth taller than she. It wasn't the worst feeling in the world, standing oh-so-close to a handsome, muscular hero, but even Bennie sensed she was getting ahead of herself, if not entering the zone of what they used to call "on the make."

"Oh, well, at least they're clean," David said. "Thanks." He'd taken a shower, and the wet sheen of his hair caught the light of the overhead lamp. He leaned down to pat Bear, who had curled into a cinnamon doughnut on the rag rug in front of the sink.

"Want coffee?" Bennie asked, pouring him a cup and handing it to him. "I have no food in the house, I've been kind of busy. I do have cream and sugar, if you want dessert."

He smiled. "I take it black."

"Why am I not surprised?" Bennie touched her hair, suddenly self-conscious. It was wet from her shower, too, but she was dry again in her favorite work shirt and loose khaki shorts. He didn't seem to notice one way or the other, though he stood sort of close and she could smell the fresh soap

smell clinging to his skin. She tried not to in-
hale. It had been a long time since she'd
had a soapy man in her kitchen. "So how do
you know all that stuff?"

"What stuff?"

"How to save dogs and boats."

David sipped his coffee. His eyes were
kind and intelligent, with a sort of benevo-
lent reserve about them. "Good coffee."

"My goal in life. So what do you do for a
living?" Bennie asked. "I already confessed
to being a lawyer."

"I'm taking some time off."

"From what?"

"From work."

"What kind of work?"

"Nothing   important."   David   leaned
against the counter, sipping his coffee. His
eyes were intense and brown, his nose
long and straight, and he had a squarish
chin. He was easily the most handsome
man she'd ever had in her hemisphere,
much less her kitchen, but he was hardly
the most animated, especially in Capri
pants. And he was clearly avoiding the
question. He drained his cup and set it
down, and Bennie felt a sudden twinge of
nervousness coming out of nowhere. She

really didn't know much about him, and she'd let him into the house.

"Forgive me, but who are you and what do you do? I may sound paranoid, but someone *is* out to get me."

"I should have thought of that. Sorry." David grinned easily. "I was assistant director of the SEAL/BUDS command. I'm an instructor. I'm taking some time off."

"You're a SEAL?" Bennie asked, astonished even though she wasn't sure exactly what that was. She just knew that it was something cool. "Okay, what's a SEAL?"

"SEALs are a division of the Navy. BUDS is basic underwater demolition training."

"And who do you instruct?"

"Cadets."

"Where did you instruct them?"

"California."

"What did you instruct them to do?"

"Become sea-air-land commandos."

Eek. "How long does it take to become a SEAL?"

"If you make it, twenty-seven weeks."

"Do a lot of people drop out?"

"If they don't drown."

Bennie was pretty sure he was kidding.

"Do I have to take your deposition, or can you tell me a little more about yourself?"

"I would, but there's not much more to tell. I'm a Navy captain, graduated class of eighty-four."

"From the Naval Academy?"

"Yep. The Southern Maryland School of Boat and Barge. Went to BUDS in Coronado, southern California. Served two years in Central America, then Desert Storm, instructed for three years, then went operational again in the Middle East. Iraq, Kuwait, Saudi Arabia."

Wow. "Fighting?"

David smiled. "Combat, yes."

"Jeez. And in all those places. I've been to Pennsauken. It's nice, in summer." This would be in the category of saying anything, even dumb stuff. Bennie knew next to nothing about the military, from a lifetime of being philosophically opposed, and also a big chicken besides. And all she knew about SEALs she had learned from Hollywood. "I mean, wasn't Demi Moore—"

"There are no female SEALs."

"How nice for you."

"Tell me more about your twin."

"Oh, is this the enough-about-me part?"

Bennie set down her coffee. It was kind of frustrating. "You don't like to talk about yourself, do you, David?"

"No."

"But you're kind of intense."

"Very."

"So, why? Would you elaborate?"

David burst into laughter, a deep, rich masculine sound. "I don't think I've *elaborated* in my life. If I were the kind of man who *elaborated,* I'd be the kind of man who liked talking about himself, wouldn't I?"

"Okay, maybe." Bennie couldn't help but smile. At least he could laugh at himself. David was like an action figure, with bendable arms. *And what arms.*

"Now tell me about your twin. Alice. What did she serve time for?"

"Drug dealing, which she did, and murder, which she didn't."

"Wonder how she knew you'd be at the river."

Bennie thought about it. "I used to row on a very regular schedule, but it was interrupted three weeks ago by this trial."

"So she's been following you for a month, at least, to know your schedule."

Hearing it out loud gave Bennie the

creeps. She sipped her coffee but the creeps were still there. Creeps are the only thing that coffee doesn't cure.

"So what are you going to do, to protect yourself?"

"Protect myself?" Bennie hadn't thought of it that way.

"Yes. You're under attack. How will you counter it?"

"Well, I changed my clothes so she couldn't dress like me. To make it harder for her to pose as me."

"You changed your clothes?" David mock-shuddered. "Tough tactics. Watch out."

"It's just the first step," Bennie said defensively. *You try losing an identical twin.* "I'll do whatever I have to. I'll figure it out. I always do."

"Do you need help?"

"No, I don't. Thanks, but I don't need help." Bennie knew it sounded like she needed help. She didn't think she needed help, but she didn't know how to make it sound better.

"I can help you. I'd be happy to."

Bennie flushed red, with the three thousand emotions she was feeling at once.

Gratitude. Embarrassment. Sheer schoolgirl crushiness. But his tone was so matter-of-fact that it didn't sound like a come-on. His tone simply matched his words. It was an offer of help, straight up. *Damn*.

"Is this a hard one?" David asked, cocking his head. "A choice. Yes or no."

"How can you help me with Alice?"

"I know stuff, as you put it. And I have the time."

Bennie thought about it. He was a SEAL, but still, would that help? All he could do was raise the *Titanic,* save golden retrievers, and defend our democratic way of life. Still, he was a complete and total stranger. And it was confusing, letting him into her life in such a personal way. Plus he was way too hot and it distracted her. "You don't have to help. Thanks, but no. I'm sure I can hire someone. A private detective, or a security guy."

"Fine." David nodded. "Though before I go, I am kind of curious how Alice got in here. Aren't you?"

"Yes, of course. Obviously it wasn't through the front door, since the cops had already broken in and nailed it shut."

"Maybe we can find out."

"But you're not trained in stuff like that, are you?"

"No, but I'll figure it out. I always do."

Bennie smiled, against her better judgment. She wasn't sure whether she wanted him involved even to that extent, but he had saved Bear, the cops were no help, and her investigator had prostate problems. She doubted that David had prostate problems. His prostate was probably pink and spongy and in perfect shape. She banished the thought. Definitely, *on the make*. "I can't see how she got in. No forced entry, and it's not like she pretended she was me."

"Let's get to work." David went over to the sink with his empty coffee mug, rinsed it under the faucet, then opened the skinny KitchenAid dishwasher and placed it upside down on the white plastic rack. That clinched it:

If David Holland wasn't Superman, he was basically the same thing.

Fifteen minutes later, he was kneeling in front of her backdoor in his silly sweatpants, running his fingertips between the glass panes like a surgeon. Beside him, Bennie petted Bear's thick glossy fur, scratching the flyaway crimps behind his ear, more for her comfort than for his. Her head throbbed. Her eyelids dropped. Her arms ached from the swim, and her shins had been scratched by the sea monsters. Bennie tried to think about what to do next, but she was fried. And she appreciated David's trying to help, but she was starting to feel guilty about it.

"David, do Navy SEALs ever give up?"

"What do you think?"

"Guessed as much." Bennie thought about calling the associates and updating them, but she was too tired. She rubbed her forehead irritably and leaned on the glass of the backdoor. "David, I appreciate it, but—" Suddenly, she felt the windowpane give way under her hand. It popped out of the window and fell outside the door to the flag-stone, where it shattered with a tinkling sound. Bennie looked over, astonished. "Jeez."

"Way to go." David rose to his feet, rising up on powerful thighs, and unlocked the door with the old-fashioned key in the lock. "You always keep this key in the lock?"

"Yes."

"Then that's what happened. She cut the glass, unlocked the door, and replaced the pane." David ran a fingertip along the inside of the pane and his finger came away with white gunk on it. "She puttied it back in place. It would have stayed that way if you hadn't leaned on it so hard."

Bennie's mouth dropped open. "Are you serious? That's kind of professional, isn't it?"

"If she's the one who did it. She could have had an accomplice, or she could simply be that professional, as you put it."

Bennie considered the possibilities, with a shudder. "But she's not that smart, is she?"

"Are you? She's your twin."

"Right, of course. I forgot I was very smart." Bennie was about to remark on his powers of perception when the telephone rang. She went to the kitchen, set down her empty mug, and picked up the receiver. "Hello?" she asked, her eyes on the broken glass.

"Bennie?" The voice on the line was one she didn't recognize, a man's. "Is this Bennie Rosato?"

"Who is this?" Bennie asked coldly. She didn't like strange men using her first name. Unless they wore Capri pants and trained commandos.

"This is Jim Mattuck with the *Philly News,* and I was wondering if you would care to comment—"

"Excuse me, Jim. You're calling my home late at night, and I have no further comment on my arrest. All charges against me will be dropped after the preliminary hearing, I guarantee it."

"I wasn't calling for comment on your arrest, Ms. Rosato." The reporter paused, suddenly uncertain. "Haven't you . . . seen the news? On TV?"

"No." Bennie felt her stomach tense. "What news?"

"I'm sorry to have to tell you this, but there was a murder tonight."

18

Boxy TV news vans littered Walnut Street, their tall microwave towers cutting into the night sky, with their logos, painted in cheery colors, incongruous in the grim scene. Red lights arched through the darkness, flashing from the bubble tops of white police cruisers that blocked the street, and a uniformed cop directed traffic away from the number street and kept it moving up Walnut. Onlookers gathered behind splintered blue-and-white sawhorses that cordoned off the area, mostly teenage boys with backward baseball caps. They tried to get on camera, waving, jumping, and flashing peace signs behind TV reporters talking into black foam microphones in pools of fake light, softened to a more flattering level by wiggly circular reflector screens held up by assistants with aching arms.

Bennie had seen it all before, but it seemed oddly new as she hurried through the commotion, her heart in her throat, hustling in her running shoes over thick rubbery TV cables stretched like trip wires across the street. She ignored the reporters dogging her with tape recorders and microphones, tuning out their questions in her pain, and she didn't stop moving forward until a uniformed cop halted her in the middle of the street, at a sawhorse wreathed with yellow plastic tape.

"You can't pass, here, miss," the cop said tiredly. He was heavyset and he'd said it thirty times already tonight. "This is a crime scene."

"I know, I'm a lawyer. My name is Bennie Rosato, and the victim was my client." Bennie couldn't believe she was saying these words. Her mouth could barely form them. Her mind couldn't process it. *Robert. Dead. Murdered.* "His name is Robert St. Amien."

"Sorry, Ms. Rosato, I can't let you through." The cop shook his head, his eyes shaded and barely visible under the shiny patent brim of his cap. "Only police personnel. If you're a lawyer, you should know that. You could contaminate the scene."

"Come on, please." Bennie peered over his shoulder and across the street. Between a florist's shop and an old-fashioned shoe-repair store lay an alley whose entrance was completely obstructed by police personnel and vehicles. The murder had happened right in Center City, the business district, and it was the second murder here in as many months. The press had flocked to the scene, spinning a story they'd already tagged The Tourist Murders, like a miniseries.

Bennie stood on tiptoe to get a better look. Between the light cast by the streetlights and the ritzy storefronts, still lit for window-shopping, she could pick out the chrome grille of the sober black Econoline that read OFFICE OF THE MEDICAL EXAMINER in yellow block letters. It was parked askew, across the two-lane number street, and its double doors at the back lay undoubtedly open. So the body hadn't been taken yet. *Robert. He is lying there, dead.* "I have to get in there! I am a lawyer, I'm his lawyer. I was with him in court today, I swear it."

"No can do. Now back off. Step away from the—"

"Who's been assigned to the case from Homicide? I know some of those guys." Bennie squinted across the street, scanning the assembled personnel. Uniformed cops, their light blue summer shirts bright spots in the gloom, stood talking in small groups that formed a clotted ring around the mouth of an alley. He had to have been killed in the alley. Against the far curb was the MOBILE CRIME van, but no crime techs were coming or going. Murder scenes always struck Bennie as remarkably static for such a dramatic, horrifying event, but this time the inactivity was driving her nuts. *Why isn't anybody doing anything?* "Officer, who's been assigned? Can you find out?"

"No way I can interrupt, miss. Now step away or I'll have you arrested."

"They tried that already." Bennie had had it. She had to get to that alley. Then it struck her. *Why was Robert here, anyway?* He lived uptown, about eight blocks west. What was he doing here? She needed answers and she needed to be at his side. Then she got an idea. She hung over the barricade and began waving her arms.

"I'm here, Inspector!" Bennie shouted at no police inspector in particular, and the cop at the sawhorse turned to look behind him.

"The inspector's here?" he asked in surprise, and in that moment Bennie ducked under the barricade and bolted toward the scene.

"Hey, you! Lady! Stop!" the cop called out, giving chase. The uniforms near the medical examiner's van turned around at the shouting, and Bennie recognized one of them. Officer Banneman, the cop who had been at her house tonight.

"Banneman, it's me, Bennie Rosato, remember?" she shouted as she ran to him, reaching him. "I'm the one at the house, with the golden retriever. Remember?" Bennie wasn't even out of breath. If she couldn't outrun a beat cop, she should turn in her Sauconys.

"Oh, you," Banneman said, with an audible sigh. "The B & E that wasn't."

"It was, we figured it out. She cut the glass, in the backdoor."

"No kidding?" Banneman looked surprised. "We'll have to get over and have a look at that. Where's your friend, the big guy?"

"He left," Bennie said. She had sent David to his Jeep with a thank-you and declined his offer to come along. For some reason that seemed hours ago. The cop from the barricade caught up with them and grabbed Bennie's arm.

"You know this lady, Banneman?" he asked, miffed. "She says she's a lawyer and the vic is her client."

"She's legit." Banneman waved him off and turned to Bennie, his eyes narrowing in the dim light. "Cut the glass, huh? You call it in, so they could make a report?"

"I didn't have the chance. I heard about this. I needed to get here." Bennie tried to look over his shoulder. At the mouth of the alley, the mobile techs had set up the klieg-lights they used to illuminate nighttime crime scenes, and the lights threw off an eerie glow from their metal stands, the calcium white light hovering close to the ground like an electrical fog. Bennie spotted a crime tech in a baggy jumpsuit bent over at the mouth of the alley, silhouetted in the klieglight, then other men hunched over, squatting. She saw nothing beyond them but shadows. She made a megaphone of her hands and shouted at the group. "Who's assigned to this case from Homicide? Does anybody know? Kovich? Brinkley?"

"Yo," came a voice from the alley, and in the next minute a grim-faced man in rolled-up shirtsleeves and a striped tie emerged from the shadows. He wore wire-rimmed glasses under a scissored spray of silvery Phil Donahue hair, and his manner was intelligent, if not downright bookish. Into the back pocket of his pressed pants he slipped a long, skinny steno pad, of the type carried by detectives. "I heard you were looking for the primary, and I don't like people yelling at my scenes." Despite his gruffness, he extended a hand. "Bob Needleman."

"Sorry." Bennie introduced herself. Her handshake wasn't as firm as usual.

"Kovich and Brinkley are on day tour this month, but they told me about you." It was too dark to determine his eye color, but he had an easy grin. "You're the famous Bennie Rosato."

"Guilty." Bennie couldn't manage a smile. "Robert St. Amien was my client. My friend."

"So I hear. My condolences."

So it is really true. Bennie had hoped he'd say that there'd been some mistake, and she entertained that fantasy for a moment longer. *"Oh, sorry, the victim of this murder is Robert Amien, not Robert St. Amien! Oops!"*

"I admire your work, Ms. Rosato. The civil rights work, not the police cases."

"Fair enough. Thanks." Bennie peeked over his shoulder to the shadows. "Can I see what happened to him? It was a stabbing, they said on the news."

"You've been to scenes before." It sounded like a statement, but the detective waited for an answer, and she nodded. He pursed his lips and took her arm gently. "All right then. This one isn't pretty. Keep your cool. If you gotta leave, leave. You know what Kovich always says, 'Leave or heave.'"

She nodded, noting the kindness in his eyes, which turned out to be light blue. She sensed that Robert would be in good hands. They edged forward, going into the alley, where a ring of personnel clustered in the middle. The coroner, an older man wearing a yarmulke over a balding head, was kneeling over the middle of the alley, and

Bennie recognized him: Dr. Feldman, one of the best on rotation. His two assistants, both black men, flanked him, bent over, working. They'd be finishing the tasks they performed at the crime scene, bagging the hands to preserve trace evidence under the fingernails and making final notations on the position and condition of the body.

Robert's body. Bennie looked away.

The alley couldn't have been more than three feet wide, with a concrete floor that dipped in the center, presumably sloping down to a drain somewhere. A tiny snake of greasy water lay stagnant in the gulley, its surface shiny with oil and littered with a striped straw, a few cigarette butts, and an old *Daily News* sports section, and Bennie tried not to think about Robert lying among the trash. *He doesn't belong here.* The alley reeked of rotting garbage from rusty blue BFI Dumpsters that overflowed at its head, and its walls were lined with old red brick, its color dimmed with age and grime, its mortar grayed and crumbling, granulated. The activity in the alley had stirred up its dirt, soot, and silt, and particulates leavened the air, sparkling as they floated into the exacting beams of the klieglight. It must have been why the light looked foggy at a distance. Bennie felt her brain returning to function.

"What happened?" she heard herself say in a hushed tone, even though she didn't know if Detective Needleman was listening. She wasn't sure she was addressing him, or anyone at all.

"He was stabbed to death. We looked but didn't recover the knife. Same MO as that murder, last month, you heard of it. He was about the same age, fiftyish, from Belgium, it happened two blocks away."

Bennie nodded, sickened.

"This body was found by a Temple kid walking by, out with his buddies, he called on his cell." Needleman checked his watch, pressing on a tiny button so its purple numbers glowed in the dark. "That was about ten-thirty. An hour ago, at this point. Tentative time of death was nine o'clock, but that's only tentative. We found the vic's wallet beside him, credit cards and cash gone. Watch gone, too. And a ring, I think. Had a slight indent on the ring finger. Same as the guy from Belgium."

Bennie flashed on St. Amien's wedding

band. The simple band, worn by a widower. She bit her lip so it wouldn't tremble.

"Cause of death, also unofficial, exsanguination. He bled to death. This is all confidential from the media, by the way. I was assuming you could be trusted, from what Brinkley told me." Needleman looked over for verification, and Bennie nodded. She knew it wasn't procedure for him to be talking to her so openly, or even to take the time. Kovich and Brinkley must have given her very good press. Needleman was saying, "The way I figure it, and it's a working theory at this point, is that this is another tourist got picked on. Whoever's doin' this is taking these tourists as easy prey and robbing them. Either your friend wouldn't give up the goods when they asked, or they killed him anyway."

Bennie tried to picture it, then tried not to. Her gaze remained glued to the bent backs of the coroner and his assistants. Steeling herself for the moment they'd step aside.

"It won't do the tourism business any good, and it doesn't help CompStat either." The detective was referring to the crime statistics the Philadelphia police had instituted under the now-legendary Commissioner John Timoney. "Now with these two murders, it throws off the numbers. Shame of it is, we decreased street crime in the Center City District last year by adding beat cops. You would think it would help with these tourists." Detective Needleman was thinking aloud, and Bennie felt reassured to see that he was questioning even his own theory. Not every detective was secure enough to do that. He continued, "But I guess not, and these foreigners, they're easy marks."

"How would somebody know he's a tourist, just by looking?" Bennie asked, hearing an unnecessary sharpness in her tone. She hated the term "foreigner" and thought about how bigotry had hurt St. Amien. In the lawsuit, and now. "Sorry, I guess I'm being oversensitive, and I think it gives street thugs a lot of credit. And I don't know why somebody would be running around killing foreigners."

"S'okay, these are all good questions, and I don't mind being backstopped. My partner's on disability and I'm solo until he comes back." Detective Needleman waved the apology away. "Foreigners, or tourists, are easy marks because they have lots of dough on them, and they don't expect violence the way we do. They don't take the precautions. They walk in dumb places, not paying attention. They think they're safe here, like they are at home."

Bennie ignored the irony. *We get killed in the streets, and foreigners are the crazy ones.* "So how can you tell St. Amien wasn't from here? Could *you* have told, with Robert?"

"Sure. He smoked those weird cigarettes, he was smoking one when he got hit. Also, from the cut of his clothes, his expensive suit. He dressed too nice for here, especially for Philly."

Bennie managed a smile that only made her sadder. That much was true. Robert stuck out in this dressed-down town.

"He had very polished shoes, a little formal. Lace-ups, and I never saw that kind here. A fancy silk tie. You could tell he was different, not from here, even if you couldn't tell he was European. Same thing with the Belgian, and he was an international banker."

Bennie considered it. It wasn't implausible. Still. "You think street thugs notice these things, like shoes?"

"Of course. They can tell Iversons at fifty yards."

"In the dark?"

"Probably followed him for a while. It's Center City, plenty of light around."

Bennie nodded reluctantly. "Also, if they confronted him, they would have known for sure. He had an accent."

"There you go. So did the Belgian guy." Detective Needleman nodded, acknowledging that she was with the program.

"Any witnesses?"

"No, at least not yet." His gaze returned to the scene. The klieglight reflected bright on his face, limning the contours of soft, almost jowly features, a short nose framed with deep laugh lines. He was about fifty years old, and he laughed a lot. Just not right now; his mouth had a grave set to it. "The vic's driver's license said he lived at the Manchester, on Rittenhouse Square. Nice place. Condos, isn't it?'

"I've never been. Robert was my client for only a few days."

"Very nice place. I went there for the notification. Just got back."

Bennie looked over. "Notification? You mean next of kin?"

"Sure, it's procedure. I got his name from the wallet and I went over."

"Waste of your time, huh? He doesn't have family in town. His wife is dead and his son's at law school, at Harvard."

Needleman shook his head. "I know, but the brother was at home. He lives in the same building. When I went looking for next of kin, they told me at the desk."

"He lives in the Manchester too?" Bennie asked, in surprise. Why hadn't St. Amien mentioned his brother? Then she remembered that he had. *You have never met my wacky brother.* Bennie had just assumed that the brother was in France. "He's a doctor, right?"

"Yes. I did the notification, and the man got pretty broken up. Name is Georges. They were supposed to have dinner that night. Nice guy. Wait, excuse me a sec." Detective Needleman took a step forward in response to one of the coroner's assistants, who was straightening up and brushing down the knees of his baggy jumpsuit. They were obviously getting ready to go. Bennie braced herself for the sight as the detective motioned her backward. "Step aside, please. They're going to take the body."

Bennie held her breath. The assistant edged out of the alley, back to retrieve the gurney, and his absence gave Bennie a clear view of the lower half of Robert's legs. Her throat caught at the sight. His feet lay askew, flopped horribly apart in their polished black shoes, and the cuffed leg of his finely tailored black trousers had been pushed rudely up, exposing a sheer black sock. He was wearing the gorgeous suit he'd worn in court today, but now it was as if he'd dressed for his own funeral. In the next minute, the coroner was helped to his feet by his other assistant, exposing the corpse entirely.

St. Amien's eyes were horribly open, fixed and unseeing, and his mouth livid and contorted with agony. His glasses were off, and his head was turned to the nearer of the klieglights, his skin as white as the beam itself. *Oh my God. No.* His tie remained carefully knotted but his suit jacket had been rent by the knife blade and lay open, exposing his chest to the klieglight, which cruelly illuminated a vivid crimson mass of sopping red blood that had spread from the many cuts. The coroner and his assistants moved expertly around the corpse, returning with the stainless-steel gurney and preparing the body to be transported, but Bennie saw them only as a shadowy blur around the elegant man who lay sprawled on the filthy concrete of the alley. The air suddenly thickened with the stench of the fresh blood, and Bennie couldn't breathe.

"You okay?" the detective asked, concerned, but she had already turned away, covering her eyes with her hands, almost involuntarily. She was supposed to be professional, but she couldn't deal with it. The horror of the crime. The very violence of the act, and of Robert's death. Bennie unaccountably thought of her father and tasted a bile that washed her palate with acid. Not Robert. Robert was a good man. An elegant man.

Bennie felt a steadying hand on her shoulder and heard the harsh sounds of the gurney snapped to its standing position, then the practiced "One, two, three" count as the body was lifted onto it, then the ungreased squeak of the covered wheels as they bumped over the trash in the alley. She could hear the heavy cases being carried off, their stainless-steel instruments jingling inside, and the people shuffling in paper booties around her, out of the alley. The *slam-slam* of two car doors closing punctuated the night: the coroner's van, which started its hollow-sounding engine and took off in the next moment. The scene was closing. The police personnel had completed their job; their notes and photos had been taken, scrapings and samples collected. It was over for them, but it was just beginning for Bennie. She took her hands from her eyes and found herself looking at Detective Needleman. He was just the man she wanted to see.

"I want to get whoever did this to him," Bennie said, in a voice more controlled than she felt. Firm, sure, furious. "I want to help you, in any way I can. I want them brought to justice. I want to know who they are. I want to know what they do. I want to know why they did this, and why Robert was even here in the first place."

Detective Needleman almost smiled. "You must feel better."

"I will when I can get those questions answered, and not until."

"I can answer one of them."

"Which one?"

"Why he was here," the detective answered matter-of-factly, and Bennie blinked.

"Why was he here?"

"His brother told me. He was out to dinner, a business dinner, at the Palm."

"I thought you said he was going to have dinner with the brother."

"He was, but then he called and canceled. Something had come up at work. I figured he was walking home when he got robbed."

"Who did he eat with?" Bennie asked, but the detective was already reaching for his back pocket. He extracted the slim steno pad, flipped it open, and ran a finger down the pages, squinting in the klieglight, which made a stocky silhouette of him.

"Here we go. He was going to dinner with another man. Herman Mayer."

19

It took Bennie a minute to absorb the shock. "*Mayer* was here with Robert?"

"Not here, at dinner. You know him?"

"Yes, he's a fellow plaintiff in a class action, a big case. I don't know why Robert would be eating with Mayer. I can't believe it." She was shaking her head. "Was the brother sure?"

"Seemed it." The detective shifted aside, taking Bennie's arm, as mobile technicians hustled back and forth for their equipment. "I don't get it. If they're fellow plaintiffs, as you say, why wouldn't they be eating together?"

"It's a long story." Bennie didn't want to explain it now. She wanted information. "Did the brother tell you anything else?"

"No, just that his brother had called late in the day, about five-thirty, and said he'd have to cancel dinner. He was gonna eat with this Mayer."

"What time was Robert expected?"

"About seven. I went over fast because the TV people got the news off the scanners, and I wanted the notification to come first."

Bennie couldn't wrap her mind around it. What the hell was going on? Why would Robert agree to meet with Mayer? Why didn't he tell her? She'd been at the river, but why didn't he leave a message? "You didn't talk to Mayer yet, did you?"

"No way, I had to hurry to do the notification, and I only got that in because they live so close. I gotta go back to the squad room and run down some leads on this and the Belgian case. I'll call him, too, though I doubt he'll have much to say."

"I wouldn't be so sure about that," Bennie said, responding before she even knew what she meant. She didn't know what was going on, and that meant she didn't *like* what was going on. All she understood was that Robert had gone to dinner with Herman Mayer and now he was dead. She tried to clarify her thoughts. "Mayer and Robert weren't truly on the same side of the lawsuit, at this stage. As a practical matter, these men were enemies. There was a major dispute over who should be lead plaintiff."

The detective's eyes were glazing over. She had to get to the point.

"Mayer wanted to be lead plaintiff, and Robert and I were challenging him. In fact, in court today, we had a huge fight and—"

"Watch out," the detective interrupted, gentling her out of the way. A mobile tech shuffled past them and turned off one klieglight, then unplugged it from a portable generator and carried it out of the alley on his shoulder, like a fishing pole. The detective watched him go. "These people got a job to do. He won't be the only case tonight."

"Let me put it this way, Detective. This case was worth seventy million dollars to Mayer, and the lead plaintiff would get the lion's share. That's what Mayer was fighting with us over."

"That's real money," Needleman said, guiding her out of the alley, and Bennie fell into step beside him, matching her beat-up Sauconys to his worn loafers.

"Real, *real* money. You see what I'm saying? I'm saying that there was a lot of money at stake in this case, between these parties." Bennie knew she was losing him. Crime techs were packing up around them, stowing the remaining equipment into municipal cars and vans. One turned off the leftover klieglight, plunging them all into darkness. The party was officially over. It took a minute for Bennie's eyes to adjust, and she could barely see the detective's face in the residual lighting from the storefronts. "You with me, Detective?"

"No," he said, turning to her. His glasses reflected the windows across the street, obscuring his eyes. "I'm not with you. I see a robbery here, a street crime with an MO very similar to another recent one, and it makes sense to me that it's the same doer. What are you seeing?"

Bennie swallowed hard. What *was* she seeing? What was she *saying*? That she thought Mayer had *murdered* Robert? Was it possible? But Mayer was a civilized man. A businessman, not a thug. It seemed crazy. Unthinkable. Then she flashed on the scene in the courtroom. Mayer's anger at Robert. Linette's anger at them both. And Robert coming up to her after court had adjourned and asking if they had won. She had answered: *They want to kill us, don't they?*

Bennie felt suddenly stricken.

"Let's get outta the way, I'm done here," the detective said, taking Bennie's arm. They walked from the alley with Bennie on autopilot and headed toward an old black Crown Vic parked at the curb. Around them uniformed cops dismantled the wooden sawhorses and stacked them on a Parks Department flatbed that had pulled up, rattling and spewing gray exhaust. The crowd was dispersing except for the TV news vans and reporters, whom Detective Needleman kept at bay by waving them off. He opened his car door, turned to Bennie, and put a hand on her shoulder. "Look, you're upset. Your client just got killed. You're not thinking clearly, and it's late."

Bennie nodded, shaken, but she couldn't listen. She just couldn't believe what she'd said to Robert in court. Why had she said it? Had she meant it? Was it possible?

"I know you're a smart lawyer, and Brinkley thinks the world of you, and that's enough for me. But this isn't the time to play cop, Ms. Rosato." Detective Needleman gave her arm a final pat. "You need a ride? Let me take you home."

Bennie found her voice, and it carried a ring of certainty that surprised even her. "I'm not saying that Mayer did it, but I'm not ruling it out, either. I don't know. But I can't pretend that Mayer didn't fight with Robert in court today, or that we didn't beat him. And seventy million dollars is a lot of motive."

"Now you're talkin' about motive? Seventy million dollars is a lot of *money,* and that's all I know right now." Detective Needleman sat heavily in the driver's seat, keeping one loafer out of the car flat on the asphalt. "Brinkley likes you, but he did say you get yourself worked up."

"Murder gets me worked up, particularly this murder. And sometimes I'm right, so will you please consider that this murder may not be what it seems right off the bat?"

"Oh, Jesus, here we go." The detective looked through his windshield with pursed lips.

"Keep an open mind, consider that maybe it's not a robbery, a street crime, whatever. And you're going to talk with Mayer, so why wait until tomorrow?

Wouldn't you like to know where he is right now? He was the last person to see Robert alive."

"I would, and I will. Now you need a ride or not?"

"No, thanks." Bennie was thinking clearly now, or what passed for clearly to the delusional. Robert had been stabbed to death. The detective had said they hadn't found the murder weapon. "What kind of knife was it, do we know?"

"A sharp knife, I gather, and there is no *we*. Later *I* will find out. *You* won't."

Bennie let it go. At least he was keeping his sense of humor. He'd need it. "What kind of sharp knife? How long was the blade? Was it a steak knife? The Palm is a steakhouse." She had been there exactly twice. She was guessing when she said, "They give you a steak knife when you order, you know."

"No good deed goes unpunished, does it?" Detective Needleman closed the door of the car with a rueful smile. "I tried to be nice to you, I talked to you, and now look where it got me. Wait'll I get Brinkley."

"Sorry." Bennie watched him turned the key in the ignition, and the car's old engine wheezed to life. She half considered taking a ride just to keep badgering him. "Any chance I can go with you when you talk to Mayer?"

"You know, I bet you read a lot of Nancy Drew when you were little. Am I right?" He raised his voice to be heard over the car engine. "Why is it that every little girl who reads Nancy Drew thinks she can be a homicide detective? My wife, she's the exact same way."

"Hold on." Bennie leaned on the car so he wouldn't take off. "Here's what to ask Mayer about. He was Robert's chief competitor in the medical-lens business, and I know there was bad blood between them over a contract with a company named Hospcare. Mayer lives in Chestnut Hill, his home address was on the complaint they filed. I can fax you over a copy, or you can call information. As for his lawyer, I don't know where—"

"I think I can do this without you." The detective released the emergency brake. "Call me crazy."

"I'm just trying to help. I know these players, and I have information you may need."

"I'll call you if I need you."

"I want to get whoever did this." Bennie leaned into the open car window. The Crown Vic reeked of cigar smoke. "And if the bad guy wears a tie, I don't want him getting away with murder."

"I don't either, and I will keep an open mind, I always do. But don't get in my face and don't go over my head. I'll keep you posted as I see fit." The detective's eyes went flinty, and his tone turned stern in a way that suggested he was a good father. "You have any questions or want to tell me something, you can call me at the Roundhouse."

"Oh, come on. Don't try and sell me that." Detectives never spent time sitting around the Roundhouse. They were always out on jobs, as they called them. "Lemme have your beeper number."

"No." The detective frowned and gunned the engine, probably so it wouldn't stall. Detectives got the worst cars in the pool and bitched about it constantly. He shouted over the breathy noise, "The best hope of getting the knucklehead who killed your client is to leave it to the professionals! Let me do my job! You get in there, you'll screw it up!"

"Wouldn't think of it!" Bennie shouted back, withdrawing from the window.

"There *is* a line!" Detective Needleman wagged his finger. "Don't cross it, *Nancy!*"

Bennie put up both palms. *Don't shoot,* said her body language, and the Crown Vic cruised off.

She put her arms down when he was out of sight. She hadn't actually agreed not to cross the line. Nancy Drew wouldn't have, either. And *she* didn't even have a law degree.

Chestnut Hill is one of Philadelphia's oldest and most exclusive residential neighborhoods, settled comfortably to the north of Center City, first by the Quakers. The neighborhood boasts spacious, graceful homes built of distinctive gray-black stones, and its main street, Germantown Avenue, winds gently through the center of town and climbs the hill that lends the town its name. Tall leafy trees line the street, sheltering quaint colonial-scale storefronts refitted with tasteful versions of Baby Gap and Starbucks. Traffic was nonexistent at this late hour, so Bennie had Germantown Avenue all to herself, though its authentic cobble-stones slowed her, destroying the shock absorbers on the Saab as she rumbled over them, *bump bump bump,* rattling her jaw and setting her teeth on edge. But that could have been her mood.

Robert. Dead. She rolled down the window and gulped in a lungful of fresh March air, waiting until the nausea passed. The night breeze wafted cool and green, full of promise, carrying the music of crickets. It qualified as a beautiful night, which somehow made Bennie angrier, for Robert's sake. He wouldn't get to see it, wouldn't draw another breath on this earth. Why had he been meeting with Mayer? Did it matter?

She pressed the gas and the Saab climbed, bobbling past one green street sign then the next, looking for Prescott Road. *Bump bump bump.* Something in her felt satisfied at dropping in on Herr Mayer. Normally she wouldn't contact a represented client without his lawyer's consent, but Linette hadn't thought twice about doing exactly that to her. Two wrongs make a lawyer.

She passed Gorgas Lane, then Cliveden. She had to be getting closer. Then a new thought struck her. She didn't have to worry any longer about seeing a represented client. Robert's death had mooted the rules of professional ethics, at least as applied to this situation. Because without a client, Bennie could be out of the class-action lawsuit. *Bump bump bump.*

The implications of Robert's murder dawned on her only slowly, and she felt guilty and selfish for even thinking of them. Robert had been the principal of St. Amien & Fils, and it was a privately held French company. God knew what bylaws governed, if any, or how its being a foreign corporation mattered. Robert had to have a successor or a second-in-command; most companies had successor plans in place. Bennie would have to find him because unless he wanted to continue the lawsuit, there would be no lawsuit, as far as she was concerned. No class-action settlement to transfuse her firm's finances, pay the rent, and get her back on her pumps. Whoever killed Robert could have unwittingly dealt a death blow to her law firm. She could lose Rosato & Associates. She could lose the associates. She could lose her *house.*

Bennie bit her lip not to think about it.

That realization had no place now, not tonight. Robert had lost his very life, and he was the reason she was here. The green street sign coming up read Prescott Road, and she could feel a surge of new energy as adrenaline dumped suddenly into her bloodstream. She wanted answers, and she'd shake them out of Mayer if she had to.

She swung the Saab onto Prescott and hit the gas.

20

"Of course I know what time it is," Bennie answered, wedging a perfectly placed Saucony farther into the front door, which was being pressed on the other side by a startled Herman Mayer.

"Then what are you doing here? How dare you come to my home at this hour! This is an outrage! It's the middle of the—"

"Let me in, Mayer!" Bennie heaved the door with such force that it sent the thin man staggering backward against the striped wallpaper of his entrance hall.

"What do you think you are doing?" Mayer's back flattened against the wall, his thin lips formed a perfect circle, and his eyes flared behind his glasses. "You have no business being here! You are trespassing! I'll call the police!"

"Do it!" Bennie closed the door behind her, then glanced around. There wasn't a telephone in the entrance, only a cherry-wood half-table that sat flush against the wall and a brass stand that contained an oversized golf umbrella. So she reached into her back pocket for her cell phone and thrust it at him. "Call 911. Be my guest. Ask for Detective Needleman and tell him where you were tonight. He'd love to know. So would I."

"This is ridiculous!" Mayer shouted, but his tone faltered. He took the cell phone but didn't open it up. He straightened his glasses and smoothed out a shiny merlot smoking jacket with a black shawl collar, something that Bennie didn't know people wore in real life. He looked like a Teutonic Ward Cleaver and he glowered at her with the same ersatz sternness used on the Beav. Mayer asked, more quietly, "Why would the police care where I was?"

Bennie checked his reaction. His upper lip stuck to his teeth; his mouth must have gone dry. His forehead furrowed deeply in the soft light of a brass candelabra. She had caught him. He was hiding something. He had done it! Fury bubbled in her blood. She grabbed the golf umbrella from the brass stand and brandished it. It was all she could do not to break it on his head, but she wanted him tried and convicted. "Call the cops, Mayer. Before I beat the shit out of you."

"I . . . cannot."

"Why not? I broke into your house. It's an outrage. I'm trespassing."

Mayer was shaking his head. His lips tightened to a line like a rubber band.

"Tell me what happened tonight." Bennie could barely breathe. He *had* done it. "I want the truth."

"Tonight?" Mayer swallowed with obvious difficulty. "Well. So. Tonight I had dinner at the Palm, with Robert."

Bennie blinked. So he'd confess to dinner. She could work with that. His stalling was calming her down. "Whose idea was the dinner?"

"Mine."

"Why?"

"I wished to talk with Robert about the lawsuit. And to apologize, for today . . . my conduct in court."

"And did you?"

"Why do you ask me? Ask your client."

"Yeah, right." Bennie clenched her teeth and brandished the umbrella, which was navy and bore a white WHYY-FM logo. She had the same one. So they both supported public radio. Still, it was heavy enough and had a rather nasty point for NPR. "I'm asking *you*, you complete and total shit."

"I was trying to persuade him to step aside. I wanted him to agree to let me serve as lead plaintiff, but I was unsuccessful."

"He didn't tell me anything about this meeting."

"I know. I asked him not to, and he agreed."

"Why?"

"This was to be kept between us, as businessmen."

"But you told Linette."

"I did not."

"Oh, please. You're telling me you didn't tell Linette? That he didn't put you up to it?" Bennie was normally better at cross-examination than this, but she'd never conducted one after seeing the corpse of a murdered client.

"It's the truth. I know you may not agree,

but oftentimes lawyers merely complicate the . . . process."

Bennie didn't disagree. "Did you speak with Linette tonight?"

"It's not your concern, but I haven't. I went to bed with a headache. After dinner, from the wine."

Bennie eyed him under the umbrella. He was obviously lying. She didn't have the best shit detector in the world, but he did all the dumb things like shifting his eyes back and forth toward the darkened living room. "What time did you finish dinner?"

"Eight o'clock, eight-thirty."

It jibed with the time of death. "What did you do next?"

"I offered Robert a ride home, but he said it was a beautiful night, and he chose to walk. Really, this is absurd!" Mayer threw up his arms, and his funny sleeves billowed. The black satin that matched the shawl collar hemmed the cuffs, too. "Then I came home. And now I'm tired and I want to return to bed!"

"You did not, Mayer!" It *was* a beautiful night. Robert loved to walk. Now he was dead. Knifed by this man. Left to bleed in an alley. "You're lying!"

"I did, I swear it," Mayer stammered. He edged back toward the wall. "Honestly, call Robert and ask him! Do!"

"You *bastard!*" Bennie heard herself shouting. "You know Robert's dead. You *killed* him! *You did it!*" She considered bringing the umbrella down onto Mayer's head, but for the shock in his eyes and the gasp that escaped his lips.

"That cannot be. Robert dead?" Mayer shook his head slowly. "That cannot be."

Bennie watched Mayer in a bewilderment of her own now. This guy was too stiff to fake it with such conviction, wasn't he? It was so uncharacteristic, it had to be real. She lowered the umbrella harmlessly, surprised by her own violence and completely confused. She wasn't sure if it was an act or not, but if he really didn't know Robert was dead, he obviously hadn't killed him. Then what was he so nervous about? What was Mayer hiding?

"Herman?" came another voice, and Bennie jumped. A light went on in the living room adjoining the entrance hall, and a young man emerged, in a matching Ward Cleaver robe. He was barefoot and evidently naked under the robe, which had slipped aside at the neck to reveal a skinny chest. "Is something the matter?" he asked, coming into the entrance hall, and he froze when he saw Bennie. "What's going on here?"

Oh. So Mayer was gay. It was no biggie to Bennie, except for that marriage part. But Mayer was doing the freak.

"Go back upstairs!" he shouted at the young man, showing the temper he'd displayed in court. "Go upstairs! Everything here is fine!" The young man turned on his bare heel and padded from the room, his footsteps disappearing in the soft rug. Mayer looked at Bennie, his thin skin tinged so deeply it made her heart go out to him.

"Herman, I don't care if you're gay. Nobody should have to be afraid of who they are. Some of my best friends are gay. In fact, my best friend *is*—"

"How dare you! Leave my house this instant!" Mayer flew to his door, his robe billowing behind him. He flung open the door and grabbed Bennie by the arm, with a strength he hadn't shown to date. "Out! Out now! You've done enough damage here!"

"Herman, relax." Bennie let herself be shown outside, in disbelief. Did people still reside in the closet? So that's what Mayer had been hiding. That was why he'd been so nervous. Silly. She actually liked him better now. If he was gay, he had to have a fun side. She could introduce him to Sam. After his divorce. "Look, I won't go blabbing. Your personal life is your personal life."

"Never come back here!" Mayer shouted, throwing her cell phone onto the pavement, where she heard it clatter, and slamming the front door shut behind her.

Bennie stood bewildered on the stoop as the light went off in the entrance hall; she could tell from the old-fashioned transom over the front door. She felt suddenly confused, exhausted, and defeated, and she reached for the wrought-iron railing as she stepped down the front steps. She didn't understand Mayer. She didn't understand anything. She wanted to know for sure who killed Robert. She wanted to go home and lay her head on a cool, thin pillow. She found her cell phone in the pachysandra, went to her car, and drove back down Germantown Avenue.

Bump bump bump. She was thinking about Robert. Trying to deal with the fact that he was dead. Wondering whether

Mayer had in fact done it. Wrapping her mind around the notion that it could have been a foreigner-hater.

And realizing that the road ahead would get even bumpier.

Bennie had no idea what time it was when she slid finally into bed, too exhausted to perform all those good-girl tasks like washing her face, much less flossing. She had showered when she came out of the river, which was basically the same thing, even if it did seem like ages ago. She turned over in bed, wondering why things always went like that for her. Nice and even, except for periods of life-threatening drama. Why couldn't she be more like the other girl lawyers?

She tossed under the light quilt, feeling a slight grittiness. It told her that her sheets were entering week three. *So what*. She'd been a little busy lately, and Bear didn't mind. She threw an arm over the dog, snoring beside her in bed, where a man would usually be. In an alternate reality.

Bennie felt a twinge of guilt. She should have called Robert's brother, introduced herself and offered condolences, inquired after the son at Harvard. But she'd been too preoccupied. Hot on the trail of a terrified homosexual with really bad taste in bathrobes. Bennie found her mind wandering to "Night by Night," the Steely Dan song that had been playing in David's Jeep.

She squeezed her eyes tighter. She had screwed up so much lately, and now everything had gone wrong. She'd have to find Robert's successor and hope he wanted to continue to press the claim. It was a legal wrong to the corporation, not merely personal to Robert, so it could survive Robert's death, as a technical matter. But figuring it out could take weeks she didn't have. In the meantime, Rosato & Associates could go completely under. She'd have to let the bank foreclose on the house. She had no idea how she'd get another place, much less start over, with a bankruptcy on her record and her credit already so messed up, thanks to Alice.

Alice. Bennie shifted on her scratchy sheets. She had completely forgotten about her twin in the awful events of the night. Alice was still out there. She had tried to kill Bear. She had broken into her house. She could still be following Bennie, even to the crime scene. And before that. Bennie thought back. Had Alice followed her down to Delaware, to the place where her father used to live? Did Alice even know their father was dead?

Oh my God. Bennie's eyes flew open. She couldn't see anything but darkness. She couldn't hear any sound but the dog. She knew there was no way she'd get to sleep tonight. Her brain had made a connection she hadn't. She'd been so exhausted, her subconscious had done the work for her. She lay still on the pillow, as if paralyzed by the thought itself:

What if it was Alice who killed Robert?

21

"No comment, no comment, no comment!" Bennie shouted to the reporters thronging in front of her office building the next morning. The sky was clear and the day pretty, but her mood was predictably grim. The morning newspaper headlines read: SECOND EUROPEAN TOURIST SLAIN. Today Bennie had to get busy and find Alice, not for her own account, but for Robert's. If Alice had killed him, she would pay for it.

Bennie kept her head down through the reporters, since she didn't have a free hand to flip the bird with. She carried her briefcase, her Coach bag, two newspapers, and a medium cup of Dunkin' Donuts coffee. She had taken the precaution of hiding Bear in the cellar at home, which he liked anyway because of its coolness, and nailing boards over the windows on the French doors. Her house looked like a war zone, or at least a fire code violation, but it would do until she could get the windows and doors fixed.

The reporters kept shouting their questions, but Bennie powered her way to the building's entrance, then shoved through the double doors, crossed the lobby, and went upstairs. When the doors opened, she got off the elevator into the reception area. At the desk, Marshall looked drawn, not to mention extra large, in her baby blue maternity dress.

"I'm just so sorry about Robert, I know you liked him."

"Thanks. It's terrible, isn't it?"

"Awful." Marshall handed her a flurry of phone messages, and the one on top was from David Holland. "I hate to deal with business, but so much is going on this morning."

"I'll say." Bennie thumbed through her messages, almost as many as in the old days. Another call was from David with his cell number, one from Sam, and Hattie, her mother's old caretaker. She flipped through the remaining messages, all reporters and creditors. "Look at all my new best friends."

"And you're not going to believe who's in your office. He didn't want to wait in the reception area, where he could be *seen*." Marshall made little quote marks in the air. "He insisted I show him in."

"Who?" Bennie asked, and when Marshall told her, she decided she was completely sick of getting caught by surprise every time she came back to her own office. This time the surprise wasn't an Italian wedding, a tower of boxes, or even an eviction notice.

But it was basically the same thing.

"We need to talk, Bennie," he began, and seated himself uninvited at the conference table in her office. A large man, he took up more space than Robert had in the same seat, not so long ago. Or maybe he just seemed bigger because his visit was unwelcome and his presence an intrusion. "Sorry about St. Amien."

"Me, too." Bennie remained standing and sipped her coffee, but didn't bother to make him any because she wasn't his professional. His face had its ruddy sunburn, and he wore a light houndstooth suit with a custom cut. His hair retained the wetness from a morning shower, darkening its reddish shade, and Bennie could still smell his too spicy shaving cream, a bit of which was stuck in his left ear. Her phone began ringing but she ignored it. "What do we need to talk about?"

"Well, maybe what I meant was that we should talk."

"We *should*? I don't see why. Our marriage is over. You keep the house in Stone Harbor and the starter Range Rover. I'll take the running shoes and the golden."

"Listen, I don't want to fight anymore." Linette flashed a peace sign, and Bennie took a mental snapshot, to be filed under Purely Ironic Moments.

"You're kidding, right? You've been trying to muscle me out of the picture since this case began, and now that it's over, only because poor Robert is *dead*, you want to kiss and make up?"

"I haven't been trying to—"

"I don't get why you're here, and in the mood I'm in today, I'm not mincing words. I don't have a client, so I'm out of the lawsuit, at least for the time being. I wish you lotsa luck, but we don't have to be friends, you and me. It's time for you to go."

"I heard you paid a visit to my client last night."

"Sue me." Bennie took a bigger slug of coffee. It was doing her good. Maybe her testosterone/caffeine theory wasn't so crazy after all. Only Dunkin' Donuts knew for sure, and they weren't telling.

"Don't get me wrong, I don't hold it against you, and neither does Herm." Linette waved a hand like the Pope, if the Pope had been president of the Pennsylvania Trial Lawyers Association. "I understand, I know you were distraught. I know you liked Robert personally, I could tell. And you had a lot depending on him, professionally. On his case."

"Robert's death is a loss as a friend and as a client. One loss is far greater than the other, but I don't have to justify which to you." Bennie set her coffee on the conference table, strode to the door, and put a hand on the knob. "See ya." She was adult enough not to add, *Wouldn't want to be ya.* But just barely.

"One last thing. It's the main reason I

came." Linette stood up, but didn't move toward the door. "Bennie, I'll just say this right out. I want to buy your law firm. With you in it, of course. You'd be the key man. Er, woman."

Bennie stood dumbstruck. *Buy my firm, with no clients, from the brink of bankruptcy?*

"I'll give you a lump sum for the business. I'm ballparking two million bucks, in structured payments. And that doesn't include your salary, with bonuses for new clients, obviously. For you, it'll be three hundred grand a year, guaranteed, to start."

Two million dollars? Three hundred grand in salary? Guaranteed? Bennie felt her mouth fall open and didn't try to hide it. The numbers astounded her. What was more astounding was that Linette would offer it. Why was he doing this? Why now? And without seeing her disastrous financials? *Huh?*

"I'd buy your practice, your clients, your files, everything. You can sell off your furniture and books, I'll give you office allowances for my place. We'll get a coupla bean counters to have a sit-down, work out the terms, and crunch the final numbers, but it has to be better than you're doing now." Linette looked briefly around her office and managed not to hold his nose. "I think two mil is fair market value for a going concern, especially one with your good name behind it."

"My *good name?*" Bennie blurted out. "I'm under indictment for theft and assault. The Eastern District thinks I'm a drunk."

"Aw, don't be so hard on yourself. Lighten up." Linette spread his meaty palms wide. "I heard about that little bender at the Chinese restaurant. Big deal. We've all been there. As for the charges, even if you're convicted, they won't suspend your license for the first offense."

"I didn't do it!"

"Of course you didn't. And if you take my offer, you won't have to steal diamonds to stay in business. So sell to me. It'll relieve the pressure on you. I mean, honestly, are you netting even a hundred grand, after payroll and fixed expenses?"

"No," Bennie answered. Well, she wasn't. Last year she had cleared $73.22. But none of this made sense. He didn't need *her.* "I just don't know why you'd want to do this."

"You're a great lawyer, lady. Simple as

that." Linette shrugged his quarterback's shoulders. "Don't underestimate yourself."

Bennie still didn't get it. "But you do class-action law, exclusively. I don't know anything about class-action law."

"Granted, you don't have much of a track record in class-action cases, but your move in court yesterday, asking for that emergency hearing? It was tough-minded. Brilliant. You turned your low mileage to an advantage. I need someone like you at Linette & Associates." Linette smiled his overbleached smile. "You know, you impressed a lot of people yesterday. Even Herm."

Bennie read between the lines. Mayer had never been loyal to Linette; she knew that from the luncheon that first day. Maybe Mayer had talked about jumping ship, and some other class members had, too. If that was true, Linette would want to buy her to keep them. He could spend two mil and change to keep seventy; it was downright economic. But did Mayer still want to hire Bennie, after that scene last night at his house? It didn't make sense. She was guessing she knew Mayer's secret, and Linette didn't.

"Of course, you wouldn't be a principal like you are now," Linette continued. "You'd be classified as an associate for payroll purposes, but that would be in name only. You'd be the most senior attorney in the firm, second only to me, accorded all the respect you so richly deserve. And we'd spin it as a merger, not me buying you out, in all the press releases."

Bennie didn't know whether to be flattered or insulted. Insulted was the politically correct answer, but frankly, part of her was definitely listening. For that kind of money, maybe she *could* be an associate again. She used to write a mean legal memo, and she still had her crayons. If you can walk, you can crawl, right?

"I'd like to get it done this week, announce it to the press, and the defendants. Get back on track after that sideshow in court yesterday. Listen to Judge Sherman. Remember what he told us? United we stand, baby." Linette rubbed his hands together, and Bennie suppressed a smile. She wasn't sure that was what Lincoln had had in mind. Linette looked at her, tilting his jaw, his blue eyes expectant. "So, lady, whaddaya say? Agreement in principle?"

"I have some thoughts too," Bennie said. The whole scene was so bizarre, she was wondering just how bizarre it could get. "What about my employees?"

"Your people? What about them? You want them or you want them gone?"

Ouch. "I want them. I have a receptionist who needs maternity benefits right away, a secretary who needs to come back from layoff, and three smart lawyers who make a hundred grand apiece." The last part was a complete lie, but Bennie was negotiating with Santa Claus.

"Done."

Merry Christmas to me. "Also I do a lot of pro bono work. There's an ongoing case for the Circolo. You must have heard of them. They're a consortium." With cannoli. "We're currently suing the government on their behalf. Bringing justice because of the Italian American internments. I got DiNunzio on it, and I'd have to fund that case fully."

"Okay." Linette grinned. "Italians are okay by me. My third wife was Italian, and you oughta see me go to town on a plate of veal parm. Anything else?"

Bennie paused. "I need a new car. Mine's dirty."

"Porsche or Mercedes?"

"Only one?" Bennie asked, and they both fake-laughed. Then she said, "Kidding."

"Of course you were. Your choice. Porsche is for boys, Mercedes is for girls."

"I'll take the Porsche."

Linette fake-laughed again. "Of course you would!" He clapped his hands together with a loud *smack*. "So, is it a done deal?"

"Let me think about it," Bennie answered, then shut her mouth before anything as low-rent as *Yes, buy me please please please* slipped from her lips.

"Fair enough." Linette gave a brief nod, walked to the door, and paused in the threshold when Bennie opened it. Up close his eyes were very blue, and she could see lapis-tinted contacts afloat on his corneas. He flashed her a blinding grin. "Don't make me wait, Bennie."

"Perish the thought," she said, and watched him walk past her three stunned associates without a hello or even a good-bye. The phone was ringing again, and Bennie was amazed. *What's with all these calls?* Bennie let Marshall get it. Porsche owners didn't answer their own phone.

Linette slithered to the elevator, and the

minute he was safely gone, the three associates turned toward her as one, sharing a what-was-that-all-about look. Bennie thought they deserved a full accounting, and she could actually use their help to figure everything out. So she motioned the kids over, and they came running.

It took Bennie an hour to catch them up on current events, starting with Linette's offer, her seeing poor Robert at the scene, and her confrontation with Mayer. She omitted the part about Mayer's alternative-lifestyle bathrobe, since his sexual preference was his business and they didn't hear much after her description of St. Amien's body anyway. They'd learned about his murder last night, of course; Bennie's cell phone and answering machine had been full of their messages, but she'd been too exhausted to return the calls. She'd known they'd figure she was in the thick of things, and they had. She ended by doubling back to her almost drowning at the river, to David, Bear, and the break-in.

When her story was over, she scanned the young faces around her conference table, sober even in their varying degrees of morning makeup: Murphy wore the most, in full mascara; DiNunzio took the middle ground, with blusher and eyeliner; and Carrier went typically a cappella, with a foundation of Dove soap and a lingering scent of Colgate original. They'd grown a lot this year. Most of it in the last few days.

Bennie folded her arms and leaned back against her desk. "So, ladies, what do we think?"

"We think we miss Robert," Murphy said, and the other two nodded.

"It must have been awful." DiNunzio's voice was barely a whisper. "What an awful way to die."

"I hope this detective is good," Carrier said. Her pink hair clashed with her grim expression, but then again, her pink hair clashed with everything. "Because I don't know if I agree with this tourist-killer theory."

Bingo. Bennie cocked her head, intrigued. She hadn't told them her concerns, so as not to taint their thinking. "Why not, kid?"

"It's so lame, and it may apply to this Belgian guy, but not to Robert. The money was too high to ignore in this case." Carrier ran a quick tongue over her unlipsticked lips. "For example, why is it more believable that somebody would kill a man for a wallet, when he could kill him for millions of dollars?"

Bennie didn't have an immediate answer. "So who then, if not Mayer? And you're discounting Alice, with your money-as-motive theory."

"Not to go against you, but I am, boss." Carrier paused. "I think she's a possibility, but to me she doesn't follow the money trail. I have a different theory, but it's not etched in stone. Which means it's a little nuts."

"Shoot," Bennie said, and Murphy leaned forward. Only DiNunzio hung back, lost in her emotions over St. Amien. She had evidently postponed her Washington trip, and Bennie made a mental note to deal with that later. The phone began ringing but they all ignored it. Bennie turned her attention to Carrier, who was gearing up.

"Let's take a long, hard look at our new best friend, Bill Linette." Carrier held up a palm like a traffic cop, a gesture Bennie recognized from her own repertoire. "Obviously, I'm thinking out loud, but here goes. Linette had the same motive as Mayer, only less so, but when we're talking millions, it's a matter of degree."

Bennie smiled to herself. *This, from a child who never met a payroll.* Still. "Go on, Carrier."

"Well, Linette comes in here, trying to buy us. By the way, we're saying no, right?" She glanced at Bennie for confirmation.

"Table that for now. Go ahead with the theory."

"Like we always do, think of who benefits from Robert's death. If Robert is dead, then the only viable competition for lead plaintiff is gone. Linette wins the jackpot, lead plaintiff *and* lead counsel fees. And he gets to represent the entire class, and get their fees, too. Just what he wanted."

"Linette." Bennie was shaking her head. "You think he'd *kill* to be lead counsel?"

"If it's worth twenty to thirty million dollars in fees?" Carrier answered. "Sure. Remember, you thought Mayer would kill to be lead plaintiff, and you were right to suspect that. Money is a powerful motive, I don't have to remind everybody of that, and look at the other facts that point to Linette." She held up her index finger, with its chewed fingernail. "First off, the timing is too coincidental.

Right after you kick Linette's ass in court, he finds another way to eliminate the competition. I mean, Bennie, you were making a serious challenge to his claim for lead counsel, weren't you?"

Bennie nodded, cringing. *They want to kill us, don't they?* She hadn't mentioned that tidbit to the associates. It hurt too much.

"And everybody in town was talking about that Belgian guy's murder, and Linette knows all about that. Let's say he figures Robert's murder would fit right in the pattern. And it does, which is why the police think it's the tourist killer. How easy is that to fake?"

Bennie bit her lip.

"Point two." Carrier held up a second finger. "There's the humiliation factor, with Linette. Bennie, let's face it, you embarrassed Linette in court, and he is the King of All Class Actions. But you took him on and you came out on top. His own client noticed, as he himself told you, and when did that happen? Probably after the hearing, he and Mayer had words, and Mayer told him he was impressed with you. Right?"

"Possible."

"Worse, Linette may have spent the afternoon on the phone, taking calls from the other members of the plaintiff class, trying to plug leaks in the dam. He could see that his plaintiffs would defect to you, and so he needed you out of the action. So he kills Robert. It's the same rationale that you're using now, to think about his offer to buy us."

"If I find the successor, we can still stay on the case."

"That's a big if, and time matters. Maybe Linette will go to the successor too. Who knows who that is?" Carrier's voice got higher, in her enthusiasm. "See? It's the perfect plan, if Linette is the killer. Take St. Amien out, cut you out, then buy you out."

Murphy raised a sharp pencil, like a schoolgirl. "But why doesn't Linette just offer to buy her, and not kill Robert? Why murder someone and take the risk of getting caught?"

Carrier thought a second, but only a second. A Boalt grad, she had the credentials of a legal scholar. "Because if he doesn't, then Bennie has St. Amien *and* his war chest. She can stay viable and even prosper, which would increase the likelihood of defections to our firm by other class members. Get it? Linette has to kill Robert to make the plan work. Also, I'm not necessarily saying he did it himself. He could have hired someone to kill Robert."

Bennie was actually considering it. The kid was almost making sense.

"We can't reject the theory until we know more about Linette. First, where was Linette last night, boss? You didn't ask him his whereabouts, did you?"

Damn. "No. I wasn't even thinking of him as a suspect. I was too bollixed up with Alice, whom I'm still not letting off the hook." Bennie felt a familiar dread at the pit of her stomach. Her eyes fell on the phone message in Marshall's neat hand from David Holland. She felt a tiny wrench in her chest and wondered if she'd be able to call him back. What had he said—*she was under attack*—which was exactly how it felt. "Carrier, you may be right about Linette, but Alice is the wild card here. And we know she's out to get me. To ruin me. And she'd kill to do it."

Murphy's green eyes narrowed. "But how would she know how important St. Amien was to the business?"

"She's not stupid or unsophisticated.

She's a Rutgers grad, on scholarship, and she can tell that a class action that hits the newspapers is worth more than Brandolini, for example."

DiNunzio didn't look up, and Bennie let it go.

"And I was thinking, we know she's been following me. What if she followed me yesterday, and was in that courtroom? Watching me and Robert? Seeing me fight for him and hearing my argument?" Bennie was convincing herself the more she thought about it. "Robert even came up and gave me one of those little kisses at the end. She could have guessed that striking at him would be a way to strike at me, both professionally and personally."

The associates listened in silence for a change.

"And we have to look beyond the motive, to the character of the person. What kind of human being are they? I'd sooner believe that Alice is capable of killing someone than Bill Linette or Herman Mayer. They may be jerks, but she's a psycho."

Murphy seemed to mull it over. "I hear you, but I stay undecided. I'm not giving up on the tourist angle, either. The pattern *is* sort of compelling." She tucked her long red hair behind her ear with a polished fingernail. "Now, for a moment, tell me about the future, Bennie. Are we going with Linette or not? I vote no."

"Why?" Bennie asked, and Murphy squinched up her freckled nose.

"He's a jerk and a lech."

"It's a hundred grand a year to you, Murph," Bennie reminded her. "And I can't promise you a future here. As it stands now, I got plenty of nothing. I'd have to find Robert's successor, and I'm sure there's committee upon committee to go through to make any decision about the lawsuit. We may not be able to stay open the week."

"Still don't want it. I'm with you until they throw us out, then we're out together."

Next to her, Carrier was nodding enthusiastically, a fuchsia blur. "It goes without saying. I would never work for Ego Boy, and I hate that kind of work. I'm with DiNunzio, Murphy, and you." Carrier grinned happily, then nudged DiNunzio. "Wake up, girl!"

Mary nodded. "Of course. We stick together." She looked up at Bennie. "Tell him no, Bennie. We'll make a go of it somehow."

Bennie's throat caught, and she had to

wait a moment for it to pass. "Thank you, ladies, but I won't tell him no just yet. Let's slow down this transaction. Give ourselves time to change our minds. We have to be reasonable."

"We won't change our minds," Murphy said.

"And we hate being reasonable," Carrier added.

Bennie smiled. "And it will also give us some time to see what happens. See if plaintiffs do start defecting, and if the phones begin to ring again." Part of Bennie still held out hope for Rosato & Associates. She was stupid that way. "Regardless of what happens with St. Amien & Fils, if enough of them come over to us in the next few days, then maybe we can stay alive."

DiNunzio shuddered at her inadvertent choice of words, and Bennie walked over and put a hand on her shoulder.

"You didn't go to D.C. this morning. Why not?"

"With what happened to Robert, I thought I'd stay around and see if you needed me. Those records aren't going anywhere."

"Thanks, but your client needs you too.

You were going on your first business trip. You should still go."

"But there will be services for Robert. I should go."

"We'll go for you."

Mary looked uncertain, and Bennie could smell the separation anxiety. She had never had a nest with a baby bird in it, but something was telling her the right thing to do was to give the baby bird a good, hard shove into thin air. *Fly, honey. You can do it. You can fly.*

"Go," Bennie said. "Get the next train, Di-Nunzio. Do good. Fight for justice."

Mary's eyes flickered. "You sure you'll be okay?"

Carrier snorted. "We'll be fine. Forget about us and go. If we want to kick some ass, we know who to call. And she's way tougher than you."

"Who?"

"Duh. Your mom, doofus."

Mary gave her best friend a good swat, and they all laughed.

Bennie's smile faded first. She had a few hundred calls to answer, but one of them to make, and it was more important than the others. She couldn't delay it a moment longer. So she shooed the girls from her office, picked up the phone, and punched in a number.

22

"Allo?" said the voice on the other end of the phone line, and Bennie felt the soft Gallic purr reverberate in her chest. Georges St. Amien sounded almost exactly like his brother on the telephone. She gripped the receiver tighter. It was still so hard to believe that Robert was really dead. *"Allo?"*

"Hello, is this Georges?" Bennie took the liberty of pronouncing it the dumbass American way, as in Curious George. It was easier, and she had no idea how to fake the French, which was where high school Latin got you.

"Yes, here is Georges."

Okay, Georges was pronounced like Curious George, only mushier. She still wasn't going there. "Georges, this is Bennie Rosato. I'm sorry to bother you at this terrible time. I was your brother's attorney, on a litigation matter for his business, and I'm calling to offer you my condolences on his death."

"Ah, *merci bien*. How kind of you to call." His tone was raw, and Bennie could hear the bewilderment behind the words. She had heard it before, in the voices of family who had suffered a loss through violent crime. They all said it made the grief so much worse, but Bennie almost couldn't imagine grief being any harder.

"Please, forgive me for not calling sooner. I got held up this morning."

"No matter." Georges paused, and Bennie heard a whispery blowing sound she recognized. He must have been smoking, like Robert. She imagined him stubbing out his cigarette as the pause stretched longer. "I have seen your name, in the newspapers. Thank you for your well wishes."

"You're welcome. I am so very sorry for Robert's death. I liked him very much. We all did, at the firm."

"Thank you. Robert thought well of you, also. He spoke of you, and your office."

"He did?" Bennie's ears pricked up. It

was nice to hear, and she hadn't known Robert was close to his brother. Maybe Georges would know something about St. Amien & Fils, like who was Robert's successor, but she wasn't about to bring that up now. "It's a terrible loss. If I may, I would like to attend the memorial services."

"We will have something here, but the funeral will be at home, in France, of course. The police, they will tell us when we can have the service." Georges paused again, but this time it didn't sound like he was smoking. "The detective, I met him last night."

"Bob Needleman. I met him too."

"Oh. Good. He is good, do you think? Smart? To catch this man who killed my brother?"

"Yes, I do." Bennie bit her lip. She had just been sitting around the conference table with the associates, shooting theories around in the abstract. But talking to Georges made it real. For him, finding Robert's killer wasn't about justice, it was about family. She wanted to give him strength. "I think the police will find whoever did this, Georges. The detectives in Homicide are very good, and I promise you, I'll stay on top of this. If there's anything I can do for you or your family, please let me know."

"Actually, there is. Perhaps you could stop in for a brief visit today, toward the end of the day. Robert's son, Julien, I think you know of him, he will be coming in today, and he would like to meet you. You judged a competition of his, at law school."

Bennie remembered. The moot-court thing. "Sure, that would be no problem. What time?"

"Around four o'clock is good. Are you free at that time?"

"You got it, Georges."

"Pardon?"

It reminded Bennie of Robert again. He'd never understood her either, which had been only part of his charm. "I'll see you then, Georges," she said, and they hung up.

After a moment, Marshall stuck her head in the door. "You off the phone?"

"Yes."

"Get back on." Marshall tottered in with a stack of pink message slips. "The natives are restless."

"Who's calling?" Bennie asked, taking them and leafing through. She expected to see creditors like Verizon and AT&T, with 800 numbers she had memorized by now. But instead the names were Quinones and Kerpov. "Wow. Not just people who want money. Class-action lawyers."

"Say what?" Marshall said with a smirk.

"Wonder if they want to buy us too." Bennie's puzzled gaze fell upon an unfamiliar name on a message. "Who's Mort Abrams?"

"Said he's with FitCo. They make medical lenses."

"Wow." Bennie was intrigued. "Sounds like another class member. Maybe he needs a lawyer."

"He wants to meet you for lunch, so call by then." Marshall rested her hand atop her round belly, a habit that Bennie noticed was a pregnancy thing. It was like carrying your own portable shelf. "I heard about Linette's offer, and my vote is no. Even though I may not be here, I still say no. He's slime." She wrinkled her tiny nose. "And Sam called again. He wants to have lunch with you too. Call him back."

"Got it. Thanks." Marshall turned and left, and Bennie sifted through the phone messages on her desk to make the call that had been in the back of her mind all morning. David Holland's. She found the message and punched in the number. She reached him immediately, and it turned out he was on his way to see her. He'd be upstairs in fifteen minutes.

Woohoo! Bennie set down the receiver, jumped up from her desk chair, and checked her reflection in the office window. She refused to run to the mirror in the ladies' room, because that would be admitting she cared how she looked, and she preferred to remain in her usual state of denial. She squinted at her reflection in the sheet of glass, trying to block out the sunny sky and office buildings. It was so bright out that she couldn't see anything except for a transparent ghost of herself, utterly devoid of important details like zits. She wore a white T-shirt with a scoop neck with her new and improved red suit, with a short jacket and above-the-knee skirt. Her bare legs ended in running shoes, but at least she had shaved. Recently.

Bennie kicked off her sneakers and went digging in her office closet for brown pumps while she raked her fingers through her hair. After she had changed her shoes, she rechecked her reflection in the office window, standing with her arms straight at her sides. She looked positively see-through, and her hair was as fuzzy as a cloud in the sky. Or maybe it *was* a cloud in the sky.

She gave up trying to look hot, went back to her desk chair, and tried to act like a mature, sensible woman. She made a phone call to get her doors and back window replaced, and convinced them to rush the job, since she had been broken into by cops *and* robbers. They'd even agreed to do it without her being there, and to leave the new front door key inside. She hung up with satisfaction, but she still wasn't feeling mature and sensible when Marshall appeared at her threshold, with David.

"Bennie, Mr. Holland is here to see you," Marshall said, suppressing a smile, and waddled off without shouting, *Bennie, a total hunk is here to see you!*

"Hey, Bennie," David said, entering her office in a white oxford shirt, pressed khaki pants, a tan leather belt, and Timberland loafers. He looked like a man in uniform, even out of uniform, but it could have been his shoulders, which were made for epaulets. Bennie was trying not to be attracted to him, but it wasn't working. A sprig of dark chest hair sprung out of his open collar, and he smelled like mint something. Mint testosterone, maybe.

"Hoo-yah!" she said, and he laughed.

"You say it like an army man."

"Okay, how do you say it?"

"Hoo-*Ah!*"

It did sound cool, and male in the extreme. "Forget it, I took Latin. Thanks for coming by. Sit down."

"Thanks." He eased into the chair across from her desk, linking his fingers loosely between his legs. He was smiling at her with brown eyes that looked surprisingly sympathetic. "I'm sorry about your client."

"Thanks." Bennie felt a pang even the hots couldn't erase.

"You had quite a night last night. How are you doing? Did you get any sleep?"

"Some. I'm okay." Bennie had already decided not to offer David coffee because she wasn't his professional. Well, wait a minute. She had made him coffee last night at her house, so the precedent was set, and this was merely a change of venue. She couldn't decide. His chest hair was intentionally confusing her. "Coffee?" she asked, at the last minute.

"No thanks. I ate already."

Bennie laughed. "You're so nice today, and very talkative. What happened?"

"I feel bad for you, and frankly, I'm worried about you."

"Me, why?"

"Because somebody got killed. Somebody close to you." David's smile vanished, and his jaw set. "I did a little research online last night about your twin. I read all the newspaper articles from the murder trial, and all the information about her. We don't know how long she's been back in town, but if you look at her moves in a series, a logical series, it's a very dangerous scenario."

"What do you mean?"

"Alice is on the attack, and her attacks are escalating. She has attacked your reputation, your home, and an animal you love. And now possibly your client." David's eyes turned dark and bored into her. "You see where I'm going with this?"

Bennie nodded. It was bad and good to have her suspicion confirmed. Ambivalent falling short, again. "You think Alice killed Robert."

David shook his head. "Not only that."

"What?"

"I think you're next."

Whoa. Bennie's heart stopped. Maybe it was the gravity behind his eyes or the authority in his voice. Or maybe his words just rang true. She felt a tingle of fear.

"It's not out of the realm of possibility, and you have to take measures to protect yourself."

"But I'm not sure she's the one who killed Robert."

"You can't take any chances. You have to behave as though she did. You have to protect yourself, and you can't let it go just because so much else is going on."

"You're scaring me."

"I don't mean to, and I know this isn't my business." David leaned forward. "I'm just saying that last night, when you found out about the murder, you *flew* out of the house. It was like everything else went out of your head, including Alice. You didn't think twice about the danger to yourself, even though we had just found out how she'd broken in. Even though she had just tried to kill Bear."

Bennie remembered. She had barely said good-bye.

"I bet you didn't think about her this morning, either, in the aftermath of last night."

"I thought about her," Bennie told him, defensive.

"What I'm saying is, you have to end this. You have to stop her. You have to get her. You can't afford to keep disregarding your enemy because your friend was killed, or because you have a law firm to run." David gestured at her wall of fame. "I read about you last night. You've accomplished a lot in your life, and you have too much on your plate. I can't even begin to imagine what it takes to run a law firm. It isn't my expertise."

Mine either, she almost said.

"My expertise lies in another area. *This* area. I teach how to wage war, and how to win. I believe it's the same whether it's a real battle, a simulated battle, or any other conflict. War is war. It can be everywhere and anywhere."

Bennie had always believed as much. Litigation was war. She had thought it yesterday in the courtroom, when she had de-

clared on Linette. And look what had happened.

"I can tell you, from my experience, that
you have an enemy who isn't distracted. Alice is following a plan of attack, and she's
acting without hesitation or remorse. She's
aggressive and she's going forward. And
you're directly in the line of fire."

Bennie was quiet a moment.

"I'm concerned. I like you, and I wouldn't
feel so great if you got yourself killed."

Bennie felt a rush of warmth even she
couldn't deny.

"It's your cooking I would miss. Also your
dog, who loves me, I can tell."

Bennie felt her cheeks flushing. It was the
L word that did it.

"My point isn't that I can and should
help." David raised a finger like the instructor he was. "That *isn't* my point. Even
though I am the best man for the job, come
completely free, and have nothing better
to do."

"Nothing?"

"All I have to do is work out."

"No job? What do you live on?" Bennie
was so curious about him. David had come
out of the blue and was entering her life in a

very intimate way. Talking about her getting killed. What if he was working with Alice somehow? Even he had said that Alice could have an accomplice. Bennie couldn't help feeling suspicious. She was a lawyer, after all.

"I'm still drawing my pay, and I'm a saver."

Now *that* was suspicious. "Did you always want to be in the military?"

"Yes. I was ROTC in high school, a battalion commander."

"Why did you want to do that?"

"It suited me."

Okay. Bennie had wanted to be a lawyer for about the same reason. "Where do you live?"

"You're getting in a lot of personal questions here. Don't think I don't notice."

"Where you live is personal? Then what's your weight?"

He smiled. "I live on Spruce, at Twentieth, in an apartment I rent month to month. I don't know how long this break will be. Long enough to help you through this."

Bennie considered the proposition. "And you think I need help, that I can't do it myself."

"I know you can't."

Bennie bristled. *Anything you can do I can do better.* "Why the hell not?"

"Because Alice knows what you look like."

Oh. Bennie hadn't thought of that. She put her gun back in its holster.

"She can see you coming. In fact, she's been following you. And, since you and your law firm represented her, she knows what all of your associates look like. She's met them, hasn't she? They were in photos together in the newspapers, taken on the courthouse steps."

"Yes. She knows all of us but Murphy, and I bet she's seen a picture of her on our website."

"And she even knows your investigator. The one you mentioned, I forget his name."

"Lou Jacobs. He's sick anyway."

"And you don't have the money to rent a cop."

"Not really."

Bennie mulled it over. She didn't have a lot of choices. And he did seem like a normal, sane man, acting selflessly. She'd just never met anyone like him. She really could use the help. It might be time to admit it. "Well, I do have an idea."

"What is it?"

"The way I see, the problem is simple. Alice is following me, but I don't know where she is."

"True. I did some searching last night and she's not listed anywhere in the city or the suburbs."

"She's made herself invisible, except that she's following me. And that's how I can find her. You follow her, following me." Bennie tried to explain. She knew it sounded bizarre. Phones rang in the background. "Be my bodyguard, just like a rent-a-cop, but undercover. Sooner or later, she's got to show herself. And you know what she looks like. Me."

David was listening. "So I track you, that's the plan?"

"Yes. It shouldn't last too long, maybe three days at most. I hate to take so much of your time, but if you're offering, it's a plan."

David nodded. "I have plenty of time, and it won't take long. Then we turn her in and they question her for the murder of St. Amien, and prosecute her for the theft of your wallet and the diamonds. I assume once we have her out in the open, you can tie her up pretty good in legal red tape."

"That would be *my* expertise." Bennie smiled. She was feeling safer already, more in control of the situation, even if their arrangement was a little strange. If it worked, this nightmare would be over. Maybe the firm could stay afloat until then. The charges against her would be dropped, and people would know she wasn't a thief or a drunk. She couldn't wait for the day.

"One thing to note," David said. "If you see me, don't acknowledge me. No matter what. If you do, you'll blow it, and I'll be useless to you."

"Pretend I don't know you? That's not hard. I don't."

David smiled. "From now on, we can't be seen together, ever. I don't want her to be able to connect us in any way. Anything you have to tell me, call me on the cell. Do you have a back way out of here?"

"Yes, through the alley. There's a freight entrance."

"Good. I'll use it when I leave. I don't think I was followed on the way here, I was checking. Also, you have to keep me informed at all times, of everything you do and everywhere you go. What's your cell number?"

She told him.

"And you have mine, right?"

"On the message slip." Bennie eyed the curled phone messages scattered across her desk. "Somewhere."

"Last point. On the off-chance that I have on some kind of cover, don't remark it."

"You mean like camouflage? Or a disguise?"

"Yes." David nodded, and Bennie burst into laughter.

"Like leaves and berries? Or devil's horns? Or a G.I. Joe outfit?"

David grinned. "You think you're pretty funny, don't you?"

"Hoo-*Ah!*" Bennie answered. But she was laughing too hard to pronounce it in French.

Just then the intercom buzzer beeped loudly on the telephone on her desk, which was Marshall's signal for Bennie to pick up the intercom. Bennie excused herself and got out of the chair, with possibilities flashing through her mind. It could be Mort Abrams on the phone, her new best friend. Or Sam, her old best friend. She reached the desk, but there was no flashing light on line one, so there was no incoming call. She pressed the intercom button and picked up the receiver.

"Talk to me, Marsh," Bennie said, and the receptionist snorted.

"Another guest for you. He's on his way back."

"I can't see anyone now. I'm still with—"

"You don't have a choice, and neither did I."

23

"Detective Needleman!" Bennie said in surprise, hanging up the phone. She straightened up behind her desk, and David stood up as if coming to attention. Maybe there had been a development in Robert's murder. His mouth had a grim set to it, grimmer than last night at the crime scene. Bennie's stomach tensed. "Find out anything new?"

"Yes. Definitely. Absolutely, I did find out something new." His bright blue eyes pierced into Bennie, even from behind his glasses. Oddly, the detective seemed not to notice David towering like a lighthouse in the middle of the room. "I found out that you went and harassed Herman Mayer, a material witness, after I told you to stay out of police business."

Oh. That. "Does this mean there are no new leads?" Bennie asked, and David glanced over. *Oops.* She had forgotten to fill him in on that point because of her estrogen haze.

"You went to Mayer's house last night after you left me, and you accused him of murder. You had no business doing that." His silver Phil Donahue hair looked clean and feathery, and his grayish suit caught the sunlight coming in from the office window, bringing out the houndstooth pattern. He pointed at her with a finger like the barrel of a Luger. "You are a private citizen, and you interfered with an ongoing investigation."

"I'm sorry, I couldn't resist. I know Mayer, and I knew Robert."

"You interfered with my investigation. My interview of a material witness is an integral part of my investigation."

"Well, you didn't think Mayer was material last night."

"Herman Mayer was the last person to see St. Amien alive."

"There you go! That's why I went over." Bennie opened her palms, but Needleman's mouth looked carved in granite.

"Rosato, I'm not going to argue with you.

Your friend Brinkley, he's a lot nicer guy than I am. If you pull anything like that again, I'm going to charge you with obstruction of justice, and I swear, I'll make it stick."

David shifted on his feet, and given his size, it got their attention. "She didn't mean to interfere, Detective. She was just trying to help."

"Who are you?" Needleman snapped, but Bennie didn't miss a beat.

"My secretary," she answered, and David almost gasped audibly. Well, she didn't want to say his name, since they might match it from the night before with Officer Banneman, and David was supposed to be undercover anyway. What a unique camouflage. The SEAL as secretary. It was positively chameleonlike.

Detective Needleman raised a skeptical eyebrow but was too politically correct to say anything. He aimed his finger gun again. "The very next time, Rosato. You hear me?"

"Got it. Sorry. So you talked to Mayer?"

"Just now, at his office."

"What did he say?"

Needleman snorted. "None of your business."

"Did you learn anything?"

"That I shouldn't have trusted you last night."

Bennie took it on the chin. "Are there any new leads, though? I do have a right to ask that."

"No, you don't, and the answer is no. You have no rights. You're not even victim's family. You're just his lawyer. You have no greater rights than his dentist."

Ouch. The truth hurts. "Okay, I hear you. I'm sorry, I gave in, it was a moment of weakness and bad judgment. Come on, let's be friends again. I said nice things about you to the family."

"What are you talking about?" His icy gaze shifted from Bennie to David and back again.

"I called the brother to express my condolences, and he asked me what I thought of you. I told him you were wonderful in every way. Now, will you tell me, out of common courtesy, if you have any leads? They invited me over tonight. I'll say more nice things. How cute you look today, for example."

Needleman scoffed. "We have none. The prime suspect is the John Doe who killed the Belgian banker. Tell the family we are actively pursuing that theory."

Bennie nodded. "Now, did the autopsy yield anything?"

"No."

"Type of knife?"

"Common."

She thought of the Palm. "Steak knife?"

"I said common."

"Any prints at the scene?"

"No."

"Blood, fibers, or other evidence?"

"Not yet."

"I would think so, there had to be some sort of struggle."

"We're working on it."

"Any witnesses?"

"No."

"You talk to anybody at the Palm?" Bennie was going to keep asking questions until he stopped her, which he did, turning to the office door.

"No. Don't undermine us with the family. The department doesn't need more of that." The detective paused on the threshold. "The very next time you step out of line, you're in trouble, Rosato. Fool me once, but don't fool me twice. Good-bye." He turned and walked away.

"Got it, Detective!" Bennie called after him. "Sorry, and thanks for coming by." She gave his back a little wave of friendship and farewell.

As soon as he was gone, David turned to her with an incredulous grin. "I'm your *secretary?*"

"My really big secretary. Why not? I love secretaries. After mothers, they're the unsung heroes of the world."

"But *me?*"

"Can't a woman lawyer have a male secretary?"

"Not this male," David said, then shook it off. "Did you really do what that detective said you did?"

"Guilty." Bennie was already reaching for her phone messages. She needed to pick a lunch partner. "You gonna yell at me too?"

"Hell no. I'm just mad you didn't take me with you."

"Really?" Bennie looked up with the same warm rush she'd felt before, and David was smiling at her. "Thank you."

"You're welcome. Now what are you doing there?"

"Picking a lunch partner. It's either my friend Sam or a potential client, Mort Abrams." Bennie found the message slips, so she had both numbers. "It's almost noon, and I can't decide who to eat with."

"Oh, you lawyers have big problems."

"Hey, it matters. At least today it does."

"I'm just the undercover bodyguard. All I care about is where you're gonna eat."

"That's all I care about too. And that, I already know."

"Aha, I see," David said, catching up, and Bennie smiled.

"You're learning, sailor."

Silverware jingled as busboys cleared empty tables, ice cubes clinked in scotch glasses carried on round trays, and waiters in white coats rustled as they moved professionally between the tables packed with lunchtime patrons, who were buzzing with laughter and conversation. The Palm was one of the most popular restaurants in the city because of location, not decor. The design was early steakhouse, and the walls were blanketed with hand-painted head shots of local celebrities, like TV weathermen. But with City Hall, the Criminal Justice Center, and major hotels within a three-block radius, politicians, lawyers, and tourists flocked to the place, gobbling down grilled New York strip steaks and humongous Gulf shrimp.

Bennie plucked one of her huge shrimp from its orangy sea of cocktail sauce. "This qualifies as a lethal weapon in most jurisdictions."

"I am above size jokes, honey." Sam scooped a cherrystone into his mouth and leaned over his plate of tiny clamshells, with a pool of gritty water at the bottom. "So tell me what progress the cops have made."

"None. And thanks for the check, by the way. I did cash it, you devil."

"Ain't I a stinker?" They shared a table by the window, overlooking Broad Street. Indirect light brightened the spot, and Sam used it to examine his fingernails after he'd wiped his hands on the thick cloth napkin. "I'm so sorry about your client."

"Me, too. Robert was a wonderful man. You would have loved him."

"I'm sure. I love anybody who talks like Pepé Le Pew." Sam sipped his ice water and eyed the traffic out the window, on Broad. "You think it was this tourist thing?"

"It's a possibility." Bennie stopped herself before she filled him in on her other suspicions, especially about Alice. Sam would just yell at her, or worry about her, which was worse. "I'm leaving this one to the cops."

Sam set down his water in disbelief. "You are?"

"Yes."

"You're staying out of it?"

"Absolutely." Bennie nodded in a way she hoped was convincing. Of course, this act could put a damper on her plan to interrogate whoever had waited on Mayer and Robert last night. She'd have to be clever and deceitful, neither of which came naturally to her. "I have too much to deal with right now, what with Alice and the firm's finances, or lack thereof."

"I quite agree." Sam's expression turned grave, the corners of his reddish mustache turning down. "I wouldn't be so quick to dismiss that somebody is out there targeting foreigners. The way the mood has been in this country lately, there's a lot more xenophobia. It's just another form of hate crime, and believe me, you don't have to convince a gay man that hate crimes exist. I have a friend who's gay *and* Iranian. He shaved his beard and went drag."

"Maybe you're right." Bennie was drawing her own parallels, to the Brandolini case and the internment camps. She'd said good-bye to Mary before she'd left for lunch and felt proud of her. "Strange things happen when people feel threatened, don't they?"

"Sure do." Sam sighed. "Anyway, I have to tell you, as bad as I felt for your client, I felt worse for you. I don't want to think about what losing his case means for you, Bennie. It's a financial disaster. You have to let me give you some more money, at least lend it to you, with your house in play—"

"Not so fast," Bennie interrupted him. "Robert's murder may not drop me from the class action, if whoever succeeds him wants to continue the suit. I already have a call in to the vice president, who should know. And I'm getting phone calls from the other class members. I even had one invite me to lunch, but I chose you because you're way more fun."

"Also I'd pick up the tab."

"Okay, that, too. Sorry. Also, guess what? I was offered two million bucks for my firm this morning."

"What?" Sam dropped his clam fork. "Why didn't you tell me right away?" So Bennie filled him in on the meeting with Linette. Sam's thin, fair skin colored with excitement as she spoke, so brightly that she thought his navy-patterned bow tie was cutting off his oxygen. When she got to the part about the company Porsche, he got so hot and bothered that he had to take off his blazer. When she was finished, he reached over and put his fine, if clammy, hand over hers. "Bennie, I have one word for you. Sell."

"Why?"

"No, three words. *Sell, sell, sell.*" Sam wet his lips. "Or how about, sell right now. Or, sell it, honey."

"I built that firm. I saw it through everything. I grew it to full staff. I worked my ass off. Why should I sell out?"

"It's not selling *out,* it's selling, and are you seriously asking me why? *Why?* You're bankrupt, you idiot! Did you *forget?*" Sam rolled his eyes behind his hip glasses. "Bennie, listen up. Some money is better than no money. This is an essential financial principle, and even you can understand it. *Take the money.* Also three words."

"But Linette's only buying us to keep the class. He doesn't care about Rosato & Associates."

"So what?"

"I don't want to practice class-action law."

"Who cares? If you're right, Linette doesn't want you to, either. Be a consultant. Show up and say hi. Put your name on the papers."

"That's not lawyering."

"So quit after a respectable time period and go lawyer somewhere else. With that kind of money, you can start another firm." Sam's eyes flared with urgency as a waiter came over with their lunch entrées. The waiter's pristine white jacket read Westley and he was an older man, and balding. With an efficient air, he set a salmon filet in front of Sam and a strip steak in front of Bennie.

"Thank you," Bennie said. She faced the waiter, arranging her face into a casual mask for Sam's benefit. "Westley, you didn't happen to work last night, did you?"

"No, miss," the waiter answered matter-of-factly. "Yesterday was my day off."

"Thank you," Bennie repeated, watching the waiter remove her butter knife with some ceremony and replace it with a wooden-handled steak knife with a sharp serrated edge. Was this the kind of knife that had killed Robert? The thought nauseated her, but she made herself pick up the knife and turn it over. It was why she had ordered the steak, after all.

"Is anything the matter, miss?" the waiter asked, and Bennie shook her head.

"No, thanks. Everything's fine. I was just curious, is this the knife you give with every steak?"

"Yes."

"There aren't bigger ones?"

"No, I'm sure this will be fine for your purposes. We use it for the prime rib and the filet mignon. Though if you wish another, perhaps I could ask around in the kitchen."

"No. No, thanks." The waiter left, and Sam eyed her warily.

"Don't tell me, lemme guess. St. Amien ate here last night, before he was knifed to death."

Ouch. "I'm just curious, okay?"

"Stay out of it, Bennie."

"I am. I will. I was just asking."

"Right. Sure." Sam picked up his fork and separated an end flake of his salmon, encrusted with dill and coarse pink peppercorn. "I'll eat while you go over and depose the maitre d'."

It made Bennie laugh, which was a good thing, because she was already hating the heft of the knife in her hand. The blade was about six inches, and she would have described it as a common knife. Without the autopsy report, she had no way of knowing whether the blade matched the depth of the wounds, and right now she didn't want to think about it.

"I know you care about your client, your friend, but you are too busy to get involved. You have a business to sell." Sam ate a forkful of moist salmon. "Besides, you have Alice to worry about. I was thinking you should call a security agency. I'll spring for it. I want you to hire a bodyguard."

"Don't need one." Bennie took the knife in hand and, when Sam wasn't looking, slipped it inside her purse, which was sitting on the seat beside her. She couldn't bring herself to eat the steak anyway. Her appetite had vanished. "You know why I don't need one?"

"Because you think you're invincible and you're stubborn as a mule?"

"No, because I have one already."

"You're kidding." Sam stopped chasing skinny string beans with his fork. "How'd you pay for a bodyguard?"

"I didn't. He's free."

"Oh, please." Sam zeroed in on a string bean, annoyed. "Stop lying."

"It's true. Look." Bennie lowered her voice, not that anyone was listening to them in the noisy restaurant, and pointed discreetly out the window with her soda glass. A white SEPTA bus blocked their view, and she waited for it to pass. Then it did, revealing a noontime Broad Street bustling with traffic and businesspeople. But across the street, leaning against the sign for the subway stop, stood a very tall SEAL in sort of a disguise. "See that tall guy across the street, in the baseball cap with the Sixers logo?"

"No." Sam squinted. "Everybody out there has on a Sixers cap. It isn't a Ralph Lauren kind of town."

"The real tall man, near the subway stop. He's reading a paper."

Sam's eyes found David, Bennie could see it. They actually lit up. "Oh my God, is he big and hot or what? I thought he was a good-looking tree."

"That's David, my undercover body-guard."

"You're shitting me."

"I shit you not." Bennie caught herself. "And that's my last curse."

Sam couldn't tear his eyes from David. "What's his name? David what?"

"Holland."

"I like it. Holland. Mrs. Sam Holland. How's it sound? Wow, I'm a country!" Sam was getting carried away. "I hear Vermont is very nice this time of year. Does he like lawyers?"

"No."

"Who does? I'll quit. Who needs it any-way? I'll work for Ben and Jerry's. I can be his Chubby Hubby."

"Sam, relax. He's kind of macho."

"Macho works for me. I can be macho. I have a cowboy hat I got in Steamboat. It has a silver medallion in the front and a feather in the hatband. Turquoise, with a hint of sienna."

Bennie laughed. "You're not macho. You like Looney Tunes. You have stuffed animals on your windowsill."

"I'll douse them with lighter fluid and set them afire. Isn't that macho?" Sam turned away from the window momentarily. "So how'd you find him, and more important, will he come over to the dark side?"

"You mean is he gay?" Bennie smiled. "I doubt it."

"He doesn't have to be gay. He could just have gay *potential.* Can he spell 'gay'? We'll bend the rules in his case. We need to recruit men like him. Manly men." Sam grunted, and Bennie laughed.

"He's a SEAL."

"I can swim. I can bark, too. Tell me about him. Everything. Tell me, tell me, *tell me.*" Sam leaned over in high-dish mode, and Bennie filled him in on last night, going easy on the part about her almost drowning in the river. But the happiness evaporated from Sam's expression like champagne from a flute. "Bennie, this is terrible! Alice is a freak!"

"I know, that's why I need David," she

said as the waiter came over. He scanned their plates with tacit disapproval. Sam had stopped eating, and she had never started. Bennie looked up. "Can you wrap these up for us to take home? I have a golden with caviar taste."

"No problem," answered the waiter, clearing the plates and arranging them miraculously along the length of his arm. If he noticed that she'd purloined the steak knife, he'd been taught not to say so. "Coffee?"

"Sure," Bennie answered for both of them, but Sam was grim.

"You don't really know who David is, and he follows you everywhere."

"Sure I know who he is. I told you what I know."

"That's not very much. He's just a random guy, and you're supposed to tell him everything you do. Why did he quit the SEALs?"

"He didn't quit, he—"

"What did he do before that? When did he graduate from the Naval Academy? And above all, why would he do this for you? Are you sleeping with him?"

"No!" Bennie blushed.

"But you're thinking about it."

"So are you," Bennie shot back, and they

both laughed. "He's safe, Sam. He's fine. He's just a nice guy."

"You're letting a *stranger* protect you."

"He saved Bear's life, and he risked his own to do it. He's a Good Samaritan." Bennie tried to explain it, because truth to tell, she wondered about it too. "Sam, did you ever think that maybe we've been lawyers too long? Maybe we've become so inherently suspicious of everything and everyone, always questioning their motives, always imagining what will go wrong in the end, that we just can't recognize it when somebody does a selflessly good thing. Isn't that possible?"

"No. You been watching *Oprah* again?" Sam's eyes narrowed as a busboy materialized, put two empty coffee cups in front of them, and poured coffee with his other hand. He didn't have a name on his white jacket, which didn't look as surgical as the waiter's.

Bennie didn't wait for him to stop pouring. "Excuse me, did you work last night?"

"No, I don't work dinner," he said, and gestured toward the wall, where the painted faces of a local bank president and an Eagles cheerleader smiled down at the sugar caddy. "Sugar's over there, and I'll bring your cream. The dessert tray will be over shortly."

"No dessert for me, thanks," Bennie said, taking her napkin from her lap and getting up from the table. "Be right back, Sam."

"Is this where you pretend you're going to the bathroom, but you take a detour on the way to the front desk?"

Bennie smiled. "Gimme five minutes."

"I'll order the key lime pie and enjoy the view." Sam looked crankily out the window at David, then back at Bennie. "Just remember, 'Who guards the guards?'"

But Bennie didn't have the time to answer.

She had to conduct the cross-examination du jour.

24

"Sir, may I speak to you a minute?" Bennie gestured from the back of the crowd to the busy maitre d', who stood behind the paneled lectern like a hyperactive law professor. Dressed in a dark suit and tie, he was gesturing simultaneously to three hungry groups complaining to be seated.

"Steingard party, we'll be right with you. Just five minutes." The maitre d' snapped his head to the left, then smoothed his hair back into its moussed helmet. "Ms. Pecora, Lorraine Pecora, please, it's only five minutes, I promise. Mr. Kranyak, Joe Kranyak, your table is ready. Please follow James, right over there."

"Sir, please!" Bennie said again, threading through the restless crowd to the lectern, where she grabbed the wooden lip and hung like a little kid over the large reservations book. "I just have a quick question."

"Do you have a reservation?" The maitre d' looked at her with a pat smile.

"No, I mean, yes, I've already eaten. I was just wondering, were you on duty last night for dinner?"

"Yes, I was." The maitre d's attention was immediately distracted by a man behind her. "Mr. Toomey, how wonderful to see you again. And how is your lovely wife? Recuperating, I hope?"

"Sends her love," boomed the man. Bennie could feel him try to press past her to the lectern, but she sidestepped and blocked him.

"Excuse me, sir, this is important." Bennie got right in the maitre d's face, which was easy because they were the same height and she could be incredibly pushy. "Do you recall seeing two men at dinner last night, named Robert St. Amien and Herman Mayer?"

"Please, in one minute." The maitre d' flashed her the one-minute sign, then waved hello over her shoulder. "Lustig, Gail

Lustig, your table is ready. Please, follow Adriana, she'll take you."

"What about me?" said another woman, flanking Bennie. "My name is Deb Haggerty, and I had a reservation."

"Ms. Haggerty, your table is being set as we speak." The maitre d' hurried around the side of the lectern to speak to the woman while Bennie eavesdropped. "I'll escort you there myself right now, and dessert is on the house."

"Thanks, I accept," the woman said, but Bennie couldn't be bought with mere saturated fats, not that anybody was trying. She had bigger game in mind than cheesecake.

She gave up on the maitre d' for the moment and took advantage of his absence to peek over the lectern at the reservation book. The book was as huge as the lectern top itself, and glowed like gold under a dim yellow lamp that curved over its pages. Names filled the lines on the page, and next to them was a row of circled numbers, presumably indicating the number in each party. Beside that were all sorts of scribbled notations in pen and pencil. But the page showed reservations for tonight, not last night.

Bennie reached over quickly and turned the page back to last night, then began reading upside down, which was a special skill she'd honed at Grun & Chase. No young associate survived in a large firm unless she learned to read upside down, most useful during evaluation time or whenever sheer nosiness struck. She skipped down to seven o'clock and read the names, going backward and upside down. It made her dizzy, but when she reached 6:45, the entry read: Mayer, 2.

"May I help you?" the maitre d' asked, clearing his throat the way only maitre d's can.

"Yes, please. I see that Herman Mayer was here last night for dinner."

"I don't know Mr. Mayer," the maitre d' said, but his brow was furrowed and he took Bennie by the arm, away from the crowd at the lectern. "I'd be happy to briefly talk with you here," he said, his voice low. "I have already discussed this matter with the police."

"Good. So Detective Needleman did speak with you?"

"Yes, he verified that the Mayer party

dined with us last night. Mr. Mayer, and Mr. St. Amien."

"Did he talk with the waiter who waited on the Mayer party?" Bennie didn't exactly represent that she was with the police department, and he was too eager to get back to the lectern anyway. Cranky people were beginning to wave him over.

"He asked to, but Dante was the waiter and he came in late today. A doctor's appointment."

"Which one is Dante? I need to speak with him."

"Please, don't keep him long. That's him." The maitre d' pointed at a short young man darting among the tables with a huge tray of full plates balanced high above his shoulder.

"Thank you, I'll be quick," Bennie said, and the maitre d' returned to his post while she took off after Dante. Even with a tray of porterhouse steaks, three-pound lobsters, and chateaubriand beef for two, the energetic waiter threaded his way through the crowded tables, past the bathrooms to the stuffed booths lining the far side of the room. Bennie waited for him to unload the lunches and make his move toward the kitchen, to block his return. He could serve, but he couldn't hide.

Dante finished at the booth, stopped to chat up an older man at one of the other tables, then hustled toward the kitchen with his empty tray. When he realized that Bennie stood directly in his path, he said, "The ladies' room is right behind you."

"Excuse me, Dante, this is police business," Bennie said in a low tone. *Well, it is police business. It's just that a lawyer is doing it.* "I understand you waited on Herman Mayer and Robert St. Amien last night."

"Yeah, I did." Dante straightened up. He couldn't have been twenty-one, and he had the thick neck and polite manner of a high school wrestler. "I mean, yes. Yes, sir. Ma'am."

"Do you recall the dinner?"

"Yeah, *yes.* Too bad about that Belgium guy, who got stabbed."

"St. Amien was French," Bennie corrected automatically. A waiter scurried around them to the kitchen, and she took Dante's arm and edged him out of the way, toward the wall. "Anyway, what do you recall about it? Anything weird?"

"No."

"Did they fight at all. Argue?"

"No."

"How did they act?"

"Normal, no fighting. Just talked, you know, quietly. Sounded like business every time I went over. Nothing special, that way." Dante flipped his tray under his arm like a notebook. "What I remember is the tip. The dude who paid, Mayer? He only left ten percent. They didn't even drink much. Only the other guy, the dude who got killed, he had wine. Knew his wines, too."

Oh, Robert. "Do you recall what they ordered for dinner?"

Dante thought a minute. "The one, Mayer, had the strip steak, and the other guy had the spaghetti and clams."

Bennie felt her heart skip. "So you gave Mayer a steak knife."

"Probably." Dante's dark eyes widened. "You think—"

"Can't discuss it," she interrupted. "Just answer the questions and I'll let you get back to work. Who cleared the table, you or the busboy?"

"I did. . . . He was catching a smoke."

"Do you remember if the steak knife was there when you cleared?"

Dante thought longer. "Nah, I don't know. Sorry."

"You sure? It's very important." Bennie waited for his answer as a busboy hurried past them to the kitchen with a clinking tray of empty plates. She edged farther against the wall, so they were standing next to the painted portraits above the wainscoting. Bennie felt eyes on her and looked over. On the wall, at eye level, floated a very familiar head with a name painted underneath. WILLIAM LINETTE. Bennie did a double take. "That's Bill Linette," she blurted out, startled.

"Sure. Mr. Linette, he's a regular. Comes in all the time."

"He does?" Bennie thought about it. "Of course he does. He's a big-time lawyer."

"*Real* big. Tips awesome. He wasn't in my station last night, though. We gotta rotate." Dante snapped his fingers in disappointment. Bennie couldn't believe her ears.

"Did you say *Bill Linette* ate here last night?"

"Sure."

"But I didn't see his name in the reservation book."

"He doesn't have to call for reservations anymore. He comes in every Tuesday and Thursday for dinner, same time. Around seven."

Bennie's heart began to hammer. Did everybody but her eat at the Palm? "Did you see him last night?"

"Sure. He even said hi. Always does. Friendly dude."

"Who'd he eat with?"

"Some guys he knows, I think. Suits. Two."

"Quinones, Kerpov?"

"Don't know them, only Mr. Linette." Dante shrugged as another waiter hurried by. He shifted his feet. "Will this take a lot longer, sir? Miss?"

"I'll make it fast." Bennie tried to think through her excitement. "Was Linette here the same time as Mayer and St. Amien?"

"Wait. I want to get this right." Dante paused, thinking. "Yes. Definitely. Mr. Linette came in later and he left later, I think. Mr. Linette likes to have his after-dinner drinks. Always picks a nice malt."

"He drink a lot last night?"

"Well, yeah. Always. But he doesn't get

sloppy, he's a classy guy. He holds it pretty good. He's big."

Bennie eyed the restaurant layout. "Where did Mayer sit and where did Linette sit? Tell me the exact tables."

"Like I said, Mr. Mayer was in seven, I mean, that's the table in my station against the front wall, in the window. In the middle, see?" He pointed.

In the window. So anyone coming into the Palm through the main entrance would see Mayer and St. Amien. Linette had come in later, so he could have seen them in the window.

"And Mr. Linette was at his table in the back," Dante continued. "Right here."

Of course. "Near his picture."

"Yeah, right."

"Now for a hard question. Do you know if they saw each other? For example, did you see Mayer or St. Amien stop by and say hello to Linette, maybe on their way to the men's room?"

Dante shook his head. "Men never use the bathroom, only ladies. They're in there all the time." He chuckled, then caught himself. "I didn't see them get together, no. I don't know if they saw each other, but you can tell the way it is, with the tables."

Bingo. Bennie eyeballed the location of the tables. "There's even a divider, that bank of booths that screens the front of the room from the back. You can't see over that. So if Mayer and St. Amien didn't go to the bathroom, they probably didn't see Linette."

"Right. They're like separate dining rooms. If you're sitting at Mr. Linette's table back here, you don't see to the front. Mr. Linette likes his table private. He does a lotta his business here. When he wants to party, he hangs at the bar."

Bennie could barely suppress her excitement. So it was possible that Linette had seen Mayer and Robert last night when he came in. But they hadn't seen him, because of the booth divider. "How can we find out what Linette ordered last night? Who was the waiter back here?"

"I know what he ordered." Dante looked anxiously toward the kitchen, but Bennie hadn't learned everything she needed to know.

"How do you know? You didn't wait on him. He wasn't in your station."

"Don't matter, he always orders the same

thing, every Tuesday and every Thursday. He always says it's doctor's orders."

Bennie's hopes sank. "What, a salad?"

"No, the prime rib. He likes to joke around, Mr. Linette does."

So Linette had a knife too.

"You're not thinkin' that Mr. Linette *killed* that dude, because Mr. Linette would never—"

"Shhh." Bennie put a finger to her lips. "Don't speculate. Leave these matters to the police." Not that she would. "Who was the busboy at Linette's table?"

"Think it was Marky, but he isn't on tonight. And if you're gonna ask him if he picked up a knife, he won't remember. The kid likes the ganja, he don't remember his name." Dante's hand flew to cover his mouth. "Oh, shit. Did I just get him in—"

"No, I'll keep it to myself. You do the same." Bennie placed an ersatz-official arm on his shoulder. "Don't tell anyone we spoke, and say no to drugs. Thanks for the help, and sorry to have kept you. You can get back to work now."

"Thanks, Officer," Dante said, and he practically bolted toward the kitchen, leaving Bennie with a promotion.

And a painted picture of a toothy Bill Linette.

Bennie and Sam chugged along, walking down the crowded sidewalk toward her office. She slipped her Ray-Bans on in case any stray reporter was out there, and also to continue her strategy of differentiating her appearance from Alice's. Also she was carrying her doggie bag. *Take that, Alice!*

"So he's behind us?" Sam asked as they walked. He had his navy blazer hooked on his index finger and thrown over his shoulder. "He's following us? David Hottie?"

Bennie smiled. "Holland. Keep your eyes front and don't look back."

"This feels strange. Having him following us."

"No stranger than having *her* follow us."

"She's following us, too? Christ, we're a parade!"

"Really." They turned onto Locust, toward Bennie's office. Sam was going to drop her off, then go on to Grun. She checked her watch. Half past one. She had her meeting at two. She scanned the bypassers reflexively for Alice, then breathed a relieved sigh.

She didn't have to be so worried anymore with every step. "I feel better knowing that he's watching."

"But he's so big, how can he blend in?"

"He's a master of disguise. He even has a witch hat."

Sam looked over. "Be serious."

"He knows stuff."

"He's a soldier, not a spy."

Basically the same thing. "He has common sense, doesn't he? He hangs back, changes his appearance slightly day to day, and he makes it work. You don't need a surveillance degree to follow somebody around. Besides, Alice isn't expecting this. She might expect me to hire a uniformed security guard, but she wouldn't expect this. And she doesn't know David. She won't be looking for him to be following her following me."

"Huh?"

"See? It's too confusing."

They passed some office buildings a block from Bennie's. The breeze was coolish and pleasantly free of humidity, and the foot traffic dying down. It reminded Bennie of the day she had walked back to her office with Robert, only to get arrested in front of him. She couldn't believe that he was dead. Whoever had killed him wasn't playing games. She stopped in her tracks and turned to Sam.

"Sam, the truth is that beggars can't be choosers. I know that the plan isn't perfect, but it's the only one I have. And it won't last forever. I think it will only take a few days. She'll show her hand very soon, and we'll get her."

Sam inhaled. "But it's like using you as bait."

"No it isn't."

"Yes it is."

"No."

"Yes."

"Got you last," Bennie said. She wasn't about to admit as much to Sam, but she *had* thought of that.

25

"Mort Abrams," the young man said, shaking Bennie's hand with assurance. He was younger than she had expected, about her own age, with a friendly array of crow's-feet at the corners of his light brown eyes. He was short, with brown hair brushed neatly to the side, and he was dressed business casual in a forest green Lacoste shirt and charcoal Dockers. "Pleased to meet you in person, Bennie," he said as they shook hands.

"My, in person." Bennie laughed and gestured to introduce the remaining associates. DiNunzio had left for Washington, and the boss was experiencing an uncharacteristic pang of maternal concern. But she still had two baby birds left, and this case was big enough to need them both. "Mort, these are my associates, Judy Carrier and Anne Murphy."

"Great to meet you," he said, shaking each one's hand, more stiffly than Robert had and with less charm. Bennie knew the associates would be remembering Robert, too; that was why she had scheduled the meeting in the large conference room. The windows lining the north wall filled the place with bright natural light.

"Good to see you," Carrier said, lifting her chin gamely as she sat down in her denim smock and white T-shirt, and Murphy extended her hand over the table.

"Nice to meet you," she said, more quietly than usual, and sat down. She wore her favorite black knit dress, sadly appropriate for today. Bennie decided not to ignore the subject.

"Mort, you'll have to excuse us here," she began, taking her seat at the head of the table. "We're all feeling pretty shaken today, with Robert St. Amien's death last night. He was our client and our friend." She gestured Abrams into a seat to her left, giving him the view of the cityscape.

"Of course, I understand." Abrams sat

down and glanced around the table, with a puckered lower lip. "I met Robert only once, but he was a fine man and an excellent businessman. In fact, I owe him a debt of gratitude. He was the one who put me onto the notion of expanding into Europe, and we acquired an English sub."

"A subsidiary," Bennie supplied, though he could just as easily have meant an English submarine, for all she knew about business.

"Yes. I'm American, obviously, and my core business is manufacturing calibrated fittings for medical equipment."

"Fittings, I see," Bennie said, though she was constantly amazed by the number of widgets it took to make a machine of any kind. The only thing she could make was a brief, and the only widgets she understood were words. "What exactly is a fitting?"

"Well, a fitting is a little ring that"— Abrams made an O with his index finger and thumb—"well, forget the details, the bottom line is that fittings are rings that fit like collars on things, in my case most types of medical equipment. My company, FitCo, manufactures them in West Chester, outside the city."

"Okay, I'm with you."

"Last year, I wanted to expand my business, so I acquired a small English concern that manufactures medical lenses. My English sub, also called FitCo, has been damaged by the trade association's boycott against foreign lenses. We've lost two contracts since the association's meeting."

"You can document this?"

"Easily." Abrams spread his palms. "I'm wondering if I can join the class-action litigation against the association."

"What were the damages from the lost contracts?" Bennie slid a sharp pencil and a fresh legal pad from the center of the table.

"Nothing in the neighborhood of St. Amien & Fils's, but significant for us. A contract with Key Medical, Inc. A half million dollars."

"That's significant, all right," Bennie said, writing it down. It was five hundred grand more than she had, for starters.

"It certainly is, and it was only the beginning for our little sub." Abrams tented his fingers. "We use outside counsel for business work, but he doesn't do much litigation, and no class-action litigation. So I find myself in the position of needing a lawyer but not knowing whom to choose. I think a lot of us smaller companies are in the same position. I thought I'd come here to speak with you."

"Thank you for giving us a shot," Bennie told him, but her blood didn't race as it had that morning with Robert. If anything, she should have been more excited about signing Abrams, because she was more broke now, if such a thing was possible. Everything hung in the balance, but she couldn't muster the requisite enthusiasm for a dog and pony show.

"I saw your argument yesterday in the courtroom. I was in the gallery." Abrams smiled in an encouraging way. "I thought it was very interesting, what you did. I didn't follow all the technicalities, but I liked how you handled yourself, and the motion you filed seemed to do the trick."

"It may have, but the judge didn't exactly rule," Bennie said, then kicked herself. Why was she talking Abrams out of hiring her? What was the matter with her? Plus she hadn't even offered him coffee. She started to rise. "Excuse me, would you like some coffee?"

"Don't drink coffee."

"Okay." Bennie sat back down. *Bad to worse.* She could hear her house selling at foreclosure, a gavel hitting a wooden block. She'd have to find an apartment that took Bears.

"I am considering retaining Rosato & Associates because of what I saw, and part of my thinking is that if Robert chose you as counsel, that's a very high recommendation. There are a lot of lawyers in this suit, and he could have gone anywhere."

"Thank you." Bennie tried to rouse herself. "We may not have the experience the other firms do, but we're more than qualified, and we can get the job done for a fraction of their cost because we're smaller. We were very pleased that Robert selected us from among all the class-action counsel in the suit."

"I'll say. My corporate lawyer says that the roster reads like a who's who of class-action lawyers. Linette, Brenstein, Quinones, and a man named Kerpov, I think. My lawyer did some asking around, and he referred me to Bill Linette."

Bennie almost gagged on the irony, considering the steak knife still in her purse. She swallowed hard, relieved she hadn't had the chance to brief the associates on what she'd learned about Linette's dinner last night. They were too young to have developed a poker face. She said evenly:

"Bill Linette is a very qualified lawyer, Mort. I'm sure he'd serve FitCo with skill and vigor."

"That's not what he says about you."

"Excuse me?"

"He said that you had no business representing a plaintiff in *any* class action. That it was malpractice for you to represent Robert, or to try to assume a leadership role in the lawsuit."

Bennie blinked, at a momentary loss for words. Most lawyers wouldn't trash others to get a client, but if the steak knife was any indication, unfair competition was the least of Bill Linette's sins.

"Gimme a break!" somebody blurted out, and Bennie's head snapped around. Judy Carrier, her cheeks as pink as her hair, had turned to address Abrams. "That's funny that he said that, considering that he was here trying to *hire* Bennie this morning, and that he wants to buy the whole damn law—"

"*Carrier!*" Bennie jumped in, alarmed. "That really won't be necessary."

"Well, Jeez, boss!" Carrier protested. "It's just absurd to let him get away with that!"

Murphy piped up, "Really, it's not true! We can do as good a job as—"

"Ladies, that's enough," Bennie said firmly, rising at the head of the table, which seemed to shut the associates up. "I know you both mean well, but we don't play that here. Bill Linette can say whatever he wants, it makes no difference to us. We are professionals here, even if we did forget about the coffee."

"Okay," Carrier answered with a teenager's huff, and Murphy folded her skinny arms, simmering in redheaded silence.

"Good. Fine." Bennie eased back into her seat and looked at Abrams. "Sorry, we are definitely feeling a little raw today."

"I see that," Abrams said, and faced the associates. "Judy, Anne, I gotta tell you, in my opinion, there's nothing wrong with a little team spirit. I'd be pissed if anybody talked that way about FitCo. I know how good our company is, and I'm proud of it."

"Thanks," Carrier said gratefully, and Murphy nodded.

Abrams turned back to Bennie. "Please,

don't feel like you have to apologize for feeling bad today. If I ever got murdered, I'd like my lawyer to feel sad the next day. I'm sorry if I offended you or your associates. I probably shouldn't have mentioned what Bill said anyway. I couldn't help wondering what your response would be."

"Well, you just got it," Bennie answered with a smile. She liked his honesty, and he seemed to be loosening up. She was guessing he had baby birds, too. "And for the record, I disagree with his assessment. We may be inexperienced in class-action law, but we're smarter than we look, and we work hard here."

Abrams smiled gently. "For what it's worth, I wouldn't take what Linette said to heart. He was well into a few drinks when he said it, and it was probably the scotch talking."

Scotch. Bennie flashed to Dante saying, *Mr. Linette likes to have his after-dinner drinks. Always picks a nice malt.* She played the strangest hunch. "Mort, when did Linette say this about me?"

"I shouldn't have said anything—"

"No, it's okay, but when did he say it?" She had assumed they'd met in Linette's office, but maybe not. "Was it last night by any chance?"

"Yes."

"At the Palm?"

Abrams looked mildly surprised. "Why, yes."

Bingo! "You had dinner last night at the Palm, with Linette?"

"Yes. We've been looking for representation since we heard about the lawsuit. We wanted to interview him about representing us, and he took me and my controller out to dinner."

So it wasn't Quinones and Kerpov at dinner with Linette last night. It was Abrams and his controller.

Bennie's thoughts raced ahead. It made sense. Everything was churning in the class action. "What time did you leave the restaurant?" The associates shifted in their seats, but mercifully kept their mouths shut.

"About eight-thirty," Abrams answered, beginning to be puzzled, but Bennie was on a tear. She didn't care if she lost the client if she could get Robert's murderer.

"Did you all leave together? You, Bill, and your controller?"

"No, I left with my controller. Our car was in valet, and Bill had to go back to the office, so he walked." Abrams was looking at Bennie as if she were nuts. "Does this matter?"

Linette had left alone. "Not really," she answered quickly. She didn't want Abrams to go blabbing to Linette that she knew about him being at the Palm. "I'm asking because I read in the newspaper that Robert might have had dinner last night at the Palm."

"Everybody eats there. Most businessmen I know, anyway. It's the best steakhouse in Center City."

"I know, it's just a coincidence, but I was just wondering if you or Bill ran into him there."

"No, I didn't even see him, and I have no idea if Bill did."

But Robert and Mayer were sitting in the window. "It's odd that you didn't see Robert when you first went in. He was sitting in one of the windows in front, right near the main entrance."

"How do you know that?"

Indeed. "I think I read it, or somebody told me."

"Oh well, we didn't go in through the main

entrance. We drove into the valet, and that's on the side. We went in the side door, and through the Hyatt."

My God. So it *was* possible. Linette could have done it, even himself. He had the motive, the opportunity, and the knife. And who knew what his dark side was like? "Oh well, let's not dwell on it. How can I help you make your representation decision? Feel free to ask me anything about our firm."

"I'm wondering if you currently have any clients in the class, since Robert's death."

"No, I don't." Bennie let it sit there. She wasn't about to make it up, nor was she about to add, *I don't have many clients at all.* "Why do you ask?"

"I was concerned that since FitCo isn't as big a company as some of the others, it might not get much attention if we went with one of the other firms, like Bill's, for example. I think he'd be too wrapped up with Herman Mayer's company to take us seriously. Herman can be a squeaky wheel, and Linette has lots of other matters, too."

"I see. That wouldn't be a problem here." *We have no other clients.* Then Bennie thought for a moment. Maybe she could get more info if she was a little smoother. "You definitely have Herman's number."

"I do, and that's part of my concern." Abrams's face darkened. "Can't say I'm a fan."

Who is? "Do I need to know why?"

"It's probably silly," Abrams said with a sigh. "It might even be prejudice. But my background is Jewish. We lost my aunt and uncle during the Holocaust, in Theresienstadt. Herman's company was founded during the war, and I have a problem with that. My parents still won't buy a BMW or a Volkswagen."

"So you don't necessarily want to be at the same firm that Mayer is," Bennie said, without judgment. She was learning that history died hard. "Well, if you decide to go with us, I think we'd make a good fit."

"I think we would too," Abrams said, rising. He took a second to brush down his neat pleated pants. "I'd like to think it over, if I may. Take a look at the other firms, too."

"That makes sense." Bennie rose with him, her feelings mixed. His tone didn't sound warm enough to go their way, but she couldn't stop thinking about Linette.

Still, she'd be crazy to let Abrams go. "Mort, feel free to come back to us another day, when we're more ourselves."

"I will," Abrams said. He bid the associates good-bye, then let Bennie walk him out. She put him into the elevator, hoping it wasn't the last time she'd see him.

And hoping that he didn't tell Linette.

"I told you! I *told you* it was Linette!" Judy was standing at the head of the table, her eyes dark with anger. "That guy is a sleaze. Sleaze!"

"Calm yourself, Carrier," Bennie said. Now that they were alone in the conference room, she reached into her purse, pulled out the knife, and set it on the table. "This is your homework."

"What?" Carrier asked, and Bennie explained where and how she'd gotten the knife, while the associate picked it up and examined the blade, teasing it with a finger-pad. "This is sharp."

"Yep. Sharp enough."

"What do you want me to do, boss?"

"Go down to the medical examiner's office. Tell him who you are and show him that knife. See if it could have been the type used to kill Robert."

Murphy edged her tiny knit butt onto the conference table. "Shouldn't we also get a copy of the autopsy report? I bet we can finagle it. I have friends in the DA's office."

"It may not be ready yet," Bennie answered, "but that's a good idea. If it's ready, get a copy. Make noises that it's public record, even though I'm not sure that it is, and maybe they'll cough it up."

"You think Linette did it? Himself, even?" Murphy asked.

"I just want to follow up," Bennie answered, and Carrier was listening thoughtfully.

"Even if it isn't the same knife, it doesn't eliminate Linette as a suspect, or Mayer for that matter. He could have used another knife. Lots of people carry penknives, and they're way easier to get than guns."

Murphy snorted. "Guns aren't that hard to get, either."

Bennie looked at her. "You have homework too, kid. You up?"

"Sure, why wouldn't I be? What do you have?"

"First thing, you have some experience

with restraining orders, I know." Bennie felt a guilty twinge, but she needed help. "I hate to remind you of it, but I need to call upon it. Draft a brief for me against Alice, and tell me what I have to do to get an order. Put in all the facts, from the wallet to the break-in to the diamonds. It may not be foolproof, but it doesn't hurt to have one in place."

"Done."

"Thanks. Second, you heard Abrams say that Linette told him he was going back to work after dinner. I want that checked out. You know where Linette's offices are, in that tall gray building. There's got to be a security desk in the lobby, where tenants sign in and out. I'm wondering when Linette signed in and out last night."

"You mean like a sign-in log? It's not superreliable."

"No, but it's a start. Think you can get the guard to show it to you?"

"In this dress? You have to ask?" Murphy smiled broadly, for the first time today. "Where are you going, Bennie?"

She checked her watch. She hoped David was waiting out there, ready to go. She'd tell him about Linette on the cell, and

she wasn't completely surprised to find herself looking forward to the call.

"Someplace sad," Bennie answered after
a moment. "But necessary."

26

Situated at the southwestern corner of Rittenhouse Square, the lovely block-square Victorian garden designed by Frederick Law Olmsted, the Manchester was the most exclusive address in Philadelphia. Still, Bennie got no charge stepping into an elevator plusher than her living room, if only slightly smaller, and letting it carry her noiselessly upward. The elevator doors slid open on the penthouse floor, and Bennie found herself not in the hallway she had expected, but smack at the entrance to a large, well-appointed living room filled with people holding wineglasses and hors d'oeuvres on toothpicks, talking in small groups, their cadences more South of France than South Philly.

"Excuse me, I'm Micheline St. Amien," said a young, beautiful blonde, gliding from the crowd in a black tweed suit that had little flares at the cuffs, a flared skirt to match, and a cinched-in waist so narrow it made Bennie's suit look like the *Hindenburg.* The C on its shiny black buttons announced that the suit was Chanel, but it could just have easily stood for Cash. Oddly, she didn't have a French manicure. Bennie would have to tell Murphy that the French manicure thing was a sham. The French had American manicures.

"Hello," Bennie responded, extending a hand and introducing herself. "I'm, I *was*, Robert's lawyer. Georges asked me to stop in. I'm so sorry for your loss."

"Thank you for your kind words, and for coming." Micheline's French accent was just light enough to register as cultured. Bennie had never known there were so many French people living in Philly. Micheline smiled pleasantly at her, though there wasn't a laugh line marring her lovely cheekbones. She couldn't have been thirty years old. "I understand Robert liked you very much."

"I hope so," Bennie said, for lack of

something better. She didn't feel completely comfortable around the woman. Her manner was cool, and she didn't seem all that broken up by Robert's death. Bennie glanced around, and nobody here did. It didn't make sense. Robert was a nice man. "Are these employees of St. Amien & Fils?"

"No, these are our friends. Let me take you to Georges. He's in his study. He's not feeling well, and he's not exactly mobile of late." Micheline turned on her stilettos and sashayed down the hallway to the right, rolling her slim hips like a runway model.

"Thank you." Bennie lumbered, feeling roughly like Gentle Ben, in Ann Taylor. The walls were covered with tasteful tan fabric, and the corridor was lined with antique prints of the Seine, which the St. Amiens evidently found more beautiful than the Schuylkill, difficult as that was to comprehend.

"Here is his study," Micheline said when they reached the paneled door at the end of the hall, and she opened it. "I'll leave you two alone and attend our guests. I know you have a lot to discuss."

"Thanks," Bennie said, as Micheline closed the door behind her. Inside was a cozy, book-lined study containing a built-in walnut desk with drawers, a cushy brown leather chair with an ottoman, and a maroon glass ashtray on a brass stand next to it. The air smelled like the stale smoke of French cigarettes. In the center of the study sat a man in a wheelchair. His back was to the door and he appeared to be looking out the window, but when he spun around in the chair, Bennie almost gasped. Georges looked like an older version of Robert, with the same sleek silver hair, same bright blue eyes behind stainless-steel glasses, but with a full brushy beard, dark brown but laced with silver. Behind the beard, his lips tilted down into a frown, and his bushy eyebrows showed the same sad slope.

"You must be Bennie," Georges said with dignity, and he wheeled over a few inches with his left hand, more a gesture than anything else. His right leg lay completely flat on a metal support, encased in a graying cast, and he extended his right hand over it to shake hers.

"I'm so sorry for your loss." Bennie grasped his fine fingers warmly, blinking back the wetness in her eyes, which had been provoked by his voice, so like his brother's.

"Thank you very much," Georges said, and when he released her hand, the chair strayed to the left. "Please excuse this wheelchair business. I'm not very good with it, I fear I never became accustomed. Please, sit." He motioned her onto the leather ottoman, and she sat. "I broke my leg several weeks ago, like a fool."

"That must have hurt," Bennie said, glad of something else to talk about. She couldn't imagine the pain he must be feeling, sitting alone in the room, wheelchair-bound. If misery loves company, Georges didn't have any. She would stay awhile. "How did you do it?"

"Riding. My horse has a bit of spirit, he forgets he is gelded. Comes the spring, he gets crazy, he believes he is a stallion. Many men do, you know." Georges winked, and Bennie smiled.

"Is that a bad thing?"

"Touché." He laughed, just like Robert. "My warmblood, Gustave, he is a very pampered, very civilized dressage horse. He thinks he is beautiful—*pardon,* he knows he is beautiful—and he also knows he belongs only in the ring, on the perfect footing for his perfect hooves."

Bennie smiled. She could relate. She had a Bear, he had a Gustave. There are different forms of baby birds. It was all about love, anyway.

"Gustave, he knows he doesn't belong on the trail, nor do I. However, I spur him on, I take him out by myself, and along comes a *little tiny* creature, smaller than a squirrel, brown with a *little tiny* stripe, what do you call it"—Georges thought a minute—"a chipmunk! Is that it, chipmunk?"

Bennie nodded. A cheepmunk.

"This chipmunk, it is so *little tiny* it is only not even the size of Gustave's one hoof!" Georges made a number one with his index finger. "Gustave, he is seventeen hands tall, *very* tall, and he leaps forward in great and terrible fear of his life, going as high as if he is jumping a Grand Prix fence, and, *mon Dieu,* he slips in the mud and goes tumbling down the hill"—Georges made a spiraling motion with his hand—"then *I* go down, and the little tiny chipmunk, he runs off and tells his friends!"

"Oh, no!" Bennie couldn't help but smile. The way he told the story made her

I-almost-drowned-last-time-I-rowed story look like chopped foie gras.

"Luckily, only one of us broke his leg." Georges smacked his forehead with his palm, and Bennie laughed again. She didn't get it. Robert had said that his brother was wacky, but she thought he was sort of cute. She could tell he was being a good host, cheering himself and her up, mixed with a little of Robert's special alertness to women. She appreciated the effort, especially in the circumstances.

"So how long will you be in the chair?"

"Any day now, then they take off the cast, and I go back to work." Georges took a minute to extract a handkerchief from a pocket of a soft cardigan sweater and dab his long, bony nose with it. "I am almost re-tired now, from my practice as a gynecolo-gist, as you may know. But Gustave teaches me much, every time I ride him. You know what is said about horses?"

"No, what?"

"It is said, 'The outside of a horse is good for the inside of a man.' Churchill says this, either he or Roosevelt, or De Gaulle, I think." Georges laughed. "I don't know who said it really, one of those. Not Stalin, I am sure of it."

Bennie smiled, then thought about it. She wondered if her father had had anything to do with the horses, where he'd lived. If he had ridden. She found herself saying, "My father worked on a horse farm, outside of Wilmington."

"I like the horses, I *love* the horses, but Robert, he doesn't like these so much. Our father, when we were very young, he taught us to ride, until our seat is perfect. But Robert, he doesn't have the interest." Georges fiddled with his handkerchief, momentarily lost in sadness. His mouth set, and his light blue eyes clouded like the sky. "I don't understand why, why would someone kill Robert? He hurts no one."

"It is hard to understand," Bennie said. She didn't add that she didn't understand it either. That wouldn't help Georges now. And part of her knew that the deep wrench in her chest over Robert's death wasn't related to Georges. Because if Alice had killed Robert, his only mistake would have been choosing Bennie as his lawyer and remaining loyal to her. Bennie would be responsible for his death. And now she sat face-to-face with the grief and pain of his family.

"It doesn't make sense to me, not at all," Georges went on. "They take his wallet, they take his watch. These things, they add up to what, a few hundred dollars? Why do they kill him for these things? Robert, he would have given them. He could afford to replace them, easily."

"The police think it has something to do with hatred for foreigners. That the killer targets them because they're easy prey and because they have money, then kills them out of hate or resentment. But usually, criminals kill during robberies on impulse or to prevent identification. They don't want to leave a witness."

"I see. The newspaper says they kill because he is French. Can this be? I do not believe it! The Americans I know from my practice, from my riding, they are kind. They have good hearts. A generous people. They share their country with the world! Bennie, do you think this is why Robert is killed?"

"I'm not sure," Bennie had to admit. He could see doubt on her anyway.

"I don't think you do!" Georges managed a smile, though his eyes shone with new wetness. "I tell my wife, I do not believe this is the reason, this hatred, but she says, no. It *is* because he is French. Silly! So I do not understand these stupid theories," Georges said, partly to himself now, rubbing his forehead, and it was all Bennie could do not to tell him everything.

"Let's see what the police come up with," Bennie said noncommittally, and Georges looked up, his forehead reddened under his silvery hair.

"I hear nothing more from them today. The whole day goes by. Nothing."

"They'll call if they have something to tell you. I know they're investigating and I think they're doing a good, thorough job." Bennie wasn't lying. Needleman was doing everything she'd want him to do, including checking the maitre d' at the Palm. She didn't blame him for not being a naturally suspicious lawyer.

Georges gave a resigned sigh. "The coroner, from the morgue, he says we can take Robert home perhaps on Monday. Then they will be finished." His upper lip curled with such distaste it showed even under his beard. "Micheline, she has made all the arrangements, for burial at home. She was very fond of Robert."

"I see," Bennie said, but she didn't. The woman hadn't shed a tear to mess up her mascara. It was enough to make Nancy Drew suspicious again, and it was always fun to speculate without any factual basis. In fact, it was downright American.

"So we will be burying Robert in our family plot. But this is too soon, too soon for Robert. He is my little brother, younger than I." Georges paused, collecting himself. "Robert was good at the business, though. Quite good."

"He sure was." Bennie considered taking the opening. She felt so uncomfortable about it, but she had no other way to find out about the succession plans. She had never met a single other person from St. Amien & Fils. "Georges, do you know much about the business?"

"Just a little, what Robert mentioned." Georges waved his hand dismissively. "But this is not my concern. Robert has his business, I have mine. We decide this, Robert and I, a long time ago, that Robert will work in the family business. I choose not. I go to the university for medicine." Georges gestured at the books lining the room. "I enjoy a study of living beings, not a study of medical lenses, for God's sake!"

"So you don't work in the business at all?"

"Not at all." Georges shook his head. "I am now on staff at only the one hospital. The insurance is so high, I go in only one day a week. I do not live to work, like Robert. He buys out my interest in the lens business, so long ago, and I don't know what he does with it. We both agree to do this."

"But you must know who his vice president is, or his successor. I have to find out if that person wants me to continue the company's claim against the trade association, or if I should just withdraw the complaint."

"Oh, you mean, who will take charge of the business, now that Robert is . . . gone?" Georges straightened in his wheelchair, hoisting himself up by both hands. "Of course I know that. Julien, of course."

Bennie perked up. An answer, and an easy one! "The one from Harvard Law. The one you asked me to meet today?"

"Yes. He is Robert's only son, and heir. Robert wants him to run the business, that's why he sends him to Harvard. Julien makes his graduation this summer, in only one month. But Robert will not—" Georges's throat caught with the thought that Bennie could have finished for him.

"Robert will be watching, I'm sure," Bennie said with conviction. She knew her mother was watching her, right now, and she'd only gone to Penn. "I'm sure Robert was proud of him. Harvard is one of the best law schools in the country."

"Robert is, was, so very proud of Julien. Julien graduates with degrees from the law school and the business school. He is admitted in some sort of special program, very difficult to get into, and his grades are quite good."

"Is he here yet? I know you wanted me to meet him, and now I think I should."

"Yes, he's here. He arrives not long ago, his flight from Boston was delayed. He was very upset, as you can imagine. He and Robert were very close, especially since his mother's death." Georges wheeled around to the desk behind him and reached for the telephone. "Julien goes to get a shower, then to lie down. He's in the guest room. I buzz him."

"Wait," Bennie said, having second thoughts. "Maybe we should let him rest. I can come back another time. It's so soon—"

"No, he is wanting to meet you. He is a great fan of yours. He says we are to wake him when you arrive. He's waiting for you."

"All right, if you think so." So Bennie prepared herself mentally to meet a young man who had just lost a father he loved. Oddly enough, she sort of had an inkling of what that must be like.

But that might have been the denial part.

27

French heartthrob came instantly to Bennie's mind when they were joined in Georges's smoky study by the young Julien St. Amien. As if his name weren't sexy enough, Julien was tall, blade-thin, and handsome, with a dark, glossy pile of thick, wavy hair. Surprisingly, he didn't look at all like Robert, with his wide, full lips and blue eyes so light she'd seen them only on Siberian huskies. Bennie reminded herself not to mention the Siberian husky part when she described Julien to the associates.

"It's *so* cool to meet you, Bennie!" Julien said, pumping her hand with some enthusiasm. His grin was broad, his manner excited—he had evidently forgotten his sadness at the very thrill of meeting her. He finally released her hand. "I'll never forget when you judged us at our moot-court competition."

"Really. Thank you so much." *This kid is getting better looking by the minute.* Bennie considered fixing him up with one of the associates. Men this young never appealed to her. She was a woman, not a girl. She wanted a man, not a boy. Even one with such superb judgment.

"You asked so many questions, and they were all exactly on point," Julien continued, his accent mercifully American. "It was an honor to have you judge us, and I admire your work so much, particularly in the area of police brutality and individual liberties."

"Well, thank you." Bennie flushed at the flattery, but she was surprised. She remembered the argument only vaguely; the students had simulated an appellate argument over some ridiculously obscure issue of criminal law, which was typical of most moot courts she had judged. She wasn't even the marquee name of that panel; the real draws were the chief judge of the D.C. Circuit and the CEO of a Fortune 100 conglomerate. Bennie had been making her token cameo as the Diva of Public Interest

Law, which was undoubtedly part of the reason she'd been going broke.

"I've read everything you've written on the subject of civil liberties in the law reviews. I even ordered the reprints of your articles on the recent developments in excessive-force law, and the political implications. I wonder if you would take a minute to autograph them for me. They're at school, but I'll send them to your office."

"I'd be happy to," Bennie answered, amazed. She hadn't been asked to sign her reprints since the Clinton administration, and she suspected that Republicans used them for coasters. She couldn't believe that anybody who liked her stuff was about to become a corporate CEO himself. Maybe the world was changing?

"Thank you so much! You know, you were in the forefront of much of the excessive-force law. Did you see that the Third Circuit is following your analysis to the letter, in the case of—"

"Julien, please, enough!" Georges interrupted, good-naturedly. He waved his handkerchief from his wheelchair. "You're embarrassing our guest. See, her face is turning quite red!"

Bennie laughed. "Georges, you be quiet! He's making me feel like Celebrity Lawyer. Don't stop him." It wasn't so much that she loved the flattery, but it was such a relief not to be sad for a minute. Small talk had many uses, and since her mother's death Bennie had decided that true grief was like windshield wipers; intermittent, and taking over in spurts, often when you thought you were almost past it. She turned to the young man. "Please go on, handsome. Tell me in detail about how great I am."

"Also your humor," Julien added, laughing. "I have been to two moot courts before that one, this is my third year at school, and I never laughed at one of them. Everybody said the same thing, after. You were funny! You took on that CEO, who was such a pompous ass."

"I was just jealous." Bennie liked attention, but this was ridiculous. "So tell me about yourself. I'm surprised you don't look so much like your father or uncle here. You must get your great looks from your mother's side."

"Perhaps," Julien said with a modest smile. "My mother was very lovely, in pictures. Unfortunately, I don't remember her.

She died of cancer when I was three. Robert is my stepfather."

"Oh, I see," Bennie said, suddenly uncomfortable, without knowing why. "So Robert raised you."

"Well, yes, as best he could, with a young baby and a company to grow. I think of him as my father. He sent me to boarding school here, to Milton, then to Harvard and Harvard Law."

"What a wonderful education." Bennie put it together. "And that's why you don't have a French accent."

"*Mais oui,* but I do," Julien said, lapsing uncannily into a Gallic inflection. "It works so well with the girls at school." Next to him, Georges laughed in his wheelchair, and Bennie smiled.

"Congratulations on your upcoming graduation, by the way. A joint-degree program in law *and* business, very impressive."

"Yes, I can run the world now!" Julien laughed. "You know, I was so happy when you agreed to represent my father. I knew you hadn't practiced much in the area of class actions, but I knew you'd be a wonderful lawyer for him. Did he mention to you that I asked for you?"

"He did, and thank you for that."

"My father really liked you," Julien said, his enthusiasm waning as he gave way to reality. "He called me after he met you, and yesterday, after court, he called and was so excited, he couldn't stop speaking in French. He said how right I was. He said you fought like a tiger for him, and for that I thank you." Julien actually bowed his curly head slightly, his expression darkening. His eyes creased with pain premature on such a boyish face, and he swallowed visibly. His neck was long and thin, but looked even longer in the black crew-neck sweater, with his Adam's apple traveling up and down. "You made my father very happy. He always sided with the underdog, and it sounds like yesterday, because of you, the underdogs won."

Bennie felt a twinge. "I am so sorry about what happened, and about his death. It's a terrible loss for you, and for Georges. For all of us."

"Thank you." Julien's voice was soft. "I appreciate your coming by today."

"I wouldn't not," Bennie said, meaning it. "I thought the world of your father, and it's been wonderful to meet Georges, and now you. I'm so sorry it had to be in these circumstances."

"Me, too." Julien glanced with concern at Georges, sitting with his head bowed in his wheelchair. He shifted over from the desk and put a hand on Georges's shoulder, then back to Bennie. "You're probably wondering what to do about the lawsuit now. The complaint against the trade association."

"Actually, I am," Bennie said, surprised. She had forgotten about it in Julien's adoration. Okay, she hadn't completely forgotten, but she really hated bringing it up, and now Julien had saved her the trouble. Still. "I hate to discuss business at a time like this, and if you wish we can talk about it later."

"No, now is fine." Julien straightened beside Georges's wheelchair. "I don't know if you know this, but I will be assuming control of the company now. I've decided to make this my first executive decision today, even before my graduation." His smile returned. "I want you to continue to represent St. Amien & Fils against the trade association. It's what my father wanted, and it's what I want as well."

Jeez. "My, thank you," Bennie said, her feelings bollixed up. It was too sad and too happy all at once. She didn't know what to do, what to feel, but Julien did. He reached for her with open arms.

"Welcome to the family, Bennie!" Tears brimmed in his eyes and he enveloped her in a warm hug. They held the embrace for a moment, sharing their loss, and when she stepped away Bennie had to wipe her eyes too.

"It's all right, Bennie," Georges broke in, hoarsely, from his wheelchair. He reached up for Bennie's hand and gave it a soft little shake. "It is what Robert wanted, and he would be happy to see his son make such a right decision."

"Thank you, thank you both." Bennie struggled to recover her composure. She couldn't think about her business yet. She felt too swept up by their affection. If it was Alice who killed Robert, or even Linette, she couldn't accept their generosity. She didn't deserve it. "I don't know if I—"

Julien jumped in. "Of course you can, and you must. I read the complaint, my dad FedExed it to me at school. You did a great job. He thought so, and so do I."

"But can you just make this decision, like that?"

"Why not?" Julien smiled shakily at her. "We're not publicly traded, there's no board of directors."

"Don't you have to consult anybody?"

"Perhaps I should." Julien leaned over and tapped Georges's shoulder. "Uncle, can I make this decision by myself?"

"Trot on, Julien!" Georges barked, and they both laughed heartily.

Bennie wiped her eyes. She didn't even know how she'd get Robert's money back. "Maybe you should think about it. Get over to the plant, talk to whoever you have to talk to."

"Whatever for? It isn't like that. I've worked for my father every summer since I've lived with him, and every holiday. I know how he does things, and he runs the show. Period." Julien cleared his throat, with a genuinely authoritative air. "Bennie, we'll stay in touch during the next month, until I graduate. I have only a few papers to hand in and then I'm finished. You fight the good fight, just like before. Call me when you would have called my dad, and don't forget, you promised to sign my reprints."

Bennie was shaking her head and even she didn't know why.

"Now, before we forget, do we owe you any money? I know it takes a war chest to fund litigation that large, and I don't expect Rosato & Associates to have to float St. Amien & Fils. Do you need money?"

"No," she blurted out. She knew it made no sense, but she wouldn't take a penny.

"You're sure?"

"Yes, thanks. I'll let you know when I do. We give a quarterly accounting." Bennie hoped he didn't hear her gulp. She picked up her bag to leave. "I'll send you a copy of the file so far, and maybe someday you can come around the office and meet my associates. One of them has pink hair."

"I used to have blue, did my dad tell you?"

"No. Did it match your eyes?"

"Hardly." Julien laughed, giving Bennie another brief hug, and this one left her with a thickness in her throat.

"Julien, I think you might just change the world as a CEO. You're direct, honest, smart, and funny. Funny is allowed when you're not publicly traded."

Julien laughed. "Here, let me walk you out."

Bennie turned, then leaned down and

gave Georges a quick kiss on his stiff, smoky beard. "Thank you so much, Georges, and please know my thoughts are with you."

"Thank you." Georges reached for her hand and gave it a squeeze. "You are too lovely a woman to be a lawyer."

"That's what I think," Bennie said, and bade him a last good-bye. Julien led the way, escorting her down the hallway with the same gentlemanly manners Robert would have had, walking her past the crowd in the living room and out the entrance to the elevator, where he pushed the button. Bennie turned. "Shouldn't I say good-bye to Micheline?"

"Oh, yes, good call." Julien's gaze found Micheline in the crowd, and Bennie caught her smile as Julien motioned to her. She excused herself from her guests and came over, wineglass in hand. Julien seemed to straighten as she approached and smiled at her. "Micheline, I was just walking Bennie out, and she wanted to say good-bye."

"How thoughtful of you, Julien," she said, almost purring, and went on tiptoe to give him a quick peck on the cheek. Bennie was struck by her attention to Julien, which was inappropriate for a family member, if not Jerry Springer material. She touched his cheek. "I'm glad to see you're feeling better. I hated to see you looking so sad."

"Thank you for having me," Bennie interrupted, and Micheline turned.

"You're very welcome." Micheline stiffened and extended a manicured hand, shaking Bennie's lightly.

"I'll take Bennie down to the lobby," Julien offered.

"Don't be too long," Micheline said, wagging a finger at him. "I have some people I'd like for you to meet."

"Sure, Micheline." The elevator came and they went inside, and as soon as the doors slid closed, Julien grew serious. "There is something I wanted you to know, privately."

"Sure." Bennie looked over. "What?"

"I meant what I said about your continuing our class action, and I will ensure that, even when I'm not CEO anymore."

"Anymore?" Bennie didn't get it. "You didn't even start the job yet. The lawsuit won't take *that* long."

"Confidentially, I'll only be running the business for more than a few weeks, just to smooth the transition." The elevator jostled slightly as it arrived on the lobby floor, but Julien hit the black button to keep the doors closed. "I didn't want you to think I'm going to be a CEO of a lens-manufacturing company for the rest of my life. I would never do that."

"No?" Bennie was flabbergasted.

"It's what my father wanted for me, but never what I wanted. I didn't want to go to B school either, he made me. I want to do what you do, I always have. Start my own law firm, prosecute police and official misconduct. I want to fight the good fight, like you do."

The child has no clue. "Julien, I'm flattered, but really, you have to think about this. *I* don't even want to do what I do. Look, I'm a class-action lawyer. Don't make any major decisions, especially now."

"I've been thinking about this decision for a long time. I know what I'm doing."

"Giving up a family business? It's been in St. Amien hands since your great-great-grandfather, right?"

"Since *Robert's* great-grandfather, not mine," Julien corrected matter-of-factly. "St. Amien & Fils will survive just fine without me anyway. There are vice presidents at the plant, like you said. An operations VP, a financial VP. One of them can run it, with oversight from the headquarters in France."

Bennie couldn't help feeling disappointed for Robert. "Did you discuss this with your father?"

"More than once. He disagreed with me, of course. He had his plan. I have mine, and now, I choose," he said defiantly, and Bennie could hear traces of resentment.

"You mean because he . . . died, you're going to do what you want?"

"Exactly." Julien looked at her, his eyes full of pain. "It does have to do with his death. Because I don't know if I would have had the guts to do this, really do this, if he had died a normal death and stepped aside for me. But that he died now, the way he died, it taught me something. It taught me that your life can be taken from you, just like that." Julien snapped his fingers, with a bitter smile. "So you'd better live life the way you want to. No matter what you've been taught to do, or whatever promises you made. No matter what you told your father. It's *your* life."

"Julien, listen, I have an idea." The elevator began to beep, but they both ignored it.

"Next week, come over to my office." *If I have an office.* "I'll show you what it's like, what we really do."

"I'd like that. I'd love that!"

"Have you ever worked in a down-and-dirty, thrilled-to-break-even law firm?"

Beep beep beep. "No."

"Have you ever worked in a law firm at all?"

Beep. Beep. "I wanted to, but my father said I was needed at the company."

"The defense rests." Bennie took Julien's hand off the button. The elevator finally stopped beeping and the doors slid open. "We'll talk about this later, maybe next week. You'll come to the office, you'll see us in action. Maybe the week after that, and I'll take you around to meet my cronies." Bennie got out of the elevator cab, with Julien right behind her. "They're true believers, who make very little money, do their own Xeroxing, and take themselves out to lunch in the park, with a veggie sandwich in a recyclable bag. It really isn't glamorous. It's hard, exhausting work, and long, long hours."

"Like a joint-degree program? I know how to work hard."

"*Not* like a joint-degree program, because that is school and this is real life. There's very little reward in it, Julien. Not even the potential of a reward. Sometimes your firm even goes bust and you lose your house." But Bennie didn't want to go there. "Just do me one favor. Don't send in your pink slip before you even get the dress, okay?"

"It won't work, Bennie. I'm out of there as soon as I graduate. I want to make my own way in this world. Be free, and do what my heart says."

Bennie wondered which Hallmark card that came from. They were in the lobby of the building, tricked out in a traditional Olde Philadelphia motif. A wafer-thin Kirman with a worn tasseled trim, a few dark wing chairs, and mahogany end tables bearing glowing lamps with oriental jelly jars. Well-dressed people were entering the lobby, and Bennie didn't want them or guards at the security dais to hear this conversation. And Julien, in his youth and emotion, didn't realize how loud his voice had gotten.

"Take a minute and come outside with me, okay?"

"Sure." Julien shoved his hands in the pockets of his Abercrombie jeans, and he and Bennie walked past the people, the desk, and onto the sunny sidewalk, which faced Rittenhouse Square. Traffic around the square was increasing; it was just before five o'clock rush.

Bennie glanced into Rittenhouse Square, verdant and lovely, a working city park encircled by a slightly pebbled pavement and people walking city dogs. But she wasn't sight-seeing today. Her gaze roamed the park until she found a very tall Sixers fan on one of the green benches to the left, his long legs crossed as he read a newspaper. Poor David. He'd have the sports page memorized by now. Bennie turned to Julien and tried to soften her tone. "Julien, let me ask you one question. Why did you tell me this, about your plans?"

"I didn't want you to think I was some type of corporate shill. I respect you. What you do, who you are."

"And I appreciate that." Bennie had sensed as much. He wanted her approval. "And I respect you too. What you do, and who you are. So could you do me just this one favor, based on our mutual admiration society?"

"Yes."

"Wait a year to make this decision. Accept my invitation about coming to the office and seeing my friends. If you still feel the same way in a year, and you decide to chuck it all and save the world, I'll think it will be the smartest thing you ever did."

"I don't know, Bennie." Julien pursed his lips. "A year?"

"I'll settle for nine months."

"How about three?"

Suddenly Bennie's cell phone rang in her purse, and she flipped open the leather flap and reached inside. She checked the bench to see if it was David calling, but he had lowered the paper and was watching her with interest. "Excuse me just one minute," she said, and Julien nodded. She flipped open the phone and turned away. "Hello."

"Boss." It was Carrier, excited as usual. "News update. I'm right, once again. It's all Linette, all the time. I talked to the coroner and he said that Robert's wounds were consistent with the knife from the Palm. He made a point of saying that it wasn't *the* knife necessarily, just that it was just one of the possible knives. His report isn't typed up yet, but you'll have to yell at him to get a copy. It's not public record, so we struck out."

"That's okay. Good work." Behind her back, Bennie heard the ringing of another cell phone. Julien's. Dueling Motorolas; it was truly a modern moment. Julien slid his cell from his back pocket and answered it, and Bennie put a finger in her free ear to hear Carrier better.

The associate was saying, "Also, Murphy drafted the papers for your restraining order, it's ready to go. But you have to appear in person and answer questions under oath."

"I figured. Wonder how soon I can get that done."

"Next week, she called the clerk. And she found out that Linette didn't sign back in at his office last night. She got a copy of the sign-in log and a marriage proposal."

Whoa. "Thanks. Call you later. See ya." Bennie flipped the phone closed, her thoughts racing. So Linette hadn't gone back to the office last night. She slipped the phone back into her purse and turned to Julien.

But he stood stunned, cell phone in hand, with his handsome features frozen into a shocked expression. He closed the phone numbly. "That was my uncle. The police just called."

"What happened?"

"They have a suspect in my father's murder," he said shakily.

And Bennie's mouth went dry.

28

Bennie pushed through the POLICE ONLY sign on the swinging half door that led to the cramped, cluttered squad room at the Homicide Division. The phones rang constantly and detectives conferred in small groups, clustered around messy desks of battleship gray, or searched file cabinets covered with Eagles bumper stickers, yellowed memos, and a stick-on decal of an Irish flag. The shirtsleeved detective manning the front desk was on the phone, and Bennie took advantage of the chaos to barrel past him.

"Stop! You can't go back there," he barked, covering the receiver, but Bennie caught sight of Detective Needleman coming out of interrogation room C.

"I'm a friend of Detective Needleman," she said, and met him as he was closing the dark blue door behind him. The suspect had to be in the interrogation room, handcuffed to a chair, just as she had been. "Long time, no see, Bob. I hear you got a suspect in St. Amien. He in there?"

"We didn't release that information yet." Needleman frowned. To his right stood a cabinet with skinny drawers labeled BODY CHARTS, SUBPOENA BLANKS, and INJURY FORMS. He was wearing his suit, and tie, and a grayish five o'clock shadow. "How'd you hear that?"

"I was with the family when you told them." Bennie put a hand on the knob of the interrogation room. "Can't I see him?"

"It's not a zoo."

"It's not?" Bennie sidestepped him, yanked on the knob, and stole a glimpse of the suspect before Detective Needleman closed the door.

"Hey!"

"Sorry," she said, but she'd gotten her mental picture. A young white man slumped in the chair, smoking a cigarette. Dressed in a T-shirt and jeans, with tall combat boots, and his hair had been shaved into a fade that hinted at a militaristic bent. "So who was that fine citizen?"

"Did you put the brother up to calling me?" Needleman pressed her away from the door, his eyes flinty behind his glasses. Two detectives bustled past, putting on their jackets with a backward glance.

"No, I didn't. He called on his own. I gave you good press, but I guess he had a few questions. He's upset."

"Whatever. You're not supposed to be here."

"Why not? I haven't interfered with the police all day. All I did was visit the family, which you knew I was going to do. You even said it was okay."

"Like it matters what I say."

"On the contrary, I crave your approval." Bennie smiled. She was trying to lighten the mood, and failing. "Of course, I had to come down when I heard. I wanted to see the suspect. Find out what you have on him. Who is he? What's the story?"

"What do you want to know?"

Bennie groaned. "Needleman, can you give me a break? I'm not the enemy, I'm just a lady who cares about this case. Is that so terrible? It's gonna be in the papers anyway."

"Okay, fine." Needleman pursed his lips. "The story is, his name is Ronald Johnson. Twenty-six years old. Unemployed. Record of three ag assaults in the nineties."

"What weapon did he use for the aggravated assaults?"

"Knife, all three times. A onetime member of a militia group, white supremacists, out in western PA. The FBI got a file on him. Fits the serial-killer profile to a T."

"Sounds like it." Bennie was trying to be supportive.

"We placed him under for the Chiamel murder. That's Claude Chiamel, the Belgian banker. He's suspected of the St. Amien murder, too, but we don't have enough for that yet. It's just a matter of time, which is what I told the brother. Georges." Needleman cocked his head. "How the hell you pronounce that anyway?"

"Just like Curious George. So Johnson is under arrest for the Chiamel murder, but not the St. Amien. He's only a suspect in St. Amien."

"Correct. *The* suspect."

"What's the evidence to support the murder charge in Chiamel?"

Needleman shook his head. "I'm not giving that up, Rosato."

"Don't be that way, Detective. I just taught you French."

"Sorry, I told you the same thing I tell the press. You're not the defense and you're not the family. End of story."

Bennie gritted her teeth. "I was with the victim's son, Julien, when you spoke with his brother. Julien wanted to come down here with me, but I told him to stay home. I didn't want to put the kid through it. You really want me to bring him? I could call him right now."

"You wouldn't."

"You're right, and maybe I don't need to. Does Mr. Johnson have a lawyer?"

"He's waiting on a public defender."

"What a coincidence! I'm a defense lawyer. Perhaps I should offer my professional services, twenty years' experience in murder cases. Then I'd be defense counsel, entitled to everything. Should I do that?"

Needleman scoffed. "You want to defend the knucklehead who killed your client?"

"I don't know that he killed my client. In

fact, I highly doubt it. He may have killed the Belgian, but I'm not buying into your tourist-killer theory yet."

Needleman leaned over. "You are *such* a pain in the ass."

"Come on, let's be friends." Bennie forced a smile. "So tell me what you have on Ronald Johnson to support the charge in Chiamel."

"Ample physical evidence."

"Is that all you're going to tell me?"

"That's it."

Bennie bit her tongue because she had officially quit cursing again. "Fibers, blood, prints? Is it bigger than a breadbox?"

"Ample physical evidence."

"Do you have ample physical evidence in St. Amien?"

"The tests aren't back. When the tests come back, I believe we'll have ample physical evidence against Johnson."

"If the results go the way you expect. But right now, you have no ample physical evidence linking Johnson to St. Amien."

"Technically."

"Technically matters. It's the difference between the right guy and the wrong guy."

"He's the doer, Rosato." Needleman's

mouth set in a firm little line that Bennie was beginning to think he should patent.

"When will the tests come back?"

"Some of them, day or so."

Bennie nodded. So that meant they had fibers and maybe a print or two. Stuff they could test here, in the Roundhouse. DNA, as in blood, had to be sent to Maryland for testing, which took weeks. "What's Mr. Johnson have to say?"

"Nothing. He's not talking until his lawyer gets here. But I'll tell you what you're gonna see on the TV news, only because one of the witnesses went live at five. Johnson bragged to a couple guys in a bar on Juniper that he was on a one-man campaign to 'clean up America.' Admitted out loud that he killed Chiamel, and St. Amien, too. Said he was gonna get himself an A-rab next. And he wasn't even drinking. Three witnesses heard it, and they're all willing to testify."

"So you got a tip."

"Yes."

Bennie considered it. "Did Johnson give you an alibi on Chiamel or St. Amien before he clammed up?"

"No, he wanted a lawyer from the jump."

Bennie was trying to keep an open mind. "You really think he's the doer in both murders?"

"Yes."

"The MO is the same?"

"Identical."

"Why don't you fill me in? Convince me." Bennie glanced around the room. "Come on, everybody's too busy to care if we actually get along. Maybe we can help each other. We both want the same thing. You tell me stuff, and I tell you stuff."

Needleman stepped closer. "Okay, I'll bite. Here's the MO. Victim is taken from behind, at the mouth of an alley. Same time of night, same type of vic. Older man, well dressed, foreign, speaks with an accent. Stabbed in the back with a common knife, dragged into an alley, turned over and knifed until subdued. Ten to twelve stab wounds, indicative of rage. Robbed and left for dead."

Poor Robert. Bennie was so glad she'd talked Julien out of coming. It was tough even for her to hear. Detectives were usually present at autopsies and heard the findings. Needleman was essentially telling her what was in the autopsy report.

"Also, Johnson lives a few blocks from both scenes, in Center City. Twice divorced. Lives with mom, she works at night. You know the profile, the skinhead type. Impulsive, angry, underachiever. Badly socialized, a loner. Can't hold a job or a marriage. Blames his problems on everybody else. A victim."

Bennie's eyes narrowed. "But this killer should be a planner, if your theory is true. He follows tourists around and systematically kills them. He's cleaning up America. It's part of a plan."

"Not that well organized a plan. Opportunistic."

"So he's a planner, but a bad one. Like me," Bennie said, and they both laughed. "Detective, I'm trying to believe, but it just isn't working, partly because the other possibilities make so much more sense to me. And if you would investigate them, maybe we'd find the aforementioned ample physical evidence. But you're not looking, and now you think you got your man." Bennie wanted so badly to persuade him. "What if Johnson didn't kill St. Amien, only Chiamel? They're similar victims, you're right, but they're still two different men. St. Amien was involved in a very contentious lawsuit, worth millions of dollars, and he was represented by a woman with a very nasty twin."

Needleman laughed again. "Okay, tell me what you know, Nancy."

"Brace yourself," Bennie began, and she filled the detective in on her history with Alice, telling him the details of the night at the river and the break-in at her house. Detective Needleman listened politely, which Bennie regarded as progress. "Well, whaddaya think?" she asked when she had finished.

"I'm trying to believe, but it just doesn't work for me," Detective Needleman answered, with a hint of sarcasm.

"Why not? We know my twin is trying to get me."

"Rosato, if your twin is out to get you, why wouldn't she just get *you?* Why kill your client?"

"She's toying with me, Detective. She's closing in. By killing someone I care about, who is important to my business, she hurts me. She's saying, I can take you anytime. Then she makes her move."

Needleman frowned with genuine concern. "If you think this, you should have security."

"I do. Thanks. And I'm getting a TRO against her, for what that's worth. Look, even if it's not Alice, there are suspects far more likely than some skinhead." Bennie launched into telling him about Bill Linette and his whereabouts last night, taking him through her interview with the waiter he had missed and about the steak knife and Mort Abrams. "Well?"

"I have to tell you, I listened to you, I really did, but I just think we got the bad guy, right in there." The detective nodded at the door behind him. "I been in this business too long, and I like this guy. I really like him." Bennie knew the term was detective-speak for he's a killer, but didn't remark on the irony. "He's the type of scumbag we're looking for. Not some broad who's got a grudge against her sister, or some fat-cat lawyer or his client. The two murders, back to back, it is too clear a pattern, especially in Center City, which never gets this kind of action." Detective Needleman nodded, more convinced as he went on. Bennie knew the syndrome. She did the same thing. "My hunches come out of thirty years' experience on the job. I wouldn't have told the brother unless I was sure. Johnson is the guy who killed both men."

"Why do you dismiss the others so easily?"

"I don't dismiss them, and I didn't. But right now I got the doer in Chiamel, and when the tests come back, we'll see what they tell us on St. Amien. If it doesn't pan out, it doesn't pan out." Needleman touched her shoulder, in a comforting way. "I know you care about your client, and I know you've been under a lot of strain. Why don't you just do your thing, and let us do ours, with Johnson."

"So you're not gonna buy it, are you," Bennie said. It was a statement of fact, not a question.

"Sorry."

"Me, too."

Needleman inclined his head. "You gonna lay off now?"

"Me?" Bennie didn't have to think twice. "Never."

Bennie hit the parking lot outside and threaded her way through the umpteenth gauntlet of reporters. They had the scent of a big story about to break and it had sent them circling and barking. They shouted questions in her ears. Shoved cameras in her face. Flew boom mikes on metal poles at her. She shot forward, pressing ahead, through the crazed reporters and out to the street. And to David. But he wasn't there.

Relax, you just don't see him.

Bennie hustled through the press. A cameraman jostled her, making her drop her briefcase. She bent to pick it up and was almost knocked over from the other side. Suddenly, it was a mob scene. Reporters surged toward her, screaming questions. Blocking her in. She couldn't go forward, she couldn't go back. She couldn't see the street over the cameras. She was trapped. Vulnerable. Unprotected. Was Alice in this crowd? Where was David?

"Get out of my way!" Bennie yelled, swinging her briefcase. The reporters kept shouting. The motor drives kept clicking, the videocameras filming. She had to get free, free of all of it. She had to save herself. She had to *go*.

She broke into a jog out of the parking lot, then accelerated to a run even in her pumps, ignoring the shock each time her foot hit the pavement. She didn't know where David was and she didn't care anymore. Her cell phone began ringing but she didn't answer it. She kept running, panting hard, her heart pumping like the athlete's heart it was, and she paid no mind to the stares of the people on the street or to the perspiration soaking her blouse and suit or to the pain in her lungs and ache in her knees. She took the pounding like the punishment she deserved, for getting Robert killed, and for causing so much pain to Julien and Georges. And part of her took the punishment for Alice, too.

For the crime of being the chosen one.

29

Bennie had thrown herself on her couch, head back against the hard wooden frame, legs splayed, trying to catch her breath. Listening to her heart thunder in her chest. Feeling the hardness of every muscle in her legs, pumped taut and engorged with blood, still racing. She had fumbled her way through the backdoor, dropped her briefcase on the floor, thrown her purse on the couch. She had run all the way home, from the east end of town to the west, well over an hour, and was only now coming back to herself.

Bear sat at her feet, swishing his tail against the floor, in sheer delight that he'd been freed from the basement, even if his mistress had lost her marbles. Bennie had no idea why she had run home. She had no idea what time it was. It was still light outside, but it was waning. Her cell phone rang and rang. She caught her breath, groped for her purse, shoved her sweaty hand inside it, and rummaged around. The cell felt smooth and familiar in her palm. She opened the phone. *Oh yes, I remember now. I'm a lawyer. I talk on the cell phone all day.*

"Bennie, are you there? Are you okay?" It was David, sounding as hysterical as a SEAL gets. "What's the matter?"

"I'm okay. I'm fine." Bennie brushed wet curls from her forehead. Her suit and shirt felt glued to her body. "I'm really fine."

"What happened? Why did you run like that?"

"I don't know."

"You weren't being chased."

"I know. I had to get away."

"Bennie, you have to answer when I call. I've been dialing and leaving messages since you got in. I was a minute from calling 911."

"Sorry." She tried to think, but her brain was too tired. The phone hadn't rung, or she hadn't heard it. "Did I blow it? Did Alice see you?"

"No. No. I let you run on, I knew where you were going. You are so *quick,* woman. You haul ass!"

Bennie smiled. "Thanks, I think."

"I don't think I was seen."

"Did you see her?"

"No."

"Have you seen her at all?"

"No, but she's there. Bet on it. This is when it matters, at night. If she makes any move on you, it'll be after dark."

"I don't know, David." Bennie raked her hair back again, wiping her cheeks. "I don't know if this makes sense."

"Why? What do you mean?"

"How long can we do this? Maybe she's not even there. Maybe this whole thing is crazy. I should just give up. I have so much to do."

"Bennie, listen to me." David seemed to bear down. "You listening?"

"No, I have calls to make. I should call the office. See if DiNunzio called in."

"Forget about work now."

"I should call Julien, the St. Amiens. I said I'd call if I had anything new to report."

"Forget it for now. It can wait until the morning."

"We got the case back again."

"That's nice, dear. Now, no more shop talk. Can you turn it off?"

"I should call Carrier and Murphy, and tell them to follow up on Linette. I should call Sam and tell him I'm back in business on the class action."

"Linette can wait. Sam can wait. Everything can wait. For now, just rest. Don't think. Breathe."

"I am."

"No phone calls. No work. No nothing. You need to get calm."

"I know."

"Nothing works if you fall apart, does it?"

"No."

" 'Ain't nobody happy when Mama ain't happy.' "

"Huh?"

"You never heard that?"

"No."

"The gist is, we have to take care of *you* now. You don't have any food in the house, do you?"

Bennie snorted. "What do you think?"

"Any booze?"

"Does Gatorade count?"

"Only original flavor. The blue sucks."

Bennie laughed. She was beginning to like this conversation. It was a working girl's version of phone sex.

"Get yourself something to drink. Water, at least."

Her mouth did feel parched. She couldn't remember the last time she'd eaten. She'd left the Palm doggie bag in the office refrigerator.

"Go now. Take the phone with you. I want to make sure you're okay."

"I'm fine," Bennie said, but when she got up, she felt dizzy. She sat back down. "Where are you anyway?"

"I'm out back. I checked your alley, your backdoor, and back windows. Everything looks fine. I like your new bars, in the back."

"Do you have your water yet?"

"Coming, Mother." Bennie rocked herself off the couch, one, two, three, and stood until the dizziness passed, then kicked off her shoes and padded into the kitchen. Her feet were wet, and between her toes her foot powder had turned to Spackle. "Here I go, into the kitchen." She left pasty Desenex footprints that Bear crouched to sniff, but she didn't tell David. Athlete's foot wasn't first-date conversation.

"What happened with the cops? And before that, at the St. Amiens? But first, drink."

So Bennie filled him in while she got herself a glass of water, took a gulp between sentences, then eased down her tile wall and sat on the floor to finish the story, cross-legged and talking on the phone like a kid in high school. It was a chummy feeling, trading sentences with David, answering his questions and hearing his views, there in the stillness of her cozy kitchen, with only Bear as a witness.

By the end of the conversation, her breathing had returned to normal and her clothes felt dry. She was feeling so good and calm inside. It had been such a long time since she'd had a man in her life that even one on a cell phone could give comfort. It had been a long time since she'd even been in the company of a man. Heard a deeper voice in her ear. Considered a different way of looking at the world. Had someone agree with her, and more important, disagree.

"David?" she blurted out, right when he was in the middle of a sentence.

"Yes?"

But she couldn't say more. She didn't

know what she wanted to say. Okay, maybe she did. She just didn't know how to say it.

"What?" he asked, waiting.

She let it pass. "Where are you now?"

"Watching your house. From the front now."

"What's going on out there?"

"It's dark out, and people are finishing dinner." David's voice sounded calm, steady, and unhurried. Unworried. If he'd been wondering what she was going to say, he wasn't wondering anymore. "An old man near you just put his trash out, only half a bag. He did a very neat job with his newspapers, all folded. Little girls who live on your side of the street are jumping on the bed, on the second floor, in the front room. There's a poster on their wall of Britney Spears. And your neighbor was washing her dishes by hand, in her kitchen in the back. Her window is open, over the sink. If you're in the kitchen, you should be able to hear her, if she's still at it. Is she?"

Bennie listened and heard it faintly. The clinking of silverware. A sweetly domestic sound she remembered from her childhood. Her mother had never had a dishwasher. Bennie leaned her head back against the base cabinet and closed her eyes. Missing her mother, and listening. She hadn't heard that small sound in years. She was never home at this hour. She missed the sound and savored it, both at the same time, holding the thickness in her throat, like a sliver of milk chocolate you knew would melt away too soon, making it all the more precious. She missed her mother so much; she was with her right now. It was a paradox Bennie had never understood until this minute.

"And your neighbor on the other side is practicing his guitar, in front of the window. He's pretty good. It's classical, but it's slow. Nice. Can you hear that, too?"

Bennie didn't know if she could; she just wanted him to go on. She kept her eyes closed, letting the wetness slip from beneath her lids. It would do her good, wash the city soot out of her eyes.

"People are walking their dogs. Somebody has a yellow lab out here, with a red bandanna. I hate dogs in clothes. God meant dogs to be naked. Hey, doesn't Bear have to go out?"

"Oh, Jeez. I forgot." Bennie wiped her eyes and sat straight up, guilted out of her reverie. Bear snoozed curled up against her foot. He hadn't even complained. The dog was a saint. "I can't believe I forgot about him."

"You had a lot on your mind."

"I have to take him out now."

"Okay, relax. I'll make sure you're okay. Take the phone with you."

Bennie scrambled to her feet. "You don't mind?"

"Not at all. This is why I make the big bucks."

"Wise ass." She padded back into the living room and slipped into her shoes. Bear followed, realizing what was going on, and began to dance at her feet, his nails clicking on the hardwood. She went to the back of the door where his leash hung on the knob and slid it off, along with the pooper scooper from the entrance hall. "Hold on, David," she said, putting the phone down while she leashed the excitable dog, since it couldn't be accomplished with one hand, then retrieved the phone. "I'm back."

"Okay, come on out."

"Roger wilco." Bennie grabbed her keys and left the house. The night was cool, dark, and quiet, and revived her slightly. Even if it hadn't, Bear would have, by tugging her instantly up the street to his favorite tree, where he squatted like a girl dog. "Cute, huh? I have no idea why he does this."

"He needs a father, obviously."

Bennie got a little tingle. *Definitely a flirty thing to say.* She scanned the street for David but didn't see him anywhere. "Where *are* you?"

"I see you."

"I don't see you."

"Damn, I'm good."

"Gimme a clue. You in disguise? Got the red horns on?"

"Are you two finished yet? Ole Bear seems to be doing a lot of sniffing."

"He's stalling. He owes me number two."

"Thanks for sharing."

Bennie walked Bear up to the next tree, looking around. No David and no Alice. Only two streetlights illuminated the street at either end, and both were far from her house. The street was bathed in darkness. She heard some shouting in the distance, then a bottle breaking. City noises. Still, it was a little creepy. No one was on the street.

"Don't worry, I'm here."

Bennie smiled in the darkness. "How did you know I was worried?"

"I just did." His voice remained soft and calm, coming out of nowhere. If God talked on the cell, it would sound like this.

"Wait, we have ignition." Bear did his business, and Bennie reached for her scooper, scooped his poop expertly, and dropped it in the sewer on the way to the house. "I think we're done."

"Head home now, keep walking. You're almost at your next-door neighbor's house, right?"

"Right."

"There's a trash bag there, a white Hefty kitchen bag, just like the kind you use. It looks like new. Do you see it?"

Bennie spotted the white trash bag, catching what little light there was in the dark. "I guess they put out their trash."

"No, you did. Walk past it."

"Okay," Bennie said, mystified. "How do you know what kind of kitchen bags I use?"

"The other night, remember? I noticed. Now go inside your house, get your trash, and come back out with Bear and switch bags."

"Why?"

"Because it's trash day. And that white bag has presents for you."

"Presents?"

"Make the switch quickly. Pretend you forgot something you had to throw out. Can you do that?"

"Watch." Bennie reached her front door, unlocked it, and went inside, locking the door. Then she went to the kitchen with her puzzled retriever, grabbed her white kitchen bag from under the sink, unlocked the door, and went outside with it to the trash bag. Bear was loving the new game, wagging his tail. "Impressed yet? Bear is."

"Very."

"Can I handle a trash bag or what?" She picked up the new trash bag and set the old one down in its place, then hurried back inside with Bear, who began jumping up on her as soon as she locked the door. Whatever was in there, he wanted it. "What's in this bag, David?"

"Open it."

Bennie set it down on the coffee table and opened the yellow tape, instantly releasing the truly gourmet smell of oregano and processed meats. She looked inside. Three wrapped hoagies leaked olive oil through their white paper, and they rested on top of loose red apples, huge Jaffa oranges, and a plastic bag of green grapes. There was even a sealed container of cole slaw and a jar of dill pickle chips. "Wow!"

"Dessert's on the bottom."

"Really?" She dug deeper to a cellophane pack of Oreos, a bag of Pepperidge Farm chocolate chips, a megasize Snickers bar, a half gallon of milk, and a few cans of Coke. It was Thanksgiving in a bag, and Bennie hadn't realized how hungry she was until she saw it. "This is amazing! Where did you get all this stuff?"

"The deli, when you were inside St. Amien's."

"When did you put it outside?"

"I didn't, I paid a little kid to do it. I'm taking no chances."

"This is great!" Bennie felt overwhelmed. It was such a thoughtful thing to do, and somehow so sexy. *What do women want? Someone else to go food shopping.* "Thank you so much."

"There's Milk-Bones for the boy, too. So. You got dinner, and you're safe inside. Don't answer the door, not for anything or anybody. If the doorbell rings, call 911 right away. Don't even worry if it's a false alarm, call them anyway. Then call me."

"Where will you be?"

"I'll stay here awhile, and when I'm sure it's okay, I'll go home. I want you to eat well, go to sleep, safe until the morning. Call me when you get up, and we'll start over."

Bennie swallowed. So that was *it?* Okay, of course that was it. Right? They hardly knew each other. What did she think was going to happen? "David, what's going to happen?"

"You're going to get through this. We're going to catch Alice. And it will all be over."

"And then?"

"I'll come over and you'll make me coffee. And I'll stay. If you want."

Bennie felt her toes curl. "I think I want. I mean, I definitely want."

"Hold that thought. And tell me good night."

"Good night, David," Bennie said, with more regret than she wanted to admit.

30

Bennie felt refreshed and energized when she got off the elevator on her floor. She'd slept like a baby, she'd eaten a provolone hoagie for breakfast, and she was a little in love with her surveillance, who had ensured her safety all the way into work.

She strode through the reception area in a crisp un-Bennie-like suit of pressed white linen. She'd slicked her blond hair into a neat French twist and she'd even smeared on pink lip gloss and brownish eyeliner. She carried her purse, her briefcase, and a box of Krispy Kremes. She was feeling excellent, especially for a murder target. In life, you have to take the bad with the good.

"What's up with *you,* girl?" Marshall asked with a smile, getting up slowly from behind the reception desk, in a bright yellow maternity dress. At her size, it looked roughly like the sun rising at dawn.

"Marshall, are you feeling okay?" she asked, vaguely alarmed. *I mean, you're a planet.*

"I'm fine. The doctor says everything is okay, and I should keep coming to work, that the activity is good for me and the baby. Here's your mail and a hand delivery from Sam." Marshall handed Bennie a huge stack of messages and mail. "Enough about me, let's talk about you. What are you so happy about? Are you wearing makeup?"

"It's my disguise. I'm back in control of my life, Marshall. Ain't nobody happy if Mama ain't happy."

"Huh?"

"You never heard that? I'm fighting back, and finally winning." Bennie skipped through the phone messages, reading them aloud. "Sam, Julien, reporter, reporter, CoreMed—whoever that is—and DiNunzio, good. What's new with DiNunzio?"

"She thinks she'll finish today, at the library in Washington. She's coming home a day early, on an afternoon train."

"Good." Bennie looked at the last message. "Mort Abrams," she said, and did a double take. "*Abrams?* That's *very* exciting. They're all very exciting. And it's time to celebrate." She touched Marshall on the shoulder. "Come into my office. We're having a little party."

"We are?"

"Yep." Bennie charged ahead, bearing her tray of hot glazed doughnuts, and she knew the smell would waft through the office and work its Krispy Kreme magic. "Carrier! Murphy! Breakfast in my office! I've been cooking all morning!"

"Huh? What?" Heads popped out of their offices, and the associates hurried after Bennie and Marshall. They all piled in, making hot coffee and passing around steamy doughnuts stuck to plates of legal pads. In no time, fresh coffee and hot pastry scented the room and they all gathered around the conference table with hot mugs and sugar highs.

Bennie raised her mug of coffee. "A toast to you, ladies. To your faith and hard work, and to DiNunzio, who will be home tonight! Our wonderful news is that Rosato & Associates is back in business! Julien St. Amien intends to continue the class action!"

"Yes!" Carrier said, setting down her coffee to throw her arms into the air, signaling a touchdown. She had on her favorite denim smock, with a hot pink T-shirt that matched her hair. "That's so great!"

"Yeah!" Murphy hollered beside her. She cut her usual curvy figure in a tan jersey that skimmed her skinny knees, and her hair swung long and free. She butter-churned her way across the room, shaking her cute tan butt. "Awesome!"

"Go, us!" Marshall clapped from her seat at the table, and Bennie raised a hand.

"Marshall, please don't explode," she said, and everyone laughed, applauding and boogying. When they finally settled down, Bennie filled in the details, including her trip to see the suspect at the Roundhouse and Julien's decision to become a solo practitioner. Somehow Julien was what they wanted to talk about first. "I'm having him over, so you can show him what you do and talk him out of wanting to do it."

"We can't do that," Carrier said, munching a doughnut. "We love it too much here. Every friggin' minute."

Murphy laughed. "Yeah. We can't get

enough, now that the long distance is back on."

Bennie smiled, despite herself, and Marshall said, "Can I go back to work, Bennie? Somebody has to."

"Sure, thanks. You gonna be okay to walk there? You need a hand?"

"More like a chairlift," Marshall mumbled as she waddled out of the office.

Bennie clapped her hands together. "Okay, moving right along, we do have other business to attend to this morning. The cops have a suspect in Robert's murder, which I think is totally bogus."

"I have a question," Murphy said, her lovely face turning grave. "What happened to you last night, Bennie? I saw you on TV, bitching out the reporters."

"I'm back on the sauce."

Murphy raised a perfectly groomed brow. "This could be the only explanation for your eyeliner."

"A for effort?"

"No. Anything more from Alice? I got you a hearing for next week."

"I'll take it. Meantime, no more break-ins, lots of new locks, and David surveilled the street last night and this morning."

"That working out okay with him?"

"Good as can be expected," Bennie answered. She suppressed: *He food-shopped for me and I think I'm in lust.* The kids didn't have to know everything about Mommy and Daddy.

"Boss," Carrier broke in, barely able to contain herself. "I did some research last night on Linette."

"You did?" Bennie asked, surprised. It was what she had been going to call the associate about before David stopped her. "What did you learn?"

"I found out he lives in a town house in Society Hill, on Delancey. I have the address in my office. It's one of those huge ones."

"Really." It would have been Bennie's first question last night. Perhaps the world *could* turn without her. "Good for you, Carrier."

"But wait, there's more. What we want to know is what Linette was doing the night of the murder, assuming he didn't hire anyone to kill Robert." Carrier barely took a breath before answering her own question. "Dinner ended before nine, according to Abrams, and at that hour there are two basic possibilities for most lawyers in America. Back to the office, or give it up and go home."

Bennie smiled.

"Now. We know that Linette didn't go back to the office, because of what Murphy learned from the sign-in log at his building. So let's give this jerk the benefit of the doubt and say that he *intended* to go back to the office, but changed his mind and went home instead." Carrier's voice took on a logical cadence. "Now, to get to his house from the Palm, it's about ten blocks. We know he didn't have a car, Abrams told us that. That means Linette could walk, go by bus, or take a cab."

Bennie nodded. "Door number three, the cab. He's too self-important to take a bus, much less walk."

"I thought so, too." Carrier held up a finger, her china blue eyes keeping a secret. "Now, we know that he didn't go back to the office. So we need to eliminate the possibility that he went home."

"How do we do that?"

"We do what I did. First question. What is the way that most lawyers, especially ones with major dough, get a cab at that hour?"

"They call a radio cab, Penn Call. We did it at Grun."

"Right, and we did it at Stalling and

Webb, too. It's easiest. They come right away. You charge it to the firm, you sign a receipt for the fare and the tip. It costs nothing and it's instant. So I made a basic assumption, that if Linette changed his mind about going to work, he would have taken a Penn Call cab home. You with me?"

"I don't know." Bennie was dubious. "It's not that hard to get a cab at a hotel like the Hyatt, where the Palm is."

"True, but Abrams would have seen Linette grab a cab there, especially because he had to wait for the valet to get his car. Abrams didn't say he had seen Linette do that. So it's logical to assume that if Linette got a cab, it wasn't at the Palm."

"Okay," Bennie said. The reasoning held up.

"So let's say Linette walks toward his office and then decides to go home. There are so few cabs in this city, it's not New York, and I think he'd save himself the hassle and do what the rich lawyers do. Phone Penn Call." Carrier paused. "So I called Penn Call, pretending to be Linette's secretary. I told them that he'd left his Montblanc pen in the cab last night, and asked if they knew which cab he took from the Palm to his house."

Bennie smiled. "Cute."

"They said if he had taken a cab, the driver would have turned in the receipt. But guess what? They had no record he took a trip from the Palm to his house, and they checked all the receipts. They even asked the drivers. And yes, Linette does have an account with Penn Call. He uses them exclusively. The dispatcher told me he even keeps them on speed dial, on his cell." Carrier couldn't hide her pride. "And by the way, they also told me they didn't take him anywhere else that night either. Linette was not in a Penn Call cab the night Robert was killed."

Hmm. Bennie was worried about something. "What if the cab company—"

"Calls and tells Linette?" Carrier held up her traffic hand. "Don't worry, I thought of that. I called back as the secretary, saying I'd made a mistake and please not to tell my boss I screwed up."

"Smooth."

Carrier grinned. "So let's review. What have we learned? That Bill Linette didn't go back to the office *or* to his house on the night St. Amien was murdered. So, where was he?"

"Interesting." Bennie mulled it over. "Of course, there *are* other places to go."

"We're talking about Philadelphia."

Murphy's lovely green eyes shifted to Carrier. "Judy, how many married men do you know?"

"My dad," Carrier answered, nonplussed, and Bennie smiled while Murphy followed up.

"Well, I know more than a few, because they hit on me all the time. I'm not bragging, I'm just giving you a field report. Nine times out of nine, if a man is hitting on me, he's married."

"You're kidding," Carrier said, so surprised she couldn't finish her second doughnut.

"If Linette didn't go home on a night he told a client he was going back to the office, I bet you he's got a chick somewhere." Murphy pushed aside her coffee. "And he's probably set her up in an apartment in town, within walking distance of his office, for his convenience."

"How do you know that?"

"It's the standard offer. Platinum AmEx, BMW convertible. It's minimum wage."

"Whoa," Carrier said, but Bennie was remembering her visit to Linette's plush offices.

"Linette has a receptionist who looks like Miss Texas."

"Now you're talking," Murphy said. "I'd start there." She turned to Carrier. "Sorry to shoot your theory, Jude."

"It's not shot, Murph. We just go digging."

"What do you mean?"

"We find some reason for you to go over to Linette's office and see if he hits on you."

Murphy sniffed. "Of course he'll hit on me. I'm practically undefeated."

"Are you two nuts?" Bennie interrupted.

"What?" they both asked, in unison. The phone started ringing but everybody ignored it.

"Have Linette *hit on you,* Murphy?" Bennie couldn't believe the words coming out of her own mouth. "It's crazy, dangerous, and *revolting!* And it wouldn't prove anything!"

"It could," Murphy answered.

"Like what?"

"We don't know yet. We'd be investigating." Murphy looked as if she were actually considering it, sipping her coffee and narrowing her eyes. "We have to find out what Linette's up to, then confront him."

Carrier joined in. "Or turn him in. Or catch him in a lie. It's not the whole picture yet, boss. It's just a piece. That's how we always do it. Piece by piece, like a puzzle."

"*What?* No we don't. It's *not* a puzzle!" Bennie wanted to tear out her moussed hair. The only problem with Mama was the kids. "I do *not* send my associates to *seduce killers!*"

"I bet we could crack this case, Bennie," Murphy added.

"Absolutely not!" Bennie's good mood vanished. She reached for her coffee but it was cold. The intercom started buzzing on her phone, and she picked up. "Yes, Marshall?"

"Got Sam on line one. He says it's really important."

"Okay, thanks. Ask him to hold while I kill my associates." Bennie pressed off the intercom and turned to the offenders. "Girls, leave my office and get back to work. Do legal work, since we're back on the class action. Leave Linette alone. And leave me alone."

"Okay." Carrier got up, obviously disappointed, and Murphy went after her, taking her coffee.

"Making a big mistake, Bennie."

"Right. See ya. Bye." Bennie hit the flashing light on her phone. "Sam, before you tell me anything, let me tell you something. I'm back in business. St. Amien's son wants to continue the case."

"Wonderful, but I'm not calling about money. I'm calling about your friend David. Did you get my envelope? I had it hand delivered."

"Uh, wait." Bennie fished through the mail that Marshall had given her, then gave up. "What's it say?"

"Read it. I would have faxed it to you, but the photo came out too black."

"Hang on a minute." Bennie reached for the manila envelope with the red hand-delivery stamp from Grun, and slipped her hand inside. "Gimme the sneak preview."

"Your bodyguard David has a past you should know about."

"What?" Bennie pulled out the piece of paper from the envelope. It was a photocopied clipping from a local newspaper in California. The headline read, SEAL INSTRUCTOR CHARGED IN CADET'S DEATH, and next to it was a small head shot of David, mostly obscured by the darkness of the fax. She could recognize his eyes and mouth, pixilated, in inky black-and-white dots.

Oh my God. Bennie's heart stopped as she read the brief paragraph:

David R. Holland was indicted today in the death of Cadet John Wellington, 23, of Encino, who died Monday morning, during training of the Navy SEALs. Cadet Wellington succumbed to a heart attack during one of the exercises supervised by Instructor Holland, comprising so-called "Hell Week." Instructor Holland, who served as Assistant Director of the training facility, was suspended pending a military hearing on the charges. The hearing is set for March 3.

"Bennie, you there? He didn't tell you that, did he?" Sam asked, his tone softer.

"No." Bennie sighed.

"I told you, people don't just take a break from the SEALs."

"I guess not." Bennie reread the article. The date on the newspaper was this year. "It says his hearing is March third. That was last month. Do you know what happened?"

"No, I don't."

"Maybe he was found innocent, or whatever they do in military trials."

"Maybe he was, but maybe he wasn't. And maybe there's been a continuance and we don't know yet. It doesn't matter. It's a material fact, and he omitted it."

Bennie couldn't deny it. "How did you find the article? Were there others?"

"I had a kid here do a Lexis search and order the original from the paper's online archives. I knew you had to see it to believe it. This is all she came up with, and the kid's a whip."

Bennie's gaze rested on the photo, a head shot of David in a stiff white cap. Under the photo the caption read, CAPT. DAVID HOLLAND.

"Bennie, I gotta go. I'm sorry to leave you with this. If you want to call me, call anytime. But I think this is clear. I don't trust this guy and I don't think you should let him protect you. You don't need him. I already called a personal-security firm and told them to send me the bill. The name's

Guardian something, and they're gonna call you. Talk to you later, honey."

"Bye," she said, and hung up the phone. Looking at the picture until the intercom started buzzing again.

31

"Bennie, Mort Abrams here."

"Yo, Mort, how you doin'?" Bennie couldn't stop looking at the photo of David. It was just too surprising. She never would have thought he could be involved in anything like this. The death of a twenty-three-year-old.

"Bennie, you there?"

Get over it. "Mort, yes. Sorry, it's hectic here today."

"I gather. The cops caught that animal who killed Robert, I hear. And that banker, too. I bet you're happy."

"Yes, right." Bennie folded the article and slipped it under her mail. She couldn't concentrate with the headline staring at her. "How can I help you, Mort?"

"Well, I'm calling with good news. I've decided to go with your firm, for representation in the class action."

Really? "Really! How wonderful. That's great news. Thank you so much for your confidence in us." Bennie struggled to keep the surprise from her voice, but she was more puzzled than anything else. She had never done *less* to get a client. Maybe she should have been doing less all along, like reverse psychology. Trash your clients, so they come running. You'll get clients with intimacy issues, but business is business.

"I look forward to our working together, Bennie. Now, when can you come out to our facility to meet the rest of my team and see the place? We'll give you the grand tour of FitCo. Our lunchroom is great too."

"Uh, well." Bennie couldn't begin to deal with it. "Here's what I'd suggest, if it's okay with you. Send me any paper and documents that arguably pertain to the suit. All the stuff on your English sub, and the contract you lost."

"Key Medical, Inc."

"Of course. I'll review the file as soon as I get it, then come out and meet with you and the gang. This way I won't waste your time, or your staff's, asking questions I can answer myself."

"Okay, good deal." Abrams sounded cheered. "And payment, how do we work that?"

"I'll send you a fee agreement for your signature. I work on standard contingency, but a small retainer could get us rolling. Say five thousand dollars?"

"That's doable. Send me the agreement, I'll sign it and send it back with a check."

"Great, Mort. Appreciate it." Bennie couldn't believe this. Two days ago she would have been deliriously happy at the cash. Now she could barely get her act together.

"I'll get you those papers right away."

"Looking forward to it." They said corporate good-byes, and Bennie exhaled audibly the moment she hung up the phone. She should have been happy, but it was impossible.

David. She had trusted him, but he hadn't told her everything. Still. He had watched over her. Taken care of her. Seen to it that she had food and rest. And he'd given her good advice last night. He couldn't have been in cahoots with Alice on anything.

Thanks to him, she'd felt great when she'd gotten up today, and great when she'd come in. Her gaze fell on the edge of the article, sticking stubbornly from her mail, and she knew just what to do with it. Tuck it back inside. So she did.

It left her facing a flock of pink message slips, with CoreMed's on top. She hadn't focused on it before, at the reception desk. She slid out the message, and there were others stuck to it that she hadn't seen. Total Lenz of Korea. Reiss, Inc. Tumflex. She didn't know any of these names, but they sure sounded like lens manufacturers. They had to be potential class members. They didn't sound like debt consolidators.

Bennie arranged the phone messages on her desk, with Julien St. Amien's on top. He was her biggest and best client ever, and if the others were new business too, she had better stop whining and pay attention. Work had always focused her. Seen her through, even when all else failed. She'd rested last night, but that was then. And this was now. It was time to get on the horn. She picked up the receiver and punched in the number.

"Julien?" she asked when a man's voice

picked up, then the accent registered. "Georges?"

"Yes, this is Bennie? How are you, Bennie?"

"Fine, thanks." A tide of guilt washed over her. "I'm so sorry I didn't call you last night after I went to the police. I spoke with Detective Needleman and saw the suspect in Robert's murder."

"His name is Ronald Johnson, eh? Detective Needleman says he's a Nazi type, a skinhead. He belongs to a group. So there *are* these people, after all, in America."

"Yes, there are," Bennie said. It felt like a shameful admission, even though Johnson wasn't the killer. For a civil libertarian, there were times even she hated the First Amendment.

"So I see I am wrong, and I am glad they have him. I hope today or tomorrow they will charge him."

"Me, too." Bennie wanted to shift the subject because she was such a lousy liar. "Julien called, and it may be important. May I speak with him?"

"He isn't in. He went out with Micheline."

Bennie's ears pricked up. "He seems very friendly with Micheline."

"They get along very well, yes. It's good that they spend time together, for Julien lost his mother when he was quite young."

And Micheline is so motherly. "What, did she take him out to lunch?"

"Perhaps, I don't know. I got my cast off this morning, and when I came back, they had left a note." Georges paused. "Bennie, I am worried a little bit about Julien. He has been behaving so strangely."

"With Robert's death, he would be."

"No, not sad. Secretive. What was it he talked to you about yesterday? Micheline told me she saw you two talking outside in the square."

Oh, that. Bennie bit her tongue. She had said she'd keep it confidential, so she told a white lie: "Just a few things about the company. It's probably what he's calling me about."

"Really? You sure that was it?" The doubt in his voice suggested he had a good *merde* detector. "Micheline said it looked as if Julien was upset, and she knows the boy quite well."

"Yes, that's all it was. Business. Please tell him I called." Bennie said a quick good-bye and hung up before Georges asked another hard question. She sifted through the messages for the next business call, then punched in the number for CoreMed, Inc. "Is Mr. Gupta in, please?" she asked, introduced herself, and was put through.

"Gupta here," said a voice with a thick Indian accent. "Ms. Rosato, thank you for calling back. It is a pleasure indeed to speak with you. I am a lens manufacturer for medical equipment, based in New Delhi, and I was a friend of Robert St. Amien's."

"It's wonderful to speak with you, then."

"I see on the news they have his murderer. It is a terrible crime. A terrible shame."

"Yes, it is."

"Well, to the point. I had the opportunity to see you in court the other day, I was watching your performance, and I admired very much the way you dealt with the situation, and also your liveliness."

Bennie smiled. "I am lively."

"I call Julien to send my respects to him and his family, and he is telling me that you will continue as their counsel. Is this true? He is quite happy about this, he tells me on the telephone."

"Yes, it is true, and I am happy to do so too."

"Then perhaps I wonder if you would consider serving CoreMed as counsel and representing my company in the class action?"

"Yes, of course," Bennie said, amazed. It was like picking low fruit off a tree, this plum thanks to Julien. And even while she was saying yes, another call was coming in, which Marshall picked up. "I'd be honored to do so."

"Excellent. This makes me very happy. When shall we meet to discuss our claim?"

"Let me check next week." Bennie got out her desk calendar and flipped the pages to the next week. Empty, empty, empty, empty. "Friday looks good to me," she said, for effect.

"Two o'clock on Friday?"

"Done. Why don't you send me all the documents that are arguably relevant to the case and I'll read them before we meet."

"An excellent idea. I value such efficiency. Now, what about the payment terms?" Mr. Gupta asked, and she filled him in. She'd send the fee agreement, he'd send the retainer check. Bennie could almost hear the *ca-ching ca-ching*. She was on her way to solvency. Paying back the money she owed. Getting her house out of hock.

She picked up the next message before the phone rang again and punched in the number for Tumflex, Inc. When the call connected, she asked, "Is Mr. Riagrelli in? This is Bennie Rosato, returning his call."

She spoke with Mr. Riagrelli, who wanted to retain her, then Mr. Grsucjki of Reiss, Inc., Ms. Lutenka of SeeMore, and after that Ms. Hurye, Horst Balshamn, Dreyer Ertmann, and Seji Yamamoto. It was a veritable United Nations of well-paying clients, and they didn't care that she had taken only high school Latin. They all wanted to speak with her, meet her, or retain her right away, based on either Robert's reputation, Julien's recommendation, or what they'd seen of her in court. Of this latter group, they liked her spunk, feistiness, courage, balls, toughness, softness, cleverness, honesty, and oh, yes, muscular legs. Go figure.

Bennie took all comers and worked through lunch, and all the time she was talking, the other phones were ringing. When Marshall brought her a tuna sandwich, which she inhaled, she also had ten more phone messages. By the time Bennie was finished returning all of the calls, she had a list of twelve new clients, nineteen possible clients, and accounts receivable of over fifty thousand dollars, to be paid within the week. It was almost too good to believe. Not only was Bennie back in business, she was back with a vengeance. And if this kept up, there would be no contest at all about who would be lead counsel.

She picked up the last message, from Linette. He had to know what was going on. If he couldn't feel the almost seismic shift of power, they all had to be buzzing about it. He had called twice while she was on the phone, but she wasn't returning his call yet. Let him sweat. He'd want to know her response to his offer, but she'd known the answer even when she was broke. Yesterday. And Bennie still couldn't believe he was Robert's killer, or had him killed. Not with Alice out there somewhere.

She checked her watch. Three o'clock. Sooner or later she'd have to call David. *What am I going to say?*

"Incoming," Marshall said, walking in with another batch of messages. "What *is* going on, Bennie?"

"It's like dominoes. When one fell, they all did." Bennie threw up her hands, astounded. "I think we got our law firm back, and you got enough maternity benefits for triplets."

"Well, congratulations to both of us." Marshall smiled, with relief she let Bennie see for the first time.

"You were worried. I don't blame you. I'm just happy you don't have to worry anymore, and I'm going to miss you." Bennie ignored the silly lump in her throat. "When this baby comes, do whatever you want. Stay home if you want to. I'll pay you for six months, full benefits and all. You have to be free to do what your heart says."

Marshall looked at her as if she were nuts.

"I read it somewhere."

"You're assuming this baby is ever coming out."

"It's gotta come out, Marshall. How's it gonna go to law school?"

"Ha!" Marshall said. She set down the messages and wandered out, her hand on her lower back, and Bennie winced just from looking at her.

"I keep telling you, I'll come to the desk and get the messages."

"Walking is good for me!" Marshall called back as Bennie picked up the first message from her desk. Mr. Cho, of Cho & Co. He could be her new favorite client. She suppressed a smile and punched in the number.

Bennie was bleary-eyed by four o'clock, when there was a very loud knock on her door. In the threshold stood Murphy and Carrier, looking very pleased with themselves. Bennie set down the telephone receiver. "I hope you're here to tell me you've been working like dogs. Because we got so much work it's not even funny."

"We heard. But we've been doing something I think you'd approve of, very much," Murphy said.

"Very much." Carrier nodded. "We totally stayed away from Linette because he could be dangerous and a killer and repulsive, like you said."

Bennie eyed them. "So where have you been?"

"Lunch," Murphy answered. "A really long, really late lunch. But not with Linette. We had a better idea."

"What did you do and why didn't you ask me first?"

"I went to lunch with Ross, an associate from Linette's office, and I didn't clear it with you because there was no risk or weirdness."

"Also you would have said no," Carrier added, and Bennie felt a tension she couldn't explain.

"Carrier, where were you while she was having lunch with this Ross?"

"We worked as a team, and I was backup. I sat at the next table, incognito, in case she got into any trouble."

"As I was saying, Ross Pacine is an associate who works for Linette." Murphy eased into a chair opposite Bennie, and Carrier into the chair next to her. "I went over to Linette's to drop off some papers—"

"What papers?"

"An extra copy of our complaint, which I know is bogus, but it gave Ross the chance to ask me out. Which he did. So I said how about a late lunch instead, and he said sure. And we went to lunch and he had a few Amstels and he dished." Murphy licked her glossy lips. "Linette is having an affair with the new receptionist, the one you call Miss Texas. He bought her a love shack at the Water's Edge, down on Front Street. Near his house."

"Ross knows this for sure?" Bennie asked.

"Everybody in the office knows it for sure. But Linette didn't go see Miss Texas on Tuesday, the night Robert was killed."

"You asked him that? Murphy, this could be dangerous."

"Of course I didn't ask, but I know just the same. Because Miss Texas had a breast job on Tuesday morning, paid for by Linette. I'm guessing she wasn't in the mood for love that night." Murphy folded her arms. "So where *was* Linette on the night of the murder? He wasn't anywhere he was supposed to be, and he wasn't even where he *wasn't* supposed to be."

"I thought he could have another mistress," Carrier interjected.

"Ross said he doesn't, Miss Texas would kill him." Murphy raised an auburn eyebrow. "We think it's time for you to talk to Linette. Ask him what he did Tuesday night, in some casual way, and see if he lies to you. Then Murphy and I can follow up."

"Follow up?" Bennie repeated. "You two?"

Carrier was nodding eagerly. "And you know what else we found out? Ross says that Linette has a big goon who hangs around him from the old days, when he did criminal defense. This guy supposedly does all sorts of sleazy jobs for Linette, and I was thinking maybe Linette hired him to kill Robert. His name is Luke Deal."

Oh, no. Bennie's mouth went dry. "Luke Deal was tried for a brutal double murder ten years ago, in Bridesburg. The case made all the papers. Linette was his lawyer, and he got him off on a technicality, by suppressing his confession."

Carrier's face lit up. "That's incredible! Maybe Deal's the one! We should definitely follow this up. I'll research Deal online and find out where he lives."

Murphy bubbled with excitement. "What if Linette was with Deal the night Robert was killed? They could have been in it together! I'll call Ross and see if he wants to meet me for dinner, and afterward I'll make up some excuse to stop by Linette's office. I wonder if there's a way I can slip away from him and sneak into the financial records and see if there are any suspicious payoffs and then—"

"*Are you two nuts?*" Bennie shouted, suddenly furious, and the associates looked at her in surprise. "Why do you think you can go running around after murderers!"

"What are you so mad about, boss?" Carrier asked, confused. "You do it all the time."

Murphy frowned. "And why do you have to get so freaked out? We know what we're doing!"

"I can take risks like that, but you can't!" Bennie shot back. Then she heard herself shouting. She *was* so freaked out. She couldn't let them get hurt solving this case. It made her realize something. She loved them. *Loved* them. The thought silenced her, at least for the moment. And the two girls, oblivious, kept chattering away.

"It only got dangerous when Ross made his move," Carrier was saying with a smile. "He tried to grab Murphy's knee under the table. Then I stepped in and saved the day, like Batgirl."

Murphy looked askance. "*You* saved the day? Please. I handled him."

"Oh, don't even start with me! *I* was the one who dropped my fork and stabbed him in the ankle, accidentally on purpose. That's why he yelped!"

"That's not why! He yelped because I

kicked him in the shin. It was nothing my Manolo couldn't fix." Murphy wiggled her overpriced designer pump, and Carrier laughed.

"No way! You needed me!"

"Who needs Batgirl when she has Blahnik?"

"Oh, blah blah Blahnik. You did!"

"Did not!"

"Did too!" Carrier gave her a playful shove, and Murphy shoved her back, less convincingly.

"Bennie, she hit me!"

Bennie let them bicker—her thoughts were going elsewhere. Her smile faded, and a chill came suddenly over her. Because she had realized something else:

She knew who had killed Robert St. Amien.

32

But there was a commotion outside her office, and Bennie and the associates jumped up and went for the door. The associates got there first and collided with a whirlwind of worsted wool, wrapped around a hysterical Vita DiNunzio. She was rushing headlong into Bennie's office, her short little legs churning in their support hose and black orthopedic shoes, so quickly that Carrier and Murphy reflexively held her back, one on each arm, in her bunchy winter coat.

"You! *You! Benedetta Rosato!*" Mrs. DiNunzio was shouting, pointing her arthritic finger at Bennie. Her magnified eyes flared behind her thick glasses, and the wrinkled skin on her face was a streaky red. Only her hair remained unemotional, a perfect swirl of pinkish cotton candy. "My Maria! My Maria! My Maria, she'sa *hurt!*"

"Mrs. DiNunzio, hello, and what are you talking about?" Despite her confusion, Bennie extended her hand, but Mrs. DiNunzio took a taloned swipe at it. How had the woman gotten through Marshall? What the hell was going on? "Mrs. DiNunzio, Mary's on a business trip. She's in Washington. I'm sure she told you, she's coming home on the train today."

"Washington! *Washington!* Maria is onna train! Onna train onna *TV!*"

"What?" Bennie asked, bewildered, and Carrier jumped between them.

"Turn on the TV, Bennie," she shouted over the din. "There must be something about Mary on TV."

"Maria! Maria!" Mrs. DiNunzio kept shouting, waving her little fists and struggling to get out of the associates' grasp. "Devil! *Witch!*"

Mary. Bennie hurried to the small Sony on her credenza and turned it on. She had wanted to tell the associates about Robert's killer, but that would have to wait. The TV came on and the screen was showing news of a huge train derailment, with car after car crumpled hideously, lying sideways like a grotesque Jacob's ladder beside a railroad track. Bennie gasped. "Oh, no. Not Mary."

"It's *not* Mary, it can't be!" Murphy said, restraining Mrs. DiNunzio as she pointed to the bottom of the screen. The banner underneath the picture read, Outside Seattle, Washington. Murphy turned to the raving Mrs. DiNunzio. "The train crash isn't in Washington, D.C. It's in Washington State! Mrs. DiNunzio, you understand what I'm saying? This isn't the same Washington! Mary is fine!"

"Maria! Maria!" Mrs. DiNunzio kept yelling at Bennie. "You no care about my Maria! You only love money! *Money!*"

Bennie tried to figure out what had happened. Mrs. DiNunzio had heard the word "Washington" on TV, had seen the wrecked train, and had made the wrong connection. There were no fatalities in the Washington State train wreck anyway. Evidently Mr. DiNunzio hadn't been around to talk sense to her, and she wouldn't listen to anybody else. Or even leave her kitchen, except to come here and try to kill Bennie.

"Mrs. D., Mrs. D.!" Carrier was shouting, holding her other arm. "Mary is fine! That's not where she is! Mary wasn't on that train! You can call her cell phone right now! She'll answer!"

"She no answer! I call, I call! She no answer! She'sa inna *Washington!*" Mrs. DiNunzio ranted as Bennie went to her desk for her cell, opened it, and punched in the number for Washington information. She waited for the call to connect to the National Archives and pressed her way through three levels of automated operations until she finally got through to a librarian in the Research Room.

"Could you page her please?" Bennie said into the phone. "She must have her cell turned off in the library. It's an emergency."

"*Devil!* Witch! You no care about Mary! You no care about nobody but *yourself!*"

In a minute, Mary's cute little voice came on the line, and Bennie handed the cell phone to her mother, who stopped struggling long enough to put the phone to her gold earring hanging from a stretched-out earlobe, and in the next second, she erupted in joy and relief.

"Maria! Maria!" Mrs. DiNunzio shouted, with a hiccupy sob that would break even a lawyer's heart. "*Grazie, Dio! Grazie mille!*

Maria! Maria!" Tears sprang to her eyes and she lapsed into rapid and deliriously happy Italian, while Carrier and Murphy relaxed their grip. "Maria! Maria! Hokay, hokay, Maria! Bye-bye, Maria! *Ti amo*, Maria! *Ti amo!*" Mrs. DiNunzio closed the phone and returned it to Bennie with new, wet, and completely adoring eyes.

"All better, Mrs. D.?" Bennie asked, and Mrs. DiNunzio rushed forward and flew into Bennie's arms.

"Benedetta, you *save* my Maria! You *save* her life!" The older woman felt soft and warm as a plump hen, and Bennie held her close. "You are angel! Angel, from *God! Grazie mille! Grazie mille!* Thank you *so much,* Benedetta!"

Bennie looked amazedly at the associates, who looked equally surprised. Then she got an idea. There was only one way to make peace with Mrs. DiNunzio, now and forever. "You're very welcome, Mrs. DiNunzio," she said warmly, accepting any and all credit.

Suddenly a terrifying scream came from outside the office, shattering the moment. "Help, Bennie! Help!" The shriek electrified Bennie, who released a shocked Mrs. Di-

Nunzio and bolted for the door, with the associates right behind her.

Waiting for them in the hallway was a horrifying sight.

33

"Bennie, help!" Marshall screamed. She was on the floor, doubled over and clutching her pregnant belly. Her pretty features contorted in agony. Tears poured from her eyes. Her skin blanched white as bone. Her forehead shone with perspiration.

"Marshall!" Bennie ran frantically to her side and knelt on the rug beside her. She wouldn't let anything happen to Marshall or her baby. She couldn't. "It's okay, Marshall, we're here."

"My God it hurts! It hurts so much!" Marshall was gritting her teeth not to scream anymore. "The baby! I was in the bathroom! Something's wrong!"

"Carrier, call 911!" Bennie shouted, but

Judy had already flipped open her cell phone.

"I'm on it," Judy called back as Murphy sprinted for the telephone on the reception desk.

"I'll call security!"

"Then call Marshall's husband. The number's on the reception desk, with the emergency numbers." Bennie squeezed Marshall's hand to steady her as she grimaced with pain. She was having contractions so severe it made her draw up her knees. Then Bennie saw it. Fresh red blood was flowing down the inside of Marshall's leg. *Jesus, God. What the hell is wrong?* "Help is on the way, Marshall. We're calling 911 right now."

"Okay, okay, Marsh," Mrs. DiNunzio whispered, easing down onto Marshall's other side and patting her hand with an Old World authority. If the older woman noticed the blood, she didn't show it, and her features stayed calm and steady. A gold crucifix and tiny gold horn hung on a gold chain that dipped as she bent over. "It's gonna be okay. Everything gonna be okay."

Carrier was repeating their office address into her cell phone. "Please come quick! She was due in two weeks! No, it's not a normal birth! She's in pain! She's screaming! And there's blood, lots of blood."

Jesus. Please. Bennie looked down. Marshall was hemorrhaging freely now, thrashing back and forth in agony. Blood coursed down both legs, staining her dress. Her blood pressure had to be dropping. She could go into shock. "We need to put her feet up! We need something for under her feet!"

"Marsh, it'sa okay, all okay." Mrs. DiNunzio released Marshall's hand, took off her brown wool car coat, and kneaded it into a bunchy ball, then tucked it under Marshall's feet. "Your baby gonna be fine, Marsh, you see."

Thank God. Bennie couldn't let Marshall die. She couldn't let her baby die. They needed an extra hand. *David.* He'd be good in an emergency. She lunged for her cell phone, dropped forgotten on the rug, then flipped the phone open, hit the speed dial, and David picked up.

"David, come now! It's Marshall! We need help!" Bennie shouted just as Murphy and a young security guard burst into the office with a white plastic first-aid kit bearing a red cross.

"Holy shit!" the employee said at the sight of the bloodstain spreading on Marshall's dress.

"Carrier, I wanna talk to 911!" Bennie hollered, closing her cell phone and taking Judy's when she rushed it to her. "Help me, would you?" she yelled into the phone. "Tell me what to do, for God's sake! We put her feet up already. There has to be something we can do. This woman is *not* going to die in my arms!"

"Whom am I speaking with, please? Ms. Carrier?" the dispatcher asked, with so much attitude that Bennie wanted to strangle her.

"You're speaking to *me* now!" Bennie shouted, and she handed the phone back to Carrier when David bounded into the room, with two uniformed paramedics hustling in with a stainless-steel stretcher and a large black duffel bag.

"Found these guys outside," David said quickly, going to Bennie's side. His expression only momentarily betrayed the shock he had to be feeling at the sight of Marshall. Mrs. DiNunzio rose and edged away, praying to herself. The paramedics took over, sprinting to Marshall, unpacking their duffel, and moving expertly around her.

"Miss, we're here and we're gonna take care of you," one paramedic soothed. "What's your name?" he asked, and when Marshall managed to cry out her name, the paramedic didn't bother trying to make further conversation. He located a vein in the crook of her arm and put in an IV shunt while the other paramedic pulled a plastic oxygen mask from the duffel and tore off the sterile plastic encasing it, then threaded it to the tank.

"Please lie still, miss," the second one said, his tone controlled as he positioned the plastic oxygen mask over Marshall's nose and slipped green elastic straps behind her head. Then he shifted over to unfold the stretcher and unbuckle bright orange restraints. "We're going right to the hospital with you. No stops for pizza, so don't even ask."

"Which hospital are we going to?" Murphy called from the phone on the reception. "We need to tell her husband."

"University of Penn," the second paramedic answered, nestling the small green oxygen tank next to Marshall on the stretcher.

It was all happening so fast that in the next second the paramedics were counting "one, two, three," lifting Marshall onto the stretcher, strapping her to it, getting her moving with oxygen, and shouting to Carrier to grab their "first-in bag" and to Bennie to hold the saline IV up high. They all hustled out of the office together with the stretcher, with David holding one end next to Bennie, and rushed into the hallway and out to the reception area. The security guard scurried ahead to the elevator bank and hit the down button, and when the cab came, Murphy held it open.

"Okay, take it easy," a paramedic ordered as the men angled the stretcher into the cab and David hit the button for the lobby floor. Carrier hurried inside after Bennie, who nodded to Murphy.

"Murph, you stay with my girl Mrs. Di-Nunzio. Make sure she gets home okay."

"Sure," Murphy said, biting her lip. "See you later, Marshall!" she called out as she slipped an arm around the little woman and the doors slid closed.

It was scary-quiet in the elevator, and

Bennie eyed the deep furrow of David's forehead. She flashed on the newspaper article, back on her desk. Had he been here before? Trying to save a life? Failing? The elevator doors slid open onto two jump-suited building employees, who cleared an aisle. The paramedics rushed the stretcher to the back of a waiting red truck that read PHILADELPHIA FIRE RESCUE, its backdoors wide open, and on another "one, two, three" count, the paramedics slid the stretcher inside the back of the truck.

One paramedic jumped in after Marshall's stretcher, the other paramedic took off to drive, and Bennie tried to board until he blocked her. "No riders! Not on my bus, lady."

"But I'm family!"

"Sorry. Liability issues."

Marshall cried out, "Let her come! I want her here!"

"I'll write you a release," Bennie said, jumping in anyway as the paramedic scrambled past her to the backdoors, slammed them closed, and twisted the inside lever to lock them, and the truck lurched off.

"Hang on, Marshall," Bennie said, squeezing Marshall's damp hand. There was a padded jump seat behind her but she didn't sit down. "Hang on, honey, we're going to the hospital."

Marshall thrashed on the gurney, trying not to scream, and Bennie held fast to her hand, appalled. Clotty bleeding soaked her sunny yellow dress, bathing her knees and calves. The paramedic rolled up a hand towel, set it between her legs to absorb the blood, and wrapped a blood pressure cuff on her arm, his dark eyes fixed on her trembling form. He appeared to be counting her breaths.

"What's the matter with her?" Bennie asked, panicky.

"We don't do the diagnosis, lady. We're the swoop and scoop crew, me and Derek." The paramedic frowned at the blood pressure gauge, then placed two fingers at the pulse on Marshall's wrist. "Everything's fine, Marshall. So how do you take your pizza? Double cheese?"

"Please!" Marshall cried out, in torment, and the sound went right through Bennie. "Is the baby okay! How's my baby?"

"The baby's going to be fine, Marshall," the paramedic answered, but the rescue truck bucked and stalled in rush-hour traffic. Sirens screamed in Bennie's head. She kept telling Marshall everything was going to be okay, though she knew the person she was trying most to convince was herself.

"Let's move it, Derek!" the paramedic called out to the driver. "BP is sixty over forty! Respiration is thirty! Pulse is a hundred ten! She's diaphoretic!"

"Goddamn it!" the driver cursed in the front seat, and the truck slowed almost to a full stop. "This Lexus is trying to turn the corner!" Suddenly there was a crackling over the radio in the front seat, near a computer keyboard and small blue screen, and the driver called back, "Change of plans. We're going to Memorial. Tractor-trailer overturned on 95, and they got the ticket to Penn. Traffic to Memorial will be lighter too." The driver hit the horn, hard, *honk honk,* and the truck finally broke free and, with a few stutter steps, took off, veering around the corner.

"Memorial Hospital?" Bennie asked. "Her husband will be going to Penn."

"So call and tell him."

"Right," Bennie said, then remembered she didn't have a cell phone. She'd left it somewhere on the floor of her office. Carrier and David would go to Penn to find Marshall. *Damn*. She'd have to find a pay phone at the hospital.

Honk honk honk, the horn blared. The siren screamed. The truck accelerated, then began to fly. Everything on the shelves rattled, even behind smoked plastic windows. Boxes read VIONEX WIPES and a container labeled GLUCOSE TUBES. Marshall's head bobbled, and Bennie leapt to hold it still. It was something she could do as they raced through the city. They were on the way to the hospital. They were going to save Marshall and the baby. They were going. They were moving. They were *flying*.

"Go, go, gophers, watch 'em go, go, go," the paramedic sang under his breath. But the tune stopped abruptly when he slipped a stethoscope into his ears and placed its bulb on Marshall's huge belly.

Bennie held her breath. She wanted to ask how the baby was, but in the next second the paramedic looked up and met her gaze. His face had gone completely white.

And something in his eye told Bennie to start praying.

34

"I'm sorry, but you have to go," one of the nurses told Bennie. They'd rushed Marshall to Memorial's Labor and Delivery floor, and a group of nurses were hurrying to prepare her for an emergency C-section. A nurse grabbed the checked curtain that hung around Marshall's bed and whisked it along its metal J-shaped track with a *zzzipp,* blocking Marshall from Bennie.

"I hate to leave her alone," Bennie said, her throat thick with emotion. "Her husband's not here. He's at the wrong hospital."

"Husbands can stay, but you can't." The nurse's brown eyes softened. "We'll take good care of her and the baby. She's getting blood now. The baby's on the monitor. The doctor will be right here. He's dealing with another emergency."

"What's the matter with her? She's in so much pain."

"We think it's placenta abruptio," she said, and Bennie looked puzzled. "An abruption. The placenta peels away from the uterine wall. It's terribly painful."

Oh my God. "How did she get that? She was fine."

"No one knows why it happens, but it does."

"Is there a phone, so I can call her husband? I left my cell phone."

"You couldn't use a cell here anyway. Use our L and D phone." The nurse pointed to the station behind them, covered with baby photos and thank-you notes, but another nurse in a puffy scrub hat was already on the phone. "There's a pay phone, but it's quite a ways, because the new labor wing is under construction. I probably shouldn't tell you this, but take the shortcut."

"Where?"

The nurse pointed down the hall and to her right, at a makeshift plywood door with a handmade sign that read NO ADMITTANCE! CONTRACTION SITE. "Take that door, go through the double doors, take a right at the sign for the elevators, and you'll see the pay phones. I think they're still there. But tell Dad to get here quick. We go in five minutes."

"*Five* minutes?" Bennie took off. She hustled down the hallway to the door, flung it open, and found herself in a construction site, with temporary drywall where corridors evidently used to be. Her house had looked like this for two years, while she'd rehabbed it. The air was warm here—the air-conditioning hadn't been put in yet. She ran down the hall of exposed drywall and raw concrete subfloor, but it ended in another corridor of drywall, which she also ran down, then stopped.

Shit! There *were* no double doors. Just another makeshift corridor. A trash bag against one wall overflowed with empty Mountain Dew cans, Tastykake wrappers, and bunched-up paper bags. There were no workmen around to ask for directions. It was after five, and they would have cut out by four.

Bennie spun around. Two glass doors lay on their side, resting on a pile of two-by-fours, and next to them hung a bright blue tarp, duct-taped over a hallway entrance to keep the dust out, which everybody knew never worked. On the tarp hung another sign that read DANGER—KEEP OUT. Maybe the tarp had become the double doors, or vice versa. The phones must be on the other side of the tarp. Bennie didn't have time to be law-abiding.

She ducked under the tarp and came out the other side, into another drywall corridor, almost finished and painted with white prime coat. The floor was bare cement, spotted with drips of paint. What had the nurse said?

Damn. Go! She ran down the corridor, which angled into another corridor, less finished than the first, partly unpainted. She ran down it, too, and it was longer, some twenty-five feet. The drywall was completely unpainted in the corridor, and the air smelled like something burning. It didn't seem more finished, it was obviously less so, and Bennie couldn't believe phones were anywhere near here.

Fuck! She must have gone the wrong way. It was like a maze of drywall! She didn't have the time to run back, but this couldn't be right. She heard a sound and spun around on her pumps.

And came face-to-face with herself.

35

"Alice!" Bennie said, startled. Her twin stood directly in front of her. She was Bennie's double. Same blond tangle of hair, same light makeup, same linen suit. Bennie could have been standing in front of a mirror, but for the gun. A Beretta, it was small, black, and deadly. And its snub nose was aimed at her heart.

"Scream and I'll shoot you dead." Alice's voice had the same tone and timbre as Bennie's. She raised the gun, sending a tingle of fear through Bennie.

Stay calm. At least Marshall is being cared for. Bennie sensed that talk was her only chance of getting out of this alive. David was up at Penn. She was on her own. "I am curious why."

"Why what?"

There are three two-by-fours on the cement floor, by the drywall. "Are you kidding? The whole thing."

"This is a hard one? To take everything from you." Alice's lips—Bennie's lips—curled into a sneer. "To take every last thing you owned, worked for, built, or created. Because you got all of it at my expense."

The lumber is about ten feet away, slightly behind Alice and to the right. Bennie took a step closer to the plywood, as if she were startled, which wasn't hard to fake. "I didn't even know you until two years ago."

"And I didn't know you either. But it doesn't mean you didn't take from me." Alice cocked the gun, and it made a mechanical *clik*. "Every day you lived in the nice house, with the boyfriend and the furry doggie, those were days that belonged to me. Things that I would have had, but you got instead. And once I knew that you had it all, I wanted it, too."

I have to get close enough to dive for the wood, then swing it at her. Bennie inched closer to the lumber. Nine feet away now. "I defended you when you were charged with murder, Alice. I got you out of jail, free."

"You didn't do it for me. You did it for yourself. You're the famous one. You're the one with the degrees and the cool job. You were the one who got the glory." Alice's eyes narrowed, and Bennie was reminded of herself. "Tell the truth, Bennie. Isn't there a part of you that feels guilty that Mommy gave me up, and not you? But for that one little thing, my life would be yours, and yours would be mine."

It's true. Bennie swallowed hard.

"You've thought about me since we met, haven't you? You've tried to find me, I know. I heard."

Bennie couldn't deny it. She looked into the eyes of her twin. Her own eyes. Denying her would be denying herself.

"So it's true. That guilt tells you something. It tells you how wrong you are, and how right I am. You want justice? I'll give you justice." Alice took aim.

"Did you know that Dad died?"

Alice blinked behind the gun.

"Obviously not."

"You're lying."

"No. I went to see him, to find you. He's gone. I found out."

"When?" Alice seemed to falter. "I was . . . going to see him."

Just like me. "You waited too long. Too bad. I guess you were too busy wreaking havoc."

Alice's lip twitched. "When did he . . . when did this happen?"

This could work. I know how to get to her, because she is me. Bennie took a step closer to the discarded lumber, eight feet away now. "Don't tell me that you care about him, Alice. You don't have a bit of human emotion in you."

"I do, too."

"You didn't even know the man."

"I knew him better than you." Alice's tone echoed a child's. "He knew *me* better than you. He knew that I was the one who cared about him, not you. You were Mommy's girl."

Bennie felt something happening under their talk. Alice wanted her to know that she was their father's favorite. And if that was true, then Alice needed her approval. Power shifted from Alice to Bennie, but the gun didn't. Bennie inched closer to the lumber. Seven feet away. "So you were Daddy's girl?"

Alice pursed her lips, just slightly.

"You were?" Bennie had had no idea. She took another step. Six feet now. *Almost close enough*.

"We kept in touch the past two years. On the phone, we talked. He wasn't ill, not that he said."

But Alice fell suddenly silent when a rustling came from the other side of the blue tarp that hung behind Bennie.

Somebody was pulling the tarp aside.

36

Georges St. Amien stood in front of the tarp, pointing a black handgun at Bennie. Her heart froze in fear. So she had been right. He was Robert's killer. And now he was after her.

"Welcome to my hospital, Bennie," Georges said calmly. His gaze shifted from Bennie to Alice and back again. "I was back making my rounds when the ambulance brought your friend in." He managed a civilized smile and reaimed his gun at Alice. "So you do have a twin, eh? I read this in the papers."

"Who the *fuck* is this joker?" Alice spat out, and pointed her gun at Georges.

"He's my client's brother. His name is Georges. Say hi, Sis." Bennie defaulted to stalling, and she wanted the truth. She had realized Georges was the killer during her conversation with Carrier and Murphy, when she'd watched them bicker. They had reminded her of sisters, and Bennie had thought of the depth of rage that sibling rivalry could breed. And Bennie had made the connection to Robert's "wacky" brother, Georges. Even the cops always said look to the nearest and dearest. But Bennie needed to hear it from Georges. "You killed Robert, didn't you?"

"Yes, I did," Georges answered. His blue eyes had gone hard as ice. "He calls and says he isn't coming to dinner that night and I know the restaurant, so I go there. He sits in the window, and I follow him when he leaves, walking home. I take him when he goes past the alley."

My God. Bennie could even hear pride in his confession. But she needed time to think. To save herself. "Your cast came off?"

"Of course. I made it myself, with a slit in the back that no one sees. Micheline is out that night with friends. I get back before anyone knows anything, home to my chair and my study."

"But why?" Bennie asked, but she was

sizing up the situation. Alice was aiming her gun at Georges. Georges was aiming his gun at Alice. She could duck and let them shoot each other, but that only happened in movies. "Robert was *your brother*."

"Ha! Robert ruins my life. He makes me a nothing, a cipher. He turns me into the un-successful one, the *useless* one."

"But why now, Georges? It makes no sense." It sounded so much like Alice, but Bennie doubted her twin would make the connection, especially at the end of a gun. With all this firepower, there was no time for family therapy.

"Because of the Belgian banker. I know the police are already thinking it is because he was a foreigner, and I say, this is my time. So I pretend I have the riding accident, put on the cast, and wait for the opportunity. Then Robert, he cancels our dinner that night, for business." Georges snorted. "Gustave doesn't throw me, not in a million years."

Keep him talking. "But what did you gain by killing him? Revenge?"

"Not only." Georges brightened behind his gun. "Money, lots of money, because now I 'ave my family business back. Now

I will own and run St. Amien & Fils, and now I will share in the money from the lawsuit. It is *my* business, by rights!"

"But Julien—"

"He will not stay with it. Everyone but Robert sees this. I cannot do this with Robert alive, so he has to go. He makes his own bed." Georges's eyes went cold again. "But, I think I will need a new lawyer, eh? You have to go too, Bennie. *C'est dommage.*"

"Why kill me?" Bennie asked. She tried not to panic. The two-by-four lay less than five feet away. Almost close enough to her right hand. She kept her eye on Georges. "I don't have anything to do with it."

"Because I know you are onto me, my dear. You tell me you don't believe the police theory. You are talking with Julien, secretly, outside my building. When I ask you about it on the phone today, you lie. You say it is business, and I know it is not. Julien doesn't get upset about business. He doesn't care enough." Georges's eyes narrowed over the gun. "Does he suspect me also? Is that what you two were discussing?"

Bennie's heart sank. She was going to die

because she was a lousy liar. It didn't seem fair. "Georges, put the gun down. You can't get away with this. There's no reason to do this."

Alice laughed abruptly. "I don't think you're gonna talk him out of it, girl." She raised her gun and aimed it dead-on at Georges's forehead. "And right now, I got this clown in my sight."

"Ha!" Georges raised his gun, pointing it at Alice's forehead. "And I you, *madame*."

"Everybody stay calm," Bennie said. She edged toward the board. Four feet away. No time left. She was about to lunge for it when suddenly she saw a murderous flickering in Georges's eyes. He was going to shoot Alice. A voice told Bennie what to do. She knew that voice. She recognized that voice.

"No!" Bennie dove in front of Alice as both guns exploded into fire and earsplitting sound. Smoke filled Bennie's nostrils. Georges's shoulder erupted in blood. He collapsed to his knees, his gun clattering to the concrete.

Bennie found herself in her twin's arms. She blinked once, then twice. There wasn't a mark on Alice. Georges must have missed. *Thank God.*

Then Bennie felt herself slipping from Alice's grasp. The room began to whirl. Her stomach turned over. The only sound was a hideous gasping. It took her a moment to understand why. Pain stabbed through her back like a hot steel spike. She couldn't breathe. "Huh huh huh," went the gasping. It was her. She fell to the concrete, her head slamming against the floor at Alice's feet.

Bennie gasped for air. Her chest seared with pain. She struggled to function. She looked up at Alice, her eyes welling with tears. She tried to speak but she choked on her own blood, bubbling hot in her mouth.

Help me help me why aren't you helping?

Alice aimed the gun down, hot smoke curling from its barrel. She cocked the gun and took aim. "Why did you save me, you idiot?" she asked, standing over her twin.

Bennie tried to scream. Blood sputtered from her mouth, falling back on her face like a warm spring shower.

Don't kill me don't kill me don't kill me don't

And then the world went dark.

37

But it wasn't dark, in the dream. In the dream it was light and sunny. Not the rumored white light of heaven, nor the sunniness of a clear sky, but the incandescent amber glow of a small lamp bought long ago at Woolworth's and set on a bedside table. Its paper shade had yellowed, its tiny flowers faded to the thinness of a butterfly's wing, their colors impossible to discern. The shade rested askew on its base of cheap yellow glass, shaped like an oversized tulip bulb, fluted at the top but too coarse to be pretty. A thick brown wire that ran from the back of the base, still bearing its round "UL Approved!" tag, stamped in authoritative black ink onto soft, thick paper.

Bennie remembered the lamp, recognized the lamp, it was one that had sat on her mother's nightstand, atop a cotton doily crocheted by hand. By her mother's hand, from when she had been well. A time Bennie could never recall in her waking moments, but which came back to her in the dream with a clarity remarkable in its detail.

The lamp rested always next to an empty perfume bottle of lead crystal, not Waterford but a quality her mother could have afforded so long ago, when she was well enough to place it, even empty, on her nightstand, in a storybook understanding of the way rich ladies lived. It was a naive fantasy her mother had, of privileged women who owned lovely items like French perfume bottles and other luxurious things, strands of lustrous pearls and gold bangles and long-handled brushes of sterling silver, engraved with monograms in incomprehensible swirls. It was Hollywood's version of wealthy women that stayed with her mother, and she would envision these lovely women who sat at vanities before bedtime, brushing their long hair until it shone—*one hundred strokes*, she always said, and *no cheating*.

And in the dream Bennie's mother became that woman at the movie vanity, her round, dark eyes serene, her lips full with dark lipstick, and she was brushing her long wavy hair in the mirror, letting her curls bounce back shiny with each stroke of the gleaming brush, a great lady of a great house, surrounded by beautiful bottles of real crystal, full of heavy, fragrant perfumes from Paris, their amber glowing like liquid gold in the lamplight and somehow shooting light like sunbeams, suffusing the place with the warm golden orange of a late afternoon in summer.

In the golden light Bennie went up to her mother, her shining mother, now seated at her vanity of light, and stood behind her for a minute, enjoying the vision she'd never had, of her mother happy and whole and finally getting everything she wanted, becoming at last the woman she always wished to be. And in the next moment her mother's dream became Bennie's own, for her mother turned glowing from the mirror, set down the precious shiny hairbrush, and smiled at Bennie with the sweetest of smiles.

"Benedetta," she said, her voice soft and familiar.

And she raised her loving arms to embrace her daughter in the light.

38

When Bennie opened her eyes, everything around her was white. White walls, white bed, white cotton covers. It was either a hospital room or a cloud with a three-thousand-dollar-a-day bill. She had an ache in her chest that seemed to encompass her entire upper body, a profoundly deep pain kept only reluctantly at bay by something more powerful than Tylenol, and infinitely more pleasant. Bennie felt surprisingly happy, but maybe that was the being-alive part.

"Welcome back, sleepyhead," said a man's voice. It was David, and he was moving from a chair in the corner of the dim room to one closer to her bed, then rolling away a tray table with a brown Formica top.

Bennie caught his smile before her eyes closed again. She swallowed with difficulty, her throat so parched it hurt. She opened her eyes to find some water, but David was already raising a Styrofoam cup.

"Thirsty?" he asked, and she smiled. Or at least it felt like a sort of smile.

"You're good," she said, her voice so hoarse it was more like a whisper.

"Wait a minute." He pressed something on the side of the bed to raise the top half slowly. "High enough?"

"No. More morphine."

David smiled. "Let me hold the cup," he said, but Bennie was already reaching for it herself. A bolt of pain shot through her chest, and IV tubes she hadn't noticed tethered her arms to the bed.

Okay, so much for the independent-woman part.

"Please, let me do it." David looped his right arm around her back, cradling her while he brought the cup to her lips so she could take a small sip of lukewarm water. Then he eased her back onto the pillows.

"That was good for me, was it good for you?" Bennie rasped, and he laughed.

"Congratulations, by the way. You're not critical anymore."

"I'm always critical," Bennie said, testing out her new throat. It still hurt like hell, but at least now it was wet.

"The associates just left. Too bad you missed them." David set the cup of water on the rolling cart, eased onto the orange plastic chair beside the bed, and hung a forearm over the molded bedrail. "How do you feel?"

"Okay." Bennie swallowed. She sensed he was avoiding the obvious. "How are Marshall and the baby?"

"Marshall is fine." David paused. "And the baby, well, the baby might not make it. We'll know later today. Its blood and oxygen supply were compromised when the placenta separated."

No. Bennie closed her eyes. "Is it a girl or a boy?"

"Girl. Named Gabrielle."

Gabrielle. Bennie felt her eyes well up, and David squeezed her hand.

"As for you, you took a shot in your lung, but it missed your spine, which is very good news, and your pulmonary artery, which is more very good news. You had a lot of bleeding, but they didn't have to transfuse you." David gave her hand another squeeze. His voice sounded calm and even. "You've been awake a couple of times, which the doctor says is normal, with the drugs they're giving you and the trauma your body went through."

Bennie nodded. She'd been lucky. She prayed to God the baby would be. She couldn't stop thinking about Marshall. What she had gone through. What she might yet have to go through. "Is Jim with Marshall?"

"Yes. You need anything? More water, maybe?"

"No, thanks." Bennie opened her eyes and blinked the wetness away. "What about Alice and Georges? Catch me up."

"Alice is the one who ran for the ER people when you got hit. She probably saved your life."

Well, how do you like that? Returning the favor.

"Nobody's seen her since, though, and Georges is fine, except for a shoulder injury, and he's already been charged with his brother's murder. What happened between you three?" David leaned closer, but Bennie waved him back.

"I'll tell you if you don't smell my breath."

"Your breath is better than Bear's."

"There's a plus." Bennie smiled. She must look terrible. She didn't know the last time she had washed her hair. She didn't know what day it was. She wished for mascara, which she'd never worn in her life. "I bet I look hot in this gown."

"Bennie, can I tell you something, quite honestly?" David leaned over, smoothed back a strand of her hair, and planted a soft kiss on her forehead. "I think you are beautiful, even now."

Bennie didn't know what to say, so she closed her eyes and let the sensation wash over her. It was about as sexy as a hospital room gets, and she was filled with a warm, strong rush that was better than morphine. Okay, maybe not better than morphine, but really really good.

"And Bear says hi. I'm staying at your house, if that's okay. Taking care of him and making sure Alice doesn't come back."

Bennie nodded. It felt good, David staying in her place. He was in her bed, even if she wasn't. Huh?

"So what happened? Georges isn't saying, and Alice can't be found. She told the cops that he confessed when he came upon you and her together. She said that when he tried to shoot her, you stepped in and saved her. Is that true?"

"Partly." Bennie smiled. *Except for that attempted-murder part.* "How did she explain what she was doing there with a gun?"

"She didn't have to. She said it was yours. It was registered to you."

"Ha!" Bennie blinked. "She must have bought it using my name and ID. Perfect."

"So what *was* she doing there with a gun?" David's forehead knitted with concern. "Wasn't she trying to kill you? And if she was, why would you save her?"

Bennie shook her head. She didn't want to tell him why. She hadn't realized it herself until this minute anyway. Instead, she told him what had happened with Alice.

"You must have been terrified."

"Nah." *Scared shitless is more like it.*

"She should be charged. She tried to kill you."

Bennie shook her head. "They won't find her. She's outta here. That's her MO."

"I'm sorry that I wasn't there when the shit hit the fan." David's tone was heavy with regret. "I called your cell when I saw you hadn't been brought to Penn, but there was no answer. I couldn't get here in time."

"It's not your fault."

"Yes it is. It happened on my watch. You were on my watch."

"David, no."

He rubbed her hand. "Let it go, don't talk. Just rest. I'm here," he said, and Bennie could hear the sadness lingering in his tone. A memory of a headline floated into her brain, from the newspaper clipping Sam had given her. The one about the cadet who had died. What had it said?

"So if something goes wrong on your watch, it's your fault?"

"Sure," David answered, without hesitation.

"Why?"

"I'm the captain, the head coach, the commander. I'm responsible for what goes wrong."

Bennie nodded. She used to think that way too. Until now. "Can I have some more water?"

"Of course," he said, and they went through their water drill again, leaving Bennie with a scratchy but moistened throat, which was all she needed.

No time like the present. "I read that about a cadet who died during SEAL training. What happened?" Bennie asked, then closed her eyes so she didn't have to see his face. He'd be too proud, so she saved face for him. Literally.

David fell silent for a moment. "You know about that?"

Bennie waited, eyes closed.

"I don't want to talk about that now. This isn't the time or the place."

"Why not?"

"You're barely conscious."

"Hey. Tell me."

Bennie heard a deep sigh.

"Well, Cadet Wellington collapsed and died at one of our exercises, during Hell Week, which is the last week of training before graduation. Cadet Wellington was under my command."

"What did he die of?"

"A heart attack. A defect of the mitral valve, which burst under the strain."

"No one knew?"

"No one knew, not even Wellington. It was congenital. No exam revealed it, preinduction. Only an ECT would have given any sign of it, and they're not required as part of our physical. His dad was a big cheese at the Pentagon, and they charged me."

"I see." Bennie kept her eyes closed. David's voice sounded more hoarse than hers, and she'd bet his pain was worse too. "They cleared you of any wrongdoing, right?"

"Once the whole medical history came to light, yes."

Bennie breathed easier. She'd normally never cross-examine with a question she didn't know the answer to, but for the first time, she'd bet on the military. "The other cadets were fine, right?"

"Yes."

"Nothing unusual about the exercise?"

"Standard for SEALs."

Bennie considered it. "But you took some time off anyway, and the Navy let you."

"Right."

"Because you felt responsible."

"I was responsible. I *am* responsible."

Bennie winced, for him. "Do the parents blame you?"

"No."

"Are they suing you, civilly?"

"No."

Bennie paused, her eyes closed. "Maybe

that's why you run around, saving dogs and lawyers."

There was silence.

Bennie opened one eye.

David's face had darkened, his lips unmoving. He was looking out the window, but there was nothing to see this high up except the red brick of the building across the street and the slowly setting sun. Bennie took his hand, dragging her IV tubes with her like spaghetti.

"Am I right, David?"

He swung his head from the window and fixed Bennie in the saddest gaze she'd ever seen. "So what if you're right? What's the difference?"

"You suffer, and you don't have to. Life isn't about pain. It's about joy. With the occasional threat of litigation."

David didn't smile.

"Did you like training cadets, before?"

"Loved it."

"If it hadn't happened, would you still be doing it?"

"Sure."

Bennie knew what she had to say, but she was getting too tired to say it. And part of her didn't want to. "Then you should go back," she said anyway.

"I don't know."

"David." Bennie collected her thoughts, but they kept coming undone. "All the golden retrievers in the world won't make up for that boy. It was his heart that killed him. Not you."

"I wish I could believe that."

Bennie kept her eyes closed, but this time it really was fatigue. Her thoughts flitted from David to Alice to her mother, and she was wondering why some people took on so much responsibility, way too much, and other people took on so little, way too little, and how both types of people came to be the way they did.

"Bennie, you should rest now," David said softly, and she could feel the bed fall slowly back down.

And her thoughts floated back to the clouds.

39

"Yeah!" "Hurray!" "Welcome back, Bennie!" came the shouts as Bennie stepped off the elevator into the reception area and a very happy crowd. They were all there: Carrier, DiNunzio, and Murphy in front, then David, Sam, and even Julien, all surging toward her, shouting and calling.

"Boss! You're back!" Carrier yelled, and Murphy was right behind her.

"Bennie, you look awesome!" Murphy squealed. "And no pantyhose! You're learning, girl!"

DiNunzio was wet-eyed. "I'm so glad you're okay, Bennie!" The associate hugged Bennie so hard it should have made her wince, but she felt too good to be back. It had been a month since the shooting, but right now it seemed like years ago.

"Thanks, DiNunzio," Bennie said, and patted her little back. "It's all right now, kiddo." As soon as DiNunzio released her, David stepped forward, took her in his arms, and gave her a distinctly wonderful kiss.

"Wow!" Bennie said, when he put her back on her feet. "Was that your tongue?"

"That was a sneak preview. I don't go back for another week," David answered with a laugh, and Julien stepped forward and gave Bennie a light hug.

"I am so sorry," Julien said into her ear, and she hugged him back.

"Forget it, and remember your promise, right? One year?"

Julien released her. "Six months, you got it."

Suddenly Julien was pushed aside by Sam, who held two huge bouquets, one of red roses and another of white sweethearts. "Honey, you're home! Take these!"

"Flowers?" Bennie asked, delighted. "From you, the red and the white?"

"Please." Sam sniffed. "The red dozen are

mine. The sweethearts are from Chief Judge Kolbert."

"The chief?" Bennie plucked the florist's card from the bouquet, opened it, and read it aloud with glee. " 'Sorry I misjudged you. Lunch on me. Best, Kate.' Wow!"

"And that's not all, folks!" Sam extracted an envelope from the inside pocket of his custom blazer and handed it to Bennie. "Check this out."

"What?" Bennie tucked the flowers into one arm, opened the envelope, and slid out some thick folded papers, then read them with amazement. "You paid off my mortgage? How did you do that?"

"Ask the femmes," Sam answered, pointing at the associates.

Carrier gestured behind her, to a wall of boxes. "Well, those boxes are the new documents and files from St. Amien & Fils, and those next to it are from LensCo, and next to those are files from Tumflex, and the four on top are from FitCo." She took a breath, and Murphy took over.

"The boxes against the wall are from Reiss, Inc., those by the coffee table are from CoreMed, and the last two are from MedLens and Cho & Company. They overflowed both conference rooms and all of our offices, so that's why they're here." Murphy grinned. In the background, telephones were ringing and fax machines were *zz-zzting*. "Bottom line is, they're all documents from all of our new and improved class-action clients. We got business coming out the wazoo!"

Bennie blinked. "You guys are working the cases yourselves?"

"Sure," Murphy answered. "Just like you taught us. We've prepared fifty-five complaints for the class-action plaintiffs, all waiting for your signature. And in two weeks, with your approval, we file a motion to be appointed as lead plaintiff. We're a shoo-in."

"We're on the move!" Carrier joined in. "And we need Marie back and two more secretaries and at least another investigator until Lou gets well. We need staff! Warm bodies! Help!"

Mary nodded beside them. "I hired a contract paralegal on Brandolini, but it will take me months to read through all the documents I got from the War Department. And the Circolo raised twenty-five grand in donations, a big hunk from a car dealership in

South Philly. So now we're paying for ourselves and then some!"

Bennie couldn't believe what she was hearing. She didn't know what to say. This was her dream, and she hadn't even realized it until this very moment, when it came true. Phones that rang off the hook, faxes that never stopped coming, and E-mail that busted the server. And associates who grew up to be real lawyers in their own right. Bennie felt a wrench in her chest, but it had to be her stitches. Okay, maybe it wasn't.

"Bennie, did you forget about me?" came a shout from behind the boxes, and Bennie looked up to see Marshall coming around the box.

"Marshall!" she shouted, and they embraced. The receptionist smelled like fresh Ivory soap and felt strong and healthy, almost back to her normal weight despite the hell she'd been through. Bennie swallowed the lump in her throat and held her out to look at her. "You came to say hi?"

"Are you kidding? I came to work!" Marshall answered, beaming. "This is my first day back, too, and boy, do you need me! I'll start part-time, and share with Marie, in the beginning. This joint is jumpin', just like old times. No, *better* than old times!"

"But what about—"

"The baby?" Marshall waved her off. "She's fine. She still has some delays, but she'll catch up, and I got the best baby-sitter ever!"

"She sure does," Mary chimed in, throwing an arm around Marshall's shoulders. "Hey, baby-sitter!" she shouted, and from behind the boxes, cuddling a newborn baby girl in acres of receiving blanket, came Vita DiNunzio.

Bennie burst into surprised laughter. "Mrs. DiNunzio is going to be your sitter? How great!" She caught Mary's eye. "Why do I think you had something to do with this, girl?"

"I plead the Fifth," the associate answered, holding up a testimonial hand, and Mrs. DiNunzio leaned over the baby.

"Bennie! Bennie! See the baby!" Mrs. DiNunzio cried, dabbing at the baby's mouth with Kleenex. "I just feed her the bottle! See her, so sweet! See Gabrielle!"

"Gabrielle, welcome to Rosato & Associates!" Bennie said, giving the infant's impossibly soft cheek a stroke with her finger.

The baby gurgled adorably in response, with bright blue eyes peeking from her blanket, a nose like a pink button, and a mouth that formed a seraph's smile. Even Bennie had to admit, she was even cuter than a puppy. "Gabrielle, did you get that present I sent you?"

"The *laptop?*" Marshall laughed. "It's a little early, don't you think?"

"It was either that or a chew toy," Bennie answered, and they all laughed. She looked at Mrs. DiNunzio, obviously in her glory. "You got a baby again, huh?"

"Yes, yes, *si!* She's a good baby, a beautiful baby!" Mrs. DiNunzio beamed behind thick glasses that magnified eyes full of happiness. She wore a flowered housedress and had shed her winter coat for the occasion. "I take care of her, me and my husband. He helps, too, while Marshall work!"

"Wonderful!"

"Benedetta," Mrs. DiNunzio whispered, beckoning her closer with her finger. "Your sister, she'sa here. To see you, in your office. She says she wants to talk to you."

Bennie blinked, astonished. "Really? Alice is here? *Here?*" She and David exchanged looks.

"I think it's safe, if you want to talk to her," he said. "If you don't, I'll throw her out. We'll call the cops when you give the word."

The associates nodded unhappily. Carrier said, "We called security, too, and David's here, and we're all standing by, just in case. We thought you might want to see her."

"*I* thought you might like to speak to her," Mary said.

"*I* didn't think you would," Murphy chimed in, "not after what she's done to you."

"Me, either." Marshall nodded, folding her arms, next to a scowling Sam, and Mrs. DiNunzio was beside herself, even with the baby in her arms.

"She's a *devil!* A *devil!* I tell her to *go home!* She don't listen! She don't care about *you*! She don't care about anybody but *herself!*"

Bennie smiled, but she couldn't deny it. Alice was a devil. But she was a devil Bennie couldn't ignore any longer. So she said good-bye to all of them, steeled herself, and went to her office. She had wondered what would happen if ever she saw Alice again, and so far it wasn't going the way she'd planned.

For one thing, she didn't have a flamethrower.

40

Bennie opened her office door into the aroma of brewing coffee, and Alice turned from the credenza. She looked better than she had behind a loaded Beretta. The hardness had gone from her expression, and her eyes were a clear blue and softly made-up. Her hair curled to her shoulders, and her lips were slick with a fresh peachy gloss. She wore jeans too low for most jurisdictions, with a smallish white T-shirt that showed her curves to advantage. Bennie was looking at herself, with a beauty makeover. And a black heart.

"Want some coffee?" Alice poured the fresh brew into a Styrofoam cup and held it out.

"I'll get it myself," Bennie said. She set

down her bouquets, briefcase, and purse on the conference table, crossed to the credenza, and chose the perfect mug for her mood. HEAD BITCH. She poured herself some coffee, avoiding eye contact. "So, Alice, come to turn yourself in?"

"Yes."

Huh? Bennie's chest tightened, but she got over it by shaking sugar and fake creamer into her coffee and watching with unusual interest as they dissolved. "You're kidding."

"No, I mean it. I'm turning myself in. I thought I should call the cops from here, to clear up the confusion, with the theft charges and all. And I wanted to see how you felt, if you're all healed."

Bennie was so astounded that she didn't know what to say. She was still getting used to the sound of her own voice coming out of someone else.

"So, how do you feel?"

"Alive. Thanks for asking." Bennie turned her back and went over to her desk with her coffee. She always felt in control there, at least she had before she'd played hostess to the twin who tried to kill her.

"Look, I know this is totally weird, but I

am very sorry." Alice went to the chair on the other side of the desk and sat down with her cup of coffee. "I'm sorry for everything I did to you."

" 'I'm sorry'?" Anger flared like a flame in Bennie's chest. " 'I'm sorry,' doesn't cut it, Alice. You tried to kill me."

"No I didn't. I could have shot you and I didn't. I'll tell the cops the way it went down, and they can charge me if they want to." Alice's tone was urgent, if oddly reasonable. "But I want you to know, I would not have killed you."

"Bullshit!" *Yet another exception to the curse diet.* Bennie set her mug down. "You were going to, I saw it in your eyes. You *planned* to kill me. You even bought the gun in my name."

"I couldn't have gone through with it."

"Of course you could! You've killed before, haven't you?"

"Only in self-defense."

Bennie wasn't asking for details. "What about Georges? You tried to kill him!"

"No I didn't. I aimed for his shoulder."

"Oh, come on, Alice!" Bennie shot back, raising her voice. "The bullet went astray because I knocked you when you were shooting."

"I'm a better shot than that. I wanted to disarm him. Girl, if I'd wanted to kill him, he'd be dead."

The coldness in Alice's tone chilled Bennie. She didn't believe her for a minute, and she couldn't process the distinction anyway. Shooting another human being wasn't approved behavior, no matter where the bullet landed, and she felt ridiculous arguing over it. It wasn't the kind of thing the other kids fought about.

"I did have a plan, but I swear, I couldn't have gone through with it. And all that was before, anyway."

"Before what?"

"Before I knew that Dad had died."

"So what?"

"So that meant you were all I had left. It hit me, when you told me." A thoughtful expression crossed Alice's face, as if she were reflecting on the moment of her decision. "It struck me, caught me up short, that we were *it*."

"Oh, please."

"It's the truth. Think about it." Alice

blinked. "Now that Dad is gone, we're the only family we have left."

"We're *not* family!" Bennie snorted. "But for some tenuous connection of bad blood and a *very* twisted strand of DNA, we don't even know each other. I haven't even heard from you in two years. And let's get real, it's not like you made any effort to stay in touch. I got you off on a murder charge and never heard from you again."

"The day you left me off at the train station, I knew I'd made enemies in town. I was framed for murder, if you remember. And then you didn't matter to me. Now, you do. We're family."

"We've never been family!"

"Of course we were, and we still are. You and I, we have the same parents, Bill and Carmella. So what if we never lived together or even knew each other? In the world, there's only us now. You and me. Sisters. Twins."

"So what?" Bennie ignored the wrench in her heart. "What follows from that? Nothing!"

"Really?" Alice's eyes narrowed. "That's not what you used to think, when you defended me on that murder rap."

"And look where it got me! You tried to kill me! You tried to kill my *dog!*" Even if Bennie could forgive Alice for trying to kill her, she could never forgive her for trying to kill Bear. She wasn't about to parse her own reasoning; she knew only that it was true. "What about my *dog?*"

"I said I'm sorry, for everything. It seems like a very nice dog."

"He's a *great* dog! He's one of the greatest dogs of all time! He never did anything to you, and you tried to run him into traffic!"

"I'm sorry."

"You're damn right you're sorry! You'd better be sorry!" Bennie grabbed the phone and shoved it at her across the desk. "You said you wanna call the cops? Do it! Why wait?"

"Hold on a minute." Alice reached into a purse on the floor, pulled out Bennie's black Filofax, and set it on the desk. "This belongs to you. Your ID's inside, and credit cards. I sent the earrings back to Tiffany too."

"What a gal." Bennie hoped that Carrier had called the DA about her indictment. She made a mental to-do list: Get acquitted. "They'll still prosecute you, you know. It's a felony and you assaulted the guard."

"I know. I'm ready to take what comes. And I'll never pretend to be you again, I swear." Alice's eyes narrowed. "I do have a question, though. If I really don't mean anything to you, why did you save my life?"

Ouch. "Everybody makes mistakes."

"You didn't make a mistake. You stepped in front of a bullet. For me. I'd like to know why."

"None of your business."

"How can it not be?" Alice laughed, Bennie's own laugh. "It's *my* life, it has to be my business."

"Well, it's *my* reason, so it isn't."

"Thank you for it, whatever the reason." Alice gestured at Bennie's wall of fame, behind her. "You know, I learned something that day, at the hospital. I used to be so jealous of you. I used to want what you had. But I got to see myself, when Georges pulled that gun. He killed his own brother, and I didn't want to become him. I don't want to become you, either. I want to become me." Alice shook her head, musing. "See, you saved my life, and now I have a second one, because of you. From now on, I want to get it right, if you can understand that." Alice's face softened, her lips curving into a sweet smile that Bennie had seen on only one other person in the world. Her mother.

My God. Bennie found herself wondering. *Is there any of my mother in Alice? Any of her sweetness, her goodness of heart?* It stood to reason that there would be. Alice was her full-blooded child, just like Bennie. And before Bennie had met Alice, she had believed that blood was all. It was only afterward she'd concluded that blood meant nothing. But maybe the answer lay somewhere in the middle ground.

"Do you believe in redemption? Well, I'm redeeming myself. You'll see. I'm starting by turning myself in. I figure I'll get maybe probation or county time for the earrings. When I get out, I'm going to stay in Philly."

"Philly? Why?"

"I have family here," Alice answered with a smile, but Bennie didn't see the humor. Her hometown wasn't the middle ground she'd had in mind. She was thinking Timbuktu.

"But what would you do here?"

"I thought I'd get a job."

"What, in sales? Cocaine or crack?"

"No. A legitimate job, a straight job. I

went to college, I majored in criminal justice. I could do something in a law office."

"You asking me for a *job?*" Bennie asked in disbelief.

"No, not at all. It's too weird, with us being twins and all, but I think it wouldn't be the worst thing if we got to know each other. I've been staying in a little efficiency in town, on Bainbridge, nice and clean, and I take care of it. I bought curtains with ruffles and ordered HBO. It's a cute place. Sunny, nice." The faint pride in her voice made her sound oddly vulnerable, and believable.

Do you believe in redemption? Bennie couldn't deny that she did. That was why she had saved Alice's life. For her, and for her mother. The weight Bennie had carried over being chosen had been lifted. And her mother could never be happy, had never been happy, until now.

"I'm changing, I really am. I'm going to change, whether I'm in the joint or out. So let's call the cops."

Bennie turned the telephone back to her, picked up the receiver, and punched in the number. Her whole legal career had been about finding justice, and she was going to see that justice was served, right now. "This is Bennie Rosato," she said when the call connected. "Can I speak to the boss?"

Alice watched her in silence, her expression turning grave.

"This you?" Bennie said into the phone when the familiar voice came on. It wasn't Detective Needleman; it was Karen Wise, the director of the Public Law Group. Alice didn't know that, yet she still didn't get up and run away, which confirmed to Bennie the correctness of her decision. It was the right decision, even if it was a little, well, unorthodox. But then again, Bennie always was a maverick.

"Karen," Bennie said, "I have a woman you might want to interview, sitting here in my office. She's about to serve some county time, about eighteen months, but she says she wants to change when she gets out. You guys believe that's possible over there, right? That people can redeem themselves? That good can triumph over evil, even when lawyers are involved?"

Alice straightened in her chair, and an incredulous smile spread across her face.

"She's smart and resourceful and I think she'd work hard. She says she wants to change, and I'm fool enough to believe her.

She hasn't been given a lot of chances in her life. I think I'd bet on her this one time. You might recognize her when you meet her. Who is she?" Bennie eyed the blonde on the other side of the desk, and when she answered, she chose her words carefully:

"Her name is Alice Connelly, and she's my twin sister."

ACKNOWLEDGMENTS

Bennie Rosato is impossible to contain, so I needed a lot of research for this book and wasn't shy about asking any number of very kind, very smart professionals. They are certified geniuses and any mistakes are mine.

Grazie mille to the National Italian American Foundation, a wonderful organization that funds and promotes the study of Italian-American culture, including the internment during World War II, a fascinating chapter in our history. In this regard, I should also acknowledge two outstanding works on the internment: Lawrence Di-Stasi's *Una Storia Segreta: The Secret History of the Italian-American Evacuation and Internment During World War II* and

Stephen Fox's *Uncivil Liberties*. Something tells me I'm not quite finished with this subject yet, and neither is Mary DiNunzio.

Thank you and a huge hug go to Art Mee and Glenn Gilman, Esq., for law and law enforcement expertise. Art and Glenn help me with every book, and I owe them big-time. Thanks to Detective Ron Milewski and the other great detectives of the Ninth District, for research and hospitality on the fly, and to Detective Howard Peterman of the Homicide Division of the Philadelphia police, for letting me hang out.

Thanks to Jerry Hoffman, Esq., attorney extraordinaire at Dechert, for his expertise and longtime friendship. Thanks to Shaun Wilson of the Pennsylvania Bar Association for an ethics assist, and to David Grunfeld, Esq., lawyer, book lover, and friend. Thanks to Neal Colton, Esq., who taught me everything I know about bankruptcy law and was so kind to me when I was a young associate, back in the day. Thanks to Mary Chase of the Clerk's Office of the Eastern District of Pennsylvania, and to Clerk of Court Michael Kunz and his staff, for all the good work they do for all of us.

Thank you to my galpal Andrea Hanaway,

M.D., for her emergency-room expertise, and to lawyer-doctor-rower Gary Zakeosian, Esq., who took the time to help me when my rowing got rusty. *Grazie mille* to Lou Battalino, crime-fighting sales associate at Tiffany & Co., and to Karen McClure of PNC Bank. *Merci beaucoup* to Susan Ostien, a wonderful, caring, and enthusiastic teacher who brushed up my French IV. And a big hug to homeboy Marty Keeley, who fills me in on military lore and plies me with his mother's delicious roasted peppers. For SEALs research, I should also acknowledge some wonderful books: *The Warrior Elite* by Dick Couch, *SEAL!* by Lt. Cmdr. Michael J. Walsh (ret.), and *Inside the U.S. Navy Seals* by Gary Stubblefield.

Heartfelt thanks to my half-sister Jeanie, whom I met late in life but who is a wonderful, intelligent, and loving sister—nothing like certain sisters herein.

A special thanks to the generous citizens whose names appear, by permission, in this book. I have a long-standing practice of allowing worthy causes to auction off character names in my books, in return for contributions to the causes. My benefit is karmic, plus I get a novel populated with kind citizens, who should be recognized here. Thanks to Lynne Maxwell for supporting the Public Interest Fellowship at Villanova University Law School; thanks to Ernest Calhoun Eadeh, for supporting The Home of the Sparrow, a haven for abused women and children; thanks to Joe Kranyak, who supports not only the Moorestown Library but also the Support Center for Child Advocates; thanks to Karen Wise for the Miami Valley Literacy Council, in Ohio, and Happy Birthday to Kathryn Kolbert of the Public Interest Law Center of Philadelphia. And a big Milk-Bone to Deb Haggerty and Gail Lustig for their contribution to the Goldstock Fund, for golden retriever rescue. Arf!

A warm hug to the Honorable Cynthia M. Rufe of the Eastern District of Pennsylvania, for supporting the International House of the University of Pennsylvania.

Thank you so very much to my amazing editor, Carolyn Marino, and to my terrific agent, Molly Friedrich, both of whom improved this book a thousandfold. I am blessed to have both of them in my life. A huge hug to A. Paul Cirone for his great suggestions and to Laura Leonard for hers, as well as her help around the clock.

And lotsa love to the gang at HarperCollins, namely SuperPublisher Jane Friedman, Cathy Hemming, Susan Weinberg, Michael Morrison, and Laurie Rippon, who have been so supportive of me and my books for so long. I'm a very lucky girl. Thanks again to the wonderful Tara Brown, and to Christine Caruso and Josh Marwell, and last but not least the amazingly patient Jennifer Civiletto.

Finally, heartfelt thanks and love to my family, and especially to my father, who has endured so much this year and has managed to survive, and even to smile. Dad, you're the reason I understand the importance of fathers.

I love you.